I0627188

Also by Mike Vance

Please enjoy these other titles by Mike Vance. They are available
where books are sold and also at www.mikevancewriter.com

Non-Fiction

Undertold Texas Volume 1

Getting Away With Bloody Murder

Mud & Money: A Timeline of Houston History

Murder & Mayhem in Houston (with John Nova Lomax)

Houston Baseball: The Early Years, 1861-1961

Houston's Sporting Life

Stand-Up Stories: Tales from Behind the Microphone

A Fire to Kindle (Two volumes)

Brenham

Fiction

The Devil's Lease

A Convenient Scapegoat

Wingo: The Remarkable Story of an Unremarkable Man

Wingo's Redemption

Zeke Gets Glasses (with John Swasey)

A Convenient Scapegoat

Mike Vance

Dos Dogs Press

Copyright © 2025 by Mike Vance

All rights reserved.

LCCN TXu 2-499-775

ISBN (hardback) 978-1-965272-06-0

ISBN (paperback) 978-1-965272-07-7

ISBN (ebook) 978-1-965272-08-4

No portion of this book may be reproduced in any form without written permission from the publisher or author, except as permitted by U.S. copyright law.

This is a work of fiction. All the names, characters, places, businesses, events, or incidents in this book are either the product of the author's imagination or used in a fictitious manner. With the exception of public figures, any resemblance to actual persons, living or dead, or actual events, is purely coincidental. The actions and words of public figures or businesses described in this book are completely fictitious and are created whole cloth from the author's imagination for the purposes of entertainment. The opinions expressed are those of the characters and should not be confused with the author's.

It is also worth noting that this book treats difficult matters of race and segregation in an historically accurate manner that may sometimes evoke uncomfortable feelings. Those feelings are the appropriate ones. Let us strive to always do better.

Printed in the United States of America

LEGEND
Central Houston
1904

1 – **Duckworth & Fein**
1107½ Congress Ave

2 – **Duckworth Home**

3 – **Harris County Jail**

4 – **Big Annie's**

5 – **John Duckworth lodging**

6 – **Turf Exchange**

7 – **Louie Swearingen bachelor apartment**

P. Whitty – Surveyor

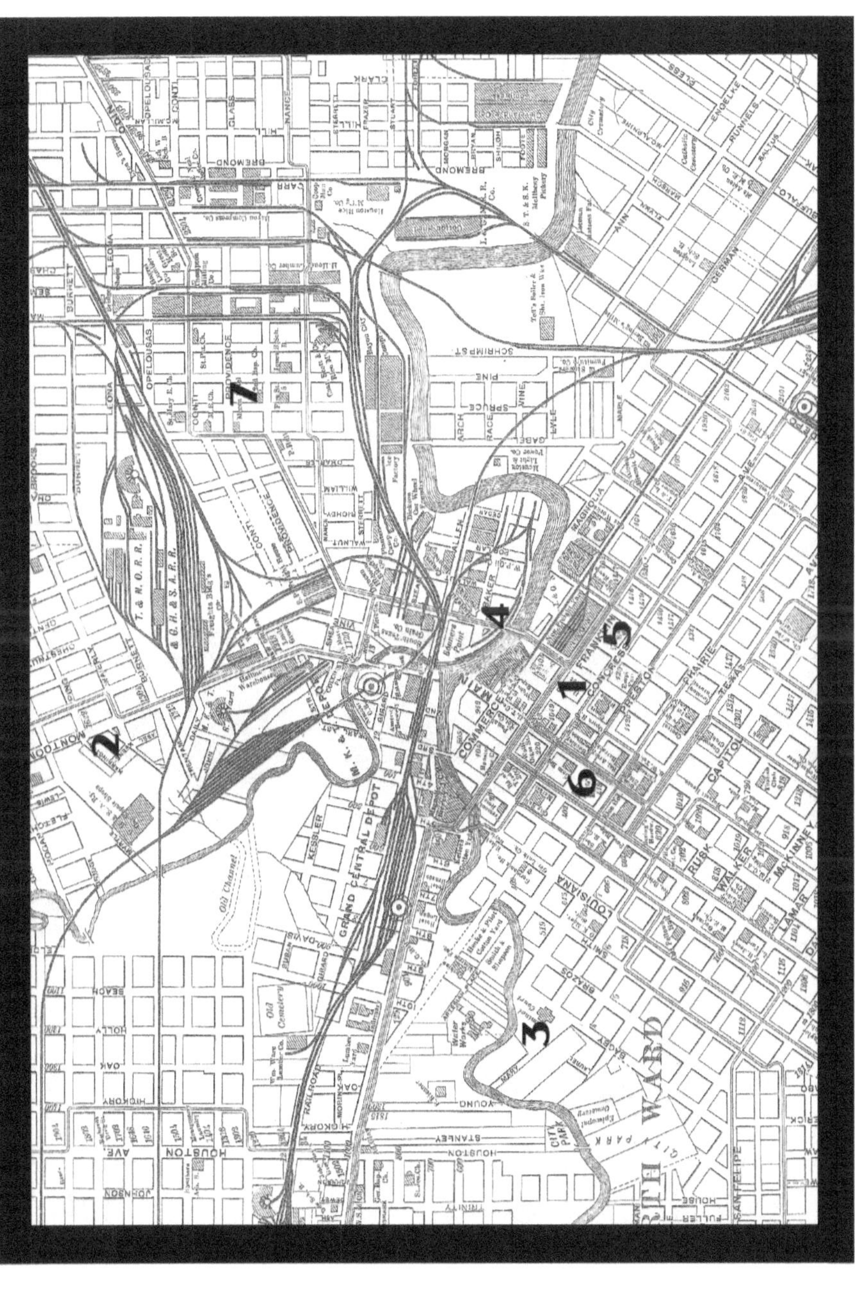

Houston 1904

Chapter 1

September 1901

Andy Green was mighty glad that it was a pleasant night because his friend Johnson Montgomery had not stopped talking for the last half hour. It was not an unusual occurrence, and though they were best buddies, Green had learned that digesting every fifth or sixth word was generally sufficient to keep him in the conversation.

"... Like some fever dream. He was just talking nonsense," Montgomery was saying. "He might as well have been rattling on about flying purple monkeys. You were there. Did you have the slightest idea what that man was talking about?"

No pause was offered for Andy Green to respond.

A few rogue fireflies lingered despite the midnight hour. The occasional breeze offered a hint that summer might eventually come to a close. Andy stepped on a tree roach that dared a languid stroll across the porch, then he took a sip from a bottle of cheap wine and passed it to Montgomery. His friend drank, and the narrative continued.

"... He come off the top of that car and landed right on his head. That's a good fifteen feet down to the gravel. If that train had been moving, Robert would be dead. You know that. Everybody knows that. But they just tell you to shake out the goblins and get on back to work."

Johnson Montgomery and Andy Green worked together as linemen for the Galveston, Houston & Henderson Rail Road. The line could well have shortened its name to the Galveston & Houston since that was as far as the tracks ever ran. Any grand plans to extend into Deep East Texas blew away like just so much smoke, gone before Green or Montgomery were ever born. Such notions fell victim to the vagaries of rich men's finances and did not bear much thought.

In present day reality, the GH&H ran precisely 50 miles and contained only two curves, one on each side of the town of Harrisburg. It had earned the nickname of the Old Reliable Short Line, and Montgomery and Green carried a good measure of pride in being two of the men who kept the trackage in tip-top order. Their sweat, six long days a week, smoothed the way for passengers and freight and allowed Galveston and Houston to read each other's newspapers fresh every morning. It was not a long railroad, but it was a good one.

The two men traveled between the Houston terminus and the stop at Genoa mostly, though some day's work took them as far as Webster. Another group of linemen worked the southern end of the route. That one was not an enviable assignment since their bay trestle had been destroyed by the great storm a year prior.

"...old Reynolds, he knew damn well that they'd reported a piece of loose track this side of Dumont, just yonder from that siding we're always having trouble with, but he just didn't want to haul his sorry ass down there an hour before supper time."

Johnson Montgomery had changed the subject yet again, and Andy Green had not even noticed. He was busy thinking about the little owl who was trilling from a catalpa tree while eyeballing for neighborhood rats. Montgomery plowed on.

"You've seen the man's wife. She'd beat any one of us half to death with an iron skillet if we looked askance, so you can see why he stays in line. Yes, sir. Either she's got her a sinful right hook or she's a demon between the sheets. And if it's the second one, I have a hard time picturing it. Keep me up nights."

Montgomery punctuated his comment with a rich baritone laugh.

The two men shared a house, a shotgun shack to be more precise, on the east side of the truncated street grid that was Harrisburg. To be fully accurate, Green sublet one of the dwelling's two rooms from his friend Montgomery. The little town was far from urban. There were elements of industry around the dock and railroads, wild animals that still ran the bayous, and plenty of loitering milk cows providing daily mischief.

The most assertive resident of their small home was a brown and white terrier named Poochie. He had wandered up one evening and plopped down between the two men as they ended the day on the tiny front porch. Montgomery cut him off a few slices from an apple, and the dog never left.

"… Not sure why I even bother putting the plants in the ground. You'd think living in town, we'd get a break from the critters, but I think there's more possums around here than we had at home. Armadillos, too. I put those carrots and collards in the ground three weeks ago, and the tops of them are already gone. Slick to the dirt."

Johnson Montgomery looked toward the small garden plot at the left side of the house though it was much too dark to see anything. His friend, Andy, thought he'd stir the pot.

"Possums got to eat, too."

"What do you know about it? You grew up in the middle of Fourth Ward. When I was a boy, my daddy would whizz all around the edge of the vegetables. Keep the deer and other varmints at bay. They don't like the smell of a man's pee. You remember when I tried it last spring. That damn Miss Jackson like to drop her marbles. I'm just a man making water and trying to protect his crops."

Harrisburg had once been a grand village at the confluence of two bayous, a legitimate rival to upstart Houston. It was more than a decade older, and the first of the Texas railroads had started within its city limits. Business fortunes came from the water, and they were lost in fire. Most notably, the big railroad shops had burned to the ground in 1870, and the line's bosses decided to rebuild them upstream at Houston, dragging all of the workers with them. No more than 500 hardy souls remained.

In Texas, though, there was always a new pipedream on the horizon. The latest was oil. The entire eastern part of the state was mad over the smelly stuff. That included Harrisburg, and Johnson Montgomery was now prattling on about making money from gas wells that were sure to be going in soon.

"Three, four years ago, man was digging a water well right over on Frio Street and hit a gas bubble. Put a sulfur match to it, and it burned bright as daylight. That's what they say."

Andy Green throated an mmm-hmm and took another swig of wine.

"This could be the next Sour Lake. Derricks like to go up all over town, down the bayous in every direction."

"Could be."

"They say that at Spindletop you can step from one well to the next without your feet ever touching ground."

"That so?"

"When they found gas down the road, there was no call for it, you know. But now, the world has changed. Coal is on the way out, and petroleum fuel is the way of the future. You heard the stories of that oil burner on the S.P. A locomotive that runs slick as goose shit. With oil or gas, you throw down a pipe, and it comes right up from the ground. No sending hundreds of men into a hole they might never climb out of. This is the future, and it's right beneath our feet."

Montgomery stamped on the porch boards twice to underscore his point. The dog shot him a dirty look.

"Yes, sir. Right where we sit, and my aim is to get my share of those royalties and retire from railroad work."

The last statement jumped out from the rest of the diatribe and jarred Andy Green into his first real response in well over an hour.

"Now, Johnson, that's pure nonsense. You don't own any land. You're not going to make any money off a rented house."

Montgomery grew slightly louder at the rebuff.

"That's not the point of the matter. There is money to be made, and I aim to collect my share of it."

Poochie the terrier raised her head and voiced what Andy Green took to be slight frustration. He was impressed that the dog was taking his side, for once, but the noise soon turned into a low growl.

The two men on the porch looked to the street about fifteen yards away across the bar ditch. Someone was there, just out of view in the night gloom. The hair on Poochie's nape bristled.

Andy Green's questioning hello had barely left his mouth before two rifle shots sounded. He vaguely saw his friend shudder in his chair before he leapt from the side of the porch and threw himself prone onto the dirt yard. Green crawled a few feet on his hands and knees. When he reached the right front corner of the house, he stumbled upright and took off running to the northwest. At age 41, he was not a sprinter, but it felt to Andy that he was flying. He did not look back.

Green was breathing so heavily that he did not hear the shooter himself run to the corner of the block two houses away where he untied his horse and galloped west. Though it may not have been intentional in the moment, the horse and rider roughly followed Andy Green's mad flight from danger for two blocks before veering left.

Johnson Montgomery's dead body sat in his favorite front porch chair for well over an hour and a half before the local justice of the peace, Applewhite Jordan of Harris County Precinct 2, made an appearance. Jordan was bare-headed, and a healthy cowlick of brown hair stood up on the right side of his head. He gave the occasional tug at his trousers since he had forgotten his belt. The J.P. was understandably fussy as he shooed gawking neighbors away from the crime scene.

Several retreated no more than 20 feet, crossed their arms, and kept watching the grisly goings on.

After scanning the faces, Jordan asked two of the people to remain, the teener boy who had fetched him and the lad's grandmother who had investigated the shots then sent her grandson on the errand. They lived next door. Aside from providing a name for the victim and recounting that they were startled awake by two gunshots that "sounded like they come from the end of the bed," neither had testimony of any value. The grandmother did complain that the two men had been "hallooing till the wee time like they do every night."

Being roused from bed at all hours was part of the job of a J.P. So, too, was often serving as official coroner. In the downtown Houston precincts, poking and prodding at a dead body was such a frequent phenomenon that a justice just might learn what he was doing. Sometimes, in the middle of the city, a designated medical doctor made an appearance and offered some trained expertise, but in a sleepy jurisdiction like Harrisburg the fine points of forensic science were elusive. Luckily for Apple Jordan, the two bullet holes in Johnson Montgomery's head were difficult to miss.

There were just the two shots, coming right together according to the neighbors. One bullet entered through the corner of Johnson Montgomery's right eye and the other went into the forehead just above that same eye. Two inches apart. Jordan thought to himself that the murderer was either very close or knew his way around a gun.

Finally, the curious neighbors retired to their beds and left the justice to examine the scene with only boisterous bullfrogs for company. He was giving the body a final going over when he heard a slow rider draw to a stop in front of the little shack. He glanced up to see a uniformed deputy sheriff tie his mount to a sapling that had almost certainly started life as a weed.

Jordan had met Deputy Tim McDougal a few times and found the young man eternally jocular in the most annoying sense. In spite of the early hour and the reason for their presence, McDougal did not disappoint.

"Looks like coon hunting season has started."

Apple Jordan raised himself from a squat with a grunt and several loud pops from his knees.

"I don't much like digging through a man's brains at three in the morning whether he's White or colored."

The J.P.'s accompanying glare sent the deputy scurrying back to the lot line in search of evidence.

It took a few minutes, but Deputy McDougal ambled back to the porch for another attempt at conversation.

"The constable is dead drunk in his bed, and his deputy is no place to be found. Someone telephoned to the jail, so I come out from Houston."

The justice continued scribbling notes without comment.

"Bet I didn't pass more than four other souls between here and the cotton shed," McDougal added.

Just as the gregarious deputy was about to give up any effort to draw the justice into a chat, the Westheimer's ambulance rattled to a stop in front of the house. The driver, used to the night shift like the deputy, called down with a chuckle.

"Navigating through Dark Town in the dark sure ain't easy. We like to never found this place."

The deputy joined the two ambulance men in laughter.

Apple Jordan groaned loudly. If the others heard, they did not acknowledge him.

There was not much to delay them. Only fifteen minutes after their arrival, the two Westheimer's men loaded Johnson Montgomery into the ambulance. With a complete lack of urgency, they lingered, and one man shared a plug of tobacco with Tim McDougal. The J.P. was doing a fine job of ignoring their lewd conversation as he jotted a few final notations. Any adrenaline that had sustained him an hour earlier had ebbed.

Apple Jordan was the first of the four men to realize that they were no longer alone. A stocky middle aged Black man was standing to one side of the porch, right at the edge of his visibility.

"Go on home, boy. There is nothing to see here."

Jordan spoke without menace, and the tiredness made his words sound soft and sad.

Instead of leaving, the man took two steps closer, his eyes wide. Jordan saw the man's agitation. Finally, the man spoke, his words tremulous.

"This is my home, sir."

"Aah."

Jordan set his notebook aside.

Andy Green surveyed the scene.

"What happened to Johnson?"

"Your friend is dead, I'm afraid."

Though Green had surmised as much from the loitering ambulance men, he still choked back a gasp. Jordan asked him a question.

"Were you here when this happened?"

"Yes, sir."

The J.P. remained seated, but motioned Andy forward. Green took a seat on the boards at the edge of the little porch, not mentioning that the White man was occupying his chair.

Deputy McDougal peeled himself away from the ambulance men and stepped to the front of the house. Andy Green glanced up at the uniformed man. He was already too afraid to register any further alarm.

"Have y'all seen my dog? Brown and white about yay big?" he asked with a spread of his hands.

Apple Jordan kept his voice even.

"No. Deputy have you seen a little dog?"

McDougal shook his head, but added a question.

"What's your name, boy?"

"Green. Andy Green."

Apple Jordan gave McDougal a quick scowl to reestablish the pecking order, then he resumed his questions.

"Your neighbors said the shooting happened just past midnight, Andy." The justice pulled out his watch. "It's 3:45. Where have you been this whole time?"

"Someone was shooting at us, so I took off running right away. I jumped for the dirt with the first report. Then I gained my feet, and I didn't stop till I was all the way up to Mr. Milby's house."

"So, you ran immediately after the trouble started?"

"There was no trouble. We were talking and laughing one minute, then there was a shot from the road the next. Yes, sir. I hightailed it."

"And stayed gone for nigh on four hours? Gone from your own house?"

"I was afraid to come back," Andy responded. He failed to stifle an incredulous expression aimed at what he considered a very stupid question.

Apple Jordan considered the answer and let loose a sigh.

"All right. I'm too damn sleepy to talk to you tonight. Come by my office in the morning. You know where that is, don't you?"

Andy nodded. He was still trembling slightly.

Jordan spoke to McDougal.

"That all okay with you, deputy? Letting this man be for now?"

With all in agreement, they prepared to go their separate ways. McDougal would follow the ambulance back to Houston. They should reach downtown just before dawn. Apple Jordan, calculating that he could get another two hours of sleep, rose from the porch chair and walked toward the road. Just as he reached to untie his roan gelding, the J.P. had a thought and turned back to Andy Green.

"Sorry. I'm worn out. I do have to clarify. You took off running, so you didn't see who did the shooting?"

The silence lasted so long that Jordan was about to repeat his question when Green offered a soft response.

"I did, sir."

"You did? You did see the man?"

"Yes, sir."

The deputy and the justice each leaned slightly closer to make sure they heard correctly. McDougal asked the next question.

"Colored man? Somebody from around here?"

Andy Green felt a shudder go through his body, and he again waited a long time before responding.

"No, sir. It was a White man. But I recognized him."

For the second time in an hour, Apple Jordan emitted a loud groan.

Chapter 2

Big Annie's had a loyal clientele. Sitting at Willow and Baker, a block north of the iron swing bridge, the drinkers were almost all regulars. The rambling one-story building, unadorned by exterior signage, was not the place for a business meeting. There were no bored out of towners looking to pass the time. No hotel clerk ever directed a guest to Big Annie's. It may be only a single block across the bayou from downtown, but it was an indisputable fact, or at least a running joke amongst her customers, that no one came to Fifth Ward unless they had to.

Yet somehow, on this particular night, a stranger had swum against the stream, eluded the metaphorical nets and discovered himself sipping whiskey at Big Annie's bar. To make matters worse, he was busily trying to place one of the establishment's habitues, a man who preferred, at least in this case, to remain anonymous.

Unlike many of the drinkers, J.B. Duckworth was not found at Big Annie's every single night, but he was comfortable there. His house sat at the corner of Montgomery Avenue and Waverly, just the other side of the vast Hardy railroad yards. Big Annie's was less than five minutes away by the Montgomery streetcar. It was his favored place for a few night-caps after his wife and daughter had gone to bed, excepting the many nights he burned the late oil at his office across from the courthouse.

This night, his older brother, John, had come north the few blocks from his boarding house to meet him. They had been each other's protector for forty-odd years, and though they were very different men, the two Duckworths thoroughly relished one another's company.

They leaned amiably on the rail, talking of sundry topics of little import and occasionally interjecting a bon mot into the overheard conversations of their bar friends. From time to time, J.B. squatted down to give his dog Maizy a long scratch on the head or hand her a small slice of the cheese that was a thoughtful treat from the bar. If the situation at all permitted it, Maizy, the little retriever he'd liberated from the streets, was by J.B.'s side.

One constant of any good, dark pub was the smell, and J.B. took a deep inhale of the sour beer, the spilled whiskey, the gas lamps, and the bygone smoke and turned to his brother.

"If Annie ever gave this place a good scrubbing, it might fall down."

John snorted his agreement.

"Held together by spilled tipple."

"I was thinking more just the fumes."

"Now why in God's green would I wipe away the sweet perfume of barley-bree? The tears and laughter of my closest friends, that is."

Annie Caverly's words boomed from behind the Duckworths, and she clapped the gents playfully between their shoulder blades. Of course, what was playful to Big Annie could well knock an average sized man off his feet. The Scotswoman's moniker was well-earned. She stood six feet tall and jestingly boasted that "I'll top 23 stone, but ten of that is heart." That was occasionally followed by a wet kiss planted square on a shocked gentleman's forehead. Once she grew to like and trust a regular drinker, it was assumed those kissed would defend Big Annie to their final breath, and she would do the same for them. Hers was that kind of tavern.

If the stranger at the bar felt at all out of place amongst such camaraderie, he did not betray it. That might be because his attention was singular. His interest in Duckworth had progressed from sidelong glances to, three drinks in, squinty-eyed staring.

J.B. was a highly observant man, even after several glasses of Old Taylor whiskey or enough beer to drown a giraffe. He certainly did not overlook the scrutiny of the thick, florid faced man wearing a rumpled suit coat over mismatched trousers. Finally, the stranger could stand it no more and walked to where the Duckworths leaned against the battered pine bar. He grasped J.B. by the wrist in an unrequested hand shake, and attempted to pull him close. J.B. flinched slightly from the man's fermented breath as he yanked his hand free. As the younger Duckworth balled his right fist, John, the older one stepped between the two, hands raised placatingly.

"I'm just trying to have a couple of drinks with my brother."

The man leaned to his left, looking around John.

"Yeah, but I know him."

The drunk man clarified by jabbing a fat finger in J.B.'s direction.

"I know you."

J.B. Duckworth took a moment to smooth his bush of a moustache and eye the stranger before replying.

"Then you are one up on me, sir, because I don't know you from a scalp on a fence post."

Duckworth made to turn back to his drink, but the stranger was having none of it.

"I arrested you in Waco."

The man's voice was plenty loud enough to attract the attention of several other drinkers, and his slurred tone had notes of superiority and belligerence.

Mark Callaway was a stone cutter at the Humphreville Company. He was not a tall man, perhaps the shortest in the place, and his squinty-eyed, perpetually lopsided grin belied any trace of evil intent. Still, Callaway had never been bested in an arm wrestling match and had a deft touch at horseshoe pitching. He stood up from the table where he had been swilling beer and retelling tall tales. Risking a placating hand on the stranger's bicep, he spoke with a smile, exaggerating the Yorkshire accent he never lost.

"You know, that's highly unlikely, mate. The man you're pointing to is one of top attorneys in this city. He spends his time keeping us good folk out of trouble, not getting into it himself."

There was not a regular drinker in Big Annie's that could fail to put the lie to that statement when it came to a combative man like J.B. Duckworth. They knew stories of his many small transgressions, but nary a snicker escaped anyone's lips. The stranger jerked his arm back from Callaway. He shook his head back and forth to clear it, grimacing as he did it.

"I don't give a shit what he is now. I know that ten years ago, when I was a city bull, I pinched him climbing in a window at the Wortham Hotel in Waco, and I shot the son of a bitch in the hand."

Mark Callaway valiantly tried to change the subject.

"What brings you in here?"

"Process serving on some Heinie that works for the railroad. I haven't found him yet, but there's another shift at eleven."

The big man looked around the bar as if checking for his mark, but he was not to be redirected.

"Then I saw that plucker. Sneak thieving bastard."

The man wiped a corner of his mouth with the knuckles of his right hand then used it to point at J.B. again.

"I shot him in the mitt. Look at him."

Several of the Big Annie patrons tried to avoid glancing at the scar they already knew to be present. If it was true that lawyer Duckworth was never at a loss for words, as he reflexively touched the back of his left hand, he at least weighed his carefully now.

"I did get shot in the hand in Waco, that much is true, but it came courtesy of some brigand bent on lifting my wallet."

"Horseshit! I've been trying to place you for a goddamned hour, and I finally put it together. It's just like I said. You were climbing in a guest room window, and when I hollered for you to stop, you legged it down the alley. I shot you right through the palm of your left hand. I can see the scar from here."

"Like I said..."

Duckworth's face reddened, but his brother again interrupted, something that was largely out of character. John Duckworth tried to pull himself to a height that matched the stranger's.

"Look, mister. You've been drinking. Hell, we all have, and you made a mistake. That's all."

The lawman gave a rueful laugh.

"I may be drunk as Lords now, but I've been sober enough to remember several days over the last ten years, so don't play me the fool. I know who he is on account of I was there. Right on the end of the trigger."

He punctuated his sentence with a puff of his broad chest and an almost well-aimed stream at the closest spittoon, but J.B. had reached his limit. With a dramatic flair, the besieged attorney slammed his empty drink glass on the bar. Maizy, who did not have a growl in her, finally rose from her slumber and stood by her master's calf.

"God damn it! I've had enough of this slanderous piffle. I don't know you, nor do I give a flying shit what you have to say."

Several minutes earlier, Duckworth had automatically felt for the pistol he often carried in his waistband only to realize that he had left it at home. Even unarmed, J.B.'s outburst turned the flow of the encounter. The Waco man took an ever so slight stumble backwards. It was a cue for the other two men at Mark Callaway's table to push back their chairs and stand. Two more of the regulars stepped closer to the Duckworth's backs. The whole clientele was now peering toward the bar.

Annie Caverly understood how bar grudges could linger, and thus she rarely intervened in disputes until they put her glassware in danger. She had been sorting beer receipts at the far end of the bar and sipping from her oversized mug, but now she ambled towards the ruckus.

"That's enough, sunshine. On your way."

The big woman deftly grabbed the stranger by the back of his coat and heaved him toward the front door. Perhaps a natural stumble, or maybe a well-placed foot, caused the Waco man to hit the plank floor face first. When he rose, his front coated in swill, hair, and dust, the man's first reaction was to fight, but a fast appraisal of some seventeen grim faces led him to pick his hat off the bar and stumble outside.

J.B. Duckworth's life narrative was fluid. The city in which he had first learned the law changed with each telling. It had become a personal game for him over the years, but he was serious about the underlying sentiment – if he kept his biography a moving target, the lies and fancies were harder to pin down. Lord knows the truth of his journey was not a confidence-building advertisement for a growing law firm, and he'd be damned if some drunk flatfoot from backwater Waco was going to cast evil light upon it.

When Annie offered to buy another round for the two Duckworths, J.B. spoke up before his brother could accept.

"Thanks, Annie, but we'll do it another time, and it'll be my treat if you'll drink with us."

That was a foregone conclusion since the ample bar owner never declined a drink with friends.

The Duckworths said their gracious goodbyes, though John still looked a mite parched. J.B. did not want to be subject to questions from his bar friends at the moment. By tomorrow, they would sober up and the details of this night would be a feather in the wind.

From Big Annie's, it was roughly the same short distance home for each of the Duckworth brothers, but John insisted on accompanying his brother to the house just in case the Waco man lingered with a hot grudge, but their ride on the car was uneventful. Joe Russo, the motorman, shared a groaner of a joke, but they laughed heartily nonetheless. The other few passengers did not join in.

J.B. Duckworth opened his front door as quietly as his current state allowed and immediately pulled a half bottle of whiskey and two glasses from the cabinet. John pulled off his boots and flopped back on the sofa, and Maizy scrambled up beside him.

Though their minds may have wanted the last beaker of bourbon, they were both asleep well before the nectar was gone.

J.B.'s wife, Lola, had learned to crochet from her Yankee grandmother. It soothed her and filled the many hours that her husband worked. It also meant that she made more things than their baby, Katherine, could use. It was a foregone conclusion that most all of their immediate neighbors possessed something that Lola Duckworth had crocheted.

The undisputed prize went to a soft rug for Katherine in daffodil yellow that the girl could not live without. When it was in need of washing, the baby wailed relentlessly until her treasured bankie was pulled down fresh from the clothesline. God save the household if it got dirty during a rainy spell.

Katherine turned one year old the month before. Lola and JB had a birthday party at the house with a few attendees, all adults save one other baby who aroused her great interest. Katherine's vocabulary had surpassed twelve words, the most frequent of which was uh-oh. She was the couple's darling. Though her father rarely saw his daughter thanks to his grand schedule of life, his last waking words were usually a whispered goodnight to his girl.

Lola roused them for work the next day. Her husband, his brother, and Maizy all snoring away. J.B. was slumped to one side of an upholstered chair holding tight to a green crocheted afghan.

Chapter 3

It was tough to fathom two lawmen more different than Archie Anderson and Eddie Isgitt. One was the best known copper in the city, and the other could likely have stood in one of his own identification lineups without being recognized. Today, they were working together.

E.P. Isgitt was the recently elected constable of Precinct 2 at Harrisburg. He was a hulking man with close-cropped sandy hair and an abnormally weak chin. He tried to hide this defect under a sparse moustache, but it somehow only managed to make it more glaring.

Isgitt had moved to the east side of Houston from Madison County three years earlier and had been in town for barely eighteen months when he ran for constable. He won by 13 votes over an incumbent who had a heart attack and died four weeks before the election. His position was not gained by mandate.

In contrast, Anderson was an easy-going Mississippian who already had a dozen years as a local deputy under his belt before he became the Harris County sheriff two years prior. His calm face was dominated by uncontrollably bushy eyebrows and a long, drooping moustache. Laugh lines radiated out from the corners of his thin brown eyes. He carried an ample belly that managed to look stately in his usual garb of a grey Stetson and dark suit.

Even their mounts were not easily confused. The sheriff rode a handsome black gelding with three white socks and a blaze on his face. Isgitt rode a gray that could have used a good brushing.

Isgitt rose before dawn that day. As a constable out of his jurisdiction, the protocol was to notify the Harris County Sheriff's Office before serving a warrant.

Depending on the seriousness of the offense, a county deputy may or may not accompany the visiting man. Isgitt was perplexed when he called the county jail the evening before and was told that the sheriff himself insisted on serving the Precinct 2 murder warrant and that the constable was requested at the jail by seven the next morning. Though he did not like it, Isgitt complied.

There was no long ride for Sheriff Archie Anderson. He lived at the big red jail on Capitol Street in private quarters with his two youngest children. His sister and brother-in-law, the Wilsons, also lived there, and they had four little ones. Scots-born Tom Wilson worked as head keeper of the county prisoners. At normal times, Wilson oversaw about 80 inmates, male and female, White and Black, American and foreign born, compliant, belligerent, and bereft.

Jennie Wilson held a place of even greater esteem. The sheriff's wife had passed away from consumption a decade before, and though he was still a young man in his thirties at the time, Archie Anderson had never even considered remarriage. It was up to Jennie to keep the county's top constabulary household in good fettle.

In front of the three-story jail, the sheriff offered his underling an amiable handshake, and the two men began to pick their way northeast from the imposing gothic edifice that backed up to Buffalo Bayou on the southwest edge of downtown. They rode down Capitol Street and were all the way to the Bering's sporting goods store before they turned north. Theo Bering, one of the owners, was placing a string of cedar ducks on the front walk for display, and he hailed Anderson in his German-accented English.

"Archie. Next month. Ducks. You'll come out with us, yes?"

"I wouldn't miss it, Theo. Save me a bed at the clubhouse. But I might need to buy a new shotgun off you. If I can get a good deal."

Bering laughed.

"I know people at this store."

The two badgemen passed the next few blocks gently arguing over the best duck marsh in the area. Anderson was partial to the prairies at Eagle Lake where he had bagged 170 mallards, redheads, and pintails in two days the previous fall.

Isgitt swore that a good hunter could do better at Anahuac at the top of Trinity Bay.

As they turned again, onto Produce Row along Commerce Street, the sheriff reined his horse to a stop next to the high sidewalk. He called to a short, dark, aproned man.

"Guido, toss me three good peaches, will you?"

The Italian obeyed.

"I've only got maybe a week's more peaches left. Soon, you're going to have to eat pears."

Anderson put one peach in his jacket pocket and handed another to Isgitt along with unsolicited advice.

"The Italians grow the best fruit. Guido's place is up in Little York. That one is going to be juicy as a rainstorm."

The sheriff turned back toward the fruit vendor and flicked over two dimes. The man shouted a thank you as the lawmen got back to their journey toward Hardy Street north of the bayou.

"My sister made hotcakes this morning," Anderson told Isgitt. "But there was trouble in the cells, and I only managed to get three or four of them down before you rode up."

A great, bushy eyebrow lowered in a wink as Archie Anderson took a bite of peach.

One trait that both men shared was the need to talk. Anderson was prone to reminisce about old friends at the least provocation, whether the other parties in the conversation knew the person or not. Isgitt was more suited to sketchy braggadocio. He was particularly fond of sharing drunken tales of his sexual exploits that were shy on substance but replete with details. Most doubted these love legends of Isgitt's based upon his looks alone, but his five young children left no doubt about his overall virility.

On this ride, as the hunting conversation lulled and silence threatened, both men were spared the worst of the other's proclivity by the subject of the impending arrest itself.

"You know this Swearingen's papa?" Anderson asked.

"No. Any reason I should?"

"He's been the town marshal out in Sealy for a coon's age. Over at Kenney before that. Good man. I've known him a lot of years."

Anderson did not turn to face Isgitt, but his point got through nonetheless. It explained the personal attention to serving this particular warrant. The constable's argument rose up like a chill wind.

"What's that supposed to mean?"

"I'm just saying I'm going to give the boy the benefit of the doubt."

Isgitt bristled. Suddenly this had the potential to go in a different direction than he had imagined. He was smart enough to know that the sheriff outranked him, but his nature would not stop him from pushing back.

"There is no doubt. I have a witness. Colored, but just the same, he saw Swearingen pull the trigger."

Across the iron swing bridge, the two horsemen ambled along next to the car tracks up Willow and jogged right on Nance. In spurts, Isgitt continued to extol Swearingen's guilt. When they passed Fire Station 5, three blocks from Swearingen's rooming house, Isgitt turned to Anderson. His thick neck was taut, and his eyes had widened. He pointed a beefy hand up ahead.

"It's right up there. How do you want to work this?"

The sheriff looked back a little confused.

"I reckon we'll knock on his door and tell him he's under arrest."

Isgitt nodded lightly.

"You want me to wait out back in case he tries to scarper?"

Anderson offered a few seconds of thoughtful expression. When he did respond, though the crinkles were still at the corners, his eyes themselves were hard as stone.

"Every bartender I've ever known is in a deep, drunken slumber at eight in the morning. And if he does run, I'd rather not have to tell Big Lou Swearingen that I got his boy killed. So why don't you just stick next to me and keep your pistol in the holster."

The men need not have worried. Louie Swearingen, reeking of booze and with a bed crease down the left side of his face, opened the door to his room and, once dressed, allowed himself to be handcuffed. The only resistance he offered was borne of confusion. It was the same look given by the preacher of the McKee Street Church who was puttering in a vegetable garden on his building's back lot. Unsure of the protocol, the reverend offered a half-hearted wave at his arrested neighbor and the sheriff.

Given the convenience of Swearingen's lodgings to the Liberty line, coupled with the fact that their prisoner did not own a horse, Anderson planned to take the restrained Swearingen on the streetcar and Isgitt would follow. The three men stood in Hardy Street next to the two tethered horses. The road surface was not quite sunbaked enough since the last heavy rain to qualify as dirt, but at least it was not completely muddy. Swearingen, nursing a bear of a hangover and craving a few more hours of sleep, was silent. Anderson kept a firm grip on his culprit's shoulder as he turned to Isgitt.

"You know how to lead a horse?"

There was a moment of annoyed hesitation before the constable answered.

"Yeah."

The sheriff spoke as if to a dull child.

"You've led a horse before?"

"Yes, I've led a horse before. Jesus, I'm not some kind of idiot."

Anderson gently rubbed the gelding's neck and shoulder while he gave the reins a once over, then he handed them to Isgitt.

"Old Beau here'll trail you just fine. Keep him on your left, and don't run off and leave us. I want you to walk either alongside or just behind the cars in case there's any trouble. I ain't expecting none, though."

Isgitt gave the sheriff a disgruntled nod. The car, crowded with workers headed into downtown, came into view at the corner of Conti and pulled to a stop. Two neatly dressed women eyed the unkempt handcuffed man being led by the sheriff and skittered forward without a word. Anderson shoved the sleepy-eyed Swearingen onto the vacated back bench.

Clean shaven and twenty-eight years old, Louie Swearingen was from the small town of Kenney in northern Austin County. He moved to Houston eight years earlier and had worked at several bars over that span. His most notable physical feature was a wild shock of peanut brown hair that sat atop the close-cropped sides of his head like an unruly nest. With most of the hair oil having transferred onto the pillow case during his too-brief night, his locks were even more mutinous than usual.

Swearingen liked bartending, and he enjoyed Houston immensely. There were abundant opportunities for fun as well as gainful employment. Not to be discounted was the fact that it got him out of his father's shadow and offered ample room to stretch himself. Since he moved to the Magnolia City, Louie was living well. That is, until this morning.

Archie Anderson regarded his charge. The boy had a handsome enough face. The sheriff also recognized a nasty morning after when he saw one. He kept his voice low.

"I know your pa, son. He's a good man, and I see where you favor him a bit."

Swearingen stifled a grumble.

"Yeah, I've been trying to live down being his son for twenty years."

Anderson, unsure of what to do with that comment, stayed uncharacteristically silent for several blocks. Just before the north end of the big bridge, a man in blue overalls stopped at the last bench as he prepared to step down in front of the planing mill. His eyes widened at the sight of Louie Swearingen's disobedient mane. The man chuckled before loudly offering his opinion.

"I've got a mare that looks just like you."

The rest of the car's passengers laughed heartily, and Swearingen, in spite of any self-inflicted pain, joined them.

Archie Anderson had no intention of holding an interrogation on a public streetcar, but he very quietly asked Swearingen if he had, indeed, murdered a man night before last. The prisoner slowly raised his gaze to meet the sheriff's. The lawman interpreted his look as earnest enough.

"No, sir. I'd have sure remembered doing that."

"You can tell me where you were? Working most likely?"

Louie started to shake his head but stopped halfway over, and his face lowered again.

"I can't recollect just now."

A touch of exasperation crept into Anderson's calm.

"Come on, son. It was just two nights ago."

Swearingen kept staring at the seatback ahead of him.

"Were you out in Harrisburg?"

The prisoner's head shot up at that.

"Harrisburg? No."

There was a pause, and the sounds of the busy city got louder before he spoke again.

"I don't think I would've gone to Harrisburg." The last words came softly as if to convince himself. "I don't think so."

Back at the jail, after one change of cars, Anderson led the prisoner in through a door on the back side of the building. Tom Wilson sat at his small desk shuffling through papers.

"Tom, this is Mr. Louis Swearingen, Jr. Word is he shot a colored man out in Harrisburg. Louie here says he didn't do it."

Anderson's wry smile vanished as he added an admonition.

"Be good to him. I know his daddy."

Wilson gave a single, formal nod.

"I'll bear it in mind, Archie."

Tom Wilson led the still handcuffed Swearingen, who was looking wide-eyed and alive for the first time that morning, through a pair of grated iron doors leaving the sheriff behind to scribble an entry into an oversized ledger. Hearing the solid heavy door slam shut with a thunderous ring, Louie looked at the business end of the jailhouse and began to fully grasp the seriousness of his newfound situation.

After handing over the newest Harris County inmate, the sheriff walked out to the side yard of the jail where Eddie Isgitt was laughing with one of the deputies and the wagon driver from Houston Packing. The latter fellow had just finished unloading the day's meat. Sighting the red van, Anderson surmised that Annie Brown, the head cook for the inmates, was already busily chopping whatever cheap cuts the slaughterhouse had sent their way.

The sheriff stood apart from the trio, hoping the ribald conversation would wind itself down, but finally sensing that the men might be at it for some time, he stepped closer and interrupted.

"Mr. Isgitt, I'd like a little parley if you can pry yourself away from your business there."

The sheriff turned from the group without waiting for an answer and took several steps toward the bayou. Isgitt followed, a lascivious chuckle still dying on his breath. Anderson got right to the point.

"I'm going to insist that you wait until tomorrow to question that boy. He needs to get his bearings. But I have to ask you. Why do you have such a burr under your saddle over this Swearingen thing?"

The constable's expression darkened like a petulant five year old.

"I just don't like him is all."

Anderson scratched at his neck and tossed a casual comment.

"I didn't think you knew him."

Isgitt gaped like a stunned catfish. It was not the first time that morning that Anderson had set the constable on the defensive. His reply was muted.

"Well, fact is I do recollect him. I heard tell that he used to tend bar at the Anchor on Frio Street before I come to Harrisburg."

The sheriff rubbed innocuously at his beltline.

"So, you dislike the young man even though you never met him personally?"

Isgitt's face darkened, and he spat into the dirt.

"Oh, I've met him. The son of a bitch tossed me out of the bar where he worked one night."

"Here in town?"

"Yep. A year or so ago. Refused to serve me any more of their swill, then he failed to step in before two overgrown hayseeds tossed me into the back alley."

Anderson's implacable silence urged Isgitt on.

"It's horseshit. He knew I was the law. He just stood there, chuckling it up with his boys."

"Were you raising a ruckus?"

The constable puffed up his chest.

"I may have got a little chippy with those two clods I mentioned."

"You were fairly sozzled?"

Isgitt offered a haughty snort.

"No more than anybody else."

Again, the silence kept him talking.

"I'm glad to bring him in. Is that what you're poking at? I knew he'd be getting his sooner or later. He's a bad egg. I just wish he'd kicked a little bit at his rooming house. Getting in a few cuffs would have suited me just fine."

Without comment, Anderson untied Beau's reins from a railing and walked the horse over toward the stables that backed up hard against bulkhead at the bayou bank. Turkey John, the man who tended to the jail's horses and handled various repairs, met him outside the open doors.

"I got him, Mister Archie."

"Thank you, John."

About three that afternoon following a hearty pork chop dinner and a short nap, the sheriff ascended to the top floor of the cells and pulled a little chair inside so he could talk to Louie Swearingen. Anderson liked the young man, but then again, he showed patience to almost every one of his prisoners, generally more so than his deputies did.

"Nobody's giving you a hard time, are they?"

In spite of the location, Swearingen looked less green at the gills than he had that morning.

"No, sir. Most of the fellows have been minding their own business."

"Yep. They hear 'murder charge' and they tend to keep a distance."

One side of Anderson's moustache rose before he followed with the question he had come upstairs to ask.

"You're going to need a good lawyer. You got one?"

"Not yet, but I'd like to get a message to J.B. Duckworth."

Anderson pursed his lips and nodded.

"You know the man?"

Swearingen responded with a wide smile.

"Everybody in Fifth Ward knows Mr. Duckworth."

The sheriff laughed softly.

"I reckon they do. And for that matter, every bartender in Houston, too."

Chapter 4

Louie Swearingen and John Duckworth talked through the cell grates. Each was trying his best to ignore the happily insistent drunk who kept inserting himself into their initial client interview. As often happened, John was the first representative of the law firm of Duckworth & Fein to gather details of a new case. Since the clients were very often behind bars, the conditions for that conversation, including in the matter of privacy, varied widely.

John was not an attorney, but in addition to being the senior partner's brother, he acted as the firm's jack-of-all-trades, serving as everything from office manager to lead investigator. He was especially adept at finding out things his brother would want to know. As he gathered a new client's details about the alleged offense, John also meandered the personal rabbit trails that often led to the building blocks of a good case.

Their uninvited friend, Pete, a recently unemployed car wheel man for the S.P., laid on his side in his hammock. Unfortunately for Louie and John, Pete was wide awake and fully invested in their conversation. He kept picking up scraps of the dialogue and blithely sharing stories from his own life. Some of them, such as the time his brother-in-law needed a lawyer, were almost germane. Others, including a brief memoir of his late cat, Eva, were headscratchers.

Swearingen and his new found pal Pete shared a cell on the third floor in what was still sometimes called the new jail. That top floor, which offered the best chance for a cross breeze, was for White prisoners. Blacks were housed on the second, and women and juveniles stayed on the ground level. In the interest of safety, inmates had duck fabric hammocks hung from the ceiling by leather straps instead of mattresses that might become a hiding place or bedsprings that could be turned into a weapon. The slung beds were all right for sleeping, but they did not lend themselves to meetings with a lawyer.

John had opened by relating why Duckworth & Fein decided to take the case. Louie's message from the jail had come in, and right behind that was a note sent over from Charlie Lusk, the owner of the Turf Exchange and Swearingen's employer. It was one of several establishments frequented by J.B. Duckworth, so Charlie's request carried some weight. It was suggested that Louie thank his boss at the first chance.

As usual in this situation, John explained how his younger brother, J.B., was the important Duckworth, the man who would steward Louie Swearingen to a verdict of not guilty. He himself was just a lackey, John said, but what the firm learned today were often the most important pieces of a client's case. He stressed that honesty was crucial and that completeness in the young man's answers would go no further than the law firm's personnel.

After confirming some basics of Swearingen's life, John got down to the questions at the heart of the matter.

"Did you have any trouble with the man who got killed, Johnson Montgomery?"

Swearingen shook his head

"I can't even recollect that I knew him."

"But you used to work in Harrisburg?"

"Yep, at a little joint called the Anchor, but it's been six years."

Duckworth screwed up his face as he searched his memory.

"The Anchor. Can't picture it, and I thought I knew them all."

Louie waved his hand dismissively. "Just a tumble-down for railroaders and rivermen. Place ain't even there anymore. Blew down in '95, eight months after I went to work."

John scribbled a note in his ledger book.

"Did you have any set-tos with any of the colored folks back then?"

"No more than anybody else."

Talk soon turned to an alibi for the night of the shooting, but Swearingen truly did not recall where he was.

"All I can tell you for sure is that I was off work on Wednesday night. I'd done a day shift. Frank was busy at the lunch counter. Tables were about half full. Billiards were cracking downstairs."

"Customers were drinking plenty, I gather?"

"Every day. I had to swap out two kegs. The more they drink, the more they wager."

Louie tossed out a genuine wink as he continued.

"Not every man wants to go home and see his wife for lunch, Mr. Duckworth."

"Did you start your drinking there at the Turf?"

"One or two maybe. I think I went around to the Drummer's. That's my usual first stop after I work days. There are generally a few sweet-looking doves to watch across at the market."

John acknowledged Louie's slight leer with a small smile.

"Is it usual for you, Louie, forgetting where you've been?"

Swearingen shot an involuntary glance at his cellmate Pete who had finally nodded off. His response carried notes of both apology and defiance.

"It happens. I'm young, and I like to have a good time. Course, I never landed up in jail before."

Louie wracked his memory for particulars, but the short of it was that he woke up in a strange room with an overly zozzled girl before he stumbled home then slept all day. John realized from the description that the young man found that narrative neither alarming nor unusual. He kept prodding.

"Was she a bawd?"

Swearingen broke into another easy smile.

"Well, she was accommodating, but I had money left when I got home, so I couldn't tell you."

"We can find some witnesses."

The client was skeptical.

"How are you going to find anyone when I don't even know where in hell I was?"

Duckworth's response was enigmatic.

"Finding a good witness is always the least of our worries."

After barely twenty minutes, John Duckworth sensed that he had gleaned everything Louie Swearingen could offer, and it was not much. He tried one last angle.

"Where do you normally drink, Louie? Is there a pattern? My brother likes to drink his way toward home, do you normally do that?"

Louie laughed heartily.

"That's no fun. Nothing personal, Mr. Duckworth, but that sounds like old man drinking."

He gathered himself when he realized that he might have overstepped. The big smile disappeared from his face.

"Naw. Every night is different. After tending bar in this town for eight years, I'm never short on drinking companions. You go to one saloon ready to bend with the wind, and before you know it, there's a whole boodle of you off to get fogged in Lord knows where."

Louie was chuckling again.

"More than once I've ended up at some shindig in another town entirely with no clue how I got there. Galveston. Richmond."

John's comment was soft but solemn.

"Or Harrisburg."

Both Duckworth brothers were good listeners. It was a talent they used frequently to wring details from clients and witnesses. Quietude from the brothers often begat answers from a stranger. Who taught the skill to the other there was no telling, but over the years, the practice for each had diverged.

No one ever called J.B. a peaceful soul. Certainly, J.B., as the wily lawyer, retreated into total silence and eschewed conversation when he was cogitating a specific problem, but what he reveled in most was telling a raucous story to a crowd of lubricated friends. John, on the other hand could happily go hours during a normal day enjoying only the company of his thoughts. When coupled with a person who needed to talk, his soft presence could yield a flood of words with just a tiny nudge. He also had an innate desire to ease people away from confrontation or disquiet.

After the realization of the last exchange settled, John changed the subject. Perhaps he could end the interview on a more positive note. He looked at the sleeping Pete then spoke to Louie.

"He'll be sprung as soon as he's straight, so you'll get the cell to yourself."

"Can't say I don't envy him a little. I could use a drink or two to settle the fidgets."

Duckworth nodded, at a loss for anything helpful.

"Can I ask you something, John? Does it rankle you, getting the hind tit?"

Louie read the perplexed look on John's face and continued.

"Standing behind the coattails of the big man every day. Never getting the sunshine for yourself."

Duckworth was wistful.

"Aw, I don't mind it, J.B. getting all the attention, that is. He's been smarter than me since he was about four years old."

That statement brought a smile of misty-eyed memory to John's face, but if he felt like sharing a story from his youth, the moment passed with it untold. He turned things back to Louie Swearingen instead.

"I know your daddy was the town marshal, right? I assume we're talking about him?"

"He's a decent man, I reckon. Never beat me or anything. Taught me how to fish and fire a gun. Did what a dad should."

Swearingen rubbed his face as he searched for words.

"I'm not sure how to describe it in a way that don't seem petty. It's just that being around him, and even before I was born, he never met a stranger that wasn't an instant friend as long as they abided by the law, and even some who didn't, come to that. He was always the constable where I grew up, the showpiece of the community. Living in a two horse town where your pa owns both of the horses, well, it didn't make for the most peaceful childhood is all. I just wanted to be my own man, as they say."

Jed Posey was the senior clerk at Duckworth & Fein. He was an overly serious young man but a solid lawyer. The firm's growing caseload meant that Posey frequently handled things such as bail, especially when the name partners were at trial in some other county. Four days after Louie Swearingen's arrest, that was precisely what he found himself arguing.

The hearing was held in front of Apple Jordan who, in Judge Gillaspie's absence, rode in from Harrisburg to make his presence known in a case that still held his interest. Some who considered themselves the cream of Houston's legal community, the railroad lawyers, looked down on a lowly justice of the peace, but the men of the district attorney's office and those scraping out a living in criminal defense saw the inside of the J.P courts much more often than the big district theatres. Though not everyone involved could be described as part of a mutual admiration society, theirs was still a tight knit club.

Posey's bail motion was made in what was ostensibly the same building where Louie Swearingen was housed. The Harris County jail and the criminal courthouse were two halves of the large red brick and white stone behemoth that squatted with its back to the bayou. A revolving metal door allowed only a single person at a time to pass between the cells and the public portion that housed the courtrooms and accompanying chambers. The district attorney's offices could also be found by anyone who ambled up the wide staircase from Capitol Street.

When Posey pushed open the courtroom doors, Phil Linzy was already seated at the prosecution table. Linzy was District Attorney J.V. Lea's lone lawyer assistant. His jug-handle ears and naturally wide eyes lent him a perpetually bewildered look, but Posey believed that Linzy was growing into competence at his job. The assistant D.A. glanced back to see who had opened the courtroom doors, and nodded a solemn hello at Jed before returning his eyes to the case at hand, a matter in which he had no personal stake.

Apple Jordan was reviewing papers at that moment and paying no mind to anyone else in the courtroom. Two pairs of other lawyers buzzed and murmured in small conversations at the back of the room. Finally, Jordan tapped the documents together and slipped on a paper clip. Three people stood before the bench - an attorney who Jed did not recognize and two nervous looking men who were clearly the parties to some legal dispute. The fact that one seemed to be unrepresented by counsel was a good indication of its triviality.

"Sorry to make y'all come all the way down here, but it was either this or wait till next week. My court's business moves with me while I cover for Judge Gillaspie. That sentiment goes double for you, Mr. Maury because you've got three days to move out of that house you're living in. A man's got to pay his rent."

The one in the shabbier suit coat started to argue, but Jordan snapped a gavel down on the wood.

"You had your say. That's my ruling."

Though Jed could not see it, the landlord apparently treated himself to a smile. The J.P leaned slightly forward in his chair.

"Don't get too jolly, Mr. Collins. I went with you this time as a straight matter of law, but you need to get that roof fixed before you let that house out again. That's as close as I can get to ordering you to do so, but life goes smoother when you treat people with respect."

There was another bang of the gavel, and the bailiff called the matter of Louie Swearingen's bail as the parties to the rent dispute shuffled toward the door. Posey and Linzy quietly took their places while the acting judge thumbed through their files.

Justice of the Peace Jordan looked at the two lawyers with a bit of a bulldog scowl on his face, but gradually he broke into a genuine grin.

"No Mr. Lea and no Mr. Duckworth, and here I am sitting in for an absent judge. Some might say that we are playing Class D ball here, gentlemen."

Phil Linzy at least tried to feign amusement, but the truth was that both of the young lawyers looked slightly wounded. Jordan resumed his scowl.

"Don't take it personal. Fact is that I view this as my case. I'm the fellow who lost a good night's sleep scribbling in my little notebook over a dead body. I know the pecking order, but that don't mean I wouldn't prefer finders keepers. What have you got for me, Mr. Posey?"

"Judge, Mr. Swearingen says that he did not commit the offense charged and that he was not even in the area at the time the crime took place. Furthermore, Mr. Swearingen is gainfully employed at the Turf Exchange, and his father is a respected lawman in Austin County. He is not a risk for flight nor a threat to his fellow citizens."

Jed shut his mouth and held the J.P.'s gaze. He had been before Jordan enough times to know that the man wanted all arguments to be quick. Judging by Phil Linzy's remarks, he knew it, too.

"It's a murder, judge. No matter how upstanding Mr. Swearingen may be, and given his employment in an alcohol establishment that is debatable, this is still a murder. Mr. Swearingen was identified by an eyewitness who previously knew him. The state does not believe it is in the best interest of the community to grant bail to a murderer."

"Mr. Posey, what do you say to that?"

Jed's words were drawn out.

"Well, judge, the witness in question..."

Jordan nodded.

"I know, the witness is not a White man. I talked to him myself, Mr. Posey. Did you forget that part? I found his thoughts pretty compelling."

The judge looked from Posey to Linzy and then back. All were silent as the stack of papers got examined once more. For the final time, Jordan placed the file back on the bench in front of him.

"All right, Mr. Posey. I'll grant bail but I'm not going to give the privilege away. Five hundred dollars. Pay the clerk."

Jed Posey promised to have the money delivered to the court clerk forthwith. Even before he completed the sentence, Apple Jordan had directed the bailiff to call the next case.

Charlie Lusk and John Irwin, the owners at the Turf Exchange, helped raise Louie's cash bail by tapping their regular customers, the men whose thirst had frequently been quenched by Louis Swearingen, Jr. Even George Voss, Tom Doucette, and Will Frame, all saloon men who had formerly employed Swearingen made their way to the Turf to toss a few greenbacks in the special bucket. The only one of Louie's old bosses in Houston who declined was Ernst Meyer, a notoriously cheap German who perpetually claimed to have just spent the last dime he had in his pockets. Never mind that Meyer's beer garden was hopping with his countrymen most every afternoon and night.

After two days and five turns at counting the money, Lusk himself added the final eighteen dollars and thirty-six cents and dispatched Sam Carr, one of his new waiters and a physically solid fellow, to carry the envelope over to the court house. Upon handing over the greenbacks, he was given a receipt which he in turn brought to the county jail. After six nights in a swinging hammock, Louie Swearingen looked forward to a drink followed by a good sleep in his own bed. Perhaps several drinks.

A J.B. Duckworth trial was generally considered a good entertainment in Harris County legal circles, but it often took some time for a client to get there. In any town, the months between a crime and its verdict were filled with insider maneuvering, but Houston seemed to be the perfect size to offer generous helpings of personal pettiness and drama that were not reported in the local press.

The city directory held an entire page filled with lawyers, but those tasked with criminal defense in Houston faced the same opponents time and again. James Vernon Lea was the district attorney, elected a year earlier when James K.P. Gillaspie vacated the D.A.'s office to run for the judgeship of criminal district court. Both men were responsible for Galveston and Harris counties.

J.V. Lea's early career rose like a rocket. He was sent to the state legislature at such a young age that the august body had to pass a special deferment so Lea could be seated as a member. He served as D.A. for a district of Piney Woods counties before moving to Houston and winning the election there.

Aside from the plain fact that they were almost always at opposing counsel tables, Lea and Duckworth were friends unafraid to laugh over drinks and juvenile sparring. The defense man regularly needled Lea about his chronic dyspepsia, and the D.A. invariably replied by saying, "Better out the mouth then out the south." In turn, Lea chaffed Duckworth about his record of taking cases on barter or low pay. "How many chickens are you getting for this defense, J.B.?" was a regular first question in court.

The relationship between J.B. Duckworth and the soon-to-be elevated Judge Gillaspie was much more complex. The men had been cordial enough when Gillaspie was the new district attorney and J.B. was a scrapping lawyer. A more precise way to state it might be that in those days, the haughty likes of Gillaspie never gave a man such a Duckworth a second thought. Gillaspie was riddled with ambition. Raised by a rigid soldier and state prison superintendent, J.K.P. Gillaspie was also devoid of humor, as surely as if it had been carefully excised by an army surgeon.

The more Duckworth's success in court brought him into contact with Gillaspie as D.A., the more evident it became that the social austerity of the one could not tolerate the wanton lack of restraint from the other.

Duckworth, often the gadder of an evening, rarely ignored an opportunity to ridicule someone he disliked. So, when blue-nosed Gillaspie worked to ban prizefighting three years prior, robbing Texas sports of major entertainment, J.B.'s insults reached the district attorney's ears where they did not induce the same laughter that the lawyer had gotten in the barrooms.

Gillaspie had been an officer in the volunteer fire companies before Houston created a paid department, and Duckworth, in a great exaggeration, liked to remind the D.A. that he almost died in the St Joseph's Infirmary fire only weeks after moving to the city.

"Escaped with the clothes on my back," J.B. deadpanned.

Each time, Gillaspie bridled at the personal affront as if hearing the defense lawyer's gibe for the first time.

Duckworth's biggest source of fodder to date was when Gillaspie ran afoul of Judge Cavin two years before by not disclosing legal fees he was charging while district attorney. J.K.P. even appealed to a higher court and lost again. The jokes flowed. Though the new judge was not the sort to bend the law to feed his grudge, J.B. Duckworth knew better than to expect the slightest extra courtesy in the courtroom of "Just Keeping Payments" Gillaspie.

Chapter 5

February 1902

Nora Reaves had long ago given up blushing when she stole a kiss from Louie Swearingen. Their engagement to be married was just over a week old, but they had been love-birds since the weather started turning cool at nights. Things were still new enough to give Nora a tingle, but she did not think twice about letting Louie plant a quick kiss on her lips right there on Main Street. Hopefully, standing in front of a jewelry store, it was even a good omen for the ring he would slip on her finger when they married.

If anyone asked Louie, he would say that he first noticed Nora waiting at a car stop on Travis Street with her friend from work. Believers in kismet might say that Nora and Louie were destined to meet eventually. She worked as a seamstress at the Parisian Dye Works on Travis near Capitol, only two blocks from the Turf, where Louie tended bar. No one save her older sister knew that, by that time, Nora had already set a cap for Louis Swearingen, Jr.

Louie thought her beautiful, dimpled, and flirty. She was only 17, but she had sparkly, heavy-lidded eyes that crinkled at the corners and a mouth that was forever upturned into a conspiratorial smile, like she knew his most wicked thoughts. Louie found the slender girl irresistible from the first.

For her, it was his enthusiastic personality. She had watched through the Turf's windows, transfixed by him laughing easily with customers, and wishing the world allowed 17 year old girls to hobnob at a manly bar, though she fully understood even in her daydreams that the cigar smoke would likely make her gag.

On this cold afternoon, they were walking to dinner at the Chinese restaurant on the Square when Swearingen impulsively bussed her smack in front of the Sweeney's clock. Not that either one of them cared, but they did not hear a single soul tut-tut Louie's romantic impetuosity. The couple giggled, as couples tend to do, and walked on.

The unrehearsed essence of things was Swearingen's natural state. One Friday afternoon, at a point when they had barely even said hello to one another, he invited her to meet at the band concert that Sunday at City Park. At the time, Louie had no idea what an ordeal it was for Nora to get into downtown, but the girl already knew that if she was to ever escape her rustic family, she must overcome her geographical undesirability. Her future lay in the big city.

The following Sunday, Nora found Louie Swearingen fifty yards back of the bandstand, spotting him in the crowd by his great shock of hair. The city band provided background music for Louie's conversation and Nora's sometimes overeager responses. Sitting on the grass, the west side of Houston invisible just over the top of the rise from the bayou, they managed to survive uncomfortable silences and their wandering thoughts. Afterwards, they strolled across the bayou footbridge and did a slow turn around the park paths. Amidst the general banter, Louie slipped in a few probing questions.

"Is there no boyfriend I need to watch out for on dark nights?"

Nora looked genuinely confused.

"No one at your dye works has been paying court?"

"Now, why would I want some old man with blue hands?"

Louie's infectious laugh made Nora laugh in return.

"Are they all that old?"

"Every last one over 30."

Louie loosed a wry smile. "I'm 28, you know."

She did not hesitate with a reply.

"Which is less than 30."

Her wit won him over. They met for Sunday walks, and then more frequently. Strolls through the park or window shopping along Main Street or elsewhere downtown. Louie still kept seeing a variety of his nighttime women, but over the next few weeks, he began to find their various flaws more glaring.

As he learned more about her, Louie realized that dating Nora would not be easy. He could hardly walk and chivalrously meet her at the garden gate. He learned that in order to get to her job at the Dye Works, his inamorata faced quite the ordeal. If she could not find a neighbor's buggy headed toward town, Nora might have to walk six miles along the Clark Street Road, all the way to Lorraine Street in the upper reaches of Fifth Ward, to catch a Montgomery line car. If she wanted to leave home while the roosters were still abed, she could ride an East & West Texas train, but the cost of the tickets would consume a third of her pay. Of course, most days, there was no shortage of wagon drivers willing to let a pretty girl accompany them into town. Usually, it was Mr. Paronto, bringing produce from his farm in Little York to the Market Square. The quiet, little Italian waited at the end of her track if she was running late, and she imagined that he would be sad not to have her companionship.

In turn, Nora knew that luring visitors to her house in the woods was nigh on impossible. She thought Louie rather rakish on his bicycle, but nine miles of pedaling down rutted dirt roads sounded daunting even for a young man infatuated, particularly when there was another nine miles home in the dark.

It was eight weeks into the budding relationship when Louie decided that Nora might be interested in knowing about his pending indictment for murder. Prepared for the absolute worst, as any sane man would have been, she took it amazingly well. Louie found out a possible reason for that resilience when he got to know Nora's father.

The first time Louis Swearingen met the family was four days after she accepted his proposal to be married. Following a morning shift at the Turf, he rented a horse and gig and collected his betrothed outside her work. At a buck and a half, it was a splurge, more than a day's wages, but since none of his friends had a buggy to borrow, it was his only choice.

To reach the Reaves abode, Louie and Nora traveled over the bayou, through all of Fifth Ward, then up the Clark Street Road for more than a mile past the Cross Timbers community before turning east down an overgrown track through the untended forest. The whole neighborhood was but nine miles from downtown but a stranger would be hard pressed to differentiate it from the East Texas Piney Woods.

The winter sun was setting, and the quiet whispers from the trees were a tad unnerving compared to the urban bustle of Houston. Along the track, the smell of wood smoke and rotting leaves stuck in Louie's nose. When they pulled into the clearing, Nora looked down with uncharacteristic shame, but Louie squeezed her hand and gave her a warm, open grin.

The Reaves family home was a tumble-down and rambling place. It was evident that at least two cottages and as many lean-to sheds had been nailed together to create the house. There had been a porch at one time, but it was now mostly enclosed with mismatched wood slats so that it could serve as the sleeping space for the three youngest children. The two little girls, Viola and Lou, shared one end of the improvised room, and the youngest child, a boy named Jack, had a cot at the farthest corner. Nora had already warned Louie that her little brother was at times mostly feral.

About fifteen feet in front of the house was a straight run of unpainted picket fence. Though it enclosed exactly nothing, it almost matched the house's faded snatches of whitewash. There was no gate, so the young couple skirted it on the lefthand side and went into the house.

The smell of kerosene lamps was strong. Electric light was in most public spaces in Houston, and where electricity did not go, gas lines generally did. The odor from what Louie quickly counted as five lamps brought a fleeting memory from childhood.

"Good evening, Mr. Swearingen."

Nora's mother was fast to the door, and though she thoroughly wiped her hands on her apron, she did not offer one in greeting.

"You can call me Louie, Mrs. Reaves."

The eyeballs of the rest of the family bore into him like so many cotton worms. Louie countered with his best smile, but that failed to deter little brother Jack.

"What happened to your hair?"

"Jacky, that ain't polite."

Swearingen heard the words in his defense but got the clear sense that Elsie Reaves wanted to ask the very same question. She struck Louie as a meek and nervous woman, perhaps a bit cowed by her husband. For his part, E.L. Reaves made no move from his chair at the kitchen table. Nora intervened with a sweep of her hand.

"Louie, this is my father."

Swearingen stepped to the man and extended his hand. The shake was firm, but there was nothing but coldness in his expression. Nora had cautioned him that her father was a hard man to like. Sullen and uncultured were her words, but she had also assured her fiancé that the man's greatest commitment was to protecting his daughters. Even forewarned, the distrust in Reaves' face was vexing.

"Pleased to meet you, sir. Nora has told me great things about all of you."

Erv Reaves let out what was either a sarcastic grunt or a stifled belch.

Nora led her beau to a spot on the horsehair sofa, the nicest piece of furniture in the large open room, and Louie found himself pinned between Nora and her older sister, Mary.

The three youngest children attended the one room school at Cross Timbers, but like Nora, Mary earned money for the family. She worked as a seamstress at home, making plain dresses for the neighborhood ladies on a hand-me-down treadle Singer that faced the back wall of the common room. A Tuck calendar hung on the bare planks in front of machine, the Tennyson verse and mounted soldier there to keep Mary company until the first of June.

Nora's mother worked, as well. She was making small talk about the little store where she helped as a clerk. It belonged to her sister's father-in-law, and he obligingly furnished her employment. Mary joined in with gossip about two dozen people that Louie well knew he would never meet. She was attractive and friendly, but lacked Nora's crackle and spark.

Trying not to stare, Louis Swearingen stole glances at Nora's father when he could. Erv Reaves was thin, brown, and leathered like a worn razor strop. Looking from profile, the old man's eyes were hazy. Louie wondered if it was from his work or if Nora's dad was half muzzy.

Reaves was a charcoal burner, turning wood into charcoal for use in the city's ovens. It was a low paying and smoky profession. Even on the rare days that Erv Reaves saw lye soap and a trough of water, the smell of him was enough to alert the fire department.

The Reaves family had moved from the community of Laceola in Madison County fifteen years earlier. Elsie offered that they might have been there still if the cane syrup mill had not closed. Like hundreds of other rural Texans, the call of better times in the city drew them in, even if the Reaves family did not make it all the way into town before dropping anchor.

After assessing her daughter's beau for an hour without initiating a single scrap of conversation, E.L. Reaves made a determination. He walked silently to the cupboard, pulled a Mason jar from the back of the top shelf, and held it out in Swearingen's direction.

"Shine?"

Louie thanked the man and took a swig of the clear liquid, then he tried his best not to cough or holler. For the first time, Erv Reaves smiled, revealing four or five remaining front teeth.

"Strong, ain't it?"

Temporarily unable to speak, Swearingen managed an enthusiastic nod. By the time his eyes stopped watering, he figured this was the best opening he would get. He got down to business.

"I'd like to speak to you alone, if I could, Mr. Reaves."

While the women tittered, Louie followed Erv Reaves out into the front yard, watching him closely in the dark. The man walked with quick, short steps, bent forward at the waist from years of scouting the woody path ahead for copperheads and moccasins. He said nothing as he bypassed the little fence to find a spot reclining against an old buckboard.

The Reaves Family did not even own a horse. Of course, neither did Louie. They did keep a cantankerous aged mule named Spartacus who may or may not be coaxed into pulling a load of charcoal into the edge of Houston. Spartacus enjoyed dragging logs through the forest, but he most assuredly would not take a single step with a saddle on his back. Either way, the wagon provided a hospitable enough place to lean and talk.

Louie forced himself to look Reaves in the eye.

"Sir, I have come to love your daughter, and I think she feels the same. I have a steady job and better than two hundred dollars saved up. We'd like to get married, and I come out here to ask your blessing."

The woods were pitch dark behind him, but the man's dirty face reflected just enough lamp light from the house to summon thoughts of a Poe demon. Louie broke the uncomfortable silence with one last thought.

"She sure is a fine young lady."

"You tend bar?"

"Yes, sir."

Crickets and tree frogs filled the void while Erv Reaves considered that.

"Where your folks at, then?"

Louie took the question as an excellent sign.

"My daddy is the constable over in Sealy, but we were at Kenney before that. Up at the top of Austin County. That's where I grew up."

"I ain't got much truck with lawmen."

Chirping bugs again soothed the silence before Reaves continued.

"But I reckon you sound like a good provider. She could do worse. I'll talk to her."

Interview over, E.L. Reaves headed back to the kitchen table.

Chapter 6

John Duckworth's leg did not bother him often, or perhaps the slight pain was such second nature that he just failed to realize it. Today, however, his childhood injury was acting up. When he was younger, he sometimes fancied that the soreness foretold danger or at least a change in the weather, but now, as he neared 48 years of age, he had long since come to grips with the fact that his leg sometimes hurt because a chunk of his calf and a significant slice of his foot were missing. It was simply something unpleasant that must be dealt with. He tried not to wince as he walked away from the Harrisburg depot, limping slightly more than usual.

Not that his brother wanted the Louis Swearingen case to go to trial anytime soon, but it was on the docket for next month, and that meant that John, as the firm's lead investigator, had to knuckle down and begin examining the situation with some urgency. This was his fourth trip out to Harrisburg in search of Andy Green, and John was firmly convinced that the state's star witness was actively avoiding him. He had failed to rouse the man once at the little home where the crime transpired, and twice he vainly cooled his heels outside a line shack on the southern outskirts of the little town while a pair of Black men smoking along the tracks whispered and smirked.

He was getting much the same reaction as he ventured farther into the Negro section of Harrisburg where the houses felt less congealed into a neighborhood. It was early on a chilly Sunday morning. Neatly dressed women and children, and a few men in cheap suits, bustled down the dirt streets on their way to church. Other men slumped on their front step or draped themselves across chairs randomly scattered in muddy front yards. A few, supposing that Duckworth might represent the law, scurried inside. None volunteered a hand in greeting. They only watched him pass.

Twice John stopped one of the church families to inquire the whereabout of Myrtle Street. Both times they dropped their gaze and pointed in the direction he was already headed. Behind him, even on the day of rest, a dredge on the other side of Brady's Island huffed noisily, scraping at the Ship Channel bottom and dropping its mud into a barge.

The house was certainly not much to look at. It had been painted at some point in the past, but most of the evidence of that event had long since mingled in with the splattered or windblown dirt. A few suspect looking trees gave shade on the right hand side of the place, and beyond that was an overgrown patch dominated by reedy okra plants that reached well above head high. A little terrier narrated John's way to the front door. When he reached down to introduce himself, the dog backed up without ceasing his tirade.

John rapped on the door frame a few times before it opened to reveal a stocky man in a dirty undershirt and blue work pants. In an instant, the fellow's eyes went from confusion to fear to woeful resignation. He stepped outside before he spoke.

"Yes, sir?"

Andy Green's voice was a medium pitched croak, as scratchy as if he had been gargling rocks.

"Mr. Green, my name's John Duckworth. My brother represents Louis Swearingen, the man who you claim killed your friend."

John did not give Green a chance to deny his identity, and to his credit, the man quieted his dog and sat down in the chair farthest from the door.

"I don't just claim it, Mr. Duckworth. I saw it with these eyes."

He looked to the dog.

"Poochie, come here."

The little dog considered the offer but scampered underneath the house instead. It was a chilly morning, but seeing no invitation to the living room forthcoming, John sat down in the other chair unasked. Andy Green winced slightly but decided to be deferential.

"Poochie was Johnson's dog, but I suspect he's mine now. Even if he don't mind worth a damn."

John offered Green a small smile, but was not pulled away from his point.

"I read your statement, but for the life of me, I can't divine why Louie Swearingen would do such a thing. According to him, he didn't even know Mr. Montgomery and was nowhere near Harrisburg on the night of the shooting. We just want to see justice done, and I was hoping you might be able to help me out with that."

The delivery was so sincere that Green cocked his ear to the side while it registered. Then he slowly and sadly shook his head.

"Mr. Louie knew Johnson sure enough. Didn't like him at all."

Duckworth feared where the story was going but betrayed nothing as he asked his next calm question.

"I don't mean to offend you, Mr. Green, but don't you think you may have confused two different people here? It just seems unlikely that Mr. Swearingen would run in the same circles as your friend."

Andy Green was not used to this level of solicitousness from a White man, but the condescension was certainly familiar enough that he brushed it aside without a thought.

"Louie Swearingen tended bar at the Anchor. Working man's joint by the bayou. He worked there back... '94, '95 maybe."

"And they served Negros?"

"Place would handle colored trade out a back window, and we'd sit on crates or lumber, what have you. It was a little horse and wagon lot covered in shell. A mess of us drank back there."

"When's the last time you saw Mr. Swearingen?"

"Well..."

Green wiped at his nose, rubbed down his arms, and stared into the distance.

"I don't reckon I've seen him since he moved over to Houston. Been better than 6 years."

John let himself breathe for a second. His job was to find points to be raised or avoided in court, and Green's last answer felt like a win. It lasted only until the next question.

"After such a long time... it's just that a man can change a lot in six years."

"No, sir. Louie Swearingen, he hit me in the head with a bottle once for no good reason. I ain't likely to forget a man like that."

The two looked at each other for the better part of a minute without talking. To John's eye, Andy Green was telling the truth. He tried for something else in the plus column.

"He never had that kind of trouble with Mr. Montgomery, though, did he?"

"Lord, he and Johnson got into much worse. Rubbed each other wrong, those two. He come after Johnson with a knife late one night. Would've cut him bad most likely, if he'd been sober enough to run him down. He's a bad man, your Louie Swearingen. Mean streak wider than Mississippi."

District Attorney Lea knew which constables he could count on for competent investigation and which he could not. Eddie Isgitt would never be called a goer. That is why he asked Archie Anderson to have one of his detectives nose around. Though J.B. Duckworth was a friend, he was also someone who J.V. Lea loved to beat in court, and this looked like his best shot in years.

The man assigned by the sheriff was Bill Bernhard, a burly six footer with deep-set black eyes that could unnerve a prisoner or suspect seemingly at a whim. His boss once laughingly compared Bernhard to a raven who convinced a criminal that he was on the verge of removing his eyes or organs with a single peck. Though no one had ever heard a claim of brutality against the man, most who looked at the dark deputy believed it imminently possible nonetheless.

John Duckworth knew full well that the prosecution would have someone poking around the same places he was going, and he was exasperated to hear a fourth bartender in a row say that the sheriff's man was asking his very questions ahead of him. For the umpteenth time, he inwardly chastised himself for not spending more time investigating the Swearingen case soon after it happened. Fact was, though, that there were so many other clients in the queue ahead of him. As the firm's lone shoe leather man, his brother had him roaming over half of Texas asking questions and poking into dusty courthouse files, and that was on days when he was not in the offices trying to sort reams of paperwork.

Since his conversation on Andy Green's porch the previous Sunday, he had found exactly nothing to help Louie Swearingen's case. The next two days were spent on other cases and office work, but he was out chasing scraps once again, and it was not off to a roaring start. At least the weather had warmed up.

It was at the second stop that Wednesday afternoon, Tony Genussa's grocery and beer parlor out on German Street in the East End, that the proprietor identified Deputy Bernhard by name. At least Duckworth knew what he was up against. He pressed his first question about Swearingen.

"Customer's business is his own," was the aproned man's heavily accented response. It took less than a minute to know that no additional comments were forthcoming. John was confident the sheriff's man left with nothing better.

Overall, John counted his chances well above any lawman's. He had developed so many contacts around Houston that he was both known and liked in most places. That was especially true of bars where the owners knew the Duckworths to be generous customers. When he was after information in another town, John employed patience and likeability. He always opened by ordering a beer and offering some small talk before inquiring into the matters at hand.

The deputies and constables, whether uniformed or not, rarely spent a dime. They flashed a badge and demanded answers. If they drank a beer, they expected it to be on the house. More than one bartender made it a gleeful habit to pass wrong information to a surly copper. It was a reason to maintain some optimism that something useful would eventually surface.

John slid down from the rented rig and tied the reins to a post. It had barely gone two in the afternoon, but almost a dozen of the beer garden tables at Carl

Dumler's place were occupied. On such a mild day, several of the men had doffed their hats to enjoy the sun, and coats were slung haphazardly across chair backs. Two pea hens absently pecked at the dirt.

Inside the converted clapboard outbuilding that passed for a beer hall, it was dark and cool. The owner himself, a balding German in his 50s, was sipping at a mug and talking with an Irishman who rented a room on the sprawling property. John greeted them both and laid a quarter dollar on the pine bar top.

"Afternoon, Carl. Pete. Why don't you draw us three?"

Dumler's eyes twinkled, and he grew a mischievous smile.

"You have a hired buggy, and you stake the first round. You are working a case, Mr. Duckworth."

John let out a genuine laugh as the barman continued.

"What's more, I know which one."

The newcomer's smile gave way to a loud sigh.

"So, Bill Bernhard's beaten me here, too?"

As Dumler filled three mugs, he recounted the deputy's visit less than a week prior. As with most everyone else, the swarthy lawman left those at the beer garden a bit uneasy. It was the primary reason people generally answered his questions.

Bar people tended to know other bar people. Eyeballing the friendly competition while enjoying a libation or two was common practice. It was not news that Louie Swearingen was well known in most drinking establishments, but Carl Dumler was the first person who admitted to seeing him around the time of the murder. Still, John hoped that for once the long delay might work in his favor.

"If he shows up at least once a month, how come that night stands out?"

"He left with a girl."

Dumler chuckled to himself and waved his comment away as one might shoo a fly.

"Yes, that is not so unusual with young Louie, I must admit. Lucky devil. But this night he got in a shoving fight with another fellow who fancied her."

"That was half a year ago. There's no way you can pin it down to a single day."

"I know it was that night because I made him settle a tab. Charlie Lusk had paid him his wages. It's written in the ledger."

John felt his stomach roll over.

"And you showed the ledger to Bernhard, too?"

Dumler cast his eyes down to the bar top and sheepishly drew out the first word of his answer.

"Jaaaa. I don't need no trouble with the law."

Duckworth hesitated a moment or two before he asked the inevitable.

"Do you happen to know the girl he met here?"

"Ja. I've seen her plenty. No name. Before you ask, I don't know her name, but she is a loosey goosey. She comes here with her cousin or brother or something, but does not always leave with them. Our friend Louie is not the first."

"She on the game?"

Carl spread his hands and shrugged.

"Any idea where she lives?" John asked him.

Irish Pete offered a leer along with an answer to the question.

"That way," he said as he pointed to his left. "Towards Harrisburg."

In the first week of each quarter, the criminal district court dockets stretched the law firm's personnel as thin as a widow's knickers. In March 1902, that schedule found Henry Fein, the second name partner, handling business in the Harris County Courthouse. Junior partner Sonny Schlottmann made three stops in East Texas, the first two seeking postponements before he finally settled down with a murder trial at Coldspring. Jed Posey was in Bryan, and J.B. Duckworth, always the one to handle the highest profile cases, was at trial two counties south of the city.

For Louie Swearingen, the court date meant dressing up and skipping work only to spend less than a minute before Judge Gillaspie. Henry Fein had filled him in upon his arrival. The district attorney would seek, and get, a postponement. As

Louie stuttered out questions, the bespectacled Fein patted him on the arm and assured him this was a good thing.

When the case was called, D.A. Lea, who faced several days' worth of business before the district court, requested that the trial be put off since the state was without a vital witness – Precinct 2 Constable E.P. Isgitt. It appeared that the constable had gone squirrel hunting. Deputies knew that he was somewhere in the woods out past Cedar Bayou, but they could not find him. Judge Gillaspie grumbled under his breath as he leafed through the pages of an oversized ledger.

"All right. This case is reset for the district criminal court session to begin on Monday the second of June. Court clerk will be in touch with both parties. What's next?"

Henry stood up from his chair and straightened his papers before slipping them inside a satchel. Swearingen eyed him, his mouth slightly ajar.

"That's it?"

"Yes. That's it. Our office will be in touch soon."

J.B. never basked in the glory of courtroom victory for more than an evening, a few hours was really the norm. Some drinks and a fine dinner allowed him plenty enough time to brag to friends and have a few laughs, often at the prosecutor's expense. Beyond that, there was always the ever-looming caseload, and it was that hard work that gave J.B. Duckworth his true strength.

So, when he walked into the office the day after he returned from Wharton and three days of murder trial that culminated in the acquittal of sharecropper George Purdy, the big win was no longer on his mind. Instead, Duckworth made a serious dive into the mass of other cases strewn across his oak desk.

He also got a briefing from his partner Henry Fein about the results in the Harris County Court which in turn led to a recapitulation of the work his brother John had been doing, and that finally led to Louie Swearingen being summoned to the law offices of Duckworth & Fein.

When the client arrived, he cooled his heels in the large communal room. From an uncomfortable straight-backed chair pushed hard against the wall, Louie watched two young lawyers he did not know toil quietly. Fein, the short Alsatian who he had met for the first time in court a few days earlier, was visible through an open door to the far lefthand corner of the space. Just as Louie, slightly hungover, was on the cusp of falling asleep, John Duckworth emerged from his younger brother's office, at the far righthand corner, and waved him in.

Swearingen was a roll with the punches type, and his assumption was that this was a routine client conference about the next moves. Henry Fein had promised to be in touch. Louie just did not expect that meant in only a few days. So, he was unprepared for the raking he received after his greeting.

John Duckworth closed the office door behind him then pointed Louie to a seat across from J.B. John took the adjacent visitor's chair without a word. J.B. did not rise to shake hands. He offered his client nothing more than a level stare. The lawyer's voice started off low so he had plenty of room for it to dramatically rise.

"The first time you met with my brother, you denied ever being in Harrisburg. Hell, from what John tells me, you claimed to have barely heard of the place."

John sat quietly, deferring to his brother. When Swearingen answered, he sounded like a kid when the teacher held the switch.

"The night was a blur. I don't recollect anything. Truly."

J.B. was not having it. He waved John's original notes as a preacher might wave a Bible.

"We investigated. We're good at our jobs, and, occasionally, so is the sheriff's office. You were sober when you woke up in some chippy's room the next morning. You told my brother here how made your way home. You knew goddamned well you'd been in Harrisburg that night!"

Louie inspected his shoe tops without comment.

"God damn it!"

J.B. slapped his desktop.

"I've got enough shit piled up against me. They have an eye witness who says you shot a man through the goddamned eye! And now I'm left with a client that lies to me."

Duckworth paused and lowered his volume.

"Your boss is paying us to keep you out of the state pen. If that's going to happen, and it is far from a sure thing, you'd best start taking this whole enterprise seriously."

J.B. smoothed his moustache as he leaned back in his chair. The chastisement was over. The three men sat in silence for almost a minute before Louie Swearingen finally mustered the courage to ask the question that was truly on his mind.

"I don't know anything about how the law works, at least the courtroom part of things."

He allowed himself a little smile.

"I reckon I know why the D.A. wanted to postpone things with that constable being gone and all, but why didn't y'all put up a fight? Couldn't Mr. Fein have pushed to hold my trial and get it over with?"

"There was no point in it. Unless a judge is on the take or out to fix your wagon, he generally sets things up for a fair match. But we want to go to trial only when the ducks are lined up in our sights."

Louie cocked his head to one side.

"You mean this may go on longer? I don't like this thing dangling over my head."

"Son, if I have my way, this won't come to trial until all the prosecution witnesses are sleeping six feet south of the sod. You're out on bail, so just go about your business. J.V. Lea did us a big favor. He saved me using one of my motions with Gillaspie. Next time, we've got one coming our way. We don't want to get in the position where we've got to go to that lousy son of a bitch for any favors."

Swearingen blanched a little. J.B. laughed, and his dark eyes twinkled." Don't you worry about that. Gillaspie'll be fair even if it makes his liver burst. It's his Achilles heel. I never leave anything to chance, Louie."

Chapter 7

April 1902

There was a whole lot of nothing on the Stella Cut Off Road. It hugged close and true to the rails on the riders' left. Even the ruts were boringly straight. It was flat, uninspiring land out this way. There were a few small plots where corn and beans were starting to grow, but most of it was sandy soil better suited to ranching. The cattle breakfasting on the dew-damp switchgrass paid the two riders no mind. A pair of old white-faced cows lolled beneath a rare scrub oak, perhaps staking a claim for summer when the shade would come at a premium. The bigger of the two mounted men shook his head, marveling at how lazy an animal could get when the day had not yet even started.

Constable E.P. Isgitt and Ben Simmons, his deputy, passed only two houses in the mile since the outskirts of Harrisburg. At the second one, as the sun broke above the coastal prairie to their left, a yellow dog rushed out from under the ramshackle porch to bark and snarl. Isgitt's gray horse was rather indifferent about the whole thing, and she kept walking without more than a couple of glances toward the mutt. Simmons' chestnut brindle was more skittish, but the deputy kept him under control. It did not take long for the mongrel to give up the game and let the men ride on in peace.

Isgitt did not much like dogs. Cats either. He was well aware of Bible verses about being kind to animals, and his preacher at the Baptist church had even prattled on about God's creatures a time or two, but the notion of spending a family's hard earned money to subsidize a wild beast was beyond him. It seemed a silly custom. He knew fully where expressing such a comment to his deputy would lead, but Isgitt could not help himself.

"They'd be a damn sight better off shooting that dog or running him off someplace."

Simmons was lost in the reverie of his own thoughts, and it took him a second to put things together, though they were no more than 200 yards past the dog in question when he took the bait.

"Won't be nobody sneak-thiefing up on the place, now will there?"

Though Isgitt, as the elected official, was the boss, he was quietly intimidated by Simmons. The deputy had been in his post for several years, and he was more respected among the law abiding citizens than the hulking newcomer. Even physically, Ben Simmons might be outweighed by a good 30 pounds, but his was sinew compared to E.P. Isgitt's dough. Normally, the loquacious constable responded to the deputy with silence or defensiveness.

"I like children just fine. Don't need no dogs."

"You better like them. You got a houseful."

Simmons accompanied that remark with a not-well-hidden sneer that his boss failed to see. Instead, the big man put on a look of satisfaction.

"Yep."

To Isgitt, his young ones were proof of his virility. With friends and acquaintances in the barrooms or even in during quiet conversation after church, he was likely to brag on such a topic, but he could not help but believe his deputy somehow doubted the veracity of his conquests. Therefore, any chance to trumpet his manhood to his underling was a good one.

"I've been teaching the two boys to fish already. Make a man out of them. They're probably too young to get much out of it, but you got to start them out someplace."

When that got no response, he continued.

"Little one's too damn noisy on top of it. No one catches fish with whooping boys pegging rocks into the hole."

He punctuated the remark with a knowing smile, but Simmons did not offer much in return.

"Mmm-hmm."

Isgitt shot a silent damnation at his deputy. His five little ones were dear to him. Admittedly, his daughters were more of a mystery. Girls were perplexing creatures. The constable doubted that any father knew exactly what to do with them, but they were his, and he assured himself that he loved them.

The gray mare had been grabbing mouthfuls of tall grass as they ambled along, but she eased to a stop at a roadside stand of particularly juicy Big Bluestem. The man let her feed for a minute or two, recovering his dignity in the silence before he nudged her along. Simmons plodded slowly ahead, but Isgitt soon caught up. He wanted to catch his quarry early.

The two men saw a handful of people stirring as they crossed the Galveston Road and walked their horses past the four or five streets that comprised Brookline. If those early risers recognized either of their precinct's lawmen, they did not betray their knowledge with a wave. When they reached Street's Switch, Isgitt turned east across the tracks and slowed his mount even further motioning Simmons to do the same.

The second shack on the left was roughly a quarter mile along, and it looked much as the constable had pictured. His snitch had offered that it sat farther back from the dirt track, and true to that report, reeds grew high in depressions on three sides. The two men kept up their slow walking pace until they were 100 yards past the little shanty before they dismounted and tied their reins to a fence post. No use calling attention to themselves by stopping on the road out front.

Isgitt gave himself a mental pat on the back. The sun was behind them and so would be in the eyes of anyone looking their direction. Even better, the tall bulrushes gave them a solid screen until they were five yards from the building.

With no instructions beyond a look between them, the two walked at the verge of the rough dirt road for the first fifty yards until Simmons gave a sideways nod of the head and climbed between the wire strands of the fence to come up behind the stand of cane. Isgitt figured that barrier for about 15 feet thick. Just before they entered, he turned to his deputy and held a finger to his lips in an unnecessary reminder to be quiet. Simmons grinned and whispered back.

"Watch for moccasins. They're really coming out."

The deputy parted a way through, and his boss followed right at the heels. Both men winced every time a stalk snapped. When they reached the far edge, the two lawmen got their first good look at the place. What was now a dilapidated shanty had clearly started its life as a mere corn crib. Several of the siding boards were no closer together than bed slats. Despite the fact that someone in the past had nailed various rectangles of scrounged lumber here and there, plenty of early morning light was visible from the other side. Openings at both front and back acted as doors.

Inside, two, or maybe three figures lay prone. One of them was even snoring.

Constable Isgitt pointed first front and then back and spread his hands as a question. Simmons tapped himself on the chest and motioned that he would take the back. Isgitt nodded.

The man they were seeking was named Will Jones, an escaped state prisoner who had given guards the slip twice. His first run was a short one from a sugar cane field near Missouri City a week or two earlier virtually into the arms of a Fort Bend County Sheriff's deputy. That lucky man had been eating his supper at a Stafford café when he spied his jailbird on the lam sauntering across a nearby lot. He nabbed the fellow and chained him up in a shed while he went to get help. Due to an overnight rain and no moonlight to speak of, they did not return until the next morning, only to find a lag bolt pried free from the rotten wall and their captive gone.

The embarrassed deputies had followed his tracks, first on horseback and foot through the muddy cotton and cane fields, and soon after with dogs. The hounds indicated that they lost the scent at the tracks of the Galveston Harrisburg & San Antonio. Since the most recent train was an eastbound freight, authorities sent notification telegrams to law enforcement in that direction as far as Lafayette, but E.P. Isgitt knew that the most likely spot for a convict to hop off was right near Harrisburg where the train stood the possibility of sitting for a time in a yard.

Isgitt did not like Black people, but he found a use for some. One of those was a teener boy named Leo who carried bags at the rail depot. It was truly remarkable what that swarthy fink could learn, and he willingly gave it all up at a dime or a quarter a pop. That was money Isgitt happily billed to the county.

The evening before, Leo told the constable that an escaped con was staying in a shack out past Brookline. One of his people had been supplying him with food. There was no doubt in Isgitt's mind that this was the escapee who had generated the telegrams. Leo may be a lowly rat, but his information was generally reliable. Nothing was set in stone, but a little bit of bounty money was already hot in his pocket.

The two lawmen hoped to time their entry from opposite door openings, but Isgitt lost sight of Simmons when he went behind the far corner of the little shack. He listened for the deputy's footsteps but heard nothing beyond the loud thrum of blood pressure pulsing in his ears. A woman's scream cut through his tension. Suddenly everyone was on their feet and wrapped in a fast blur of motion.

Isgitt's eye caught briefly on the undershirt of the shapely young colored girl, probably not even 20 years old, but those carnal thoughts vanished in a blink. The pair had been laying with their feet toward the back of the crib, and the deputy's footfall squeaked a loose rough-hewn board as he stepped up from the ground. It woke the girl who commenced to hollering and had not yet quit. The natural instinct of their convict was to beeline for the far side of the shack, and that's exactly where Constable E.P. Isgitt stood, his bulky frame silhouetted against the gray and pink sky.

Will Jones was fully committed to running that direction, and he dipped his shoulder in hopes of knocking the big White man off his feet. It worked, but it also took Jones down. The two men tumbled through the opening at the south side of the little building and landed hard on the damp ground.

They did not fall together. The Black man had hoped to land on top of the big fellow blocking his escape, but he hit dirt instead. It took the wind out of him for a moment, and that was all the time the constable needed to land two hard slaps on the escapee's ear. It was not a strategy, but the pure luck of it was effective. With a loud ringing that would not stop, the con cried out as he rose to his knees.

"I ain't done nothing!"

Before he could stand to run, Jones was knocked back flat to the dirt by the flying body of Ben Simmons who had launched himself from the elevated doorway. As soon as the deputy landed, he placed an elbow on the back of the man's neck and ground the side of his face farther into the dirt. The constable fished a set of handcuffs from his pants pocket and tightened them onto the dark wrists. Behind them, the girl had managed to pull a dress over her head without stopping her caterwauling for even a second.

As soon as the handcuffs were secure, Deputy Simmons hoisted the prisoner to his feet, one of which was bleeding. The man wore nothing but a pair of stained duck canvas pants that looked about three inches too short. Even though his hair was cropped close, the curls were lousy with bits of hay.

Eddie Isgitt made sure that Simmons still had hold of the man from the back as he positioned himself in front.

"Look at that pretty face, Ben."

The big right hand came in from the side and smashed Jones right in the mouth. Immediately, Isgitt regretted the punch. He shook out his fist, but it hurt something fierce. His next blow was with his left, and the surprise of it, as much as the brute force, doubled the convict over at the waist. Isgitt did not wait until the man was upright before adding an open-handed right to the side of his head.

"We're fixing to run you downtown to the main jail so I can see about what-ever pay I got coming my way, but nothing says you need to arrive unharmed."

The handcuffed man tried to spit, but it was gravity that impelled the red viscous liquid to the ground. When he was standing, Ben Simmons spoke loudly into the man's ear.

"You tell your poke to quit her hollering and get on out of here, or me and the constable are damn likely to take our turns riding her."

The girl heard Simmons clearly. Though her noises did not cease, they did recede into the distance as she lit off across the pasture to points unknown. The deputy let out an earthy laugh.

The Precinct 2 constables discussed making their prisoner walk all the way to the Capitol Street Jail, but his foot had a nasty puncture, likely from stepping on a nail in the old corn crib, and they most decidedly did not want to be all day delivering him into Houston before getting home to Harrisburg. In the end, Constable Isgitt pulled rank, and the con rode double with Ben Simmons. Periodically on the ride, Isgitt felt a few more punches and slaps were warranted just in case their charge developed any more notions of rabbiting off.

The little party picked their way across Brays Bayou on the railroad trestle just north of Brookline then caught the Telephone Road up into the outskirts of Houston. Along the route, their prisoner found his wind and his mouth. He vehemently denied being the man they were looking for and became so adamant once that Isgitt was compelled to yank him down from the deputy's gelding and give him two more blows to the stomach. The constable had learned his lessons about hitting this one in the face.

By the time they reached the side door of the county jail, the captured convict had bruises on both sides of his face and a large knot had risen between his left ear and eyebrow. He also limped badly on his foot between the hitching rail and the building.

The head jailer himself, Tom Wilson, answered the rap on the outer door and watched as the two precinct men shoved a bloody, bruised, and handcuffed man in before them. As he secured the latches, Wilson heard a bit of shuffling behind him. He turned in time to see Eddie Isgitt throw a strong uppercut into the restrained prisoner's chin. The man slumped to the floor. With a smile in his eyes, Isgitt turned to Wilson.

"Looked like he was breaking for the door."

Wilson shot the constable a look.

"He's bleeding all over my damned floor. What the hell happened to his foot?"

"Nail or something. Happened when we caught him."

They were speaking about the prisoner as if he was nowhere in sight, and the man had, in fact, remained on the floor moaning. Tom Wilson plopped down in his chair and opened the big ledger.

"Who is he and what's the charge?"

Eddie Isgitt answered with a good measure of pride.

"That's Will Jones. The state con who run off from Missouri City."

Wilson placed his fountain pen on the table in front of him and leaned back with a sigh.

"You jacking me up?"

Eddie Isgitt scowled and could feel the tightness rise in his neck and shoulders.

"Don't you think for a minute you're fixing to cheat me out of whatever bounty money there is on this boy."

The kneeling prisoner mumbled more protests through his cut and swollen mouth, but his words were drowned out by Tom Wilson's laughter.

"Bounty? Son, they caught that fellow two days ago over at Winnie. He's likely back inside the Walls or in the hole at whatever farm they shipped him to."

Nobody said a word at first, then Wilson let loose another wry laugh.

"So, who is this poor fellow you've beat half to death?"

"That's... what I've been... telling you."

The Black man was struggling to his feet, and his words came fitfully and muted.

"I told that... sheriff in Stafford, too... My name is Bobo Carter."

Isgitt's words were not ready to give up the idea of a reward, but his face betrayed a suddenly growing doubt. He tried to bargain with Tom Wilson.

"How do you know it ain't the law over at Winnie that got it wrong? Maybe my guy is the right guy."

"The state prison boys got that one themselves. I reckon they'd recognize their own prisoner, don't you, now?"

Bobo Carter, the man who was not Will Jones, had reached his feet to lean against a wall. His breathing was growing close to normal, but his voice was still weak and slow.

"I don't know why they grabbed me. I was just walking to the store. I ain't done nothing. Please take these cuffs off me, won't you, sir? Sheriff's man in Stafford took me and chained me up in a shed. Along about midnight, I prised out that hook and I ran..."

Carter's woeful story continued, but as he rambled and pleaded, Eddie Isgitt snatched the keyring from the jailer's hook and fumbled the lock mechanism open to the outside. He tossed the ring down on top of the open ledger and left without another word. After a wry shrug, Ben Simmons followed.

Few lawmen enjoyed paperwork, but it was a necessary task to keep the county auditors at bay. If he wanted his paltry pay vouchers to keep coming, E.P. Isgitt had to complete reports. One thing his small Madison County school had taught him was good Spencerian penmanship, even if the lessons had come at the expense of innumerable sharp raps across his knuckles with a ruler or switch. They might be tedious to compose, but the constable's forms looked elegant and tidy.

At the thought of his pristine reports, Isgitt brushed crumbs off the paper in front of him. His wife had wrapped him up two cheese and pepper sandwiches for lunch, and he had brought one out a little early. The wife was awfully good to him, and she knew well enough that her husband enjoyed two snacks during the day rather than a single lunch. His normal duties took him out on patrol, and Elsie understood that her man worked up an appetite. The thought of her made him pause until the subject of his scribbling snapped back to the fore.

Isgitt had considered not even filling out a report about his pursuit and arrest of the man who turned out to be someone other than who he sought. He realized, though, that the circulation of horrible rumors was inevitable. It was a certainty that everyone in the sheriff's department and likely the Houston Police were already whooping it up at his expense. The new commissioner for his precinct was Heinan Dunks up at Highlands, and it was possible that he did not yet know, but that felt like a matter of time. Dunks would be expecting to see the write-up.

When Applewhite Jordan stuck his head into the constable's small office, Isgitt could tell immediately that a roasting had arrived. Jordan's denigration of the man who shared the spare little Precinct 2 court building was a constant. The J.P. showed no restraint in his opinion that the new constable was incompetent, stupid, or even inherently slow. The smirk of the moment was especially foreboding.

"Word around town is you got your man, Isgitt."

A thundercloud washed over the constable's face, but he said nothing. His writing stopped lest he make a mistake.

The J.P. adopted the syrupy tone of false camaraderie.

"They all look alike, them darkies, don't they Isgitt?"

Though he felt fit to burst, Isgitt maintained his composure.

"I found the man that run off from Stafford. Found him in the middle of damned nowhere, an old corn crib on the prairie. I ain't ashamed of that of that kind of work."

Jordan switched to condescension.

"But that still don't make it the right guy, now does it? I heard tell that it took Tom Wilson an hour and a half to get that poor fellow you beat to quit telling his story."

The J.P. popped a couple of pecan halves into his mouth to punctuate his remark. Still his target held back the ire.

"It was the deputy down in Fort Bend who chained up the wrong jig, not me. All I did was hunt down his mistake. If Fort Bend offered a bounty, I ought to be able to collect. I got the man they were after."

Jordan pushed away from the doorframe where he was leaning.

"Bounty? Is that what's got you fit to be tied? There's no bounty. You're a goddamned elected official Isgitt. You're supposed to know how these things work. If the state has anything to give you, they'll post a reward. You don't get to decide for them. Hell, if you'd waited another week before you found him, they might have gotten around to it. But for that, you'd need to find the right man, you dumb son of a bitch."

Jordan shook his head and laughed. He filled his mouth with more pecans as he wandered back toward his own office.

Chapter 8

May 1902

Harris Peterson waved as his friend J.B. Duckworth stepped through the door of the Gentlemen's Restaurant and Bar and scanned the room. Cigar smoke hung in the air like a fog bank, and though several ceiling fans swirled the bluish haze, they did not dissipate it. The Café Sauter was crowded, but Peterson had secured one of the prime tables, toward the back next to the window overlooking Preston Street. Gustav and Mina Sauter ran what was widely considered the best restaurant in town, and after 20 years, they were helped out by their children, Fritz and Pauline. It was young Fritz who followed Duckworth to his seat and watched frustratedly as the lawyer pulled out his own chair.

"When I read the note that you were buying, I put my entire caseload aside."

Peterson graced the remark with an easy laugh.

"Louise is down at Brazoria visiting her mother for what may be a whole week. She took little Henry with her, and the rest of the brood are old enough to fend for themselves. Well, as much fending's as required with a maid at your disposal."

He waved the talk of his teenaged children away with the back of his hand before appending an afterthought.

"I told them it was business, but we can fit that little paragraph in after a couple of drinks."

As if summoned by the magic word, their long-aproned waiter appeared.

"Old Taylor, Mr. Duckworth?"

"All night, Axel. My best friend Peterson here is paying."

Harris Peterson hung his head in mock resignation and motioned to his half full whiskey glass. It would be empty by the time the new one arrived.

"You won't break me tonight, J.B.. You remember that grazing land I bought out past Waller? I sold it yesterday for a good packet. You really should have gone in with me."

"Shit, Harris, I don't make your kind of money, so I'll just have to settle for the occasional free meal from your spoils."

Harris Peterson was not only J.B. Duckworth's closest friend, he was the city's top real estate attorney and a former judge. With Peterson's expert guidance, the defense lawyer had joined in more than a dozen investments. In spite of the fact that his own home was cramped and in a decidedly undesirable part of town, slowly, but steadily, Duckworth had begun building some small personal wealth of his own.

After another round of whiskeys to warm them up, Peterson flagged their waiter, Axel, over from the service bar. Like the owner's family, the man was Prussian. German immigrants were seemingly everywhere in Houston, and, unlike the Italians, they had begun to assert themselves in polite society. Still, the accents could be hard to navigate for some inveterate Southerners. After years of dealing with restaurant patrons, the sharpest dialectical edges had worn off the staff of Sauter's.

"I think I'll start with some oysters. Are they the Blue Points?"

"No, sir. They are Galveston oysters. Fresh off the barge and likely the last we will see this season."

Duckworth spoke up.

"All the better. I want to taste that briny bay before summer punches us full in the face. Bring me a dozen, too."

The sky outside was now fully darkened, but the foot traffic on the other side of the glass was as robust as ever. In spite of the clatter inside the downstairs dining room, occasional scraps of passing conversation pierced the glass. An Irishwoman was giving her man what for. A pair of street urchins stopped to make faces, and a city police officer in his tall helmet tapped the pane with his nightstick and smiled at Harris Peterson. When he recognized Duckworth as the legal scourge of law and order, his grin vanished.

Beyond the sidewalk, various gigs and drays and carriages, open and closed, rambled past on the dirt avenue. There were single riders a plenty and one young Black couple mounted double on a game looking strawberry roan. Any noise from Preston Street was drowned out by the lively conversation among the tables. At this time of the evening, every man in the place was at least three libations to the better, and the volume had risen accordingly. That went double for the patrons at the bar. Surely, the din even intruded into the ladies-only dining room.

Duckworth and Peterson were finishing their main plates – rare steaks and asparagus spears in lemon butter. There had also been a plate of fresh tomatoes in vinaigrette. The men had laughed and filled the night with bawdy gossip about bygone days. If Harris Peterson did have any actual business to discuss, it had slipped his memory. As District Attorney Lea stopped at their table for a greeting, the mood could not have been better.

When the hellos stretched into small talk, Lea borrowed a chair from a neighboring pair of elderly gents and made himself at home. His own dinner meeting had adjourned, and he seemingly had time remaining on his hands. The ebullient Peterson signaled for another round of drinks.

"There is one thing I wanted to mention to you, J.B. Gillaspie brought your name up yesterday in chambers."

Duckworth's face darkened immediately while Lea continued his story.

"It wasn't flattering, either."

"I wouldn't suspect it to be. The son of a bitch won't even speak to me outside of court."

"Well, I doubt if you'll be hearing anything about this either unless it becomes official. He got wind of some fracas you had at Big Annie's a while back."

J.B. was genuinely perplexed.

"Fracas? I've had no run-ins at Big Annie's. And for the edification of all the high and mighty likes of Judge Gillaspie, Annie runs as peaceful a tavern as any on this side of the bayou. Nothing against you two, of course, but why does everyone need a stick up their ass about Fifth Ward?"

The D.A. offered a shrug.

"I couldn't tell you. It had something to do with an accusation against you in Waco."

Harris Peterson could read the slow dawning and building wrath in his chum's face. Within half a minute Duckworth's brow had clouded and the hinges of his jaw throbbed.

"Why'd he bring this up to you?"

J.B. was already reaching conclusions, and J.V. Lea knew it. That caused his slight hesitation before responding.

"Well, he asked me to look into it with Ollie Cross, the D.A. up in McLennan County."

The answer and its ramifications sat heavily between them. Suddenly Duckworth pounded his fist on the table. It was hard enough to make the silverware jump and cause the other two men to grab their whiskey glasses in defense against spillage. If that failed to turn a few heads in Sauter's big room, the loosed epithet certainly did.

"Goddamnit!"

The outburst relieved at least enough pressure to lower J.B.'s volume a notch, but he remained livid. His lips pursed into a thoughtful pout, and when he smoothed his walrus moustache, it was firm and deliberate.

"That no good son of a bitch aims to bring this up as proof against my moral standing to practice law."

Peterson placed his palm down on the table in front of his friend, and he drummed his fingers. His tone was placating.

"Come on, now, J.B. There's no mechanism to do anything other than embarrass you. On top of it, you've got friends on the bench, if it ever came to that. You drink with Judge Cavin, for Christ's sake. He'd speak up for you. There'd be fellow attorneys, too, on any panel Gillaspie could convene, but you're crazy if you think it'd ever come to that. He can't hold a conduct hearing on his own."

Harris chuckled and took a sip of his bourbon.

"Besides, the murdering public likes a little roguish panache in their defense lawyers. Even if he did bring something up, just consider it advertisement."

Sensing that the storm was passing, Lea spoke again.

"For the record, I'm not planning on asking Ollie Cross a goddamned thing. I'm a busy man, and Gillaspie will have to keep hounding me before I write any letters."

Again, the three sat in tense silence before Lea's curiosity got the better of him.

"I got to ask, though. What the hell are you supposed to have done?"

James B. Duckworth might be quick to anger, but he was also lightning fast on the recovery. He sipped his Old Taylor and raised one corner of his mouth in a teasing smile.

"Well, what that drunk bastard at Annie's was prattling on about was me getting shot in the hand outside a middle rate hotel. As long as it goes no further than this table, J.V., I'll tell you that much. The cretin back in... whenever, he meant to make me out as some sort of thief, but it all had to do with a woman."

Duckworth leaned back in his chair and nodded his head conspiratorially. Peterson held his tongue, but Lea was lured in, albeit skeptically. Men were certainly prone to the occasional peccadillo, but no one in Houston had ever heard such rumors about James B. Duckworth.

"I've never known you to be that kind of Lothario."

J.B. flicked the remark away with his hand.

"It was years ago. Before I ever came to Houston."

"Then why are you so afire to keep it a secret?"

Duckworth's reply was just bristly enough to sell it.

"I know you two cads don't think so, but I do have a reputation to protect. I may have been a single man at the time, but there's no use in risking the tales of such hijinks getting back to Lola, is there?"

Before Harris Peterson could say anything, Duckworth shot him a furtive glance. J.B.'s work had increased considerably in the past two years, and the quality of the cases had improved just as much. That was the positive reminder that Harris Peterson offered as a way of changing the subject.

"When I met you, you were sitting on the back bench at arraignments, wearing a moth-eaten twelve-year-old suit and flagging down those lamentable slobs in the courthouse lobby."

"Those fine citizens needed a good lawyer."

"My point is you've grown. I'm not saying you're untouchable, but you've got plenty of friends in our cutthroat little legal community."

Lea chimed in.

"Same goes for me, J.B. You got nothing to fret about.

Peterson had another thought.

"At least you're not in front of him this month. He'll forget it."

"That petty bastard? He never forgets his slights. He knows exactly what I think of him."

"It's not like you've kept that a secret, J.B."

The comment was intended as a joke, but Duckworth gave a solemn answer.

"And this is just how he'll try to pay me back. He'll be blabbing to his friends."

"What friends? This is Gillaspie. He's less likeable than a rabid weasel."

J.V. Lea chuckled at his own joke then held up his empty glass. The silence would have been a bit uncomfortable if the three friends had not been so far in their cups. Lea broke it with a sigh.

"I am dry and should be going."

He rose a tad unsteadily.

"We are a minute behind you just as soon as our rich compadre Peterson settles the damages."

After the handshakes and fare-thee-wells, Duckworth and Peterson did not follow, however. J.B. had more to say.

"The part that has me most concerned is what this is going to cost me."

Peterson narrowed his eyes in question as his pal continued.

"John Mitchell just asked me two damned days ago about joining the defense team for his boy."

Harris Peterson was never an easy man to impress, but he whistled in appreciation.

"The station massacre? That'd be big."

"Hell, yeah, it would be. It's one of the biggest goddamn cases in the history of this city. A thing like this from Gillaspie, and it may put Mitchell off his feed. What if he gets wind of this and doesn't believe I'm up for it?"

Though every column inch of James Duckworth's newspaper persona said otherwise, it was Captain John Calhoun Mitchell who had offered him a start in the lawyer business. The old man was in Richmond, but his connections easily extended into Harris County. Peterson knew that fact as well as J.B. did.

"Mitchell's known you a long time…"

"Which is why he still thinks of me as a protégé, a kid."

"He can look at that gray in your moustache and know better than that."

Duckworth did not rise to the bait.

"He may not run in the Houston circles to see any success I'm having, but he'll damn sure hear about the failures."

"Hell, J.B., you're in the damn papers every other week. John Mitchell's plenty smart enough to know what he's buying. He wants his boy set free, and he's a goddamned railroad lawyer. He needs you as much as you need him. Now, what we need…"

Peterson consulted his pocket watch.

"…is a nightcap. It's barely ten."

Their faithful waiter was soon beside the table, and Duckworth managed a small gleam in his eyes.

"Axel, bring me a bottle of Magnolia. I need to sober up with some beer. I have to go back to work for a couple of hours. I've got a trial down in Galveston to get ready for."

As a trio of the city's best known attorneys drank at Sauter's, Louie Swearingen was out for his bachelor ramble not three blocks away. He and his friends had started at the Turf where Louie tended bar. By 10, they were at stop number three but had moved only as far as the Cabinet, a few doors down Main Street.

It was a happy little foursome. Otis Kurz and Lat Shiller had run together with the prospective groom since they were toddlers in Kenney. Like their pal Louie, the two had moved to the big city in search of the adventurous unknowns of youth. Shiller worked at the Mosehart & Keller Carriage Company on Franklin and Caroline. Kurz may have fled the small town life, but he found work in the same line of business as his father – making and selling sausages at Gieselmann's Meat Market on Travis.

The fourth man who had signed on for the duration was Willie Hinton, Louie Swearingen's next door neighbor at the rooming house on Hardy. Hinton was also the one who sold Swearingen his bicycle. It was a four year old Columbia, and Hinton talked his boss into letting it go for just $27. Though Willie's social and conversational graces were seriously debilitated, Louie had often let him tag along ever since, as if he was the boy who had pulled a splinter from Swearingen's paw.

The point of a bachelor ramble was to visit several establishments, and Louie Swearingen, with his ready smile and easy manner, was welcomed by shining faces into every one. Among drinkers, bartenders were always the most popular people in town. The group had not had to reach into their pockets for drinks at the Turf Exchange. There were plenty of regulars ready to stand Louie and his friends.

At the other bars, there were a handful of those who knew the bridegroom well enough to pony up for a beer. Likely, they hoped that Louie would return the favor next time they drank at the Turf. The only one losing in that scenario was Charlie Lusk. Still, as fast as the foursome were drinking, Swearingen spent his own coins freely. They were, after all, out for a good time, and what better thing to spend one's money on.

At the Merchant's Exchange Saloon, the four revelers squeezed into an open place at the bar better suited for two. The cacophonous din, and especially the alcohol, forced the loudness of their conversation. At least half of the talk at the Exchange was in German. At one point, Lat Shiller even responded to a general wisecrack in that language. Eventually, a salesman pressed up at Louie Swearingen's back gave him a nudge in the ribs.

"Listen to them babble on. You'd think they'd have learned to talk English by now, wouldn't you?"

The salesman laughed at his own gibe, a comment that had been plenty loud enough for Shiller to overhear. Lat stepped up to flank the man, blocking his exit from the bar, while Swearingen turned to face him head on. Shiller was about the same size as the stranger, but Louie stood a good head taller. Lat pushed the man's shoulder to get his attention.

"Bub, you're in a German bar, not an Episcopal church. We'll speak whatever the fuck we want."

The Texas-born Shiller's German accent came and went. When he tried, it was hardly discernable. Now, he was laying it on thick.

"My father and my brothers ran into a fellow who made them feel unwelcome. They never found his body. Do you know why? Because they never checked the hog shit."

As soon as his friend Shiller had finished talking, Louie spun the salesman a quarter turn in the opposite direction.

"You see that squarehead with the big, hairy arms? That's Theo Thielepape, and he owns this place. He's even meaner than my friend Shiller's brothers. And while we're pointing things out to you, little man, you might want to know that my dear mother is one of those Heinies."

Swearingen gave a tug on the man's shirt front then flicked his shirt collar, popping a button and knocking it askew. With a final glare into his antagonist's eyes, he turned back to the bar and picked up his beer as if nothing had happened at all. The shorter man with the broken collar scampered through the open front door onto the sidewalk leaving what Otis Kurz considered a wasted swallow of whiskey. Not having heard a word of the short confrontation owing to the noise, Otis shrugged, reached behind the others and helped himself.

Willie Hinton drew back, a bit wide-eyed as he looked at Louie.

"Is that true about your mother?"

For a split second, Louie bristled, but then his usual wide grin spread.

"Close enough. She's Bohemian. When we kids played the fool, you should have heard her. Accent so thick, you'd never catch a word. You just ran for the barn."

Swearingen slapped his neighbor on the back.

"Let me get you another beer."

Unfortunately, a search of his pockets turned up empty. Louie laughed.

"Stake me to two dollars, then I'll buy you a beer."

By quarter to midnight, Louie and his friends were sloshing full of beer and much worse the wear from whiskey. They had adjourned to Dixie Darnell's boarding house in the Hollow, with the term boarding house being an openly acknowledged misnomer. It was one of dozens of bordellos in the district that ranged from the shabbily respectable streetside edifices to the warren of cribs that sat up a pitch dark alley and hope for the best. Dixie's fell happily in between.

The beer that a sullen teener Black girl fetched them cost twice as much as the Main Street bars and was almost certainly watered down, but it was on offer. So were the three girls arrayed in Dixie's parlor, a spare, dimly-lit room of grimy chairs and questionable sofas. A framed poster from the nearby Magnolia Brewing Company, likely a gift from a regular customer, was the lone piece of art adorning the walls.

Otis Kurz nudged his buddy Lat Shiller who dutifully extracted a Morgan dollar from his watch pocket. The two glanced briefly at Willie Hinton before shaking their heads with resigned smiles. The wide-eyed bicycle man would not be contributing. Kurz and Shiller each dropped a dollar into Louie Swearingen's hand. Lat nodded toward the women.

"Which one you fancy?"

Louie's attempt to keep his voice at a whisper failed spectacularly.

"They all look kind of scrawny to me."

"You want some or not?"

That had come from the fairer of the three, a dishwater blonde of indeterminate age. The other two, mulattoes who looked 30 but were more likely 20, stared back at the four men with indifference. Otis clapped Louie's shoulder in genuine bonhomie.

"You can wait on one of the ones upstairs, if you think they'll be better looking. I got enough change for two more beers."

"Nah, I'll go with the mouthy one."

He grinned and followed her up the squeaky staircase. The shorter of the two remaining courtesans looked back at the rest of the ramblers.

"Well, what about y'all?"

Lat Shiller shook his head and patted his belly. His Texas-German accent had gotten thicker over the course of the evening.

"Sorry, ladies, we have consumed our week's pay in beer and whiskey. Unless you are having discounts?"

The women did not dignify his joke with a response, but went back to their low conversation, awaiting the next drunk to stumble in.

"What's your name?"

"Laura Ann."

Louie tried to personalize the experience a little. Normally, his style of strumpet was the woman who hung around the bars. He chatted them up before the money changed hands. It almost felt like a date.

Laura Ann had finished at the wash basin and was crouched in front of Louie who sat on the foot of the small bed without his pants. She had oiled her hand and was sliding it up and down his not-yet-hard member.

"I'd kind of sworn off whores for the last two or three months except for a time or two. I'm getting married tomorrow evening."

"Good reason to get that dick hard. You'll need it tomorrow."

Her goal achieved, Laura Ann straddled Louie Swearingen and slid him inside. He exhaled with only a tiny sound. He grasped her small waist then ran both hands up under her dirty camisole and pinched her nipples. She made a low noise in return. She was so thin that he could feel her ribs as he brought his hands back down. Outside on the street there was a shouting match that floated in loud through the open window. What sounded like a tinner's wagon clattered past. Shadows played off the lone lamp. Laura Ann was moving her hips faster and leaning back. They slid together. Hot. Louie squeezed her waist tight as he shuddered and moaned. His panting took a while to subside.

"Well, hell, drunk as you boys are, I reckoned that was going to take longer."

The woman was rubbing her hand lightly across the exposed part of Louie's stomach, tracing the stream of hair that came down from his chest.

"You got at least another dollar, don't you? Let's give you a better sendoff that that."

She lay on her side next to him and started tugging again.

On the Louisiana Street sidewalk, the four celebrants said their raucous goodbyes. The west side of central Houston was a dark one, but tonight there was something more than a quarter moon and a few dozen scattered window lights.

Kurz and Shiller were headed across the Franklin Street bridge to their boarding house in Sixth Ward. Hinton and Swearingen were going north. Their rooms were hardly walking distance unless it was necessitated by them missing the connection for the last car. They made it just in time with a bit of unnecessary hollering and staggering, earning a faux dirty look from the motorman.

The two were still a bit unsteady on the feet when they stepped down from the streetcar. The first order of business was to stop and take a leak in some vacant lot bushes. Both men had been making faces and failing to stifle their loud giggles and base conversation ever since the swing bridge. There were no decent folk about at this time of night, so they took their welcome relief in the fresh night air without fear. Before they were completely empty, Louie gave Hinton a shove, landing him smack in middle of the overgrown weeds.

Swearingen reeked of cigar smoke and a splash of cheap bourbon that had slopped onto his coat sleeve. As he shed at least some of his clothes and climbed into his spinning bed, Louie caught a passing whiff of the scents of his whore. The last thought before he passed out was a sharp pang of guilt.

Chapter 9

Dud Lawrence's right leg was asleep, but he dared not try to shake it out. When he leaned up against the low branch, he figured that it would serve him as a partial seat while he waited, but over the course of two silent hours, it had only managed to cut off the circulation from his hip all the way down to his toes. That and the relentless mosquitoes were unbearable, drilling at his face and the backs of his hands and neck. If he was camping in the woods, he'd smear himself with camphor and pennyroyal, but that smell would give him away sure.

There was almost a half moon, but once he got deep back into the trees north of Cross Timbers, it mattered little. Dud could barely see his bait – a shiny half dollar and an almost empty bottle – that he had left on a tree stump. He knew he was in the right place. He could faintly smell recently cooked mash. His gut told him that he would be making an arrest anytime. He'd never seen a moonshiner yet who could pass on a sale.

As usual, the patience required on the job was stretched to breaking. Trying not to move in total blackness leant itself to an imagination running wild. Every shape in the woods shifted into a menace. Every scurrying mouse became a slithery cottonmouth, and every breath of the wind a wolf. It was lonely work being a revenuer, and universally unpopular, sometimes to the point of violence. Dud's recollection of how a friend's body had been found in the woods up at Gainesville, the back half of his head shot away, made him stand up straighter and finger the blue steel revolver in his jacket.

The snap of a twig broke his waking nightmare just before he felt the barrel of a gun press the bone behind his ear.

"Easy now."

A stream of chewing tobacco fluttered the dry leaves, and Dud felt the stranger's hand pull the pistol from his coat pocket. As careful as the revenue man had been to find a place downwind from where he suspected the still to be, he was at a loss how he failed to scent out the man who now had the drop on him. The odor of perspiration and wood smoke was overpowering. Maybe that was the answer – the smoke blended in to the natural aromas of the piney woods.

A safety match flared behind him just long enough to make Dud night blind again, then it was quickly blown out.

"I don't know what you want out here, mister, though I can figure. But I'll tell you this: the fellow that lives here is one tough old son of a bitch. You're damn sure lucky I found you instead of him on account of you'd already be a corpse halfway to a short grave out in the bog yonder. Now walk."

The gun barrel tapped the back of Dud Lawrence's ear. The revenuer could not hear anything but the howling wind noise that he knew to be his own racing pulse. For the next half an hour, or so it seemed, there were no words, only a tap of the gun on one side of Dud's head or the other to indicate a change in direction. He knew from the distance and the sound of breathing that the man behind him was herding with a long gun, mostly likely a break-down 20 gauge like that owned by every grown male in Texas. His captor also had an uncanny knack for knowing when Dud's eyes were finally adjusting to the forest dark. Right on cue, another match would flare.

Lawrence knew full well they were marching in circles, but he had no concept of where they were. The zig-zags and the eternal blackness did their jobs. The longer they marched, the more comfortable Dud became with the notion that this was not his night to die. Then, just as he was on the verge of taking his first easy breath, Dud Lawrence heard the man behind him stop walking and cock the shotgun hammer.

"This'll do."

A hard kick to the back of the revenuer's knee dropped him to the damp ground.

"Stay right there and don't you turn around none. You ain't going to want your mama to see you with no face."

The loud blast dislodged a rafter of roosting turkeys who put up a terrible din. Dud Lawrence did not hear them. By the time he recovered his senses and got a lungful of air back, he was alone. It took him the best part of an hour to stumble out to the edge of the Clark Street Road, though he had been left within 300 yards of it. By that time, Erv Reaves had quit smiling to himself and was already back tending to his shine.

Louie Swearingen's sore head and the throbbing in his eyes were subsiding just a bit by two in the afternoon. The plate of eggs and sausage that the cook at the Turf Exchange rustled up for him had helped, as had the two short beers he allowed himself to take the edge off. It had been at least an hour since he had last claimed to be through with whiskey, and he viewed all of these things as progress. It was important since he was due to be married at three.

The two justices of the peace who covered Harris County Precinct 1 were located in a county office building on Preston Street just across from Courthouse Square. That was a mere block and a half from the Turf, another fortunate thing for Louie. The bright sunshine was doing him no favors, though, and the back of his clean shirt was soaked through from the heat.

When Louie reached the J.P.'s outer office a clerk on the telephone shooed him out to the hallway. No sooner did he breathe a sigh of relief when his bottom hit the bench than his soon-to-be in-laws entered. Elsie Reaves and her two grown girls led the chattering way. The young ones were engaged in their own wide-eyed conversation, and Erv, still leaning forward out of habit, was at the rear of the column. Presumably he was watching for potential missteps by the youngsters.

E.L. Reaves looked at Louie, and a smirk rose from his weary face. The dark bags under Reaves' eyes suggested to the groom that the father of the bride suffered the exact same malady that he did. Words were not exchanged, but the moment was satisfying to Louie Swearingen nonetheless.

Though there would be no formality to the ceremony, Nora was referring to her sister Mary as a bridesmaid. Mary had her own beau on the hook, but she welcomed the chance to live vicariously for an afternoon. She had been working for a full month in her spare time making nice dresses for both her and Nora to wear for the occasion. Try as she might, Mary had yet to master the puffed sleeves that were the fashion, and Lord knows that she could not afford any diaphanous fabric for them at any rate. She did manage to cadge enough cheap lace to add a flourish to both their wrists. New hats were expensive, so the girls had piled each other's hair that morning, and the 90 degree heat had wilted less than half of it on the long and dusty ride in.

As the women and children continued their tittle-tattle in the hall, Erv Reaves stuck his head into the clerk's office.

"We're all here for these two to get married."

Jay Rogers, the same clerk who had moved Louie Swearingen with the back of his hand minutes earlier, glanced up prepared for more of the same. Reading the impatience in the rough man's face, he let out a nasally breath.

"I'll let the J.P. know."

It took another ten minutes for the group to be shuffled into the office of Justice Walter A. Malsch. They pushed the two visitor's chairs against the corner file cabinet, and crowded in front of the desk.

Malsch was a friendly-faced, clean shaven man of about 40. With rote experience, he arranged the participants, stopping to glower toward Jack Reaves who had picked up a ceramic boot from atop a side table. Jack's father snatched it away and slapped the back of the boy's hand before he returned the item to its original place. The J.P. signaled his thanks.

"Well, then, let's proceed."

Walter Malsch did not dally. The ceremony was over in about four minutes. He shook hands all around, even with the young hellion who was eyeballing various other curios, then repeated his thanks until the wedding party vacated his office. Louie gave two dollars and a winning smile to the clerk.

As the young couple turned toward the Preston Street door, a grizzled old man with a cane sat on a bench in the little lobby. He offered Louie a scowl and a voice dripping with sarcasm.

"Good luck."

On the sidewalk in front of the building, E.L. Reaves stuck his weathered mitt out for Louie.

"Be good to her. Can't say I ain't glad to see her married off. Can't afford them no how."

Swearingen heard only the positive parts of the comment, and he pumped his father-in-law's hand twice.

"Thank you much. Y'all fixing to come with us for a drink?"

Reaves wet his lips and briefly mulled the offer.

"No. There'd be nothing to do with the little ones. And there's work needs doing."

With that he gave Louie a curt nod and herded the rest of his family down Preston to the east.

The newlyweds walked the opposite direction. They cut over to Congress and strolled into the Big Casino. Louie's friend Jim Givens, a bartender there, pointed toward a round table in the restaurant. The Casino would be a comfortable place for the women. Swearingen had also chosen it because he figured it had been a while since he had done anything embarrassing inside its walls.

Olive and Ida, Nora's friends from the dye factory, were already there and ready to celebrate. Until Nora and her new husband arrived, the ladies had been loitering on the street outside. They would not risk going into a drinking establishment alone.

Lat and Otis arrived shortly thereafter, both looking quite the worse for wear. Still, they were young and happy to make a game effort on behalf of their friend. The previous night's misadventure was still fresh in mind, and Otis Kurz offered up such a blatantly sheepish smile when he was introduced to Nora that it made Louie cringe.

Three off duty bartenders from the Turf made an appearance. Two of them shared the first name of John and were among Louie's most reliable drinking companions. Good men, each with a ready laugh. Charlie Lusk had let them leave work an hour early in a friendly nod to the occasion. The third was Sam Carr. He had to go to work at 6, but judged there was time to stop by for some celebratory drinks.

Carr, in his middle thirties, was the oldest one at the party. His moustache was neatly cropped, and his well-oiled hair was parted in the middle. He most assuredly paid more fussy attention to his appearance than did Louie Swearingen. Still, he was an outgoing fellow, an inveterate cigarette smoker who was always quick with a safety match for his smoking customers. When it came to his own drinking tastes, Carr was avant garde. He liked both mixing and consuming the latest cocktails. He had a gin gimlet in his hand when he clapped Louie on the back.

"So, old son, no family of the bride or groom at this party?"

The fact was that Louie had not yet told his parents that he was getting married, but he planned to take Nora out to Sealy for introductions and Sunday dinner the first chance they got. He shot Sam a winning grin.

"Nora's folks were at the ceremony, and mine were tied up. You know how it is. Besides, we can let our hair down."

Swearingen punctuated his answer with a fake punch to the stomach, and Sam playfully roughed Louie's wild mane.

"I don't think your hair'll come down, kiddo."

Nora set out to nurse a glass of wine, but with others ordering for the table, she neatly went through three or four without it appearing so. Her new husband had to steady her getting up from the table at one point, but everyone was having such a good time that no one noticed.

It was after nine o'clock when Louie and Nora gave their hugs and handshakes and said their goodbyes. The Liberty Line cars stopped just two blocks away. They were both in an expansive mood as they boarded, and Louie loudly announced to all that he and Nora had just gotten hitched. Joe Russo, the motorman known to everyone in the Fifth Ward, offered hearty congratulations and most everyone else on the streetcar applauded with varying degrees of enthusiasm.

The Swearingen wedding bed was the single iron frame back at Louie's rooming house. There was no prohibition from the landlord about a couple living there, but none did. Nora was invading a bachelor's retreat. Aside for the narrow bed, there was no stove in the room, nothing but a cold water sink. Toilet facilities were a one-holer in the back yard that was otherwise utilized by men only. In spite of the fact that Louie owned very little in the way of worldly goods, those few possessions filled the small dresser. Clearly the couple would need to finalize their accommodations as a married couple at the very soonest.

The two had already enjoyed sex a few times, but both were still atingle as they began to undress one another between long kisses. Suddenly, Louie pulled away and plopped down on the bed with his suspenders hanging and his shirt gone.

"Nora. I'm so sorry. I just can't hold it inside. The boys bought me a woman last night. A goodbye gift to the single life. It was nothing important. I swear it. But I just had to let you know."

When he finished, he dropped his head whether out of embarrassment, emotional fatigue, or dramatic effect, it was impossible to know.

Nora stood unmoving in her petticoat and chemise. Her lips opened once, then they closed again. After what felt an eternity to Louie, his young wife sat down next to him and patted his hand.

"I love you for telling me. That was very sweet. I forgive you."

Even glassy from wine, a twinkle returned to her eyes, and her ever-alluring mouth twitched upward.

"Just don't make this a habit, Mr. Swearingen."

She put her arms around him and nuzzled his neck. She forgave him. And she felt no need to tell her husband about any of the neighborhood boys who lifted up her dress and gave her a poke out in the woods.

Louie Swearingen's lawyers learned of their client's nuptials when they read about it in the *Post's* legal notices. Sonny Schlottmann brought it to J.B.'s attention and added an editorial.

"Maybe it'll calm him down some. He's like an untrained puppy, that one."

Duckworth nodded thoughtfully.

"Yep. We just can't be sure he's not the one who peed on the rug."

Chapter 10

June 1902

"You keep your official calendar. Summer is here."

Henry Fein stood by the open windows holding his glasses in one hand as he wiped sweat from his eyes with the other. Across the main room of the law office, Sonny Schlottmann was yet again re-aiming the firm's Graybar fan in a brave attempt to maximize the airflow. Two ceiling fans turned overhead, one rather noisily. Nothing mitigated the heat.

A new Harris County Criminal Court session opened the following day. Six times a year it necessitated the lengthiest of Sunday conferences. Houston courts did little business during the summer, and early June was generally quite pleasant, but this year had proved to be a brutally oppressive exception. The last ten days of May all topped 90 degrees. There had been no rain to cool things down or tamp the dust. J.B. Duckworth tried and failed to blow a piece of grit off the end of his tongue as he placed paperwork in front of his fellow lawyers. They each quickly topped the new sheets with a book or something heavy. Charlie Dixon, the office boy for Duckworth & Fein, had already made two heroic snags to stop a case from fluttering out the window this morning. It was not yet noon, and the thermometer on the wall read 92.

"Sonny, can you drag that fan any closer?"

Like the rest of the group, Jed Posey was down to shirtsleeves.

"Jed, it doesn't work without it's plugged in. So, no."

Perhaps it was the heat. Perhaps it was the dour mood that Duckworth had brought with him to the office that day. By the third hour of trial preparation, tempers in the big room were frayed. Each successive case review seemed longer than the last. J.B. shot down what seemed to be every suggestion regarding the case he would be trying in Travis County, if in fact it even went to trial. He had expressed the view that it would not, but he insisted on being in Austin just in case. Duckworth always tended toward the perfectionist when it came to the law, but his nitpicking on this searing Sunday was relentless.

Jed Posey, the firm's lone law clerk was holding down the cases in Harris County while the other attorneys dealt with murder trials in other towns. Posey would handle the usual slew of lesser felonies including a curious one in which they were defending a one-legged man who was charged with the afterhours burglary of a jewelry store. There were also seven postponements to request in local murder cases. No one considered that there was the slightest danger of any of them going to trial, yet Duckworth was grilling Posey as if the lawyer was a grammar school child.

"All right, that's Robbins. What's the next one?"

"Swearingen."

There was a general sigh. Even Maizy, J.B.'s dog who was lying on her back underneath the open windows, let go a sleepy whine. Sonny Schlottmann had a question.

"Is Lea still moving on that one with one of his witnesses under indictment?"

Posey nodded.

"I've heard nothing otherwise. Not an inkling."

Duckworth turned to his brother with a hint of exasperation.

"John, tell me we have some kind of alibi for that boy."

"Not particularly. He may have picked up a whore the night of the shooting, but we can't find her. The girl that old Dumler pointed out swore a blue streak at me for even asking."

"Goddamnit. Is he lying to us, or is he just stupid? Or both?"

Sonny interjected his thoughts.

"I suspect he's stewed most of the time. Of course, as you say, that doesn't mean he's not lying to us."

J.B. leaned forward over the large table.

"We started asking him questions, what, less than two days after the murder, and he still can't give us a clue as to where he was? Shit, any jackass would know to at least try to make something up."

He sat back and returned his attention to Posey.

"Your motion is written up?"

"It's on the stack there in front of you."

As soon as the gibe left his lips, the clerk regretted it. J.B. pounded his open hand on the tabletop.

"Jed, if I wanted to read it, I would have. You wouldn't even have to be here for that. You could be galivanting around town with whatever skirt you're chasing. So could the rest of us. But you'll notice you're here, aren't you. Do you know why? Because I want to hear you make the goddamned argument."

He exhaled as if a small bit of pressure had been released from a valve. Jed Posey, who was fortunately thick-skinned, laid things out.

"Missing witness. I'm telling the court we have identified a woman who can provide an alibi, which I have lined out in detail, but we have reason to believe she is visiting family outside of the county. We are endeavoring to locate her."

"Are you naming her?"

"I was going to be very vague and go with the most common name I could muster. Mary Jones, though I'll tell the judge she may well go by another name, as well. That should cover our bases."

Duckworth pursed his lips and waved the notion away.

"Say that given the delicate nature of the alibi and the fact that the young lady comes from a good family, you don't feel that it's proper to have her name entered into the court record."

Posey nodded. He was a serious young man, and it showed in his face.

"Yeah. That's better, except for the fact that we're talking about a whore, here, not some girl from a good family. Gillaspie's not going to forget that when we finally have to produce someone."

Again, J.B.'s ire erupted.

"I've been arguing cases in front of or against Gillaspie for long damn time, and I know what he goes for. If you refuse to give a name, he'll be afraid of crossing some potential political backer. That's all he cares about. People make mistakes with names and circumstances all the goddamned time. Even lawyers. Do it like I tell you."

Jed Posey pushed back from the table and rose to full height.

"If you're that all fired worried about how I do my job, why don't you stay and argue the motions yourself. None of us understand why you want to run off to Austin for a case you admit won't come to trial. And a colored defendant at that. You always talk about publicity. Well, you're sure not getting any from that one."

For what seemed a small eternity, the room froze. Henry Fein and John Duckworth stared down at the papers before them. Sonny Schlottmann, with his mouth ever so slightly agape, watched Jed Posey, and J.B. Duckworth chewed the inside of his cheek as his black eyes blazed at his clerk. It was Fein who broke the silence.

"J.B.," he said with his soft accent. "These are our partners and friends. I think we should not hold them in the dark."

Lawyer Duckworth's jaws clenched with intensity, but it was his brother John, acting on the slightest glance, who spoke.

"J.B. and I were at Big Annie's one night a few months ago, and some belligerent drunk spread a story about the time Jamie got his hand shot in Waco."

The other lawyers all knew of their boss's scar, but none knew the story behind it. Their attentions were grabbed.

"This fellow was running his mouth and making out that J.B. had committed a felony in the process, and ..."

John shot one last quick look at his younger brother.

"... anyway, it's made it back to Judge Gillaspie somehow, and that pious son of a bitch is lording it over him."

There was a pause as the other members of the firm processed the news. Henry Fein picked up the narrative.

"So far, Gillaspie has said nothing directly, but J.B. believes that it might be best that he does not appear in that court this session. I told him I agreed."

When J.B. Duckworth finally spoke of his situation, his words were measured.

"My worry is that Gillaspie means to embarrass me, and I don't aim to let that hurt the firm."

Sonny Schlottmann was both stung and put out that he had not heard of this earlier. He was a junior, but a partner still the same. His words betrayed building anger.

"Embarrass you how? By making this public? You don't expect him to sanction you somehow, do you?"

"No!"

Duckworth's first word came out loud and harsh. He lowered his voice immediately.

"It crossed my mind, of course, but I've talked to Harris about it two or three times. That's who told me in the first place. Y'all know Harris doesn't miss much. He says there'd be no backing for Gillaspie to hold a hearing."

"How long ago did Harris tell you?"

The answer came quietly.

"Two, three weeks."

Schlottmann narrowed his eyes for a second.

"And no one else has heard about this?"

"They've not come to me."

John Duckworth signaled agreement and Henry Fein offered a thought.

"Perhaps that is the point then, J.B. Gillaspie wants only to scare you and do nothing more?"

"The only point I've been feeling is the Sword of fucking Damocles over my tender neck for the last two weeks."

Following the tension and the revelation, the team of lawyers worked until supper time. As J.B. Duckworth often preached to them, it was thorough preparation and hard work that won cases. But whatever careful effort Jed Posey had put into his motion for the Swearingen postponement proved to be for naught.

Thanks to a pair of intricate murder trials, one on a change of venue from Bellville, Swearingen and the other postponement motions were not called until late on the fifth day of the court session. Judge Gillaspie, worn down by the previous proceedings and the unabating heat, granted the others with minimal discussion.

When the court clerk called the name of Louie Swearingen, J.V. Lea beat Posey to the switch. The state desired a postponement.

"Your honor, Constable E.P. Isgitt is facing a charge of murder in this very court, perhaps in a matter of hours."

"I'm aware of my own docket, Mr. Lea."

"Yes, your honor. The state feels that giving testimony in this trial might be a distraction for the constable, to say the least."

Gillaspie looked to Jed Posey.

"It also may not help the constable's credibility if he's convicted, your honor."

"I didn't ask for an editorial, Mr. Posey. Does the defense have any objections to a postponement?"

"No, judge. The defense does not."

"In that case, my clerk will be in touch with a date. Most likely October, is that right, Oscar?"

"Might be December, judge," the court clerk answered.

With that, a relieved J.K.P. Gillaspie hit his gavel a single time and adjourned for the week's end, reminding District Attorney Lea that he would see him again Monday morning.

The trouble facing Eddie Isgitt was serious on the face of it. He was up on a charge of murder, recommended by Sheriff Anderson and, after careful consideration, filed by D.A. Lea. Six weeks prior, Isgitt had killed a Black man named Nelson Horton who Isgitt claimed "advanced on him with a knife." No one could back the lawman's story, and there were a dozen witnesses whose side of things were quite different. Without those bystanders, the charge would have never been proffered.

Veteran observers of the local justice system could not fathom a scenario in which a White lawman would be convicted of murdering a Black man, but, strictly speaking, it could happen. Stranger things, as the saying goes. Still, no one in Houston had any memory of such an event.

J.B. was still absent in the state capital. Just as he surmised, the Richards case there had not gone to trial. The prosecution was not ready, nor was Duckworth. Rather than return home, J.B. chose to remain in Austin an extra two days. He was taking no chances on making an appearance before Judge Gillaspie.

Eddie Isgitt's trial was called to order on the third Friday of the month, likely the final day of the June criminal session in Harris County. To his credit, J.V. Lea called both of the White witnesses who were willing to take the stand and walked them through detailed testimony. Three others had thought better of pushing their statements, and the remaining witnesses were Black. Lea saw no future gain in those men and women making an appearance.

Aside from two friends who swore to his good character, Isgitt was the lone witness for his own defense. He gave an impassioned recounting of seeing Horton skulking between two buildings down at Almeda. Isgitt described the guilty look on the Black man's face and how he had turned with a knife drawn. Under Lea's cross, Isgitt could not account for why none of the several onlookers had seen Horton with a weapon or observed the dead man doing anything remotely criminal. The constable put that anomaly down as one of the great mysteries of life. The jury acquitted him after a 17-minute deliberation.

The small Duckworth family sat on their front porch in the dark. The night-time noise from the train yard rang in the stillness. A crew was still working at the repair shops, and the competing odors from the cottonseed mill and Finnigan's hide house fought for supremacy. In this stifling cauldron, though, the porch was better than the house. One could at least hope for a passing breeze.

Katherine had tossed, turned, and whined in the heat, and two hours past her bedtime or not, she was now nestled in her father's lap. J.B. was home from the office early. Crime had not taken a holiday, but it could wait for a few hours.

The past two weeks were the hottest ever recorded in Houston – a string of 100 degree days broken only by the rare respite of 99. Everyone in town was desperate for an iced drink and a spot of shade. Nights dropping only into the 80s offered no respite. The sweat produced by the local citizens was probably no more than a normal June scorcher, but the complaints had definitely ratcheted up a notch.

Lola and J.B. softly exchanged the news of the day hoping the low hum of conversation might lull their almost two-year-old daughter to sleep. The Jackson streetcar extension opened just in time for the city's Negroes to go to their park for Emancipation Day. Duckworth had slipped Charlie Dixon a half dollar to buy sodas for his mother and siblings. Mrs. Stallings from around the corner on Keene Street had been taken to the infirmary with gallstones. She should recover. Harris and Louise Peterson were off for ten days at Hot Springs. The Dealy Print Company down from the law office had a big fire last night, and a frequent client of the firm was nabbed just after stealing a savings bank from the Affiliated Laundry.

"Hot Springs sounds marvelous."

That bit of news had certainly caught Lola's fancy. This type of night was tailor made for holiday dreams.

"Jamie, why can't we go away for a few days?"

"I can't afford a summer cottage in Maine. I'm not a rich man, sweetheart."

"You and Harris have bought three new properties this year. Could you not have set a little aside to take your family on a vacation?"

"I'm planning for the future, Lola. And it's not as if Katherine would remember wherever it was we got off to."

J.B. nuzzled his daughter's hair. Her eyelids were closing. Lola's were not.

"And I'm not talking about Maine or Cape Cod or even Hot Springs, Jamie. Mightn't we at least go to the seaside?"

Duckworth reached over and squeezed his wife's hand. He whispered his reply.

"I'll see what I can do."

Then he gestured with his chin to Katherine who had finally fallen asleep in his lap.

Heavy clouds had been promising rain for hours, but after 34 straight days of drought, it was clear that clouds were often liars. That was why the downpour caught J.B. Duckworth unaware as he was winding up a Sunday afternoon client visit at the jail. The dark skies opened suddenly with a tropical vengeance like the sultry monsoons of Kipling tales and Siamese pirates. It was a four block walk to the closest stop on the San Felipe line that would let Duckworth connect for his house, and he did not relish a soaking. A man would be drenched to the skin after four steps. Facing four whole blocks of this deluge, a body might drown. He would wait it out.

"Sure is a welcome sight, ain't it?"

The sheriff was standing beside him at the open vestibule door wearing a look of satisfaction. The entire city was no doubt relishing this moment. After a fashion, J.B. felt compelled to explain his presence.

"I wasn't looking forward to a dousing. Not that I want this to stop, but I was thinking it might let up long enough for me to hot foot it over to Milam."

Sheriff Anderson raised his chin and studied the sky.

"Don't look like that'll be happening anytime soon. Come have a drink with me out front."

Duckworth's moustache twitched up.

"Now Archie, it won't do me any good with potential clients for me to be spotted talking to the sheriff."

The easy grin was returned.

"We're the end of the line before the bayou, J.B. We got no passersby. This is one of the quietest corners of town, particularly on a Sunday in a typhoon. I think your practice is safe."

He punctuated his thought with a friendly slap on the shoulder.

"Come on. I got a half decent bottle of bourbon in my parlor, and we can sit out front so we don't bother my sister and the kids."

The two men were soon seated on the comfortable porch outside the sheriff's quarters. Each clutched a generous glass of whiskey. Duckworth laughed to himself, and Anderson turned to see why.

"You laughing at the country's good fortune?"

"No. I was just thinking that if I'd gotten caught up at the city jail, they'd have probably kept me. Well, at least Blackburn would've. Ellis is all right."

The sheriff smiled, and the men sat for a time in companionable silence before Anderson spoke to no one in particular.

"I like living here. I really do."

They watched the water dripping off the eaves of the jail. It was likely too late to salvage a good portion of the region's cotton and corn, but the general relief of watching copious amounts of water fall from a suddenly boiling sky made the two philosophical. Anderson nudged his hat a little farther back on his head.

"I sure do enjoy the smell of the rain. A thunderstorm ought to be smelled, don't you think?"

They passed small talk and twice refilled their glasses before Archie Anderson brought up a matter that classified as legal work.

"How's Louie Swearingen doing?"

The sheriff was still looking straight ahead at the rain.

"He got married last month."

"Yep. I saw that in the paper. I delivered a prisoner out to his daddy last week. Nasty fellow who stole a horse out in Sealy and may have interfered with a young girl, 12 or 13."

Duckworth turned to face his host with an earnest expression.

"I doubt things go well for that man."

Anderson let go a snort of laughter.

"No. I reckon not. Depending on who that little gal's pa is, the fellow I hauled out there may not even see trial."

J.B. nodded.

"Where'd you find him?"

"Precinct 5 constable up by Rose Hill overheard the fool bragging about the horse to his cousin in some slapdash rum house out that way. Boys were both drunker than a boiled owl. Didn't even see that Degenhardt was wearing a badge."

The two men chuckled at the stupidity of the criminal class.

"Swearingen, the old man, asked how his boy's prospects were looking," Anderson continued. "He's worried about his boy. You got any handle on when the case might go to trial?"

"If I have my way it'll be never. The kid's out on bail. I know he'd like to be rid of the stigma, but he's living his life."

Sheriff Anderson knew his question was a pointless one, but he asked it anyway.

"You don't think he did it, do you?"

J.B.'s eyes gleamed a little.

"You know better than that, Archie. None of my clients are guilty. It's just that a few of them are misunderstood."

Anderson nodded thoughtfully, not ready to laugh the subject away.

"Well, I've known his daddy a long time, and I wouldn't wish him anything but good."

The sheriff paused and looked directly to Duckworth as he completed the thought.

"He's real concerned about his boy."

Chapter 11

July 1902

The general consensus among the men out near Cross Timbers was that Mary Reaves did not get the same blessing of good looks that her sister Nora enjoyed, but still she was judged to be a comely woman. Unfortunately for Mary, that description did not apply when her face was red and swollen from sobbing.

Comforting his children did not come naturally to her father. E.L. Reaves winced and his eyes darted around the room as he patted his oldest daughter's shoulder. He made another face when he saw that his filthy, charcoal covered hand left a smudge on the back of her clean dress, her special dress. Reaves thought better of giving that a mention.

"He ain't worth a damn anyhow."

The words were the wrong ones, and Mary's bawling continued. Reaves changed tack.

"Maybe he's just caught up someplace. The man has a job, maybe that's holding him."

He gave Mary's shoulder a couple more absent pats. Finally, she turned to face her father, and the crying slowed ever so slightly.

Reaves had used everything he could summon to placate his distraught daughter. He wanted to help, but nurture was not something that came easy to him. The two looked at one another for several seconds before Erv Reaves let go a deep breath.

"Well, I'm going to head back out to the wood yard. I'll check back. Send one of the little ones to fetch me if he comes."

He paused before correcting himself.

"When he comes."

The man in question was James Fisher. Though Erv Reaves did not much like the man who had been sporadically courting his daughter for over a year. Fisher had taken the time to visit with the father only once. Since then, when he fetched Mary for an outing, he jumped down from his little buggy just long enough to help her up onto the seat. Reaves noted that Fisher's hands had grown all the more familiar at that task.

Today was the day that Fisher was to either fetch Mary to the justice of the peace at Westfield or bring the J.P. to her. The couple were supposed to finally tie the knot. They did not share their feelings with Mary, but the rest of the family carried some skepticism. Fisher had postponed the vows twice before. Mary's ultimatum, as insincere as it might have been in her heart, finally spurred him to swear a solemn oath that today was the day. It was why he even went so far as to suggest bringing the official to the Reaves house in the woods. Mary's great distress was because it was now 30 minutes past the appointed hour of 11 o'clock, and there was no sign of her beau.

Fisher was a secretive type, but Mary had caught his eye one day when he walked into the little store at Cross Timbers. It was pure happenstance. Mary visited her mother at work often enough – it was her escape from the house in the woods – but to be there when the handsome Mr. Fisher walked in was kismet. She was delivering a new dress for a regular customer, and her blushing gaze fleetingly met Fisher's. His eyeballing had been far less timid.

James Fisher worked as a private detective, and business took him all over the county and well beyond. He was an older man. He told Mary that he was 33, but she suspected he might be a few years past that number. Some people had described Fisher as rather unremarkable, which would doubtlessly be a help for his profession, but Mary had seen a spark in his eyes right from the start.

On his second visit to the store, Fisher inquired with Elsie Reaves about her eldest, and was so bold as to send a note asking to meet her there the following week. They sat and talked on the porch of the little store, and not long after, Fisher called for Mary at their house. That was the time when he met her father.

Mary lost her virginity to James Fisher the first time he took her out to the café up at Spring. The special moment had passed too fast. Their dates were always to Spring or Westfield since those provided a lengthy drive through the sparsely populated country and an opportunity to duck into the bushes for a quick, or sometimes not so quick, tryst. They had done right on the seat of the rented carriages, too. Mary relished the attention from James Fisher and the long, deep conversations, but mostly she wanted to get married so they could make love as often as she wanted.

It was just shy of one in the afternoon when a sweat-soaked James Fisher rode up in front of the Reaves place. He was two hours late, and Mary chastised herself for not being more angry about that fact. She could not even muster a stern look when she went into the yard to meet him.

"I see that there's no wagon, so is the J.P. coming here?"

She put her arms around Fisher's shoulders. Late or not, disheveled as he might be, this was still going to be her wedding day. It took one good look at her lover's face, though, for Mary's joy to come crashing down.

"I'm sorry, precious. Old Berry West told me he was too tied up to travel out today. Some old fellow died all the way up on Spring Creek, and Berry had to ride out to look at the corpse. Had to make certain there was no foul play."

Mary's smile fell and tears welled up in her eyes. Fisher pushed back enough to look into her face.

"Oh, now. Don't cry. He'll make it up to us. We can go next week. I'll hire a wagon, and we'll ride up to Westfield. No more excuses from him."

The suitor mustered his best smile, but Mary was slipping into full pout, and the tears spilled down her cheeks.

"You're lying. We'll never get married, and I'll never get out of here. I'll spend my life stuck in these woods."

She tried to push away, but ended up crying into Fisher's shirt instead. He was so wet with perspiration on the steamy day that the fabric was already glued to his skin.

Slowly, the soothing pats on her back changed to circles, and soon Fisher dropped his left hand down to cup Mary's bottom. He brought his right around to squeeze her heavy breasts. Gradually, the tenor of her sounds lowered. James Fisher was quickly swollen hard, and Mary stood on her tiptoes to grind against the front of his pants. She grabbed his hand and pulled him toward the house.

"Daddy'll be out at his woodyard all afternoon, and Mama went back to work."

Fisher was breathing hard. There was a moment of trepidation. They had certainly never done the deed at Mary's house, but he followed her without a word of protest. Mary turned around to him.

"I'll send the little ones out to play."

Mary insisted on removing her dress to keep it fresh for her wedding day. She had spent weeks trying to achieve something close to a pigeon front, and thought it just shy of perfection. It was carefully draped across her sewing table in the other room. Her shoes had been quickly unbuttoned and discarded somewhere, and her petticoat followed. She rarely wore drawers since she began sharing herself with James Fisher. It left her straddling her man wearing only a low neck chemise, one she sewed from a Butterick pattern, and that was pulled all the way up to her waist.

Fisher laid back on Mary's bed, an iron-framed single in the room she had shared with Nora as long as she could remember. She had never made love in her childhood bed before, but now, here was James wearing nothing but his wet shirt, whimpering underneath her even as he thrust so deep inside. Just a few months earlier, Mary had no idea that such physical feelings existed, such intense flashes of bliss. She could not stop herself from crying out as she felt him finish.

She had been ignoring the noises from her younger siblings ever since she realized that they were watching through the open window. James had jumped at first, but Mary pushed him back down on the quilt and sped the rhythm of her ride. She felt him stiffen again, and now he was pulsing and twitching inside her. Kids had to learn about the world sometime.

The next noise was different. A guttural growl. Mary looked at the window just in time to see the children running. Their father had shoved them away.

"You sorry son of a bitch! I'll kill you!"

With that scream, E. L. Reaves turned toward the house's back steps.

It took but an instant for James Fisher to snatch his pants off the floor. There was not even a glance back at Mary as he ran into the main room of the Reaves house. He had left his shoes behind, and he gave a loud yowl as his foot smashed into the corner of a hulking piece of nondescript furniture. It was some sort of ill-made sideboard or cabinet. All Fisher knew was that it had likely broken his toe. It slowed his pace, but he kept hobbling toward the front door holding his pants in his right hand.

Erv Reaves slammed open his back door hard enough to knock a framed print from the wall. Glass shattered, and he crunched across the shards as he darted for a gun. He considered himself a well-armed man. His single barrel shotgun generally stayed in the hide for his still. There was an old Colt pistol in a kitchen drawer and the Winchester rifle that was propped in the corner. It needed a good cleaning which Reaves had not gotten around to, but it was the more reliable varmint gun, and that was what he reached for now. As he did, he saw James Fisher's bare butt fall off the front porch.

As soon as he cleared the front door, Fisher tried to pull on his pants without slowing down too much. He had completed the maneuver before, but this time he could not raise his throbbing foot high enough, and he went tumbling off the step and hit face first in the dirt. With one foot through the leg hole and the other not, Fisher scrambled on all fours through the picket gate and behind a rear wheel of the old buckboard. His horse was tied to a tree limb in the shade. It was a good 80 feet away.

The younger Reaves children had recovered their wits and followed their father through the back door, eager to watch the entertainment. Mary, still half naked, was at an open window at the front of the house screaming insensibly.

"Girl, stop your hollering."

It was all E.L. Reaves muttered as he moved Jack out of the way and stepped onto his front porch. His anger was up, but he still took a few seconds to assess the situation and make sure that the scalawag Fisher was unarmed. Knowing that the man was not wearing pants offered great reassurance.

Reaves certainly did not like finding his eldest girl rutting away with some virtual stranger inside his very house, but that was not his primary concern. He was bothered by his intuition that Fisher was a dishonest snake. As much as Erv Reaves struggled with any form of eloquent expression, he loved his children. His job in that regard was to protect them, and the one time that James Fisher had been man enough to face the father of his supposed girl, the man had struck Reaves as a slick, mealy-mouthed salesman who looked down on the likes of Erv and Elsie Reaves. He just did not like the man one bit. Watching his daughter bawl that morning on the potential of being spurned had torn at Reaves' gut, and the more he let Mary's tears percolate in his mind, the madder he got.

Under cover of the wagon, James Fisher finally pulled pants on successfully, then, with hands raised, he stuck his head and torso out to try to reason with E.L. Reaves. Fisher had eyeballed the distance to his horse. Even without the limp, it was too far.

"Mr. Reaves. Hold your temper now. Mary and I are going to be married. There's no harm..."

Reaves answered with a shot from his rifle. Splinters of sun-bleached wood chased the cornered man back into hiding. When he gathered himself again, Fisher scooted a few feet to his right, nearer the front wheels of the buckboard and, ultimately, his horse.

"Mr. Reaves, I'm really sorry you found us that way, but I love Mary. Please don't hurt me."

The Winchester barked loose a low shot that kicked dirt up into Fisher's face.

Mary was still screeching from the window.

"Daddy! No, Daddy!"

If she could have formed her thoughts, Mary would have implored her father to stop shooting at the man she loved, but that was not how Reaves interpreted her cries.

Instead, he stepped around the edge of his wagon and faced the no good man who was hurting his daughter. Fisher's eyes screwed closed in fear, but his smart mouth flopped open to say something, to plead. No words came out because Reaves placed a bullet near the man's heart on the left side. A single bullet, and a report loud enough to momentarily stop his girl's screams. Then the old rifle jammed. With a few choices curses, Erv Reaves beat Fisher over the head with the gun until the stock broke off.

Chapter 12

Erv Reaves grumbled to himself as he walked down the Clark Street Road. It was the hottest part of the day, and anyone he knew was twenty times as likely to be heading north rather than into town. In fact, a neighbor, Jerry Denny, with his shoe box head and a permanent expression like he smelled something bad, had reined to a stop to visit, but Reaves shook him off with a dismissive growl. Another old fellow he recognized by sight did offer a lift, but Erv turned that down, too. He was hardly in the mood for small talk.

For the second time that day, he had tried to console his daughter Mary, but there was no gain in it. She had managed to bring her piercing screams down to boiling sobs, but she would not let go of James Fisher's unmoving hand. In the end, Erv Reaves gave her another futile pat on the back, told her to get some clothes on, and started his long trek to find a deputy sheriff someplace.

It was a good four miles to the edge of the city, and more miles beyond to reach the jail, but he was sure to locate a lawman of some sort long before that. Still, he was feeling the day. It was a scorcher. Somewhere along the way he seemed to have developed a little hitch in his step. Something at the top of his hip was catching, and it just served to make his mood all the more sour.

Mary regained her senses a little thanks to her sister Vi who threw her arms around Mary's neck and cried with her there in the dirt. There was a five year gap between Nora and Viola. It represented two miscarriages that brought lasting pain to their mother, Elsie. Mary was seven when Vi came along, and she recalled her mother smothering the new baby with love for two full years until she became pregnant again with Lou. Now 13, Vi understood that a tragedy had taken place, and her affection was a comfort.

Eventually, Mary staggered inside and cleaned herself up in the wash basin. The front of her was covered in dirt and sweat, blood and dried tears. She pulled on a plain dress, implored Viola to mind the two younger children, and set out for the store at Cross Timbers. It was the closest place with a phone. Every bit of her understood that James Fisher was dead, but a part of her heart told her that if she could only get a doctor to him, something might be done. Her walk turned into a run. Twice she tripped over a tree root or a cypress knot, and by the time she made it to the store, the front of her was dirty all over again.

It was difficult, but between bouts of loud crying, Mary choked out the story to her mother, and it was Elsie Reaves who made the call to the sheriff's office in Houston. There were few details in the telling. Mary certainly was not forthcoming about the compromising act in which she and Fisher had been found, so Elsie's telling of the story was vague. It was enough to convey that there had been a shooting, and deputies would be dispatched forthwith.

Thanks to the telephone call, news of the incident beat E.L Reaves into town by good margin. Two deputies and Sheriff Anderson himself met him just north of Quitman Street. Reaves saw a glint of sunlight off a badge before he recognized the sheriff, and he angled out in front of their horses. Anderson's black took in a nose full of charcoal smoke and exhaled loudly in protest. The sheriff reined his gelding back a step.

"I'm Erv Reaves, and I've been looking for y'all. Didn't reckon I'd find the man himself. I shot a fellow out at my place back up the road."

Reaves moved his head to motion behind him, mindful to keep his hands in view.

"He was messing with my daughter."

Anderson's tone was as relaxed as if he was shooting the breeze with an old friend.

"We got us a phone call, Mr. Reaves. We were just riding out your way. You feel like telling us what happened?"

Reaves gave a tired nod.

"My girl Mary is 20. Ain't no girl, I guess, but she's a quiet one. And this fellow's been nosing around her. He's slick. Been stringing her along in my book. I come back for lunch and found him grinding her."

The man swallowed hard before continuing. One of the deputies stifled a giggle, but Reaves ignored him.

"As soon as he saw me, he lit out like a scalded cat, and she commenced to screaming. I shot him."

Reaves looked down to inspect his feet as he added an afterthought.

"He ain't no good."

Archie Anderson rubbed the back of his knuckles where the skin felt dry, then he glanced at his deputies. He leaned forward in the saddle and took a deep breath of consideration before looking back down at Erv Reaves.

"Sounds like she's a grown woman, Mr. Reaves. And you just can't go shooting people. I reckon you know that already."

E.L. Reaves kept his eyes on the ground. He had said his piece. The smaller of the two deputies broke the silence.

"You want me to take him back to the jail?"

The sheriff thought for a moment before answering. When he spoke, it was to Reaves.

"You give me your word not to do anything stupid, Mr. Reaves? If you do, I'll let you ride up behind Deputy Robertson here. You've likely done enough walking for today already."

Reaves bit the inside of his cheek but gave his quiet assent.

"We're going to handcuff you just in case you change your mind. But Harry and me, we're going to ride on out to your home place and take a look. You mind telling us which road we want? It'd save us some time, and I'd like to get my supper before dark."

Anderson punctuated his request with an easy grin. Reaves told the men how to spot his road then Ricky Robertson helped him up onto the dun horse in a spot just behind the saddle. Erv Reaves was not an old man, but his strength had left him for the moment, and, for once in his life, he did not fuss at the extra hand. Once he was mounted, the deputy tightened cuffs around Erv's wrists.

The sheriff tried to offer a cheery parting word.

"Who knows, maybe you'll get lucky, Mr. Reaves. Maybe your fellow ain't even dead."

Reaves aimed a wad of mostly dry spit toward the dirt.

"Oh, I made sure of that before I started walking."

He did not say another word during the entire half hour ride back to the jail.

The lawmen took their time ambling out the Clark Street Road, and an ambulance from Westheimer's came along not long after. Deputy Harry Lauter waited at the turn off to direct them, but the wagon could not make it down the lane.

Ahead of them, Archie Anderson found the body of James Fisher right where the man had fallen. His clothing was disheveled, his top pants buttons still unfastened. The sheriff surveyed the situation including the three solemn-faced children standing by the open door of the house. The boy was holding a skinned down stick, and Anderson suspected that he may have been poking at the body earlier.

Inside the house, Mary Reaves alternated between a thousand yard stare and sharp intakes of breath. She was cried out for the time being. She was no immediate help to the sheriff's gentle inquiries, and he did not press the matter. When the two ambulance attendants loaded Fisher onto a litter to walk him back to their wagon, Mary quietly retreated to her room.

The crew of three sat with their backs against the shed at the Genoa Road crossing. Shade was a tough commodity to come by on the coastal prairies, and the trio were crowded together on the east side of the tiny building which stood along side of the tracks. Later in the afternoon, the shadow would stretch out, but as the men dug into their lunch buckets, their legs, from the knees down, were roasting in the sun. Their once bright blue denim pants seemed to be fading by the minute.

Andy Green had been eating on the same pot of navy beans for the past five days, and Dory Cooper was giving him the needle.

"Same lunch for two weeks now. How big's that bean pot of yours?"

"He's got to finish them off so he can take him a bath come Saturday."

The last gibe came from Tom Jorgenson, and it earned a big whoop from Cooper. Andy Green tried to give some back as he spooned up another mouthful.

"I ain't got no woman to do my stove work. A real man learns how to feed himself."

Cooper gave a cluck.

"What's that real man going do with a winter night when he needs a companion?"

Tom Jorgenson wiped his brow with his bandana.

"I doubt we ever see another winter around here. This heat wave likely to last forever."

"I can buy me a woman when I need one," Andy responded. "And she don't get to stay around and nag me day and night."

"I'll take a little nagging if it means I don't have to eat on the same damn pot of beans for two weeks straight."

Cooper punctuated it with a superior snicker.

"Five days. Made them Sunday. These beans are just coming into their own."

"Them beans'll be old enough to start school by next week."

Even Andy Green joined in the laughter on that one.

WHAM!

The loud bang came from the other side of the shed wall, and it made Andy jump to his feet and take off. He ran about ten feet, almost to a nearby barbed wire fence, still holding his lunch bucket in his left hand, before he regained his composure. His friends were convulsed on the ground. Finally, Tom Jorgenson choked out some words.

"It's just a hoe or something fell, Andy. What the hell is wrong with you?"

Green turned back to the shed but he was still breathing hard.

"Son, I've had a case of the nerves ever since they shot Johnson."

He shook his head.

"Any sharp noise, and I'm liable to come right out of my skin. Don't know if I'll ever get over that."

Like Andy Green, Dory Cooper and Tom Jorgenson were railroad lifers, and though they had not known the man as well as Green had, both worked crews with Johnson Montgomery for years. Since the murder, the GH&H had allowed this gang to operate almost half of the days with just three men. Reynolds, the supervisor, told them several times that a replacement was on the way any time, but the gang was expected to pick up the slack. There was no forgetting the loss of Montgomery in that regard, either. Cooper looked in Green's direction, his voice softer.

"He'd talk you to death, make a man think about killing him your ownself, but I got to say that I sure do miss Johnson sometimes."

Cooper smiled.

"That big old belly laugh of his. Shake the very Earth."

The frequency of Andy Green's drops into melancholy had waned, and they definitely had gotten shorter. Just brief flashes, like a shadow passing over a grave, but he felt one now.

"It does get mighty quiet and lonesome around that old place. Landlord has lowered the rent for seven months now while I look for a new room somewhere. Not that anybody in his right mind is clamoring to get in there. I just ain't been able to find the right spot."

It was only the following Sunday when the surprise came. Andy Green and Poochie were sitting on the small porch, praying for a breeze, when a young couple came walking down the street and stopped at the other side of the bar ditch. Andy did not recognize either one of them, but the man and woman exchanged a silent glance then jumped the ditch and started towards his door. The young man held back, but the girl came right up to the edge of the porch. Poochie, who was normally a growl first kind of mutt, wagged his tail.

"Mr. Green?"

Andy was skeptical. She was a nice looking girl, maybe 18 years old. Dark, clear skin and wearing a Sunday dress with lavender flowers on it. Certainly not the type of visitor he or most of his neighbors expected.

"Yes."

It came out as almost a question.

"My name is Helen Perigault. But I was born Helen Montgomery."

Green cocked his head and crinkled his eyes.

"Johnson Montgomery was my daddy."

He had not meant to be rude or hateful, but it was not until after he invited the couple to come up and sit down that Green realized the potential hurt of his statement that Johnson had never uttered word one about having a child. It was the truth, though, and it was the first blunt thing that popped out of Andy Green's mouth.

He still could not get over it. He had been staring at the young lady for 15 or 20 minutes, and, though there was a most strong resemblance to his late friend, he still struggled to believe it. How could Johnson have carried on with thousands of stories and tall tales, many spun right on that very porch, and never mentioned once that he had left a family behind in East Texas?

Helen Perigault had been raised by her mother near Kirbyville, the nearest town to the woods where the family lived. When she was little, about nine or maybe ten, they had moved south to Beaumont where her mother took work sewing canvas tarpaulins. Her mother had married again. Though there was no divorce, the woman was certain that Johnson Montgomery would never come back to contest anything.

Two months ago, Helen and Rod jumped the broom, so to speak. The boy was painfully quiet, but he was a good man. It was Rod who had convinced Helen that she needed to come to Houston to put her father's memory to rest, though he had to be convinced that there was not a haint living in the house after the murder.

Helen said that growing up any words about her father were few and far between. Her mother loathed the man. When his name arose, her mother took on an expression as if she were about to spit, but being a lady, she never did.

Over the years, though, when her mother was not around, a cousin or some family friend would let slip enough of a story that Helen began to gather a mental picture of her father. She assembled a patchwork quilt of what he might have been like as a man. She had yet to cobble together any reason that Johnson Montgomery may have run out on his wife and young daughter, left behind a sawmill job, and absconded to Houston.

There had been another child of Johnson's, a little boy who came behind Helen. John was his name. He was only two years old when he fell down an abandoned well at the back of their place and died. Their mama was pregnant at the time, and the ordeal made her lose the baby. Helen believed that Johnson left somewhere during those bleak days. Maybe he was unable to cope with tragedy, or maybe it was something else entirely.

With each new addition to the tale, Andy Green felt like he knew his best friend a little less.

"Mama only said that he was a good time man, never serious and never taking responsibility."

Andy could not square that with the man he knew. His friend Johnson liked to enjoy himself, sure. Who did not? He had been known to chase after a woman now and again, but much less frequently than some of Harrisburg's Don Juans. But between the jokes and drinking and ceaseless yarns, Johnson Montgomery had a dour streak. If anything, at those times, he was too serious. Maybe people do change, thought Andy. Maybe Johnson was bearing a deep pain from his lost family, and maybe he had just learned to push it forever down beneath the surface.

Green voiced none of this to Helen Perigault. He did not want to hurt the nice girl's feelings a second time.

She had lived with her imaginary daddy all these years until an aunt heard through the grapevine that Johnson Montgomery was shot dead in Harrisburg. It was not a subject Helen would dare to broach with her mother, but it ate at her until Rod offered a proposal to put her imaginings to bed. They took the morning train from Beaumont, then the bayou boat out of downtown Houston. Now here she was on Andy Green's porch.

Poochie took to Helen right away, and the young woman did not even mind when the little dog clambered up onto her lap. Slowly, as they exchanged memories of two seemingly different men, Andy Green warmed to the young woman, as well.

It was well into the conversation, after any awkwardness had worn away and everyone was visiting like old friends, that Helen quietly asked why her father had been murdered. Green took his time before answering.

"Yes. He rubbed some White man the wrong way. Your daddy could get under folks' skin, but Johnson never meant no harm."

The comment was short, and nothing else was forthcoming. The incident was still raw for Andy Green. They talked for two hours, then Rod, who had not said more than five words for most of that time, nudged Helen that they needed to walk back to the dock if they were going to connect with their eastbound train home. The three of them said their goodbyes, and she held Andy's hand before she hopped down from the porch.

"According to my mama's stories, he was the devil himself, but my memories of him are all pretty good. Sure, I recollect them two hollering at one another, and the screen door slamming when he'd walk out to work or off to the blind tiger down the road."

Helen smiled to herself, comfortable with her story.

"You know my most real memory of my daddy, Mr. Green? Holding hands with him and counting stars."

Chapter 13

The more Erv Reaves thought about what he had done to James Fisher, and the more other people, inmates and deputies alike, bucked him up during the night as having chosen the right path, the better he felt about his chances. He wasn't exactly smug, but his worry had ebbed.

After breakfast, they had brought him to a small holding room with two other inmates, one Black and one White. It was no more than 10 by 8 feet. One heavy iron door led to the tight, revolving passageway into the courts building, and the other, a slab of steel, took them back to the cells. One by one, the men would go into the courtroom for the morning's arraignment. There was a sheriff's deputy who shuffled the men and another who remained with them in the holding room, leaning against the wall and eyeballing them with vague suspicion.

The other White man had been gone only a moment when the Black prisoner spoke softly. So quiet that Reaves had to look up to determine that the man was even talking to him. The deputy paid them no mind.

"What you say, boy?"

The other man averted his eyes a few degrees but repeated himself.

"Sorry, boss. I was wondering if you were one of the Reaves from Laceola up in Madison County."

Erv sat up straighter and considered the question for a few seconds. He could find no harm in answering the man.

"Yeah. I'm E.L. Reaves. What of it?"

The Black man opened up a warm smile.

"I reckoned I knew you. I recollect seeing you around the Fairey Store."

Laceola was a very small and scattered community, roughly split between the races. If there was anything remotely approaching a town center, it was Richard Fairey's store. Everyone for some miles around traded there. Reaves nodded, and the other man continued.

"My people lived back on Brushy Creek."

That earned another nod from Reaves. It was a small but welcome distraction to hear a bit of home. He missed it on those rare occasions that he gave such things any thought. This was certainly not the place he expected to reminisce, or the company for it, but he replied.

"My daddy worked in the corn syrup mill. I did, too, till they closed up shop. Killed the whole place. We're down here now."

"Yes, sir. The mill sure enough killed it."

There was a long lull while both men sat silent. Not much else to share under the circumstances. After a couple of minutes, Reaves used his head to indicate their surroundings.

"What'd you do?"

"Nothing."

The man's exasperation was evident.

"They said I stole case of meat out of the back of a butcher's, but I didn't."

The conversation was interrupted by the big circular door clanging. The second deputy led the first man back into the holding room and shoved him down on the bench. The man wore a glazed look that indicated his morning was not going well.

"Reaves, you're up."

As soon as he got to his feet, not the easiest task with his ankles shackled, E.L. Reaves reached both of his cuffed hands toward his pocket and fished out his plug of Dixie Queen Tobacco. He thought about biting off some for himself, but remembered that he was about to face the judge. Instead, he tore off a piece with his teeth then held it out for the Black man. He also offered an ever so faint, crooked grin.

"I shot a man."

E.L. Reaves had regained his feistiness by the time he stood in front of Judge Gillaspie for arraignment. The action itself was uneventful. He was indicted for murder. Given that Reaves had caught a relative stranger having sex with his daughter, even if she was 20-years old, Gillaspie kept bail low.

Reaves' son-in-law had gone through the very same rigamarole less than twelve months earlier. At first, no one with the sheriff's or district attorney's offices made the connection.

If the lawyers at Duckworth & Fein had their druthers, that piece of knowledge would remain unnoticed, but Reaves himself guaranteed that it did not. With more than a small measure of braggadocio, quite late on the evening he was booked for murder, he asked the jailer to get a message to J.B. Duckworth, "He's the lawyer for my daughter's husband."

Tom Wilson and some of the deputies got quite the chuckle, and Archie Anderson placed a personal telephone call to ask Duckworth, in an excellent deadpan, if the firm was now offering a sale price for families.

Erv Reaves was only back in his cell for six hours, just long enough to eat a tin dish full of ham and beans and doze off a little before Jailer Wilson fetched him.

"Your family's here, Reaves."

"Family?"

"You got one, ain't you?"

Wilson rattled his key ring. Per protocol, all prisoners in the cell were supposed to stand against the far wall when a jailer opened the door, but the inmate bunking with E.L. Reaves was snoring and wheezing in his hammock, dead to the world. The man had been tossed in during the dark hours of the morning. The night deputy said he was disorderly and drunker than five lords. Tom Wilson looked at the pitiable figure through the small grate for half a minute then opened both locks on the cell door.

"He'll feel it enough when he wakes," the jailer mumbled under his breath as he swung back the steel door.

Downstairs, Elsie Reaves waited in the ante room. Watching the steel doors banging opened and closed had turned her pale. Behind her stood Louie and Nora Swearingen. They accompanied Elsie to help sort the situation and lend support. Though no one had mentioned the indelicate fact that Louie must know his way around the intricacies of imprisonment, it had crossed everyone's mind.

For some years, Elsie Reaves had tried to set aside at least a dollar from her pay at the store. Her husband knew nothing about the subterfuge, but Elsie was intent on buying herself a full set of crystal glassware. It was a silly conceit, she knew, but she dreamt of elevating her circumstances just a hair. She passed the goal many months back but had never quite gotten around to going into downtown Houston to select a pattern. Instead, the money had been handed over to a dry-faced court clerk to get her husband out of jail. She reached into her small handbag and fingered her empty coin purse without realizing it.

Tom Wilson led Erv Reaves through the second of the doors from the cell rotunda and pointed him to the book to sign. He handed over the Case knife they had taken from the prisoner upon his arrival. If Reaves had been carrying any change that needed returning, it was not mentioned. Instead, Erv showed a sour face.

"Not that I wanted your hospitality, but I'd shoot Fisher all over again, if I had the chance."

Elsie touched her husband's arm as a caution to mind his words, but it was Wilson who spoke next.

"Ah, you don't know, do you? Well..."

Wilson rocked back on his heels as if to savor his secret for one last time.

"Here's the horsefly in the ointment. Your Fisher wasn't Fisher. He was Jim Farnsworth. He's a private detective all right. Doc Larendon recognized him right off when he looked over the body."

The jailer paused for a smile.

"And Jim Farnsworth was a married man."

Elsie Reaves let out a loud gasp, and Nora covered her mouth. Erv narrowed his eyes to slits, unquestionably reinforced in thinking he had done the right thing. Nobody heard the low growl that resonated deep in the bottom of his throat.

Wilson continued his news report despite the fact that Elsie Reaves had gone a bit weak in the legs and was looking for a place to sit down.

"Yep, we just put two and two together this morning. Archie sent Bernhard to notify the widow, so God help her."

Even before the sheriff's deputy could get by to break things to the new widow, *Post* reporter John Hooper, J.B. Duckworth's friend and occasional drinking companion, had shown up at 1418 Congress, the Farnsworth home. Hooper heard a rumor that smelled like a small sensation, and he wasted no time before knocking on the modest oak door.

June Farnsworth was a competent-looking woman trying to cling to the final vestiges of her softness. A fresh-scrubbed toddler hid behind her legs when she opened up. Mrs. Farnsworth was a bit perplexed that a newspaperman would come calling, but her answers were honest. She had not seen her husband since breakfast two days before. Detectives often had to work strange hours and were frequently away from home. It was normal behavior for Jim Farnsworth. Nature of the job.

Hooper was still asking his background questions when the tall Deputy Bill Bernhard walked up behind him. Happy to avoid being the bearer of the news, the reporter stepped back several feet to a distance where he could clearly take in the tableau as the "stricken widow fell to her knees on the front step while her sobbing children clung tightly to her shoulders." Yes. There was most definitely a good story here.

It took barely 24 hours for Duckworth & Fein to decline to defend E.L. Reaves. As usual, the most business got done after hours when the office was free of clients. Normally, working after dark in the summer was a bit more comfortable, as well, but in the ongoing heat wave, the night time temperatures were no improvement. The attorneys sweated even in shirt sleeves.

After Reaves' late night request for Duckworth's services, Jed Posey met with him at the jail just after dinner that day. Posey had two other short client conferences in the cells so there was little extra effort involved. Still, his view of the Reaves case was mostly predetermined before he ever saw the man. He could not find an upside.

"Charges will probably be dropped anyway," Posey told the lawyers in the main office that night. "He shot a married man who came into his house and was…"

Jed was momentarily flustered, so Sonny Schlottmann made a suggestion.

"Joining giblets with his daughter?"

Before the juvenile laughter subsided, Posey, slightly flushed, resumed.

"If you like. The point is I don't see the charge lasting."

J.B. Duckworth had only one question for his law clerk.

"Is there a quick dollar to be made? Arranging his dismissal?"

"The man doesn't have two nickels to jangle in his pocket. And the pocket probably has a hole in it to boot."

That understandably led into a discussion about Reaves' son-in-law who had become a frustrating client to pin down. Schlottmann knew he was risking J.B.'s wrath by asking about the elusive witnesses, but he did anyway. The boss started out calmly.

"Not a one, and at the moment, there's not enough money to hire any, either. If John was here, you could ask him yourself."

John Duckworth did not generally burn the late oil like the lawyers did, and his brother briefly wondered which bar John was leaning against at the moment. He banished the thought of a drink and continued his assessment of the Swearingen defense.

"Nobody's doing us any favors with that case, and it comes up again in the fall. I sure as shit don't want to be the one to ask Gillaspie for a continuance. Maybe it's your turn, Henry."

Fein gave an acknowledging nod as J.B. went on, getting a bit more exercised.

"Hopefully it'll be granted as a matter of course because otherwise I'll be conjuring a defense like a Pantages magic act. One of my few hooks so far is that the kid was too pixilated to aim a gun."

Schlottmann made a face at that notion.

"He was what, 10, 15 yards away? If he can handle a gun at all…"

"His father is a lawman," J.B. scoffed. "You know he taught him to shoot. Bound to have. I think all we can do in that regard is go with the liquor. Damnation, the man can't remember where he was. You're going to tell me that he can squeeze off two patterned shots?"

Henry Fein cleared his throat.

"Well, from hearing you lot describe the boy, he's a drunk, and the only time their hands are steady…"

Henry ended his thought with an Alsatian shrug, and that in turn, ended the evening's discussion of Louie Swearingen. Talk turned back to the never-ending heat, and Jed Posey launched into an explanation that the term dog days of summer had nothing whatever to do with dogs but rather was derived from the star Sirius. Duckworth quietly walked into his office and closed the door.

J.B. Duckworth stopped off at Big Annie's for a drink or three before catching the final car to take him through the train yard. As usual, the household was asleep when he reached Waverly Street, and all but Maizy stayed that way. She stretched, yawned, licked his hand, watched him look in on Katherine, then followed him into the bedroom and curled up on the floorboards next to his side of the bed. J.B. had long ago acquired a small rug for that spot. Earlier, the dog had been quite put off that she was not going to the office, so Duckworth was pleased to find himself forgiven.

Lola Duckworth did not move when he climbed under the sheet. Luckily, given her husband's late hours, she was a sound sleeper. J.B. gave her a gentle kiss on the side of her head and was snoring less than five minutes later.

She rose the next morning with the sun and tended to the breakfast needs of her family. Once her Jamie was gone to downtown again about eight, this time with a tail-wagging Maizy in tow, Lola heated water for a bath. She was having lunch at a neighbor's. Compared to others in Fifth Ward, the Schmidt's house was just as unexceptional as the Duckworth's, but it was unsparingly clean. Lottie Schmidt kept it scrubbed to within a proverbial inch of a dustball's life, and Lola may have worked the washrag harder than usual.

The table was tidily laid. Egg salad sandwiches with all crust trimmed neatly away from the bread. The drought and heat had doomed everyone's tomato gardens by the start of June, so a plate of homemade pickles, goat cheese, and Saltine crackers rounded out the fare. Mrs. Schmidt, being a German Lutheran, served sweet white wine.

Lola's biggest goal of the day was to tell her friend about her recent seaside visit. She had wanted to take a week and travel all the way to Corpus Christi or Tarpon, but J.B. could not spare the time. Instead, the family spent two nights at the Surfside Hotel, a straight shot down the International line to Velasco. Lottie Schmidt was duly impressed.

"Was it expensive?"

"Two dollars a night."

Lottie let out a small breath.

"Well, I suppose you must pay for the luxury of sea air."

The more she described the trip, the more animated Lola became. When she was there on the beach in the moment, she had moments of slight anxiety trying to keep her husband and daughter entertained. In that respect it was no different than being at home.

J.B. did not fish. She had never even heard him mention it as anything either desirable or nostalgic. On top of that, sitting on the long veranda made him restless after more than 20 minutes at a stretch. He went on walks along the beach with and without her. She could tell that he was often laying out some legal argument in his mind, but then he would take her hand as they strolled and all was well again. She told how they found relaxation in books, and that Katherine seemed to thoroughly enjoy sitting at the edge of the water picking up handfuls of wet sand. Lola did admit to despairing ever so slightly about transporting those grains all the way back to Fifth Ward.

Lottie did not laugh at that. Perhaps the mere notion of battling sand was disturbing, but she eventually put the fear behind her and asked more questions.

"What was the best part?"

"The food was very nice," Lola thought. "Especially the fresh caught snapper. Lottie, it was the sweetest fish I have ever tasted. Even better since I didn't have to cook it. Oh, and I was afraid that Jamie was trying to eat his weight in shrimp."

Across town that night, Louie and Nora Swearingen tried to get comfortable enough to sleep in the heat. They were well settled into their rented room at the back of a house on Chenevert for these past two months. It was several blocks south of the creamier locations and on the wrong side of the street, but they got the room, a bath down the hall, and breakfast for three dollars a week. A discount if they paid the month in advance.

Their lone window faced west, though. That meant the room heated up during the day like a dreadnought's oven. Since they moved in, the nights were spent on top of the sheet wearing as little as possible, and they still woke every 90 minutes or so in a wet tangle. They had invested in a used electric fan, and that made things more bearable at a time not long before midnight.

In spite of that hardship, it was pure luxury to Nora to be in the city and away from the woods, but Louie missed certain eccentricities of Fifth Ward. He had no doubt that he would learn his new neighborhood in time, but since he left Austin County, he had never lived south of the bayou. It felt busier and impersonal, which was saying something to a gregarious bartender who worked downtown. He had yet to find anyone who could make peach puffs or anything remotely close to the goodness of Mrs. Gates who had a bakery stand on Nance Street. On the other hand, he and Nora could each walk to work.

They laid together in silence for what surely must be hours, neither one sleeping but each afraid to wake the other. Nora debated all day whether to tell Louie about her sister's latest troubles. The decision was made, so she did not see the point. When Louie gave a disgusted grunt and sat up in bed, however, Nora blurted it out.

"Mary asked to move in with us."

She felt her husband turn toward her in the dark.

"And do what? Live in the chifforobe?"

"I already told her no. Twice."

"I'd sure as hell hope so."

Swearingen realized that he sounded uncaring and rubbed his wife's bare back softly.

"Sorry, hon. It's just, you know that's an impossibility."

"Of course, I do. I just feel so sorry for the poor thing. She's not spoken to our father for several days. She moved her sewing machine into her room. Dragged it with just a little help from Vi. She's thinking about setting up her work at the store, but they don't have room, either. She just feels like there is no place to go."

They were quiet until a question made its way through Louie's drink-induced fog.

"When did she tell you all this?"

"She rang here this evening. I eventually had to rush her off the line. I was getting nothing but guff from Mrs. Lord. Though it's beyond me why the house has a telephone if we're not allowed to use it. You could have taken up for me, if it hadn't taken you three hours to make your way home from work."

Nora had promised herself that she wouldn't harp on that topic either, but her restraint was weak. It must be the heat. She tried to soften her words with a tease.

"I was afraid you'd gotten lost again and found a roommate you liked better."

Louie was convinced he was trying his honest best not to drink too much. Admittedly, he had gotten into a little trouble when he wandered into the wrong boarding house and walked in on some old man. News of that episode had somehow reached their landlord and subsequently his wife. His defense was half-hearted.

"Well, it was new. The whole place was still confusing to me. We'd only lived here a week."

"Three."

There was an uneasy pause before Nora grabbed his hand without turning her gaze from the window. She let out a sigh and spoke with great mock concern.

"I truly hope you'll not cause me to start attending Temperance meetings. Those old biddies give me the creeps."

Louie busted out a long laugh, and the two fell back on the bed together.

Chapter 14

October 1902

Over the last several months, Louie Swearingen had grown increasingly frustrated with life in legal limbo. The first anniversary of his arrest for murder came and went. The district attorney had postponed his trial twice, and his own lawyers assured him that was a wonderful thing. He could not bring himself to share in their confidence. Each time they reminded him that he still had no alibi for the time of the killing, it only served to make Louie angrier. Why could he not remember big pieces of his life. There were one or two brief interludes when he almost questioned his own innocence. He shook them off quickly, but it still ate at his mind. He considered himself an easy going man, but it was becoming more and more difficult to suppress his feelings of helplessness.

Things rose to the forefront again when Louie was summoned to the law offices at midday on the Wednesday that started October. He was due at the Turf Exchange at two. Nora left for the dye works long before he awoke. He drank the last cup and a half of cold coffee and ate the last slice of mediocre banana cake, but he was still carrying a lot of rough edges when he trudged up the stairway at 1107 ½ Congress.

Sonny Schlottmann waved Swearingen over to his desk, and though the lawyer was his general happy, smiling self, the news he imparted did nothing to soothe Louie's worries. The following Monday marked the resumption of the year's criminal court calendar, and the case of Texas v. Swearingen would probably come up in the latter half of the month. This time it was Duckworth & Fein who would be asking for a continuance. The reason was simple. J.B. Duckworth was their best trial attorney, and he would be working a case elsewhere. Either Bay City or Anahuac, depending on how things broke. Texas had no shortage of accused murderers.

Schlottmann lifted his chin and gave a grin.

"You don't know how lucky you are that your boss likes you. He got you a crackerjack lawyer."

Louie stared back at him sullenly, or perhaps it was the hangover.

"What happens if the judge decides that we start the trial right then? I know Mr. Fein promised that doesn't happen, but what if? Where does that leave me?"

Sonny shook his head and flashed a reassuring smile.

"Henry told you right. It would take a special kind of bastard to make a person go to trial without his lead attorney."

Even as he said it, Schlottmann thought of the still-pending trouble between Duckworth and Judge Gillaspie. He tried to add reassurance.

"It would certainly never happen to a man on trial for his life."

A shudder ran up Louie's back. This was not starting out as a banner day.

"Gillaspie owes us on this one."

"Enough said, J.B. You have told me 20, 30, 400 times. You will get ulcers with your fretting over Judge Gillaspie."

The October court session was more than a week old, and Duckworth had again managed to avoid appearing before J.K.P. Gillaspie, but Henry Fein was weary of the deliberately juggled schedules.

"You cannot let this imaginary threat simmer. Figure out how to resolve this. Stand up to the man. Give in to the man. This is on the verge of hurting the firm."

Fein's manner, as always, was affable, and his soft Alsatian accent never failed to wrap velvet around even the most strident words. Even though he was quite a bit younger, Henry Fein started the practice of law 18 months prior to J.B. Their merging of practices raised eyebrows around the Houston legal community, at least among those criminal lawyers low enough on the totem pole to notice such goings on. Henry Fein was undeniably Jewish, plenty enough reason for some to shun him outright, but it had never given James Duckworth a moment's pause. As it turned out, the arrangement, forged at the small law library in the courthouse, had proven nothing short of perfection. Caseload soon increased for both men. Henry, with his full law degree and quiet, bookish bent, was such a great complement to the scrappy Duckworth that it was soon impossible for either man to imagine practicing law without the other.

When the Swearingen case was finally called, Henry Fein was there to ask for and receive the desired postponement. There were barely any questions. Gillaspie granted it as a matter of course. In fact, the judge seemed to Henry strangely distracted through the entire proceeding.

Henry Fein sent a wire to his absent partner – "Swearingen pstpnd till March."

Duckworth, springing for a few extra words, replied "March 1920 if have my way."

James Duckworth started the October court sessions defending a man in Milam County. It was as far away from Houston as J.B. had ever tried a case before. Word had begun to spread about his prowess in securing a verdict of self-defense.

It had taken less than two full days of trial to gain an acquittal for a Rockdale hosteler who shot and killed one of his guests. The lodger was belligerent over what he claimed was an undercooked piece of beef. When the innkeeper replied that he ran a hotel not a tannery, the diner pulled a knife. Duckworth had everything on his side – a local over the out-of-towner, a victim who was armed, and a jury that appreciated a civilized steak. His quick securance of the verdict allowed him to take up another murder trial in Anahuac the following week.

That case proved to be more of a challenge. The deceased was a 57-year old woman who had been done in by one of her sons, or so the Chambers County attorney alleged. Between the two stops, Duckworth had a day to spend in Houston. He wanted fresh shirts from home and to replenish his supply of lemon stick candy, his latest obsession. Somewhat to the chagrin of Lola, though hardly a surprise, J.B. also stopped in at the office. He promised his wife a "short visit to get a few papers," but it turned into three-hour conversation with Sonny Schlottmann.

Evening hours were generally quite busy in the Duckworth & Fein offices, but, as the first week of the session ground to a close, Jed Posey was still traveling several counties to file motions, and Henry Fein was observing the Friday night sabbath. John Duckworth received his brother's instructions the day prior and was already in Anahuac trying to scare up anyone else who could be helpful on the stand. Consequently, the firm's junior partner was the only one still working at eight in the evening when J.B. climbed the stairs to find the door locked.

"I had three people come in here asking questions between six and seven," Schlottmann explained. "Two of them fuddled, none of them coherent, and definitely not even a modest retainer to be squeezed from the lot of them. I finally locked the door so I could get some work done."

He laughed at his own wit.

"I didn't expect you. I thought you were headed straight to the next case."

J.B. hung a hat on the rack.

"Wanted to see Katherine and Lola. I'll take the train tomorrow night so I can review the case in peace before Monday."

Duckworth pulled up a chair opposite Sonny's desk, and the two attorneys caught up on small talk. That segued into updates on other cases, then Schlottmann asked about the upcoming trial in Anahuac.

"The old woman was a real shrew from what they tell me. Never shut her gob, and not a kind word come out of it. But it's not the same as disparaging a man."

Sonny raised his shoulders.

"Every man knows a fishwife."

Duckworth shook his head.

"Not the same," he repeated. "Hell, it may remind them of their own dear harridan of a mother."

"There is no question he did it," Schlottman said.

Having been part of earlier discussions, it was a quiet statement to himself, not a question.

"When the older brother walked into the house, it was just two people there, and one of them had been chopped on pretty good with an ax. Sheriff over there says that the younger one, Kenneth, was sitting in the corner of the room, sobbing and covered in so much blood that the flies wouldn't leave him alone."

Sonny opened his eyes wide and let out a plume of air.

"That is a pickle, of course, but you still think the diminished capacity will get the boy acquitted, yes?"

Duckworth made a ticking noise with his mouth.

"I reckoned a long time on that, and there's not enough evidence to hold it up. He was drunk. Yeah, that's diminished, but it's self-inflicted."

Schlottmann smiled.

"Even sober, he's not the brightest of boys, if I recall."

"There's lots of stupid people Sonny. They don't all attack their own mamas with a goddammed ax."

Duckworth's acid comment was answered with a shrug.

"We've been talking diminished capacity for three, four months, J.B.."

Sonny paused, then gave an almost imperceptible shake of his head before going on. His senior law partner had certainly been known to change his angle of defense at the last minute, but Schlottmann never got used to it.

"What are you thinking then?"

Duckworth tugged at the right side of his moustache.

"I'm going to blame it on the other brother. The one who found him. Or at least create a very reasonable doubt."

"Isn't that our client?"

"No, That's the man who's paying us. Our client is the fellow whose neck is on the line."

The ticking of a wall clock was the only sound as the two lawyers looked at each other, daring the other to go next. Schlottmann blinked.

"Have you told him?"

"Don't intend to. I need him outraged in court."

"That can't do wonders for his reputation, J.B. The man may want to know before you despoil his good name."

"The ones who hire me are asking for one thing. A verdict of not guilty. I'm under no obligation to seek their counsel on how I get there."

"Surely there must be some better way to go about it."

"I sure as shit don't know what that would be. Do you, Sonny? I've come up with the same thing I always look for – the most straightforward way to hear 'not guilty.' I don't need to go around the barn to get there."

When J.B. returned home, Lola was already asleep, but she had neatly folded three clean shirts into his grip along with underclothing and socks. She found a new washing and ironing woman a few months back, a sweet but harried mother of several children. The woman lived only four blocks away, a neighbor, really, though Lola certainly did not think of domestic help in such a way. This one was so much more reliable than the last. Picking up the dirty laundry and returning it pristine in under 36 hours. Lola still had not settled exactly on how to use her extra time.

Tommy O'Neill's saloon was not especially crowded when Louie Swearingen stepped through the front door. Several of the dozen drinkers turned to check the new arrival, and three called out his name in a chorus.

Louie had made a solemn promise to Nora that he would not dally so long on his walks home. He meant it. He wanted to spend more time with his sweet and pretty wife, but a customer had been chatting him up about the Fifth Ward that afternoon, and Louie made another promise, this one to himself. He would make a point to stop up that way and say hello to some of his old pals. When Charlie Lusk cut him from his shift a half hour early, it seemed that there was no time like the present. Louie took the cars across the bayou and up Hardy Street, and he swore that two drinks was his limit.

After his fourth beer, possessed of every intention of leaving, someone shoved Louie from behind. It was just enough for him to take a staggering step forward, doubtless an accident. Louie was in such an expansive mood that he was not even angry, but when he turned to see who bumped him, it was clear that the other man was.

Swearingen was tall and lanky, but the man he faced had him by 3 inches and at least 50 pounds. The fellow was red faced, though whether from drink or anger, Louie could not immediately tell. Something about him looked familiar, the weak chin and the paltry moustache, but Louie could not discern that either.

The big man's fist clenched and he took a half step toward Swearingen. Louie could smell his beery breath. His glowering stare froze Swearingen in his place, but the man said nothing. Finally, he turned away, downed the dregs of a beer glass a few places down the bar and left O'Neill's with a slam of the door.

"Did you know him?"

Timmy O'Neill, the owner's son and usual bartender, was looking at Swearingen. Louie opened his mouth to say no, then the epiphany hit. His answer was a rush of astonishment.

"That's one of the guys who arrested me."

He knew fully that the murder charge dangling over his head was common knowledge across the city, but the embarrassment of it still stung. He lowered his voice.

"Damn it! I knew he was familiar. He would have had my hide the day they picked me up if it wasn't for the sheriff."

"He's a right bastard. Isgitt's his name. From what I've seen, he makes the round of a few bars every month or so, measuring up others for a fight. My da has removed him from here a time or two over the years."

Louie shook his head.

"Here's me minding my own business, and I can't escape trouble."

"Next one's on the O'Neills."

Timmy drew another mug of beer and placed it in front of Swearingen. All promises to leave at a decent hour were soon forgotten.

Tommy, the old man, appeared behind his son and extended a hand toward Louie Swearingen.

"Give me a shake, boyo. Time for you to move along home now. I'll be locking the doors soon enough in any event."

Kicked out. It sounded fitting to Louie Swearingen who took his banishment good naturedly. The sparse crowd of drinkers was down to less than a handful, and the owner instructed his son to see to Louie Swearingen.

Out on the street, the bartender steered his friend one block over to catch the car. Louie rehashed the same old story twice before Timmy O'Neill approached the motorman, a face new to Swearingen. Louie clapped O'Neill on the shoulder.

"I've been gone too long, Timmy. Should never have moved."

"Don't tell that to your bride, boyo."

O'Neill smiled then turned to the motorman.

"I'm pouring this one aboard. Kindly see that he dismounts at Franklin and point him south. We don't want him staggering into the drink."

The driver laughed and nudged the car forward. Though he was firmly seated, Louie lurched forward and grabbed the seat rail. He tried to focus on the back of the motorman's cap as he silently recited his apartment's address in his head.

"Ow!"

Swearingen rubbed the back of his throbbing right hand. He had misjudged the width of the door opening and smacked his knuckles hard on the door frame. Now Nora was wide awake and most assuredly unhappy.

"Just this morning, Louie. Just this morning you swore to me that you wouldn't stay out all night. Yet here you are, rum-soaked and yowling. Not even 24 hours!"

Nora took a moment to look around the pitch dark apartment.

"Though almost."

"I'm sorry. I really tried. I had good intentions..."

"I'm tired of your hollow promises, Louie. You can't go cadding about town like you used to. You're a married man."

"I know, sweets. But there was this man…"

"And he was buying the drinks. I've heard the song a thousand times."

Nora punctuated her remarks with a small primal shriek. That, in turn, brought a banging on the common bedroom wall. Louie fumbled with his watch and flexed his eyebrows until he could focus on the shorter hand. It was between two and three. Louie's voice dropped to a slurry stage whisper.

"Not that kind of man. A bad man…"

A soft light came on overhead as Louie finally succeeded in finding the light switch on the wall behind him.

"He was bad. He was a lawyer. No, lawman. A constable, or deputy, and I think he hates me. He's the son of a bitch who arrested me last year. He's no good. Timmy said he's no good."

Swearingen's voice had risen again, and the knocking on the wall resumed once more along with an impolite admonition to quieten down. Nora picked a mug off the drainboard and slammed it back down with a crack.

She was genuinely enraged at her husband's behavior, and Louie seemed to realize it for the first time. He threw both arms around her in a drunken bear hug. Nora pushed him away, in no mood to forgive, much less have the stink of smoky barroom on her clean nightgown. In shoving back, she looked down and suddenly let out a gasp. There was a large spot of blood, the size of a pomegranate, soaking through her husband's trousers just below the knee. With the ceiling bulb illuminated, she could see that there were drops on his shoe and now on the floor.

"My Lord, Louie. What did you do?"

Her husband looked down and let go a loud breath. For the first time in his adult life, he felt a burn in his eyes as tears welled.

"I don't have any idea, sweetie. No idea at all."

Chapter 15

Two days after the dressing down that Louie Swearingen endured in the wee hours at the hands of his wife, there was a loud knock at his door. Louie was still abed, but Nora was readying herself for work. Louie offered a faint groan and dug himself deeper under the covers.

Nora expected to see one of the neighbors, popping upstairs to ask a favor or share a juicy scrap of gossip, but she was met by a fiftyish man in the blue tunic of the Houston police. His glum face managed the briefest passing leer upon seeing an attractive young woman with three blouse buttons undone and her hair askew. She gazed at him with irritation until he spoke.

"You Mrs. Swearingen?"

His South Louisiana accent was unmistakable.

"Yes."

She scrambled to think what this might be about.

"I'm Officer Andrus, ma'am. I'm here to arrest your husband, Louis."

Nora stumbled back a step as if she had been slapped. Across the room, Louie slept on, his snores audible. Nora responded with as much indignation as she could muster while keeping her voice low to avoid eavesdropping neighbors.

"My husband is out on bail. For a crime he did not commit, I should add."

Andrus gave a world weary nod.

"Yes, ma'am, that's what I hear, but this is for another matter."

He reached into a pocket and produced a scrap of paper which he held out for Nora as he recited the details.

"Louis Swearingen, Jr., 1446 Chenevert St. Apartment 7. Yep. I'm in the right place, and I'm picking your husband up for armed robbery."

"Armed robbery! Are you crazy? Louie hasn't robbed anyone."

"Y'all going to have to take that up with the detective. He just sent me to bring the man in."

With that Andrus brushed past Nora into the small apartment.

"I reckon that's him snoring in the bed?"

Before the policeman could make the few steps to the bed, Nora had screeched her husband's name loud enough to wake him. Decorum be damned. Louie's head emerged from the quilt, his face a ball of confusion.

"What?"

"What did you do?" his wife implored.

Swearingen was having trouble understanding the situation, but the policeman dangling handcuffs at his bedside finally brought things into focus.

"What the hell?"

Louie raised himself on one arm, but before any more words escaped him, Andrus pushed him back down on his face.

"We ain't going to have no trouble now."

For a man of his age and size, the patrolman showed good strength. Swearingen was still groggy, but the policeman pulled the covers back and fastened the cuffs without difficulty, pulling Louie to a sitting position as he finished. Nora hollered at Andrus.

"Let him go! He hasn't done anything! He doesn't even own a gun."

Victor Potts, the curmudgeonly machinist who was fond of banging on walls, edged around the door frame.

"What's going on over here? What's your drunk husband done now?"

None in the apartment responded.

Billy Andrus, deciding that his perpetrator was not a risk, leaned down to Louie's face level.

"I'm fixing to help you pull on your pants. After that, if you promise to be a good boy, I'll unhook you so you can put on a shirt and your coat. How's that sound to you?"

By the time Swearingen, dressed and re-cuffed, and Andrus reached the ground floor, the downstairs neighbors were standing in the tiny hallway at the front of the house. Mrs. Lord, the landlady glared at the unseemliness. In a quieter moment, Nora would be fretting a potential eviction, but she was busy chattering into the telephone by the foot of the landing. Henry Fein was on the other end of the line, and the moment Billy Andrus' feet hit the bottom of the stairwell, Nora motioned him to the receiver.

The dismayed policeman hesitated but took the handset and spoke a hello. A firm but tinny voice responded.

"Officer, this is attorney Henry Fein with Duckworth & Fein. Do you have an arrest warrant for my client?... Hello?"

Andrus held the receiver away for his face for a moment and did a poor job of stifling his grimace.

"No, I don't, but we'll sort that out once I get him over to the station."

"I don't think so. You know the law, officer... Who am I speaking to?"

"It's Billy Andrus, Mr. Fein."

Though much of the Houston police force carried a decided hatred of J.B. Duckworth, several of those same officers had shared drinks with his partners. Yadon's Saloon just downstairs from the firm's offices was a frequent point of intersection. Andrus, being one of the patrol elders, had passed the time with Henry Fein on many occasions and over many a glass. Fein's tone softened a note.

"Ah, Billy. You certainly know the difficulties we've had with the department before over the notion that you can pick someone up without a warrant."

Fein paused for a response that was not forthcoming, so he continued.

"It never turns out well for the police, as you recall. I'm saying that you need to release my client, and someone from our firm will bring him to the station for an interview."

"Look, Mr. Fein, ...Henry, all I know is that Detective Kessler sent me over here to pick up Swearingen, and that's what I'm planning to do."

"Yes, Kessler. I might have known. He is a stubborn one who has trouble learning, doesn't he?"

Andrus's try to hold back a small laugh failed.

"All, the same, I'm not looking to get a roasting from Kessler."

"I can promise you, Billy, that if you take my client without a warrant, you'll be roasted by Chief Ellis. It will not be good for you. Everything I know shows that he has his men following the law. Let Mr. Swearingen go, and you can tell Kessler that we will bring him in with counsel, as it should be."

Billy Andrus stood silent and stared at Louie Swearingen. The entire assemblage in the foyer had heard the conversation, and all of them waited with anticipation. After what felt like an eternity, Andrus unlocked the handcuffs.

"Y'all better be over there today, or I'll come and find you again, and this time no lawyer, not even Mr. Fein, is going to save your ass."

Andrus turned toward Mrs. Lord.

"Pardon my language, ma'am."

John Duckworth was at the Swearingen flat in about 40 minutes. Apologies were relayed to Charlie Lusk at his home. Louie would not be making it to work that afternoon. He was "badly under the weather."

Within an hour after John's arrival, Nora Swearingen was calm enough to head in to work. There was no point in endangering both of their jobs. She told Mr. Fernandez at the dye works that she had a sick husband. It was not entirely a lie since Nora fully intended to remove a piece of his hide when she next got him alone.

It fell to Jed Posey to be the man who broke the news to the Houston Police that Louie Swearingen would not be coming in for that interview just yet. He first took a rasher of abuse from Detective Will Kessler, and then heard several less than choice words from Chief Ellis. The stoic lawyer was the perfect person for the task. The policemen may not have been assuaged by Posey's relentless quoting of the statutes, but they at least stopped hollering at him eventually.

The desired arrest warrant had been issued minutes before Posey crossed the police station threshold, but the best that he was willing to promise the department was that Duckworth & Fein would produce Louie Swearingen along with an ironclad alibi within the next 48 hours. As he was saying it, Jed hoped to God that it was true. The young attorney offered one last look of deadpan seriousness before he departed George Ellis' office.

Less than two miles north, John Duckworth installed Louie Swearingen in the New Florence Hotel under the name of Nelson Altgeld, a tongue-in-cheek homage to John's favorite Progressive. The New Florence easily ranked among the least desirable hostelries in Houston. It occupied a corner in an otherwise industrial section of Fifth Ward. From a grimy window at the rear of the hotel, Louie could overlook a neighboring foundry. Thanks to the missing corner of a pane, he could also hear the relentless thrumming of machinery at factories making cotton sacks and boxes and clanging at compresses for grain and cotton seed. The rationale was that nobody in their right mind would be looking for anyone remotely respectable at the New Florence. Swearingen did stand out in one respect - he was among the minute portion of guests who paid by the day instead of the hour.

It was excruciatingly dull, but Louie was complying with instructions that he not leave his hotel room except to visit the toilet down the hall. He had just awoken from his third nap of the day and started his second pass through one of the Leslie's Illustrateds that he had managed to cadge from behind the manager's desk when John Duckworth knocked at the door. John handed Louie a sack which the sequestered man quickly opened.

"It's a ham sandwich and an apple," Duckworth told him. "It's all I could snatch from Yadon's without raising suspicion."

"An apple? I don't think I've had an apple since I was a kid at Christmas. Never really cared for them."

John Duckworth reached for the fruit, but Swearingen yanked it away.

"Hell, no. I'm damn near perishing."

Louie gave Duckworth a curious eye.

"I don't suppose you brought any whiskey, did you?"

"No. And funny you should bring that up…"

John helped himself to a seat on the end of the bed.

"…The particulars of the crime they're after you for is sticking up a grocery in the Second Ward, and all the robber made off with was a bottle of hooch. A pint of Atherton to be specific. Didn't touch a dime of the money. Just the bourbon. Waved a sawed off shotgun around at the little Italian gent that owns the place. Scared him half to death to hear him tell it, though I got the notion that he had some kind of hogleg pistol under the counter for anybody who dares to step near the till."

Louie Swearingen had slouched down against the wall of the room.

"I didn't do it. And before you ask, no, I have no fucking idea how I got home. There'd been some trouble, and I was blue blind when they booted me out of O'Neill's. I admit it."

"You sure were from what they told me."

Swearingen registered surprise.

"It's my job, Louie. I talked to them this morning. They told me they poured you onto the car that dropped you at Congress. That leaves you walking who knows where."

Louie sat sullenly, his long legs splayed out in front of him on the dirty hotel room floor. When he finally spoke, it was barely a whisper.

"I don't even have a gun. You can look."

John raised his hands in supplication.

"I'm not saying you did it, Louie. And the gun thing ought to clear you, but you need to know what the coppers'll be throwing at you. That's why we want to show up with an alibi in hand. If they revoke your bail, you're in for a good while."

"I don't want to go back," Louie croaked. "I swear Nora would leave me."

Duckworth nodded.

"We need to find someone who saw you, or at least someone willing to say they did."

"You mean flat out lie?"

"I'm not a lawyer. I'm just an investigator, and right now the idea is to keep you out of the jug. This'll never get to court. It's just the meantime we're trying to fix."

Swearingen stared at the dingy wall as he took that in. Finally, Duckworth broke the silence.

"So where do you suggest I start looking?"

Louie Swearingen stayed hidden at the New Florence Hotel for 38 hours. When he and Jed Posey walked into the police station on Caroline, they were accompanied by Sam Carr, the bartender from the Turf Exchange. Detective Kessler went out of his way to be unyielding. The questions were fast and strenuous, and Louie lost count of how many times Kessler called him a liar. Carr endured the same grilling. In the end, though, the painfully vague description of the robber and Carr's stubborn insistence that he and Swearingen spent almost all of the night in question drinking at Carr's flat left the dick no choice. Kessler blustered and threatened, promised to keep looking for clues, but the arrest warrant went into a drawer, and Louie Swearingen walked out onto Caroline Street a free man for the moment.

It did not take long for Sam Carr to call in the first favor. Less than 18 hours. Carr had worked an extra shift, as had two others, while Louie was in hiding. Swearingen, having missed work, was equally eager to recoup some income. It was Carr's pointed suggestion that Louie hand over two dollars in tips to compensate for the shift he unfairly had to cover. He did not like it, but Swearingen held his tongue and forked over two silver dollars. He could not help but wonder what else was coming, nor could he afford to make an enemy of Sam Carr.

When Detective Will Kessler allowed Louie Swearingen to walk out the front door of the Houston Police Station, the hope was to put the matter into cold storage. In reality, it stayed there only until J.B. Duckworth, back from his acquittal verdict in Anahuac, heard about the latest development in the life of their client. Duckworth's moods were not always predictable, and the man who had brilliantly created enough doubt in court that a blood-soaked defendant walked free was nonetheless choleric when he stomped through the law office come Monday morning.

Duckworth & Fein was a growing practice by Houston standards, four attorneys at work on a thick caseload, but it was still plenty small enough that no detail escaped the notice of the firm's principle. The district criminal sessions for October might be complete, but a slew of small counties met in November, and Harris County courts would have a full docket come December. It was a planning day, and J.B.'s brother sat in the inner office and offered the briefing. Reading the situation perfectly after a lifetime of practice, John presaged the topic with a deep sigh then told James about the Swearingen arrest.

"We're not getting paid enough for this shit. At least with the career criminals, even back in the days of Sid Preacher, you knew there was going to be a steady stream of income. A little revenue every time those idiots fucked up and got nabbed. But this son of a bitch…"

He threw both hands in a dismissive wave.

"…He's not even enough of a Hooligan to bring us reliable income. Shit, I took the case as a favor to Charlie Lusk. It's always good to keep the better bar owners chirping, isn't it."

J.B. offered his brother a brief upward twitch of the moustache then resumed a frown as he continued.

"But after this robbery... armed robbery, I can't see Charlie keeping the fellow in his employ, can you?"

"For whatever it's worth, I don't see any way the fellow did it."

"How'd they settle on him in the first place, then?"

John Duckworth let loose a snigger.

"There was a mysterious phone call to the station desk. Some unknown man rang up and named Swearingen for the grocery holdup."

"That must've fluttered their bloomers. Nothing those tomfools like better than to have their suspect hand delivered."

John nodded.

"Yup, especially someone on bail."

"Is this ultimately headed to court?" J.B. asked.

A shrug from his brother.

"I doubt it, but you never know."

"Well, shit. Swearingen's got no money for his own defense, and now our thuggish friends over on Caroline Street have a hard on for him? I don't see the benefit here for the firm, do you? I'll stop by and talk to Charlie Lusk. He'll owe us another big chunk when we finally get around to trial. He'd be better off spending it on someone else. That is unless he's ready to cast this boy adrift altogether."

James B. Duckworth chose to break the news to Charlie Lusk in person. Anytime business could be combined with a few stiff drinks made for a good day. He walked into the Turf Exchange with the full intent of quitting as Louie Swearingen's attorney. He was finishing his second glass of Old Taylor with a beer back when the bar owner made it downstairs from his office.

"J.B., I know why you're here..."

Duckworth cut him off.

"Look, Charlie. There's no use throwing away good money. Your boy hasn't given us anything to work with, and he keeps stepping in the shit."

Lusk laughed softly.

"I know. He can be his own worst enemy, but he's a good kid. Good hearted. You know me. I like to keep the good ones. Plus, that wife of his is a corker. Just having her walk in the door makes half the old lechers in the place buy another round."

Duckworth used his index finger to wipe some drops away from his mouth then smoothed the ends of his bushy moustache.

"Eventually we'll have to take this matter to trial, and that's going to cost you notably more than it did the first go around. I'm not sure a collection jar on the bar is going to cover my fee."

"I know. I just can't believe that Louie could coldheartedly kill some man. It's just not in him. He may be a donkey sometimes, but he's not got a callous thought within him, I don't believe. I can part with enough money to see him find justice."

Duckworth stared straight ahead into the bar mirror until Lusk spoke again.

"And I'll tear up your tab when you leave today."

The two men had a good laugh at that, but the decision was made. Duckworth & Fein would keep the case.

The Turf Exchange was a higher end bar. Most drinkers left a few coins for the bartender. A man whose wagers got good results over the wire was apt to leave more, but paying a quarter to Sam Carr following every single shift began to rankle Louie Swearingen. He knew the stakes, but the money added up. He was giving away a meal almost every day, and he when he got his new tormenter alone after three plus weeks of the new arrangement, Louie finally spoke his mind.

It was a blistering rant that none of his Turf co-workers had witnessed from Swearingen, but Sam Carr listened with a smile plastered across his phiz. When Louie was done talking, Carr gave him a condescending pat on the shoulder.

"Oh, now, Louie, what's two bits between old friends like us? It won't be forever, but I'll have to let you know when we're square."

Chapter 16

November 1902

The Houston Police were off the scent of Louie Swearingen for the moment, but until the firm could make certain that no one connected to the district criminal court had caught a sniff of the foul accusations of armed robbery, Sonny Schlottmann had warned Swearingen, or it was perhaps more of a reprimand, to lay low. Home and work, the lawyer told his client.

"If you need a drink so bad, pick up a bottle... that you pay for... and have your friends loiter around your flat. Your missus'll probably hate it, but she'd hate it worse were you to be tossed into the brig again."

The good natured Schlottman left believing that he had stated the consequences as sternly as possible. He also knew he would not wager a V nickel on Swearingen actually following the directions.

While Louie may or may not have been being a good boy, his father-in-law most definitely found his way into trouble. Unlike Louie Swearingen, E.L. Reaves normally did his drinking alone at home. He was not the most social of people nor was he a hermit. When restlessness got the better of him, Reaves sometimes walked the three miles to George Vetti's store on Clark Street. Like many other small groceries, there were tables in back for neighborhood men to boast or joke or grouse as the mood struck them. For Reaves, it was usually grouse. Since his oldest daughter disowned him, Erv was even more disagreeable than usual.

George Vetti was a Sicilian. He had left his home town of Bisacquino in 1894, headed for New Orleans after the girl he loved. In his first hours off the boat in the Crescent City, he discovered that his inamorata had married someone else. He never unpacked. George Vetti drank within sight of the levee for four days, carrying his cardboard suitcase from bar to flop house to bar, then he bought a ticket to Houston. Though he found a wife in Texas, Lisabetta Barrone, daughter of a Sicilian farmer near Dickinson, Vetti never lost the veneer of anger that he acquired on the New Orleans docks.

An ever present dominoes game was in progress at one of Vetti's back tables. Four grizzled old men who had probably known each other all their lives were enthralled with a game of 42 at two bits a mark. With such serious stakes, their conversation was minimal, but after a short outburst of laughter and taunting at the end of a game, one of the men stepped out the back door for a pee and another came for beer and food while the two at the table saw to the shake for the next game.

Lisabetta Vetti cooked a single pot of food every day. It kept the drinkers at the back of the store longer. On a good day it may have prompted a customer to buy a link of homemade sausage or even a wedge of cheese aged in the quarter cellar under the floor. All of it made for a powerful fragrance inside an Italian grocery. Some of the Anglo customers loved the aroma, others did not. Erv Reaves had once grumbled to his wife that Vetti's store smelled like old feet.

The domino man at the counter took two beers back to the table then lifted the lid from Lisabetta's stew pot that was barely warm on the iron stove. Reaves, nursing his beer alone at a smaller table, eyed the man. When the fellow tipped the pot to ladle the last of the bean and celery soup into his bowl, Reaves pushed back his chair and walked over.

"Why'd you take the last of that? I was fixing to get me some."

The man let loose a snort.

"I'm hungry, that's why."

"Well, you didn't have to take the bottom of the pot."

"All I can tell you is you should've been quicker on the draw."

With that, the man returned to his game of dominoes leaving Reaves alone to sulk and peer into the empty vessel. As his lip curled up into a resentful sneer, he spotted Lisabetta.

George Vetti had learned just enough English in the past eight years to run his store and bar. His wife, who did not deal as much with the customers, spoke even less. So, when Erv Reaves turned his displeasure on Lisabetta, she struggled to understand what the man was saying or exactly why he was upset.

"You need to bring another pot of soup."

The confused woman shook her head at him. Reaves pointed to the empty pot, and this time spoke louder, expecting that to help.

"I'm still hungry. More soup."

"Aah," Lisabetta responded with a nod and a shy smile. "Zuppa finita."

Reaves gave her a glare that she did not read.

"You like?"

"I never got any goddamnit."

His voice was now just short of a shout.

"Bring out another pot."

George Vetti was next to him now.

"No more soup. All gone."

The keeper pointed toward his shelves.

"You buy can meat. Crackers..."

Vetti gestured to cans of Vienna sausage.

"...you buy sausage."

"I don't want to buy a goddamn thing. I want the free food. You gonna pay for my sausages?"

Reaves used his chin to point at Lisabetta.

"You tell her to get back in the kitchen and make some more soup."

The store owner's face changed. He grabbed Reaves by the elbow and tried to move him to the front door.

"Erv, you have enough. Go home."

Reaves' brow reddened as he shook his arm free of Vetti's hand.

"If they wanted me at home, I'd be there. What I want is another beer and some of that free soup like they got."

He waved his hand dismissively toward the dominoes table.

Again, Vetti grabbed Reaves' arm and tugged him toward the door.

"No. You go."

The dispute turned into a scuffle. Reaves pulled loose and shoved the store owner as Lisabetta let out a small shriek. Her cry earned little more than a quick glance from the dominoes table, but George Vetti reached behind the counter and snatched up an ancient revolver. It was a worn, flat-sided pistol that had passed from hand to hand for the past 30 years, but it was still effective. There was no further discussion. No warning. George Vetti simply fired a .32 bullet into the middle of E.L. Reaves.

The gun shot brought a delay to the domino game while the men all walked over for a look at the prone Reaves. The little bullet had gone through his intestines, but there did not seem to be an exit wound. Vetti, still holding the gun, was finally convinced after some argument to let Tug White, one of the domino men, make a phone call without spending the usual nickel.

It took just over an hour before a Houston patrolman reached the store. He found Reaves propped against the steps in front of the darkened store. The Vettis had moved upstairs to their residence which also showed no lamplight. The other drinkers had grumbled and complained at the sudden closing, but Tug White was the only one to remain. Though White would stop short of using the word friend, he had visited with Reaves a few times at the grocery and even bought a few jars of shine from the man. The least he could do is make certain that Reaves did not die alone.

Westheimer's ambulance arrived a little before one in the morning. E.L. Reaves was still conscious, but only just. When doctors at the Infirmary examined him, they pronounced his condition serious, but told the policeman that he would recover. By dawn, the bullet, lodged in Reaves' hip, had been removed. Elsie and the children did not get news of the shooting until the afternoon, and the woman immediately wondered how much more anguish the family could endure.

The shooting of Erv Reaves was a notable story in the press for two days. By the time J.B. Duckworth stood at the Turf Exchange bar later that week, it merited only three sentences of conversation between the attorney and his client. Swearingen largely shrugged off his father-in-law's predicament as being out of his control.

The lawyer did not broach the main subject at hand for two full drinks. Charlie Lusk had talked him into staying on as Swearingen's lawyer, but he wanted to get a feel again for the man who would face trial, to reassess his client. He was not second-guessing. He was measuring like a tailor for a plausible defense.

Louie was an easy laugher and had a knack for making customers loosen their tongues beyond the natural loquaciousness brought on by alcohol. But he was no match for J.B. Duckworth. For the last ten minutes, not counting the moments when he stepped away to serve someone else, Swearingen had been telling J.B. about his home town.

"Did you know they assembled Kenney by moving half the buildings there from someplace else? The grist mill was where it always was, of course, but two of the churches, the hotel, a couple of stores. Even the back part of the gin, they dragged those in from around the countryside."

Duckworth grunted.

"Was it a good place to grow up?"

Louie thought about that for a minute, considering his personal situation. Then he gave his lawyer one of his best smiles.

"Well, Mr. Duckworth, I can't say that there weren't challenges for me, but I reckon Kenney had its charms. Or Kenneyville. That's what they called it back when I was little."

J.B. egged him into more detail.

"What do you remember fondly?"

This time there was little hesitation.

"Rock candy from Freitag's store. And Polka music. That whole country is thick with Germans and Czechs, and there was polka dancing most every Saturday. You'd start in the afternoon, soaked in sweat within the first five minutes, and by dark you were hoping to talk one of those cute girls out of their dress."

Louie punctuated his story with a little laugh and a tap of the bar, then he went to fill some glasses.

A few minutes later Louie Swearingen returned and picked up Duckworth's empty drink and shook it.

"Not just yet. I'd like to ask you a couple of questions outside."

He looked around the bar. It was steady, but not cheek to jowl.

"I think they can spare you for a couple of minutes."

The two men walked through a door underneath the stairway that led up to the club and restaurant. Louie was a bit off his guard, unsure of the reason he was being called outside. The attorney's dark eyes bored into him. Even in the blackened alley, Louie felt the intensity. The two stared at one another unspeaking. Finally, Duckworth looked up toward the lighter patch where the alley opened onto Main Street. He let out a loud breath before he started talking.

"I'm not going to broach the subject in front of people, of course, but you need to tell me what kind of cracked marbles are rattling around in that brain of yours. I spend a fucking year trying to work up a good defense, and you go and rob a goddamned grocery store?"

The vehemence in his lawyer's voice took Louie's wind as surely as if Duckworth had punched him in the breadbasket.

"I didn't do it."

"Anybody vouch for that? I mean really vouch for it. Cause we all know that your pal behind the bar is lying, and all the store owner seems to recollect is a gun."

Swearingen's look was sullen but his answer lacked emotion.

"No."

Duckworth shook his head and rocked back on his heels.

"Jesus, kid. You've got to learn to drink better."

Louie began to bridle. Forgetting himself for a moment, he raised himself to full height over the shorter man, but J.B. cut him off before he could utter a word.

"I'm sure that Charlie Lusk didn't breathe a whisper of it, but I was ready to quit this case."

"What do you mean?"

"I mean quit, goddamnit. To stop representing you. Money's one thing, but I don't stand for anybody wasting my time. And don't you ever think for two seconds that I won't follow through with it if this sort of shit happens again. It's good to have friends, but it only carries so far, kid."

Again, Louie was physically stunned by words, but he tried to salvage some dignity.

"I'm not a kid, Mr. Duckworth. I'm 29."

"Then act like it."

The ire slowly dissipated from Duckworth's face. Finally, he patted the tall young man on the arm as he made for the door.

"Why don't you come pour me another whiskey?"

East of the city, Eddie Isgitt was in his cups. He and some friends were having a rousing time at a small Harrisburg saloon. The talk had turned to women, and one indiscreet comment nearly resulted in fisticuffs when Gene Soujourn remarked in small detail about his carnal desire for a certain Harrisburg shop clerk. The woman's husband happened to be drinking two tables back, and by that time of night, there were no more quiet words. The sound of a chair scraping the wood floor was drowned out by the talk and general din of the place, but suddenly the man loomed over their table.

"That's my wife you're talking about, you son of a bitch."

Soujourn put up his hands in supplication as he stood. He did not want to take a punch sitting down, but Fred Sparks, a chipper old man drinking to his immediate left, spoke before Soujourn was even out of his seat. Sparks had been a dockworker back when Harrisburg could provide work, but now he mostly drank with odd jobs in between. He had swapped many a story with the aggrieved husband.

"Shit, Terry, Gene here didn't mean nothing by it. You ought to take it as a compliment."

"Stay out of it, Fred. You don't talk about a man's wife like that."

Sparks was chuckling even more now.

"Hell, if you'd seen Gene's wife, you'd know he's got to think of somebody while he's fucking."

This time it was Soujourn who turned on Fred Sparks with a reddened face.

"That ain't right to joke about, Fred. I like my wife just fine."

Though it was a most helpful skill for a lawman, Eddie Isgitt was not the kind of man to diplomatically diffuse a tense situation. He may have never done it before in all his 37 years, but that was the result of his sotted interruption.

"Y'all are going to tell me I'm off my gourd, but you know who gets my pecker stirring every time? It's that teacher over at the colored school. She'd be a fine piece of ass. Tried to talk to her, but she informed me that she was a college woman."

Isgitt paused his story and laughed to himself before summoning a last bit of bravado.

"I thought I was going to crack her one night. I watched her go into her house, but some old buck come sniffing around. Shame."

The other men around the table, including the shop clerk's husband, stopped their bickering and stared at the drunk and oblivious constable. For a second, there was quiet, then the men erupted into laughter. Gene Soujourn shook his head and stuck out his hand toward the clerk's husband.

"Apologies to you. I meant no harm. Let me stake you to a beer."

Chapter 17

Louie Swearingen was frustrated.

"Why do you say it like a B if it's spelled with a V? It should be Vain-Tay."

"No se. But you say B."

"Makes no sense."

"Vaca. Also B. Remember?"

"Still makes no sense."

"You explain though, through, and tough. Then get back to me."

It took Louie a second to spell the three words in his head, but then he busted into a laugh.

"Yeah, you got me with that one."

As a side project during slow times at work, Swearingen had being learning a little Spanish from one of the cooks. Since the scare over the grocery robbery, he truly had made an effort to curtail his drinking. Or at least limit it to beer.

Fidencio Valdez was a wiry young man from Benavides in Duval County who cooked in the bar kitchen at night and operated a chili stand during the day. There were not many Mexicans in Houston, and Valdez had imagined that his stand would quickly be teeming with hundreds of hungry Anglos ready to plop down a nickel for a hearty bowl of red. The chili stands in San Antonio were everywhere. It only made sense, but the White men of Houston would rather have a cheese and pickle sandwich every day. It was worst with the Germans who turned up their noses at the South Texas spiciness. Consequently, Fidencio worked nights at the Turf. The gueros might not know good food, but he still had to pay his rent.

At the start of his self-improvement plan, Louie paid 15 cents at Pillot's for a dogeared decommissioned textbook called *Hand Book of Spanish Conversation* by L.F. Mantilla. He quickly figured out that learning pronunciation from a book was a veritable impossibility. That was when he roped Fidencio into the process, and over the past few weeks, the two had developed an easy kinship. For Louie, it was a nice workplace distraction from the bullying Sam Carr.

J.B. Duckworth did not need a reason for a final stop at Big Annie's on his way home, but on this night he could honestly tell himself that there was business to conduct. He had invited his brother, John, to discuss a delicate matter that he preferred not even his law partners be fully privy to. Now, the Duckworths leaned on the bar, each man with a boot resting on the rickety rail as he savored his third big glass of beer. There had been a shot of whiskey, and there would probably be more. Newly acquired jokes had been told. Rumors shared. Silent thoughts enjoyed in quiet companionship.

John used a lull to change the subject.

"All right. I reckon you're primed to talk. What exactly did you want to see me in private for?"

J.B. did not hesitate in his response.

"I've got to do something to put this shit with Gillaspie to bed. Put it to sleep."

John let out a puff of breath.

"About damn time. I couldn't for the life of me figure out why you've waited."

"I had my reasons."

"You hid for half a year, Jamie. Every district court session, and that's not like you."

"Goddamnit John, I worked too hard to get us here. I wasn't going to let some persnickety milksop waylay us. When I saw the election results, I figured Waco was dead and buried, just like it was before, but then he pulls this shit."

As most of the political observers in Southeast Texas expected, J.K.P. Gillaspie had stood for the area's Congressional seat instead of his district judgeship. He finished third in a four-man race, and it was widely believed that when his term ended on the final day of 1902, Gillaspie would resume private law practice. It had been enough assurance that J.B. Duckworth returned to conduct his legal business before the lame duck judge with confidence. But the day prior, Gillaspie had closed the door to his chambers and, with leering malice, told J.B. that the election setback had one silver lining – it would give him more time to settle some scores.

The lack of all subtlety was unanticipated, but once the surprise wore off, J.B. Duckworth had seethed. He confided news of the encounter only to his brother and Henry Fein. The latter offered some expressive faces and general dismissiveness, but Duckworth knew that he could only get to the heart of the thing with John.

"How much can the Waco thing really hurt you? Months ago, Harris told you it can't, that no one likes that son of a bitch enough to help him. And with him leaving the bench, he'll have even fewer friends."

J.B. gave the smallest of nods.

"Maybe. Harris is a smart man, but I can't stand having things hanging over my head."

John Duckworth laughed aloud at a memory.

"That's an understatement. Like that time in Pine Bluff with old Gardner and the goat?"

It was an episode from two lifetimes past. J.B. had pestered their boss at a dry goods store to write out a recommendation, but it was never forthcoming. Finally he had shut a hungry billy goat in the man's office overnight. The results were everything the brothers envisioned and then some.

John emitted another snort.

'I may not be able to read it, Mr. Gardner, but at least I finally got your correspondence.'"

His brother's bushy moustache twitched upward for a flash before the worry returned.

"So, how do I get the drop on Gillaspie?"

John had a good mind for planning. Whether John had learned his skills from his younger brother or whether J.B. had taken lessons from John and built on them was anyone's guess. The two had relied upon one another since early childhood, and though J.B. often forgot to give credit where it was due, he knew that at the bottom of it all, his brother was, at least occasionally, indispensable to the thinking process.

"What's a favor you could offer him? A good old-fashioned deal?" John asked.

"Before I can do anything for him, I need ammunition. You know that better than anybody. Now, before you get your feathers bent, I'm not criticizing. I know full well how you've tried, but I've got to have something to threaten him with. I need the stick."

John opened his eyes wide and threw up his hands.

"I'm out of bullets, Jamie. I've looked at everything I could think of, trying to dig up the shit on him. Every man has skeletons, but I'll be goddamned if I can find his."

J.B.'s answer came battered in sarcasm.

"He's the original goody two-shoes, John. We should understand that by now."

"Well, except he's a man."

"Oh, now, I'm not quite willing to wager on whether J.K.P. Gillaspie has a pecker."

They laughed. Then John got a glint in his eye.

"You know, just because I didn't find him playing away from home… maybe it was because I didn't throw the net wide enough. Maybe he keeps it out of town. He hears cases in Galveston and has done for years. Maybe his fancy girl is down there on the island."

J.B. waggled a finger at John's suggestion and followed it with a slap on his brother's shoulder.

"I like that notion. What do I tell you? The best ideas are at the bottom of the glass."

He took a deep gulp from his beer to punctuate the comment. They drank in thoughtful silence until the lawyer had something to add.

"Who says it has to be true? What if we made up the story about his embarrassing little mistress, and then our favor is not telling anyone about it. I could go to him and let him know the rumor I gleaned in passing. After all, I am as earnest telling a tale as any man alive."

John Duckworth did not like the idea. He much preferred to manipulate the truth to get results rather than lie outright, and he knew his little brother did, too. He also knew that when J.B.'s devils stepped from the shadows, the better angels generally followed to tamp down the damage. Consequently, he held his tongue, but instead of silence, J.B. began to dramatize his pending conversation with Gillaspie.

"Well, now Judge, I know we haven't always seen eye to eye, but I'd still hate to see your reputation sullied across half of Texas. We're all men of the world here, aren't we, and a piece of quim shouldn't derail a fellow's whole career, should it? Not to mention his home life."

J.B. reviewed his own performance with a small snicker. Before John could verbalize his disdain for the scheme as it currently stood, Big Annie's voice boomed from a conversation not far to the left of the two brothers. She had added volume as her story reached its climax.

"So, I told the fellow, she must've had two in each hand and one up the jacksie!"

The railroad men listening to the ribald tale roared and slapped the bar. At the same time, J.B. shot John a knowing look. This time John shook his head vigorously, but J.B. spoke up first.

"It's no different than what he's been doing to me."

"Well, ..."

J.B. cut his brother off cold and with adamance.

"No. We have no idea what is true about Mr. Gillaspie just as he has no idea what is true about that night in Waco."

From behind the two Duckworths came a question directed at Annie.

"Hey, Annie, What's up the jacksie?"

She took two steps toward the round table.

"In the bunghole, son," Big Annie said as she gave Mark Callaway an endearing pat on the back.

J.B. was as silent as possible as he came into the house. There was one small stumble that spilled a hat from the hall rack, but he congratulated himself that he had picked it off the floor and returned it all quiet as a proverbial mouse. He more or less draped his clothes over the bedroom chair back and was soon passed out in bed next to Lola.

She was partially awake when he climbed under the covers, but she did not risk speaking and waking herself up entirely. Instead, she just gave his hand a squeeze, a gesture he returned even as he began to softly snore.

It had been a satisfying few days for Lola. The highlight was Katherine's first time recognizing an animal at the zoo. Several of them to be more precise. They rode the cars to Sam Houston Park taking advantage of the perfect weather, and, with no prompting, Katherine pointed out "bird," "possum," "deer," and "dog," with the last one being a wolf.

Now Lola was looking forward to their little Thanksgiving dinner. It would be just the three of them plus John, but it was still special. She had reserved a turkey at the butcher, and would bake a pecan pie. She flashed a very sleepy smile and stroked her husband's arm. He smelled of cigar smoke, pomade, and whiskey. In other words, he smelled like a successful man. It had taken her quite some time to get used to it after they were married, but she had grown to find the odor comforting. She snuggled next to him and pulled the quilts higher.

Over the past few days, Louie had been rehearsing a few marginally dirty Spanish phrases that he wanted to try out on Nora. Now that he was ready to employ them, his memory and pronunciation were both failing him. Luckily, his impassioned kisses on her neck were making the point even if his butchered attempts to woo his *querida* with words fell flat.

Nora was not a giggler, but she could not help herself as her husband worked his way south while stumbling through his gibberish. They undressed quickly. Louie was atop his wife, willing himself to go slowly, and still vainly trying to recollect his titillating Spanish love talk. Nora moaned lustily, and though neither of them voiced it, they each anticipated the man next door pounding on the wall at any moment.

What they were not expecting was an explosion. The bullet slammed through the window and into the wall about a foot down from the ceiling. Glass from the shattered pane showered down on Louie, the sheets, and the floor. Though nothing hit Nora directly, she let out a loud scream and covered her face. Predictably, the banging on the common wall immediately followed.

The next morning, Louie Swearingen was waiting halfway up the stairs at 1107 ½ Congress when a bleary-eyed John Brockman opened the door from the street. Louie's face also betrayed a lack of sleep, but for once it had nothing to do with drinking. Swearingen was shaken and angry. John tried his best to calm the man, and Sonny Schlottmann, who arrived at the office some ten minutes later, took up the task, leading Swearingen to a seat at the desk.

"They tried to say it was some stray shot, that it came from some bar fight," Louie ranted. "There's not a bar anywhere close to that building. Nothing within five blocks, and the damn policeman couldn't rightly say there was any trouble anywhere else in the first damn place."

Schlottmann motioned for calm.

"Maybe they'll figure it out when they investigate some more."

Louie answered with a rueful laugh.

"You serious? They're not going to investigate shit. They barely wanted to show up to my call. They sent a patrolman. That almighty Detective Kessler said he had better things to do than chase after than some kerfuffle between murderers. Can you believe that?"

Sonny nodded and gave a sympathetic chuff.

"From Kessler I wouldn't expect anything less. He's a miserable man."

"My wife was in there. She could've been killed! And I got glass all over my bare back."

Schlottmann looked at Louie with a wry smile, and Louie answered with a blush and a shrug. A small layer of his anger dissipated.

Swearingen was honed in on the point of his visit when J.B. Duckworth and his dog arrived. It forced him to restart from the beginning. Hearing Louie's animated description of the incident interspersed with commentary from Sonny, J.B.'s eyebrows shot up.

"That goddamned Kessler is a no good bastard," J.B. grumbled. "We'll send somebody around to make them get off their padded asses and look into this."

Rather than placate Louie Swearingen, the lawyer's promise only riled him further.

"I don't care about that. Whoever did it was taking a shot at me. No doubt about that, but they're not going to catch him. The only important thing anymore is that we get this to court and over with. I can't live like this anymore."

He paused for a second before adding a mention of his primary motivation.

"And neither can my wife."

J.B. had been standing next to Schlottmann's desk, headed to his own office. He had not planned on staying in the conversation long, but he stared at Louie for a few beats before pulling up a stray chair in the big room. It was before normal office hours, so the usual buzz of clients had not yet begun. It was only the four men, Maizy, and the hum of activity through windows which John had opened. Maizy perked up at a bark in the distance, but otherwise there was a pause until J.B. spoke in an uncharacteristically paternal tone.

"Look, Louie, I know it's hard to sit and wait, but you want to stay out of prison, don't you?"

Swearingen looked as if that was the dumbest question on Earth. His attorney continued without giving the client a chance to speak.

"Well, right now we don't have shit that's going to keep you out of lockup for the next ten or fifteen years. I've already told you more than once that you getting blind drunk and forgetting where you've been is killing this case."

The kind tone was gone, and J.B. was working himself up.

"Other clients try to help themselves. They figure out alibis. The only time you've done that it was your work pal who was the most transparent hoaxer I've seen in years. It worked well enough with the police because they're stupider than a box of shoe nails, but that kind of horse shit won't fly with a judge and jury. Goddamnit, you need to get it through your thick head that I'm the expert. Charlie Lusk and your own damn customers are paying me to get you out of this, though God knows why they care. The best thing for you is to string this out for as long as we possibly can. The bad shit is behind you, whether you did it or not..."

Louie opened his mouth to protest, but Duckworth only raised his voice louder.

"...only good things can happen as I stretch it out. Let me do my fucking job."

In past months, Louie Swearingen would have accepted the same explanation he had been getting and that would be that, but this time was different. He leaned forward in his chair, almost coming off the seat with his angry words.

"I'm innocent. I've told you that, and I'll keep on telling you. Somebody fired a shot through my bedroom window last night. I don't care what the reasons are. I want my day in court, and I want this whole sorry mess behind me!"

John and Sonny clenched their jaws just a little in anticipation of the inevitable outburst. Like all lawyers, J.B. Duckworth was used to clients questioning his tactics and even raising their voices, but none of that meant he took it graciously. John had even seen his brother throw a punch at a particularly mouthy robbery suspect, but this time J.B. only countered with a spiteful stare.

"All right. If that's what you want, Lord help you. John, when does Swearingen next come up on the docket?"

John answered from memory.

"March."

"March it is then. We'll be ready for trial. And son..."

The derogatory word rankled Louie.

"... bring some old clothes to change into that day. The guards at Huntsville will keep your good suit."

Chapter 18

December 1902

Eddie Isgitt was uncomfortable, but he was trying. His wife Elsie was helping the midwife tend to Becky Glenn, a neighbor and friend in the throes of childbirth, and that left Isgitt to send his five children off to bed. The boys were easy enough. You point them in the right direction and tell them to go to sleep. For the daughters, however, that operation did not happen without ceremony. Specifically, their small coterie of dolls had to be tucked in before the girls would climb into their bed.

"No, daddy! Miss Dee can't sleep on her belly! She has a hurt nose."

"Oh, right. I didn't notice. We can't have that."

Isgitt turned the doll onto her back and readjusted the scrap of old blanket.

One of the boys was already sawing logs, but Eliot, the oldest at nine, lay propped up on an elbow, leafing through a battered copy of *American Boy* magazine. Most of the articles were above Eliot's level, but the ads had pictures. The boy had no money to spend, but he was still deciding whether he would blow his imaginary funds on a liquid pistol or a baseball uniform.

"Miss Cleo's thirsty."

"Oh, brother."

That comment came from Eliot in the peanut gallery.

"Shut your gob, boy. We're trying to get everyone situated for sleep."

The constable turned his attention back to the girls and Miss Cleo.

"Does she need real water?"

The girls giggled, and Eliot scoffed.

"She's a doll, daddy."

Isgitt pantomimed pouring water into the doll's mouth, but that brought more chiding from his youngest daughter.

"You're supposed to make the noise."

Eddie cleared his throat and hesitantly supplied gulping sounds. A few minutes later, with everyone under their covers, he pulled the string on the light bulb.

Isgitt closed the door to the children's room halfway and walked back to the kitchen table. He was restless, and there was nothing to do at home. Elsie should be back soon enough. The girls were all in bed. He looked in, and they were sound asleep. It was already dark outside, and he knew they wouldn't wake until morning.

There was no work there especially, but Isgitt decided to go back to his office. It was a ten minute walk, and he did not feel like saddling up his horse anyway. He may want to stop off for a drink on his way home, and that meant putting all the tack away drunk in the middle of the night. No need for that kind of effort.

The offices of Harrisburg's county building were quiet and ink well dark. Isgitt turned on the overhead light and eyed the short stack of reports that needed finishing. The first order of business was taking a pull from a pint bottle in his desk, then he picked up the paper on top. Like every sane copper in America, Eddie Isgitt believed reports to be nothing more than a tedious annoyance. You picked up the offender and stuck him in a cell someplace. The only thing he should have to write down is when to let the no good scofflaw out. On top of it all, most of his work load was due to the indisputable fact that Ben Simmons was a sloppy record keeper. Isgitt reached back into the drawer and gulped down another mouthful of whiskey.

He had not bothered closing the front door to the tiny county building at Medina and Sycamore. It was a quiet Wednesday night approaching nine o'clock.

Isgitt was enjoying the low sounds of the town – a screech owl, a distant boat whistle from the bayou. Then he felt a presence in the room. In the doorway to his office was a young Black girl, obviously agitated but something else. Frightened maybe.

"Yeah? What do want girl?"

She stammered a few noises before her words came out.

"My mama sent me, sir. There's a big ruckus, and my mama said there should be a lawman 'fore somebody gets killed."

Isgitt narrowed his eyes.

"What kind of ruckus? Where is this?"

"She said to tell you there's a big fight going on between Mat Thorn and his wife. Breaking things. Screaming bloody murder. We can hear it all the way over to our place."

The constable nodded. He had no clue who the girl was or where she lived, but he knew Mat Thorn. So did everyone in Harrisburg for that matter. Louisiana Red they called him. He was an intimidating mixed race man with a reputation for violence, though little of that had been seen locally. People just took the tales as truths, and most gave Thorn a wide berth based on the estimation that it was the wise thing to do.

Without a word to the girl, Eddie Isgitt pulled his holster down from its peg and strapped it around his waist. He would investigate. If Mat Thorn was on a rampage, it might be some kind of terrible fracas, to be sure. The young lady stood in the doorway for a few moments, as if waiting for instruction, but then vanished as quietly as she had appeared.

Isgitt locked the office door and started walking in the direction of the Black part of town. He already regretted his decision to leave his horse at home. It was an almost moonless night, and though he saw no one in the blackness, he felt as if he was being watched. These were businesses and homes where he did not feel welcome, and he imagined a predator lurking. Isgitt summoned up his bravado and kept walking.

He was two blocks from the Harrisburg depot, the place where he would give up any cursory search and turn back for his office. On his left was Blanchard's grocery, a store and beer joint for the colored trade. It was one of dozens of Black businesses that never saw Whites cross their threshold. Isgitt had no intention of looking inside, but he was thankful that a decent amount of light spilled out from the open door and window. He sucked in a reassuring breath. This was close enough. He would head back now.

As he spun on his heel, Eddie Isgitt gave a start. There was a figure walking toward him, only 20 feet away. The lamps from the back of the grocery were enough to illuminate the seeping scratches down the side of Mat Thorn's face.

Thorn was not nearly as big as Isgitt, but he exuded an air of power and fierceness. Still the constable could see a sheepish smile from the man.

"A girl come running and said you had a fuss with your wife."

Thorn's grin grew wider.

"Oh, it wasn't nothing."

"Then why've you got those marks all down your cheek, boy?"

Mat Thorn threw up his hands and let go a little laugh.

"My wife is a hellcat, deputy. You know how it is."

The words had barely crossed the man's lips when the big lawman shoved him to the ground with both hands.

"You leave my wife's name out your mouth, boy! I'll kill you for that sass."

Isgitt's kicks found Mat Thorn's ribs, then the constable shifted a bit, and a scuffed boot toe caught the prone man's chin.

Onlookers were now out of Blanchard's, and Isgitt heard grumbling at the back of the circle. Thorn was pulled up in a ball, trying to cover himself on the ground, but as Eddie eyed the dozen or more bystanders, his victim pushed himself up on an elbow so he could speak and be heard.

"Am I under arrest, deputy? I didn't ..."

Isgitt cut him off.

"Shut up, boy! You don't get to ask questions."

As he berated Thorn, the constable pulled his gun. He quickly turned it in his hand and smashed the butt down on the side of Mat Thorn's head. The Black man fell back to dirt. Blood welled up from behind his ear.

The murmur of complaint from the small crowd grew louder, and Isgitt spun on them, this time with the barrel of his gun waving back and forth from man to man.

"Back the fuck up. This ain't..."

However Eddie Isgitt intended to rebuke his unwanted audience, it went unheard. The man known as Louisiana Red had produced a revolver from his coat pocket. Simultaneously, he fired and swept Isgitt's feet out from under him with a vicious swing of his right leg.

As he fell, the constable squeezed off three rounds, but they hit nothing. The drinkers from the bar had scattered with the first loud report. Isgitt's shots flew noisily into the night as he collapsed on the cool ground, two .38 long Colt bullets having passed clean through his liver.

It was more than 45 minutes before a man drinking at Blanchard's finally decided to roust Apple Jordan. Almost half of the drinkers had slipped off for home. The remainder spent the time guzzling more beer and arguing over what to do. Gunfire was not all that rare in Harrisburg. There were always varmints being chased from garden patches, but that many shots near the center of town was another matter. The consensus was that someone from the depot was bound to come poking around soon. Running home to hide may solve the problem for the moment, but it took just one person to drop a name, and a man could be deep in the soup. Run from the scene of a shooting, and a fellow looked guilty as all hell. On top of it all, the men left in the back of the store wanted more drinks. It had not even gone ten o'clock.

The discussion then turned to the safest way to break the news. The closest telephone was two blocks away at the train depot, but this time of night, they would have to call into the sheriff's office in Houston. They knew that their local justice court was long since closed.

Finally, the decision was made to send the storekeeper's eight-year-old son to rouse the justice of the peace. He was a fair enough man and unlikely to escalate the violence. Still, sending a child was a safe bet. Some of these White lawmen were as volatile and unpredictable as they came, but even the worst of them were unlikely to hurt a small boy.

As it turned out, the J.P. called to the county jail since no one had the foggiest notion of where Ben Simmons was or what he might be up to. At least no one willing to tell the tale. It would take more than an hour for any deputies to ride out from town. Maybe two. Jordan let out a resigned sigh and told his wife that he might be awhile. Unlike Eddie Isgitt, the justice took the time to saddle his horse. He would ride the few blocks to the crime scene.

A few people stood off at a respectable distance watching the goings on. Jordan paused and scanned the faces with a palpable tiredness. He spied the young man who had come to his house earlier then shifted his gaze to the lights still coming from Blanchard's Grocery.

"You know, son, I wouldn't say no to a bottle of beer."

As the boy walked toward the grocery on his errand with a dime from the J.P. in his fist, Apple Jordan fished a paper and pencil from his inside coat pocket. He knelt down beside the body of the man with whom he had shared an office and looked him over. After a fashion, Jordan carefully pulled back Isgitt's coat and tried to manipulate his bloody shirt front with the pencil end. Apple assumed that Isgitt's body would be taken to the infirmary out on Washington Road. Given that he was a lawman, the county would want an accredited physician to take a look, but the local justice still had a report to file.

Along with the notes, Jordan scribbled a little diagram and noted with heavy dots where the shots hit. He looked around him in the pitch dark. He would give a cursory ask if anyone saw anything, but he already knew the ropes. People would avoid his gaze, no one wanting to be too cooperative in front of their neighbors.

Tomorrow, a few wary citizens would slink into his office to offer up information. He shook his head sadly and spoke to the prone figure with a whisper.

"Damn it, Eddie. You were a noxious idiot most of the time, but why'd you have to go and get yourself killed?"

Three Sheriff's deputies out from Houston began searching the neighborhood at daybreak the following morning. They turned over two dozen houses spanning several sparsely settled blocks on the east side of Harrisburg, disturbing the residents and physically tumbling some from their beds. It took them less than 40 minutes to make an arrest. There was a great deal of back slapping over their success, and before hauling the man back into Houston and the jail, they handcuffed him to a drainpipe behind his house and started an interrogation.

The prisoner's wife screamed protests that they had the wrong man, and her caterwauling brought a few neighbors who said the same. When one of the lawmen knocked the shrill woman on her backside with a shove to the chest, the neighbors retreated indoors.

The deputies were joined not a quarter hour later by a red-faced Ben Simmons who, expecting a day off, had been holed up with a woman up at Clinton. Since the lady in question was married, no details were immediately forthcoming.

Simmons rode up on the scene, dismounted, and tied off his horse. He pushed up next to the knot of deputies and assessed the handcuffed man. One eye was already swollen shut. The sobbing wife was still seated in the dirt where she had fallen.

"Ain't him," Simmons told them.

The deputies largely ignored him and continued to alternate between blows and questions to the put upon man. Simmons raised his voice louder.

"Knock it off, goddamnit. That ain't Mat Thorn."

He ended his remark by grabbing one deputy by the arm to spin him around. The man bowed up, but Ben stepped close enough to smell the deputy's breakfast.

"You're beating the shit out of the wrong man."

The three, each man out of breath from the exertion, were now all facing Ben Simmons. The ruddy faced one squinted out a question.

"What do you mean it ain't him. He matched the description that old buck at the grocery gave us."

If Simmons had been in a sour mood when he rode up, he was now boiling with frustration and anger. His words came slowly, loud, and enunciated.

"It's the wrong fucking jig. They call Mat Thorn "red" for a goddamn reason. He's light skinned. Mulatto...."

Simmons jerked his thumb at the cuffed, slumping figure.

"...This one's dark as a panther. Thorn has a scar on his face. This poor sucker probably will, too, now, but you three jackasses put it there."

That remark brought a brief scuffle, but nothing came of it. In due course, the victimized man was let loose from the drainpipe, and his wife led him back inside for salving of his wounds. The deputies and Ben Simmons did not part friends, but the men from Houston got on their horses and headed west on the Harrisburg Road.

Before the day was over, the death of Eddie Isgitt was an above-the-fold headline in both Houston newspapers. Sheriff Archie Anderson had announced a $150 reward backed by a fund for slain officers of the law, and, eager to collect it, a posse formed in Harrisburg. Several local men were ready to avenge their own.

Chapter 19

The salacious newspaper headlines surrounding the killing of a local lawman faded away to the lesser pages after about four days, but that did not mean the act was forgotten. J.B. Duckworth was as interested in the shooting of Eddie Isgitt as anyone in town outside of the constable's family and the police fraternity. Isgitt was a significant witness against the firm's client Louie Swearingen.

Duckworth's brother, John, had a seemingly endless list of tasks on his ledger, but J.B. asked him to go to Harrisburg and see if anything pertaining to their case might have changed with the constable's death. J.B. had already inquired of his friend the district attorney, but Lea informed him that, though Isgitt had been prepared to paint Louie Swearingen as a violent troublemaker when the young man got in his cups, the D.A.'s office still had a formidable case. The centerpiece remained the eyewitness to the murder, Andy Green.

John's inquiries in Harrisburg were not any more productive this time around. Green managed to dodge him again, so he left a business card with a note on the back. He sat it on the front porch chair and weighted it down with a stone from the yard. For good measure, John spoke to the old woman next door, the only person on the street who would give him more than a single sentence, and asked her to tell Andy Green that John Duckworth from the lawyer's office paid a call. For his trouble, John got a ten minute recounting about the woman's bunions. They evidently hampered her ability to walk to the neighbor's.

Duckworth stopped by Isgitt's former office. Though he was out patrolling somewhere, Ben Simmons had already claimed the small room as his own. Justice of the Peace Apple Jordan was amiable enough, but most responses he provided came in the form of questions. Jordan was particularly interested in any machinations of county government that John might have picked up on.

After a good half day wasted, John took the boat back to the foot of Main. He assuaged his annoyance with a bowl of chop suey at Jim Wing's and chased it down with a glass of Lemp's before heading back to the law office.

Two days later, perhaps as a result of John's trek east, Elijah Branch, a Baptist preacher from Harrisburg, came into J.B.'s office leaving the door to the big room open behind him. Duckworth motioned him to a client chair. The man had telephoned ahead for an appointment, stressing that he wished to speak with the head of the firm. John Duckworth put fifteen minutes on the books for his brother, and the distinguished looking fellow, dressed in a Sunday suit, had duly arrived 20 minutes early.

"What can I do for you, Mr. Branch?"

The preacher held a black rolled-brim derby on his lap, and he glanced down at it solemnly. It was an expression that probably opened a thousand sermons.

"I'm here to talk about Constable Isgitt's demise."

"Yes?"

Duckworth offered no platitudes about the shooting being a tragedy, and Branch made no noises to that effect either.

"I am a man of charity, Mr. Duckworth, but that constable was a scourge to my community. I might say that the majority of the colored people in Harrisburg feel better being shed of him."

"Just the coloreds?"

"Last few years, since he come to town, that man was always getting into scrapes and tussles with all races. Looking for heartache since he was born, I suspect."

"That may be. I never really knew the fellow."

"He was not one to make my people feel safe."

"As the saying goes, I've got no dog in that hunt, reverend. What do you really want from me?"

Branch was a bit taken aback, but just in case he was not offended the first time, J.B.'s follow up was more blunt.

"I'll put it another way. This meeting is a courtesy, and at this firm, those meetings need to quickly lead to billable time."

The preacher nodded, understanding where he stood.

"I'd like you to handle Mat Thorn's defense. My congregation can take a collection. I'm prepared to offer a retainer."

Elijah Branch produced four well-loved five dollar notes from his breast pocket and laid them on Duckworth's desktop.

Duckworth stared at the preacher without a response as the wall clock ticked. Other men might feel the need to shift in their chair, but Elijah Branch sat still as a mouse in church. Duckworth broke the silence

"He's not even been arrested last I heard. You know where he is, reverend?

"No, sir, but they'll find him. I hope alive."

"I wouldn't count on that."

J.B.'s comment was low and even. Reverend Branch nodded.

"He's not the bad man they say, Mr. Duckworth. A little troubled."

Duckworth lowered his chin.

"You going to tell me that big scar they talk about came from a horse kick or something?"

"No, sir. I suspect that scar was attained in a knife fight."

Outside a streetcar bell clanged.

Duckworth eyed the money in silence for a bit then jabbed his finger at the fancyback U.S. Treasury note on top of the little pile.

"That son of a bitch George Thomas was with Sherman when they destroyed my family homestead, and here he is on my office desk."

He glanced at his visitor.

"Sorry, reverend. I've got the vocabulary of a lawyer, and I don't truck much with Jesus."

Branch sat stoically and did not respond. His thoughts may have dwelled on the political perception as much as the language. Finally, J.B. pushed the bills back toward the preacher with a mischievous lift of an eyebrow.

"If you want to revisit the matter when the proper time comes, let us know. Now, if you'll excuse me, I've got a list of cases longer than Goliath's pecker."

It was one of those warm, winter afternoons on the Gulf Coast. There was not a drop of rain from the overcast sky, but everything was still wet. Water seeped up through the stones, bricks, or dirt. People took a rag and wiped off the seat of the chair lest their trousers became soaked through, and everyone remarked that they should not be swatting mosquitoes in December even though they did it most every year.

Dory Cooper finished a joke, and both men offered a respectful laugh as though they had not heard it a half dozen times before. Cooper was sitting on Andy Green's little front porch. In the months since Johnson Montgomery died, the visits had become almost a habit. What started as an obligation to a friend turned to enjoyment and expectation. They rehashed the same gossip, jabs, and wisecracks as they did at work, but the company was good. The excuse of checking on Andy also got Cooper out of the occasional household chore on his day off.

Just as everywhere else in Harrisburg, the conversation eventually got to the shooting of Eddie Isgitt.

"A mean man met his match. That's how I see it. Hearing folks talk now makes you wonder who voted for that constable in the first damn place. I reckon the town is better off with him gone. What do you think Andy?"

"Don't change nothing."

Green stared at a big patch of chickweed in his yard, and a heavy shiver ran over him.

"Shadow crossed your grave," Cooper said.

"No. There's bad men still out there, and bad men put poor old Johnson in the ground."

Cooper's expression was quizzical.

"What's that doubletalk supposed to mean? A White man ain't likely to go to jail for shooting Johnson. You and I both know that, but that don't mean he's coming after you."

Andy looked up, his brief trance broken.

"Maybe, but his lawyer sure does like coming around. They had somebody by here the other day. Got Miss Jackson all up in a tizzy."

Dory gave a sympathetic grunt.

"I just want it to end," Andy said.

The long shadows of the courthouse darkened the east side of San Jacinto Street when Harris Peterson stopped by Duckworth's private office. He carefully extricated the bottle from the bureau where it sat amidst stacks of case files and poured two drinks. Peterson then lifted two Cuban cigars from his coat and handed one to J.B. as he took the client chair. Only at that point, when his friend's eyes were smiling, did Peterson speak.

"First off, I'm just delivering the message, J.B."

Duckworth laughed loud enough that Jed Posey looked over from his desk in the big room. Peterson rose and shut the door before resuming his seat.

"That is a hell of an entrance, Harris. The message must be mighty important to cost you such a fine Partagas. On the other hand, you've soaked me for a glass of whiskey before you've even said hello."

Peterson proceeded to suggest to Duckworth that some rather powerful men around town had gained a sudden interest in Louie Swearingen's case. Without elaborating on this murky cabal, Harris let his friend know that a potential out for the defense may lay in pursuing the alternative notion that Mat Thorn killed Johnson Montgomery. An overly suspicious mind might even infer that someone in the court system itself was privy to such a conversation.

"Nobody down at the county or beyond wants to see that White boy go to jail for killing a colored one," Peterson said.

"What do you mean beyond?"

J.B. was expert at picking out the crucial words in a sentence.

"Just rumors, J.B."

"The county judge?"

Harris grinned a little at his friend's prescience.

"That's who I talked to. Yes. Fact remains you've got an unflappable eyewitness and a client who may or may not have robbed a goddamned store on top of it all. This might be a neat little package open to you here. Chances are fair that Thorn boy won't be coming home to testify in his own behalf, but if he did, well, the nut cutting of it is that there might be an issue according to these other friends of mine."

"I'm hurt. Here I was thinking I was the only friend you had, Harris."

Peterson got a good chuckle.

"These are people who don't associate with the likes of you. You wouldn't know them."

They both snickered.

"I think their big worry is that you're going to take Thorn's defense. Are you?"

"How in holy hell did anyone know anything about that? I've not agreed to anything or even taken a retainer."

"Just tittle-tattle going around, I suspect."

"What you're proposing..."

Peterson cut him off.

"Just the messenger, remember?"

"What your alleged friends are proposing is circumventing justice. I'm an officer of the court, same as anyone else."

Peterson stopped his friend again.

"No. No. No. Nobody is saying anything about illegalities, though I doubt these folks are nearly as true to the scales of justice as you reckon yourself to be. Maybe it was the whiskey vapors, but from what I recollect you telling me several times, you still don't have a solid sense of whether your boy is guilty or not. I know your libretto, J.B.. Chances are damn good that you have an alternative theory or two at the ready as we speak. I think they're just suggesting that you put this forth as a tangible possibility, and then it's up to our pal Lea to run with the ball. Everyone still gets a square trial."

"Is he on board with this nonsense?"

Peterson shrugged.

"I can't fathom he would be," Duckworth said. "J.V.'s a good man. And usually honest...for a prosecutor."

Despite any good natured jesting, Harris knew the conversation had pushed his friend to the edge of anger, and he sought to squelch the smoldering fire.

"Look, I'm in the middle here, too. Got thrown in it the moment they put me on the spot as your friend. You tell me what you want me to say, and I'll deliver it. I'm looking to be shed of this."

J.B. smoothed the ends of his moustache and gave a loud sniff before he answered.

"You tell them I haven't made any decisions about defending Mat Thorn. Most all my clients have been arrested for something. That's the nature of defense law from what I've gathered. You're also free to mention that there is no part of me that appreciates any of the bloviating gentry sticking their gilded fingers into my pie. In short, tell them J.B. Duckworth sends them a hearty fuck you."

Harris Peterson rose from his seat sporting a lop-sided smile.

"That's my boy. I've kept my word, and I heard exactly the answer I hoped you'd give. I'll pass the report along to my...," Harris gave an exaggerated wink. "acquaintances. You know, it's quite the compliment, having those muck-ety-mucks afraid of you."

Duckworth waved the comment away.

"They're not special. I want everybody to be afraid of me. You know that."

Peterson opened the door to the big room but could not resist a parting shot.

"You realize, of course, that the other respectable lawyers in town are regularly asking questions about me associating with the likes of you, a ne'er-do-well criminal attorney."

Duckworth nodded, straightfaced.

"What do you tell them?"

"I say you owe me money."

Chapter 20

After the flap with her husband and his shooting of the constable, Mat Thorn's wife had scampered out of their house. She was scared, but mostly tired of the drama brought on from living with a heavily conflicted man.

Effa Thorn was far from blameless. She had come to enjoy baiting her husband over the years. His job as a stevedore did not bring in enough to keep her in the new dresses she desired. The one and only time he ever bought her jewelry was the thin silver ring he slipped on her finger at the church. Like rain on sandstone, it had worn her down. Every time a neighbor strutted out in a newly sewn frock, Effa fingered her shabby clothes and picked at her spouse.

Usually that turned Mat sullen and brooding, but the evening before he shot Eddie Isgitt, Mat had exploded. At first there was hollering, then name calling. Effa clawed at her husband's face, and he in turn threw a punch so hard it knocked his wife halfway across the parlor of their three-room house. Three and a half days had passed, but Effa's back still twinged every time her left leg moved forward.

Now she cowered under the bed at her mother's house in far off Fulshear. She knew that Mat was likely to come after her, and here he was, pounding hard on the front door of the tidy little house out past the ball field.

"Goddamnit, Effa! I know you're in there! Open this door afore I break it down."

Dee Terry, a feisty and ramrod straight 60-year old, yanked the door open and looked up at her son-in-law.

"Mat Thorn, you'll do no such thing. You touch my front door, and I'll have your hide. You know it, too."

Thorn took a step back, propelled by the woman's force of will, but the retreat lasted just a few seconds. The anger dripping from his voice was unmistakable.

"Mama Dee, then you tell Effa to get her ass out here. Now."

"Don't you dare cuss at me, boy."

The man swallowed his first reply.

"This is between man and wife. You just tell her to get out here."

Dee, still on the offensive, gave Thorn a few moments of evil eye before she spoke.

"She ain't here. She was, I ain't going to lie to you, but she's gone back to Harrisburg in a wagon with her cousin to get her things."

Mat eyed the woman suspiciously.

"When'd she leave? I didn't pass any wagon."

Dee looked to the sky as if gauging the time.

"Three, four hours back. I don't suspect she'll be back till tomorrow."

For all the wrath inside him at that moment, an even darker cloud cast its shadow on Thorn's soul.

"You tell her I'm going to catch her. And I'll kill her for being the start of this mess."

Dee Terry did not cow under the threat. Her voice dropped an octave and her look was all steel.

"Keep away from my girl."

Mat Thorn could have waited, though he knew his mother-in-law had a shotgun and would use it. There was no desire to hurt the woman. He might have ridden the waves of rage and hung around until his wife returned, but the hairs on his neck did not feel right. He pointed a last warning finger at Dee Terry, moved off the porch, and started walking back toward the tracks. He would stay out of sight somewhere until nightfall, most likely. That meant keeping a couple of miles from Fulshear's little San Antonio & Aransas Pass station. Train stations had a vigilant eye. If he got a good sense of things, he could make up some distance that afternoon. Thorn did not even know which direction he would head, but it would come to him.

Thorn's reputation was that of a tough and a gambler. He sported a dent in one cheek, the wound from an old fight, and his left arm was stiff at the elbow from a bygone gunshot. He had been a brawler, for sure, and he encouraged it in others. Over the years, Thorn had tried talking self-defense to Blacks in Harrisburg, to stand up against oppression, but they told him there was nothing for it but to go along. If Mat Thorn believed that Whites had not taken notice of his agitating, he was badly mistaken.

The five-man posse that roamed the prairies west of Houston most likely had an inflated opinion of the danger that Thorn posed, but their suppressed fears made them hold their weapons close.

The sheriff and deputies Peyton and Reed chased Thorn, or reports of him, around Harrisburg for the better part of two days, then they turned the task over to others. Word that Thorn's wife had run off to her mother's stayed within the Black community for a while, but eventually, it leaked out.

Ben Simmons, eager to both avenge his boss's death and prove his value to the citizenry of Precinct 2, imagined himself in command. In truth he was joined by a pair of other deputy constables whose rank made them equals - Irv Greer, from Pasadena, and Willie Bouknight, from Middle Bayou. Also itching to catch the fugitive were Mill Freeman, a Harrisburg saloonkeeper who considered Eddie Isgitt an old friend, and Georgie Phelan, the manager of the Capitol Hotel in downtown Houston. Phelan's was a high-profile job at one of the city's top hostelries, but in his heart, he yearned to be a policeman. It was perhaps the product of a boyhood spent reading dime novels. This was not the first posse Phelan had joined.

Six miles east of Fulshear, the five men came upon the camp of an old man and two boys, his grandsons. The grizzled gent told the posse that he and the boys were hunting birds, but Ben Simmons noted no guns, no shells, and certainly no string of cleaned bird carcasses. The little campfire, on the other hand, looked well-established. He suspected that the thrown together lean-to was a permanent home for the three.

Irv Greer did most of the talking at first. He described their quarry, and with each detail, the old man's resignation and nodding grew a bit stronger.

"Yep. Scar right here," he said, indicating the right side of his face.

"That's him," Greer told him.

"Polite fellow, really. Offered us a dime for a cup of our beans."

The man paused then hurriedly added an afterthought.

"We didn't take it, of course."

Simmons figured that they most assuredly had, but the man did not want any ill-gotten proceeds confiscated by men with badges.

The eldest of the boys was wide eyed over a fugitive having stopped and shared their food.

"Do you think he was up to no good?"

Greer suppressed a smile. Having eclipsed 50, he was the oldest of the five. He had long ago understood that his employment would never surpass deputy constable, and that suited Irv just fine. He was an inveterate lawman and had no desire to be anything more. He was comfortable with all his bumps, and he retained his sense of humor.

"Don't know son. Most likely."

"Do you think he had a gun with him in his pack?"

"Probably so."

"What about a knife."

"Can't rightly say, but he's a dangerous fellow."

The posse determined that they were about three or four hours behind their quarry. They were mounted, and Thorn seemed to be afoot, though earlier reports suggested he may have a horse. Upon reaching Fulshear, they asked for the local constable, but could not locate the man.

As had become customary during the pursuit, the five searchers talked through their options democratically. Personalities had emerged. Freeman and Phelan, the two amateurs, were generally keenest on decisive action. Irv Greer was apt to take things slow. It was the bartender who made his case.

"Why don't we just head out to Darktown, barge into a few of those shacks and ask our questions?"

"Shacks? They're nicer than your house, Mill."

"Fuck, you, Irv."

True to form, Georgie agreed with Freeman.

"It's clear that the boy has friends here. Bust a few heads and they'll talk."

Ben Simmons raised his palms to slow the rhetoric.

"Word'll get back to Thorn, and that defeats our whole point of being out here."

They decided among themselves by a four to one vote not to ask too many questions around the colored quarters lest they alert Thorn and give him a chance to slip away. They also agreed to wait until the wee hours.

The men grabbed some welcome shuteye after dinner at a small grocery. Boiled beef with rice and gravy. None among them would call it savory, but each took a second helping off the stove. Grudgingly, after watching the pots of food dwindle, the store owner nodded his chin toward a flour sack covered door.

"If you need 40 winks, there's the storeroom. Won't hold all of you."

Three of them kipped in the low, attached space. It allowed for no more. Ben Simmons snagged the best spot. He nestled in some grain sacks and was almost instantly asleep until a mouse started a run up his pant leg. Bouknight and Greer were the odd men out, but they did little complaining. They sat outside on the back step of the building and nodded off leaning against the wall. The cricks in their muscles later made both long for a bedroll on flat ground.

The first of them stirred around midnight. They roused one another and readied to go back out looking among the houses of Fulshear's Black residents.

Even though the neighborhood looked quiet, the approach was cautious. Four of them waited a good distance away for a scouting report. Irv Greer came back at 2:30. He sported a wide grin.

"I found where everybody is. There's a big gang of coons about four blocks over yonder. They're on the ground floor of a boarding house shooting craps."

"Boarding house? You mean whore house, don't you?"

Willie Bouknight was trying his hand as a swellhead, but Greer cut him short.

"I didn't see any girls, and we ain't here for you to wet your wick."

Bouknight grumbled epithets under his breath. Mill Freeman was again the contrarian.

"You think he's in there with them? Why would he stop to shoot craps?"

"There's rooms upstairs, you dullard," Phelan shot back. "Let's surround the place and bust in."

Greer told them it would not be so simple.

"They got the doors thrown wide open." He added a snort of laughter. "I reckon they know when their lawman sleeps around these parts."

The posse turned out to be no match for the dice throwers. Greer and their lookout had missed one another in the dark. That was owing mostly to the young sentry sleeping, but when all five men began creeping forward, the fellow, a boy about nine, let out a loud whoop and ran. The gamblers scooped up their pot and scattered with the night breeze. Mill Freeman managed to scrape 17 stray cents off the wood floor, but he supposed more than that had fallen through the cracks.

They did discover two aging prostitutes upstairs and one drunk old man, naked from the waist down. Willie Bouknight did not let Irv Greer hear the end of it for some time.

Two days later, the weather had turned colder after a norther passed through. Temperatures stayed above freezing, but there was frost in the grasses at night, and the men wished for heavier coats. Phelan tied a bandana around his ears, and all pulled their hats down tight.

The posse worked their way slowly east. They tried to be thorough in their search but were mostly chasing the shadows of the latest rumor. Despite protests from Phelan and Bouknight that it was a waste of time, they had ranged through the German settlements up around Fairbanks and Hillendahl. One never knew.

This night, after a farmhouse dinner, they were following the Jeanetta Road south. They stopped at a watering hole on the flat, open plain to let their horses drink their fill. The men reached the houses at Piney Point about dusk.

It was an old freedmen's community. A peninsula of woods along a southerly twist of the bayou jutted out into bare prairie, and there a group of farmers and wood choppers settled after the Civil War. Houses lay scattered at various distances from a spare Baptist church, and a dilapidated schoolhouse leaned slightly against the horizon. Only a few candles flickered in a window here and there.

With guns drawn, the five possemen, in great need of bathing, pushed their way roughly through the spread out neighborhood for the next four hours. For the most part, the residents were quiet and dour. Only the elderly dared grouse in the face of five armed White men.

They left convinced to a man of two things – Mat Thorn was not there, but the men they had rousted were lying about not having seen him.

The ground was wet. When they happened through a prairie mudhole, one of the lawmen, if the mood hit them, struck a sulfur match to examine the terrain. That was how Willie Bouknight lucked into finding a man's shoe prints a mile or two along from Piney Point. The going was slow on such a dark night, a horse could easily break a leg with one misstep into a critter burrow. It was hard to follow given the conditions, but eventually the tenuous trail led them to an empty house about half a mile southeast of Jeanetta, not that the community had much of a center.

Ben Simmons had cemented his control on the operation, and he outlined his plan. He would go to the back left corner and Greer to the back right. Each of them would have to crawl about 200 yards on their hands and knees. They would then hide themselves in the darkest spot they could locate, hopefully behind some brush cover, but where they would not lose sight of either the side or back of the house.

Deputy Greer griped that they could crawl half that far without being spotted.

"A man couldn't see his own dick on a night like this."

"I knew Indians who could," Ben responded. "We can't take the chance."

Greer kept his mouth shut, but he already resented Simmons' newly superior attitude. He also doubted seriously that Ben Simmons ever knew any Indians.

The other three men, with Bouknight in charge, were to rush the front door. This would flush Thorn out to where one of the two senior lawmen would get him, alive or dead didn't matter. If Thorn decided to make a fight and shoot to the front, Simmons and Greer would come into the back of the house and take him from behind. Those who voiced an opinion agreed that it was a solid plan.

Partly out of necessity and partly pure petulance, Irv Greer squatted to release his dinner behind a scrubby little hackberry. When he finished, hoping that the leaves he used were all safe, he got a bit turned around in the pitch blackness. He was late getting into position.

On the opposite side of the building, Simmons crawled unknowingly within 60 feet of where Mat Thorn had set out his blanket and pack in a tangle of pipevines. Just after Simmons settled into place a lightning show exploded. Blam. Thorn knocked Ben Simmons hard on the back of the head with a two and a half foot piece of tallow tree limb. The next blow came across the back at the kidneys. As he fell, Simmons popped off four scattered shots across the prairie.

The three men in front panicked. They fanned out in ineffectual confusion. A shift in the buttermilk clouds freed just enough starshine for George Phelan to see a shadow, and he fired at the running figure.

Willie Bouknight fell with a scream.

The shot had flown low. Catching him through the back of his thigh, it just missed shattering his femur.

It took Irv Greer just shy of ten minutes to locate Ben Simmons who was by that time unconscious. Greer screamed out and kept hollering until Mill Freeman found them.

As Phelan was tending best he could to the man he'd shot, Freeman roused the trainman at Jeanetta, and the groggy fellow telegraphed the sheriff to send a doctor and dogs. Both arrived near daybreak.

The hounds searched until they were tuckered out, but they were never able to strike the murderer's trail. Mat Thorn was gone. Vanished into the ether.

The worst of it was that he had taken Simmons' chestnut brindle. The deputy constable was apoplectic, but the men agreed that they had heard no rider, not even a neigh or a nicker. They had hobbled their mounts a quarter mile away, but they should have easily heard someone riding off. By Greer's estimation, Thorn must have walked that horse for a full mile before he pulled himself into the saddle.

"My horse is skittish as all hell with strangers. There's no way that buck could have walked him out without me hearing."

"You were cold as a wedge, Ben."

Simmons winced as he instinctively rubbed at his head.

"Well, y'all would've heard something. Bound to. It's like the Earth just opened and swallowed him."

The next morning's *Post* reported the posse was drunk at Jeanetta and maybe even at Fulshear. Georgie Phelan adamantly denied those charges via a letter that ran in the next day's edition, alternately putting it down to petty jealously on someone's part and at the same time doubting that any lawman from the western side of the county would make such a statement at all. They had all behaved very kindly to the posse, Phelan wrote.

Three days later, with the small band of manhunters returned to their regular pursuits, Archie Anderson sat at his desk in the Harris County Jail Building. He thumbed through the small stack of posters that had come with the afternoon mail. Alone in the office, the sheriff shook his head. He thought to himself of the great irony given that Isgitt had gotten bent out of shape over loss of pay from his mistaken convict, and now the state offered a $700 reward for Isgitt's killer.

Chapter 21

Lang's Oyster Parlor on Travis at Preston, across from the city hall, advertised itself as the oldest exclusive oyster parlor in the South. John Lang started selling oysters fresh off his own boat at the city market just after the Civil War, and the operation had grown decidedly upscale over the years. Lang's had almost fifty tables covered with starched white cloths and sporting all the potions and powders a diner needed to concoct the cocktail sauce of their dreams. Though James Duckworth dined at Lang's as often as three times a week during season, he could count on his own two hands the number of times he darkened the formal dining area. Duckworth preferred the bar.

That was where he stood now. Dark oak, brass foot rail, and marble top. A whiff of polish occasionally sneaked through the various competing scents emanating from the diners, but the glorious smell of fat oysters fried in cornmeal reigned supreme at Lang's. Even the bar customers all the way to the front of the long space could take a deep sniff and imagine their next plate coming from the busy kitchen at the rear.

Duckworth's usual began with a cool Magnolia beer and a dozen of the Berwick Bay oysters on the half shell. Lang's brought them in fresh from Louisiana daily. They cost twenty cents a dozen while the briny beauties from Galveston or Matagorda Bay were but fifteen. It may have been the psychological appeal of ordering top of the line, or it could have been the cachet in case he was observed by a potential client. Truth be told, J.B. loved them all. When the first round was done, the lawyer invariably ordered another mug and another dozen. Only then could he gauge how hungry he was. Sometimes it would be off to lunch or supper elsewhere, perhaps another bar, or he might fit in an oyster loaf. Whoever the German had cooking back in that kitchen made the best ones in town. Butter, mayonnaise, tomato, and a full dozen fried oysters on warm sliced bread. The cocktail sauce came on the side because two or three golden bivalves always managed to escape from the sandwich.

In addition to the holy food, the bar at Lang's was often crowded with top lawyers and a judge or two. A couple of the city's biggest merchants were regulars, and since it was next door to one of the Cotton Exchanges, those trader types were found slurping down oysters from mid-morning till closing. Swapping hellos with men of that caliber never hurt business, Duckworth believed. As opposed to the denizens of J.B.'s late night haunts, these fat cats were unlikely to kill anyone, but you could never tell. Everyone had problems.

The jowly fellow feasting next to J.B. looked familiar. Downtown Houston was not so big that the convivial sort did not encounter the same faces. The fact that Duckworth could not produce a name to go with the man on his right bothered him very little, and that did not stop the two from engaging in a lively conversation. Such was one of the best attributes of a good bar.

The two had already dispensed with the Venezuelan problem by agreeing that Admiral Dewey's ships would set the Germans and British right, though they did believe that knowing someone owed them a million dollars would have them miffed, as well. The man started to comment about the local street paving bonds but noticed the mayor five places farther down. Thad Holt was a middling lawyer as far as Duckworth was concerned, but he was one of the few Houston politicians who treated defense attorneys with any respect. J.B. offered Holt an acknowledging wave.

Sometime during the second dozen, another customer slapped his new friend on the shoulder and called him Grissom. The fellow was obviously pleased when J.B. wove the name into their conversation.

Mr. Grissom was a railroad auditor, and he tried to steer the talk into a paean on that morning's meeting with his top boss who was visiting the local office.

"Mr. Trice is the general manager of the entire I&GN system. The meeting was in his private car. Had seven or eight of us in there."

Grissom dropped in a low whistle for effect. He then patted the marble in front of him.

"Paneled wood. Tufted banquettes. It's as nice as this bar, except it's on wheels!"

"I'll bet his oysters aren't as good."

J.B. signaled for one more beer, quickly and deftly turning the conversation to something that at least marginally interested him. At the same time, he started weighing his next stop.

"I read that Corbett's people are trying to ink another bout with Jeffries," Duckworth offered.

His companion made a face and a wave as if a bull had just farted.

"Corbett. He's a piker. Threw that fight with McCoy, he did. His own wife said so."

"Former wife," Duckworth corrected. "At least last I checked. He changes them faster than a harlot's linens. I can assure you getting a scorned woman to accuse a past husband is one of the world's easiest tasks."

Duckworth took a swallow of beer, and Grissom rallied, still hoping for a conversational win.

"Do you think they'll catch that darky who killed the deputy?"

Isgitt's shooting had been a popular topic for days, but J.B.'s personal interest had waned mightily. It was just a dead opposition witness, and it would not affect his plan for court. Still, his curiosity made him bite. At least for the half minute it would take him to finish his beer.

"Oh, I'd say fifty-fifty. Not that I have faith in the police, but criminals are not the brightest. What do you think?"

"If the people chasing him are anything like the deputy he killed, then the boy is Scot free."

Grissom let go a low laugh at his own joke before pressing on with the tale.

"I watched that flatfoot get tossed out of a bar one night."

Duckworth gave him a nod of encouragement. He had been planning to leave, but with the new turn, he reconsidered. Casually, J.B. put his hat back on the hook.

"You know, I changed my mind. There's always room for another dozen and another beer."

J.B. signaled his order, and the shucker behind the bar began his work. Grissom continued, delighted to have a willing audience.

"He was a surly fellow. I'd wager most people were scared of him because of his size, but not that night. He was standing at the bar alone, giving everyone the fisheye. Nobody wanted to talk to the gump, you see."

Grissom, warming to his story, became more animated.

"Well, two spots down these old boys are talking, minding their own business. One of them is a barber, and he's recounting a story about giving a haircut to a cantankerous hotel guest. The deputy sort of lurches over to him, he was well sozzled, you see, and he points his finger and says, 'You're a damned liar. There's no barber shop in that hotel.' The barber, he's not a big man, starts to turn a little red. 'I've had a chair in that shop for eight years, mister. I know where I work.'"

Duckworth smiled a heartening grunt.

"So, at that juncture, the deputy pulls out his badge. Of course, they don't wear a uniform, and he's making out to be the big intimidating guy, but he's slurring his words something fierce. 'I'm a constable, you suck-egg son of a bitch.' The barber has gone positively purple."

Unable to fully contain his enthusiasm, Grissom let go a chortle.

"But before anything could happen, the bartender steps over, picks up the deputy's whiskey off the bar – it was about half full – he calls him by name and says, 'You're done for the night.' Like I said, that deputy was a beefy man, and he started to squawk like a chased goose, but this skinny bartender, a tall, young kid, comes around the bar, apron and all, grabs him by the coat collar, and leads him to the door. Just matter of fact, as if he tosses out belligerent badge men every day. And the deputy, he tries to come back through the front door two more times. By then there's both bartenders standing there, and the other one finally shoves the deputy onto the sidewalk with a boot to the prat. Just like a music hall show. I reckon the deputy steered clear of that place for a good while. If he remembered it, that is."

Grissom wiped a small tear from his eye. Duckworth was grinning, and now he raised an eyebrow.

"What bar was that?"

"Oh, I can't recall. Somewhere close. I do most of my drinking within a few blocks of the office. It's over on Main, you know."

"But you don't recollect?"

"Well,... It wasn't Thielepape's. That's right next to the offices. The Cabinet maybe. The 66?"

The man was getting disappointed that Duckworth had not enjoyed the story more, but J.B. asked again.

"Could it have been the Turf?"

"Might have been," the crestfallen auditor answered. "I couldn't say."

Louie Swearingen was due for his first pre-trial meeting the following Monday. He had barely settled into a chair next to Sonny Schlottmann's desk when J.B. Duckworth walked over for a word. Like most every bit of information the man gleaned, the chance encounter at Lang's had remained lodged in the lawyer's mental arsenal. Being a busy man, Duckworth spared no niceties.

"Did you ever throw Eddie Isgitt out of a bar?"

The sudden question confused Swearingen. He needed a second or two to even place the name.

"I don't recollect it. Why?"

J.B. puffed out his lips.

"A fellow described an incident to me, and the bartender in the story reminded me of you."

Louie shook his head, but Duckworth did not pause.

"Isgitt already told the sheriff about it way back when they arrested you, but nobody bothered to tell me. I had John ring a few people up yesterday, and Sheriff Anderson shared what he heard. Hadn't thought it was important."

"Well, is it?"

"Not really. The man's dead, and that's a win for us. But the bigger point is that you need to tell us everything connected to your case. We're the only people between you and the gallows."

Swearingen jerked upright in his chair.

"Gallows? What... that can't..."

Duckworth's moustache turned up at the corners, and his eye's twinkled.

"Of course not. Nobody's going to hang you, but it's goddamn important that we know everything."

"Hell, I threw out a thousand of those pixielated goldbricks, Mr. Duckworth. You can't expect me to remember them all, can you?"

J.B. had no answer to that. Instead, he gave a final admonishing look to his client and then tapped his junior partner, who had remained silent throughout the exchange, on the shoulder.

"Sonny here will walk you through everything. I want you to start thinking hard, scouring your brain for anything that can help us. What we use will be up to me alone, but we need all the ammunition either way."

With that, the firm's senior partner wheeled and returned to his private office. Sonny gave Louie a reassuring look. He had not forgotten the recent gunfire incident, and he gently broached the subject.

"How have you been doing? Or I should ask how your wife is doing? She was pretty shaken up last I heard about it."

Swearingen let out a loud breath and lowered his head.

"It was rough. She fed me a shovel full four or five nights running. I don't reckon she'd have left me, but she had me pigeon-livered over the notion."

Sonny nodded with mock solemnity.

"I imagine most women worth their salt would be upset over somebody firing bullets into their bedroom."

Swearingen missed the humor.

"Least Nora's back to being more worried about my drinking than anybody else taking a shot at us. I suppose that's good, but it ain't exactly making my life easier. She's such a good woman. Do you think maybe it's because she's so young? She even went so far as to go to a Salvation Army meeting, but she said she couldn't stand it."

"God bless her," Schlottmann said. "Those people are a scourge. They will go to their grave believing that drink is a sin requiring repentance."

"I've tried to please her. I swear I have. I even invested forty cents into some tonic the druggist said would purify my blood and take away any craving to drink spirits. Gave me the shits something fierce and made me squiffier than a pint of Van Hook's."

His head shook over his plight.

"The advertisements in the papers go on about the Keeley Cure. I swear I thought about it, but it's nine dollars a shot. Shit, Mr. Schlottmann, I don't make that much in two weeks sometimes. And I can't stand needles on top of it. The sight of one makes me weak kneed. I'm not proud of it, but well,... there it is."

"It has gold in it," Sonny leaned a little nearer out of deference to a woman in the waiting chairs. "You're liable to end up with a hobo panning in your pisser."

He resumed his regular position but kept his voice low.

"It wasn't our case, so I'm violating no privilege to tell you that people right here in town have sued over the gold cure. Four weeks and four of those syringes a day, and the patient, or rube, if you prefer, was passed out on a street corner again within ten days. Rousted by the law. The word around the courthouse was that there is strychnine in there. I'm no doctor, but I'm smart enough to think that if they use something to kill rats, the same compound won't put a healthy glow back into your cheeks."

"It's not like Nora is fixing to commit me to a drunk ward or something," Louie told him. "But I don't want to let her down. Sometimes I go three or four days with nary a drop. Thing is I like to drink. The best times I've ever had, I had with my chums. We have a few drinks, and we laugh till we hurt."

"And there is no harm in it, Louie. You've just got to stop and go home while you still remember where that is."

Swearingen smiled sadly.

"I behave when I'm drinking. I do. I've never raised a hand toward Nora. I swear I'd never do that."

"I'm not a priest, Louie. I'm just a lawyer."

That elicited a wan chuckle.

"I just wanted you to know."

Schlottmann reared back in his chair, settling in for a story.

"I had an uncle. Well, my father's uncle, really. One of the ones who came from Germany. I heard tell that in his youth, he was a hale and hearty fellow. Would split logs for hours. Could lift a young hog over the pen fence by himself, if the need arose. But none of this could you prove by me. What I remember was a shambling, dissipated shell, sitting in a wooden chair in the garden at holidays, pulling on a bottle. The drink made him that way. Others in the same family, his brother, Heinrich, even, were strong as oxen right up until the week they died. And let me tell you, Heinrich loved his beer. At 87 years, he could still, as they say, drink me under the table."

Sonny jerked a thumb toward the office behind him.

"Maybe it is as the boss in there says, 'Beer is not drinking.'"

He laughed at the familiar joke then summed up his thoughts.

"Some people can handle it all. Some are good with beer but not whiskey. And some I've seen, and no doubt you have, as well, take half a glass and become a very rough fellow. None of it is fair."

Swearingen was soft but firm.

"I'm no rough fellow. That's what I want everyone to know."

Sonny's perpetual smile quietened.

"You've gotten rough with some men, though, when you're drinking, yes?"

Louie nodded.

"Mmm-hmm. That's one of the problems we have with your defense. If we put you on the stand, the D.A. will be asking you about those instances from now until Sunday."

Even on nights when the press of a court session was not looming, some of the attorneys of Duckworth & Fein were apt to be at their desks until supper time, but all was not equal. Henry Fein kept a reasonable balance of work and family. Sonny Schlottmann was known to skip out early when a good time beckoned. John Duckworth tried to maintain business hours, though his schedule was driven by the needs of cases just the same. In Jed Posey, J.B. saw a passion for the law, but Posey was young, still in his twenties, and youth sometimes had its own ideas.

Charlie Dixon almost never stayed late, but here he was at eight o'clock, in the spot he seemed to prefer, seat on the floor, back against the wall, reading. How the boy could see in the dim lamplight was a mystery. J.B., who had not risen from his desk for several hours, had no clue how long Charlie had been there or why. He knew that he was ready for a beer and some food as he worked his way home, and he imagined that Maizy was ready for a walk.

"That must be a fine book to have you so spellbound at this hour."

Charlie Dixon nodded.

"What is it?"

"Black Beauty."

Charlie held up the colorful cover, and Duckworth aahed.

"You ever read it?"

"No. It wasn't written when I was your age. She, the woman who wrote it, was dying at the time. Passed over just after it came out."

Charlie made a noise of acknowledgment, but he was back to reading. J.B. watched him for a full minute before speaking again.

"You know I encourage your studies, but I'm of a mind to get out of here. What say you finish the book up at home?"

The boy looked up with slight alarm.

"The little kids won't let me alone, and my mama'll have chores for me, and mostly, I got to hand this book in tomorrow at the school."

Charlie Dixon attended Gregory School in Freedmen's Town.

"Library book, huh?"

Charlie Dixon was a serious youngster who rarely betrayed emotion, but J.B. thought he sensed a hint of pout. The lawyer fished a coin from his pocket.

"You keep it another day. Tell them you forgot it at home, and use this to pay any fine that might incur."

"Why do folks treat horses so bad? The horses in this book, there's some of them get beat, poked, their tails cut off, and when they're not good looking enough anymore, their owners ship them off to haul coal wagons. Ain't right."

As if summoned, Maizy gave Charlie a good sniff and a nuzzle. He ruffled her coat then smoothed it back down, much to the dog's satisfaction.

"No, Charlie, it ain't right. We need to take care of those who need the help."

Even though J.B.'s stomach had voiced a few grumbles, the lawyer pulled a chair away from Jed Posey's empty desk and sat down.

"You know, it's a damned important lesson learning about animals. I was reared on a farm, at least when I was real little. I'd just got to the age of tending to the chickens. John had charge of the hogs, and I'd pad along behind him. That barnyard part of my life went away, but I've had dogs as long as I've had a place to lay my head. Couldn't fathom being without one."

J.B. smoothed his moustache as he mulled.

"I've been thinking about introducing Katherine to a pet. That girl loves the zoo. She's two and half, not old enough for a real pet that requires taking care of, but something to call her own seems good. I was thinking about a turtle. It'll make her feel like she's responsible for something, but there's no taking it for walks, and she can poke at it without either of them getting hurt. Just hold out a leaf of lettuce, and she'll get a charge out of it."

The idea earned a solemn, thoughtful nod from Charlie Dixon.

"Do you have pets at home, Charlie? You've never mentioned one that I recall."

"No, sir. My mama says we don't need any more mouths to feed, but she still slips some scraps to a couple of tabby cats that come around. One of them is fierce skittish, but the gray one lets me and my sisters pet her. If you scratch her back of the ears and on her belly, she'll sit on your lap and purr."

"How do you know it's a girl."

"I figure no boy would let a girl do that to him, would he?"

"Hmm. Not till the boy's older. I imagine you're right. Anyhow, with these last few warm days, do you think there are any red eared sliders out sunning in the bayous?"

"If sun's shining, I reckon there will be."

Duckworth considered the matter.

"You have a swimming hole, don't you?"

"There's a couple we can go to. A spot at Vinegar Hill ain't too bad. Best one's at that bend back of the cemetery, but... it's just for older boys."

Charlie meant White boys, but as long as he had been around the lawyers at the firm, none had ever heard him reference matters of race.

"If I hired you to find me a game looking turtle for Katherine's Christmas, could you do that for me? A business arrangement, mind you. I'll be paying you, so I want a good one. Not too old and not too big. And no snapper. I don't want my little girl losing a finger."

The young man was always up for paying work. Sonny had joked that Charlie would have enough to buy his own house by the time he was 14.

"That sounds fair. When do you want it?"

"Christmas Eve? Provided it's sunny maybe you can fetch me one that afternoon. I'll find a suitable box so I don't have to carry the thing home in my suit pocket."

J.B. patted his leg and made a snicking noise, and Maizy grudgingly left her scratches. Charlie Dixon carefully tucked the school library book inside his coat as Duckworth turned out the light and locked the door for the night.

Chapter 22

Christmas Day 1902

The Duckworth Brothers had hauled dining chairs into the yard and were smoking cigars and drinking glasses of wine. J.B. was hardly a connoisseur of the grape, but John Latreyte, three doors down from the office, pointed him to a French Bordeaux that "would make for a memorable Christmas." Duckworth ordered six bottles to be delivered to the house and threw in a couple of bottles of Madeira for good measure. Two liquor stores shared the block with Duckworth & Fein, and like everything else, J.B. tried to spread his trade around. There was never enough good will. He imagined Latreyte would remember the splurge the next time he needed an attorney.

Katherine was chasing her turtle around the small dirt back yard, though between an easily distracted two and a half year old girl and a red eared slider, the chase was decidedly low speed. A crisis had been averted when Monkey Doodle, as she had dubbed her new pet, explored his opportunities underneath the privy. Uncle John relocated the beast, but the brothers agreed it was only a matter of time. The hope was that if Katherine kept handing lettuce to Monkey Doodle he would stay where the food was and not plod off.

Lola had been busy in the kitchen since before dawn. It was a warm day. Though the nights had been cold all week, temperatures quickly rose to the middle sixties, and the sun shone. The small room on the back of the house was dominated by her stove. Not out of size, but out of heat. Two years ago, J.B. had ordered a four-burner Acme Princess with a reservoir direct from Sears Roebuck. It replaced a wobbly wood-burning affair half the size. Lola loved the convenience, but now that they had stepped up to coal, the heat in the kitchen was even more oppressive. She expected that cooking a full meal in the summertime was akin to wearing widow's weeds in the Sahara Desert.

With the mild weather, Lola opened the small kitchen window and propped the back door open with a mop bucket. It was still stifling. The back of her dress was long ago soaked through. She could hear J.B. and John talking in the yard and the occasional shriek of joy from her daughter. They would scare off any neighborhood strays lured by the aroma of food. She would not soon forget her fright at finding two feral cats cozying up to her baked fish one afternoon. She thanked her stars that her busy husband ate most meals away from home. Lola longed for a modest, rightful place in Houston society befitting the wife of a lawyer on the come, and she knew women confined to household drudgery were wrung out by age 40.

The Christmas menu did not vary much in the Duckworth household, though this year they did not have to purchase the main course. Her husband had brought home a nice goose the day before, a gift from a grateful but not guilty murderer from Chambers County. Lola was roasting it with pecan stuffing. There were also creamed parsnips, boiled potatoes, cranberry jelly, and steamed onions on the stove top. If she found good looking snap beans at the market, those were also a regular part of the feast. This year's had been a bit too dry to suit her.

Once the goose came out of the oven, Lola's bread pudding would go in, then she would make gravy on the spare burner. She baked two chess pies just after sunup, and they were cooling on the drainboard. One of them she would trade with Mrs. Schmidt for a pear tart. Lola had pampered herself by making her brother-in-law pick up a pan of yeasty rolls from a bakery near his boarding house. They may be a day old, but she would warm them back to life with a damp dish cloth.

Two hours later, through her efforts alone, Christmas dinner was served. Lola had freshened up in the bedroom wash basin and put on a clean dress. A glass of the Bordeaux had just begun to melt the knots in her back, and the compliments on the food helped. The brothers' raucous conversation betrayed that they were halfway through the third bottle, and it may have spurred Lola to drink a tad faster than her usual sips.

A knock at the door came about five minutes into the main course. John answered it, but did not opened the door wide enough to provide a view from the table. Still, the young voice and the fishing for a loose coin was all the others needed to know. Soon, John handed his brother the familiar small envelope.

"Telegram for you, Jamie."

J.B. wiped butter from his hand.

"You should have given that poor boy a cookie. Having to work on Christmas Day."

The lawyer's mouth was full of goose and potato. He opened the message at the table and read it without comment, slipping it into his coat pocket.

"I'll need to go out tonight, but don't think I'll be late. Just in case, a cold goose supper and another slice of pie will suit me fine. Just throw a cloth over them, if you go to bed."

He winked at his wife.

"And don't drink both bottles of that dessert wine."

Across the bayou, Louie and Nora Swearingen were enjoying their first Christmas. The day began tentatively. They slept late. Each made a trip to the outhouse in the chilly hours of morning then climbed back under the quilts.

For Nora, it was her first holiday away from the little patch of woods where she was raised. Louie had spent the past several Christmas mornings sleeping off many snootsful from the night before, and truth be told, there was a touch of that still. In those bygone times, he dragged himself to work and poured more drinks for that class of customer who believed his fellow bar patrons to be family, which in fact, they probably were. This time, when the day arrived with no place to be, neither of them fully knew how to act.

Her mother had phoned from the store asking that they come home for Christmas dinner, but Nora did not want to go. Things between her sister Mary and her father were still unpleasant, and though Nora sympathized with her younger siblings and missed them, this was a time to enjoy married life. She very much wanted a full day alone with her husband, to put the newlywed quarrels aside. She believed that if they could spend more time together, if she could make a home like the idyllic places in the stories, Louie would give up his errant ways.

The uneasiness also stemmed from the fact that neither were used to being home for an entire day, Christmas or otherwise. Work days were long, and they either met for a few glasses and supper, or Louie stayed out while Nora sat in the apartment and read.

Despite having been compelled to help in the kitchen, Nora never took to domesticity like Mary did. Not that the tiny old stove in their flat was much of a help, either. She had planned to roast a chicken in the oven. Nothing larger would fit. She also bought some sad looking string beans at the market. She managed to botch them both. The chicken reached a dark gold on the outside, but the breasts, Louie's favorite part, were decidedly pink close to the bone, and the beans could not have been more limp if she'd soaked them in the Gulf of Mexico. Louie laughed about it, Nora cried about it, and then he held her until all was good. They struggled through the bland beans and ate saltine crackers and the salvageable parts of the chicken, those being the appendages that cooked properly. Even Nora admitted the legs and wings were not half bad.

After dinner, which happened later in the afternoon, the two played a card game - whist. The first few hands were pleasant enough, but then both of them grew bored. It was Nora who initiated sex, and she thought it especially grand. There had not been much drinking, only a bottle of Christmas wine almost evenly split, but all the same, the two of them fell to sleep in each other's arms after the third bout.

It had gone dark when Nora woke to her husband's muffled cries. He was sleeping on his stomach with his face dug into the pillow, but clearly he was being visited by some phantasm. She could not make out words, but he was caught in some ordeal. If he got any louder, he might wake the neighbor through the thin wall. She paused for a second remembering the childhood warning that waking someone from a nightmare might kill them. Dismissing it as fluff, she gently rubbed his bare shoulder.

"Louie. Louie. You're having a horror dream."

Swearingen muttered something and twisted away. His wife shook him a bit harder but kept her voice soft.

"Louie. Boo. Wake up."

He bolted upright in bed, frantically looking around the dark room before he placed himself. He took his wife's hand. Nora let go a giggle.

"That must have been something awful getting you."

Louie's voice was that of a scared boy.

"I don't want to go to prison."

Archie Anderson and his family celebrated Christmas in their rooms at the county jail. His sister, Jennie Wilson, and Edna, the sheriff's daughter who was now 20, made a fine ham with sides of oyster dressing and potatoes. After the main courses, the jailer and the sheriff enjoyed seconds of the pecan pie, but Archie, Jr. took the prize with three slices, though one came surreptitiously from his cousin Lizzie who was watching her figure.

Seventy-two inmates spent their Christmas in less comfortable parts of the Harris County Jail. The sheriff and the district attorney had conspired to release eight men and two women who were almost at the end of their short stints the night before. Annie Brown and two helpers came to work in the large kitchen just as any other day, and they made sure there was a bit of extra meat in a cauldron of turkey and gizzard stew for those in the cells. She also baked eleven sweet potato pies, enough for each prisoner to get a decent sized piece. It was the Lord's birthday, after all. Turkey John was there in the morning to look after the horses, and Annie sent him home with three slices.

Around three that afternoon, happy to walk out some kinks and let his dinner settle, Archie Anderson made the rounds of the cells doling out yuletide wishes to all who would listen. Most returned his greeting, but a handful snarled and turned away. None of it changed the sheriff's contented mood. He also carried two apples out to Beau. Horses might not know the significance of the day, but they could enjoy a present just the same.

In the small house in Harrisburg, Andy Green sat with the front curtains drawn and the door closed. This beautiful day was meant for open windows or porch sitting, and the two sashes at the back of the house were pushed up for fresh air, but anyone passing down the street would believe that nobody was home.

Green had two invitations to join friends for Christmas dinner, but told each that he had other plans. It was a day free from work, and he looked forward to the quiet. No responsibilities and nobody to please but himself. He had some good links of deer sausage. His plans were to eat four meals, drink two bottles of wine, and take two naps. Sadly, when the day finally came, the past would not let Andy be. To make things worse, it was not even his own past.

His Christmas memories were good. Roaming parties traipsing between the shotgun houses on Robin Street. The teachers at his school decorated the recitation room and all the students sang songs and ate sweets. He recollected sugar cookies sprinkled with white and red.

No. The Christmas pasts that haunted Andy Green today were Johnson Montgomery's. Every year at this time, his friend fell into the fantods. Johnson carried his melancholia for days each December. He had generally stayed drunk and was even more argumentative than usual. Given his normal behavior, that made Johnson insufferable.

It never made sense to Andy until today. It was Helen. There was no good reason his best pal should keep the story of his family a secret except for shame. It had to be. Every year when he saw children giddy with expectation, Johnson must think of his daughter. Any man would. They could not help it. What might have been was a powerful force on a man's heart, and the whole notion made Andy very sad.

That evening, well after sundown, J.B. Duckworth opened the stairwell door of the House Bank Building on Main. Normally that intersection with Franklin, the heart of the city's financial and railroad enterprises, would be leaping. With so many businesses closed for the holiday, it was not. Pedestrians were scarce, light displays dark, and the red and white striped awnings hung monochromatic in the gloom.

The lone door at the top of the second flight was unlocked. It admitted Duckworth into a room of rich, wood paneling - quarter sawn oak, most likely, but stained a mahogany hue. The colossal carpet in the middle of the floor was undoubtedly imported, and the spittoons and jardinieres scattered about were highly polished brass. It was a chamber designed to impress, and the contrast with Duckworth & Fein was stark.

It was not a large firm as the number of attorneys went, but its political reach was as long as any in town. The golden glow from the far left corner of the otherwise unoccupied space marked the private office of Congressman Shelby Arnold. J.B. was expected.

"Merry Christmas, Mr. Duckworth."

Arnold motioned J.B. to a nicely upholstered chair.

"Wasn't easy getting a car over," Duckworth answered. "They're running a light schedule, I gather."

"Have a drink. That'll soothe your nerves. It's imported Scotch. One of my many vices."

The Congressman smiled with supreme self-satisfaction. Duckworth made the assumption that the man carried that expression often. The whiskey was definitely better than his Old Taylor, but J.B. did not voice that opinion. He merely savored the smoky taste as he waited for Arnold to take the lead. He knew full well why he was summoned, but he refused to make the first move.

"I know the timing of my request is unconventional," Arnold said. "But I reckoned this was a fine time to speak since anybody in his right mind is spending the day with his family. I trust you enjoyed a fine Holiday meal. Our cook outdid herself, so you'll forgive my loosened tie. I don't want to pop any buttons."

Arnold reinforced his statement with a pat of his belly as if he were a music hall comic playing for the back row. He was a railroad lawyer, a stalwart of the top class of Texas legal professionals. The last five representatives from the recently renumbered Texas District 8 were railroad lawyers, and it was likely the next ten would be, as well. As long as the railroads held the most power, their trusted legal henchmen would carry their legislative water.

Having covered the preliminaries, the Congressman could not resist one last bit of gladhanding as he got down to business.

"Let me start by saying that we members of the legal community need to stick together."

If Arnold expected the fine trappings to soften J.B. Duckworth's sharp edges, he was mistaken.

"Are we part of the same community? I always surmised that hot shot railroad lawyers wouldn't know the difference between a defense lawyer and a bug on their boot heel."

It got a short cursory laugh in reply.

"That's likely so, but it doesn't mean we can't help each other out. You're still a constituent, too."

He paused for a reaction, but getting none, forged ahead.

"There are some of us in civic leadership who are worried about this E.P. Isgitt ordeal."

"Civic leadership? That sounds important."

The congressman's expression hardened.

"People I've spoken to are concerned about the message the shooting might send to the criminal classes."

"Is Judge Gillaspie one of those people?"

The laugh from Arnold was sudden. The question had genuinely surprised him.

"The honorable J.K.P. Gillaspie wanted my job. Still does. He'll likely run against me next time, too. And if I stand for reelection, Duckworth, I'll beat him again like a red-headed step child. I see no reason to help him out. No, Gillaspie is not my type of fellow, to be honest. I'll let you in on a little secret - I like to play the dealmaker. It gives me pleasure. Gillaspie, he's more of the law library man."

The congressman had been reclined, but now he leaned forward.

"Here's the crux of the matter as I see it - Mat Thorn, the darky who shot that constable, may have a self-defense claim from what I hear. Isgitt just got acquitted of murdering one colored man in cold blood, so there's no guarantee what would happen if Thorn was to draw a good lawyer. Now, my old friend Harris Peterson tells me that you are not going take Mat Thorn's defense, is that a true statement?"

Duckworth was impassive.

"I've not taken it yet."

"I'll be blunt. We want to see that boy swing, and we'd even consider offsetting your fee."

"Who's we?"

"Well, the powers that be, as they say. No matter how off-putting Isgitt may have been, he was still a law man, and letting colored boys kill officers of the law is not a good precedent. So, you can see how Thorn being convicted of another murder would be helpful. It's a safeguard. My friends and I think Louie Swearingen's case might fill the bill. He's the son of a lawman, too. Folks I've talked to think that if Swearingen walks free that he's not likely to kill anyone else. An innocuous sort, wouldn't you agree?"

"I don't agree that he's killed anybody in the first place."

J.B.'s glass was empty, and he willed himself not to request another. Seeing the situation, Arnold topped up his own glass but neglected his guest's.

"Oh, come now, counselor, there's an ironclad eyewitness. On top of that, the boy held up a store at gunpoint."

Duckworth bristled at the notion.

"That was a set up, and if you know about the incident, then you know damn well that Louis Swearingen didn't rob any grocery."

The congressman continued unflustered, as if he had not heard J.B. at all.

"Plus, his own father-in-law is a murderer."

"Pshaw. The father-in-law is not my client."

"Same difference. It's his family."

"By marriage."

"Meaning he chose to associate himself with those people."

Duckworth cast away the final shreds of deference he may have carried into the Congressman's office and brought up something close to home for Shelby Arnold.

"So, if your brother-in-law gets caught with his hand in the accounts, that's on you then, Congressman?"

Arnold's face flushed crimson at the mention of a personal scandal that was largely kiboshed in the press.

"Watch your step, Duckworth. I'm talking about cold blooded murder, and you've got two peas in a pod on your hands."

"No. I've got nothing of the sort. The old man came to me with his grimy hat in hand, begging for my representation, and I sent him walking. Louis Swearingen is my only connection to this matter."

Shelby Arnold considered that idea for a moment and sipped his Scotch.

"It comes down to this - If Mat Thorn was to have shot the victim..."

He looked down at his desk for notes, but could not find them. Duckworth sat silent, not about to supply Johnson Montgomery's name. Arnold quickly gave up the search of his papers with a dismissive wave.

"You get my gist. If we can't work this out, your Swearingen client is likely facing a decade up at Huntsville, or worse yet, hired out on a work gang with God knows what sort of ruffians. Good looking boy, I hear. I'm sure he'll find a prison barracks most congenial. Perhaps most important of all, some little upstart defense lawyer will have greatly disappointed some powerful men. Hypothetically, of course."

The congressman's condescending smile returned.

"That's the thing about criminal lawyers, Mr. Duckworth, they deal with criminals. It can't help but rub off now, can it?"

Chapter 23

The little girl did not say a word as she reached up and gently touched his scared face. Mat Thorn closed his eyes.

"I had a baby girl once. She'd be bigger than you."

A choke stopped his voice.

The girl's father chided her very softly.

"Leave the man be, honey."

Before she climbed down from the day bed, the girl looked Thorn in the eyes.

"I wish Santa knew you'd be here."

Thorn let go a breath. Though the couple had let him into their home, he was still uneasy. He sensed that the man was a fighter like he was, but his days on the run had made him wary. He appraised his hosts by the light of the lone kerosene lamp.

That afternoon, Mat had watched the man repair a rafter tail for better than half an hour before he approached, and the fellow had shown no hint of skittishness. He looked at Thorn square on and said he was welcome to stay.

"All the same," the man had told Thorn. "I'd feel more comfortable for my family's sake were you to be gone around daybreak."

It was certainly isolated, this little farm. The woods were thick as clabber, and a ground fog had come on just after dark. The only sounds outside the cabin were some barking and yipping a mile or more away. Mat briefly worried about hounds, but identified them as coyotes. The fatback and cornbread had been good, too. Peppery like his mama made.

"I appreciate this hospitality. If it's all the same, I'll go sleep in the shed so as not to bother you folks in the morning."

The man nodded and stepped outside with Thorn. The little shed was attached to an open stall that housed an old mule. There was just enough moonlight in the clearing to make it out some 40 yards away.

The man's high voice did not match his farm strong frame.

"I've had plenty of run-ins over my years. It ain't always hospitable country around here. I just want you to know I've seen plenty of White folk accuse a colored man of things he ain't done."

Thorn did not hesitate.

"Oh, I done it."

The two looked at each other for a moment, then Mat extended his hand.

"Obliged."

There was an unexpected knock on the apartment door two days after Christmas. Nora Swearingen blinked her eyes and looked up at a thicker, older version of her husband. The hair was cropped shorter on top, but it still carried a whiff of the unruly. The face was a tad jowlier, and the temples had grayed. Instead of her husband's clean upper lip, there was a carefully waxed moustache. She had never met the man before, but there was not a whisker of a chance that she might fail to recognize him as her father-in-law. Her offered an amiable smile that was impossible to resist.

"Well, hell, you're cuter than a bug's ear, and just a slip of a thing, on top of it. Junior's done good."

He stuck out his meaty hand.

"I'm Lou Swearingen, but Big Lou'll do me just fine."

The two of them stood looking at one another for the better part of a minute before Nora's shock abated, and she asked him inside and pointed him to a worn armchair.

"Louie's at work, and I don't imagine he'll be home for hours."

Big Lou's winning smile did not waver, but Nora immediately spotted the change. The happy lines at the corners of his eyes remained, but the light in them was dimmer. For a moment, she put it down to the late afternoon sun falling behind a cloud, but that was not it.

"Oh, I knew he wouldn't be here. Me and Junior, well... we don't always cotton to one another. He's always been a rebellious boy. It just ain't..."

Swearingen slapped both his knees.

"It's you I've come to see, little girl. His mother got your letter about you expecting, and a grandchild is something I've been looking forward to. His mama convinced me that it's time, and I had to be over here on business. I wanted to meet you seeing as we're family."

"I don't guess you make it to Houston often."

If there was any shame in his next statement, Big Lou Swearingen did not betray an ounce of it.

"No, something'll drag me to Houston every couple of months. I just never saw call before now to go hunting up Junior."

"Well, you still haven't, have you?"

Big Lou gave a charming grin. Just as her husband had told her, the man possessed them in endless supply.

"No, I reckon not."

He stayed for no more than 15 minutes of small talk during which he extracted her promise to come visit at Sealy once the baby arrived. His response to an entreaty to reconcile with his son brought the winsome grin and vague words. Big Lou gave his daughter-in-law a hug when he left.

Despite having made her laugh out loud half a dozen times, barely a minute after she closed the apartment door, Nora felt mostly sadness. She already dreaded telling her husband about his father's visit.

James B. Duckworth felt like stretching his legs. The sun was shining, and a temperate south wind pinned the industrial smoke of Fifth Ward to the other side of the bayou. On many days, he would have handed such minor paperwork to Jed Posey to carry across Congress Avenue to a court clerk while he continued to bury his face in a law book or stare out the window and scheme out a case. Today, though, the outdoors was calling. He was thinking about the New Year as he opened the street door. It was a mere 33 hours away.

He might even be able to stand a beer or two after his errand. This time of the afternoon, his buddy Walter Malsch was usually bellied up at the Opera House Saloon just a few steps across Fannin.

J.B. did not make it four paces into the courthouse lobby before he nearly headlonged into J.K.P. Gillaspie. Duckworth had avoided court appearances before Gillaspie for several months, but now was the time to stand his ground. He stopped square in the jurist's path to the exit. For well over a year he had studiously avoided using the term "your honor" where Gillaspie was concerned, and in less than two days, every other attorney in Houston could comfortably do the same.

"Judge."

Gillaspie had expected to pass without acknowledgement, now the low attorney standing in his way discomfited him. He looked J.B. in the eyes but did not speak.

"Oh, what a tangled web we weave," Duckworth declaimed a tad too loudly. "Are you a fan of Walter Scott, judge?"

Gillaspie stood impassive. If he thought his silence would draw out anything else, he was mistaken. Instead, Duckworth changed direction.

"You might not be my biggest rooter, ..."

As Duckworth began, his hands raised up in straight-faced supplication, but a leer spread over his face as he continued.

"...and the Lord knows I'm not fishing for gratitude, but you're probably aware of the favor I did you by keeping word of your dalliances away from the press when they came sniffing around. They were hounding me over your little moll down on the island, but I kept mum. Oh, the things they said about you and her."

Gillaspie gritted his teeth and dropped his voice to a whisper.

"None of that is true, and I think you know it full well."

J.B. sucked in air through his teeth.

"Well, it's been my observation that the hoi polloi are always interested in rumor over truth. Wouldn't you say?"

The judge seethed. J.B. turned his body as if to walk away, then suddenly shifted back for a parting thought.

"I don't expect I'll be hearing anything more about that Waco business... or anything else that might endanger my livelihood."

The two men locked eyes for the briefest moment. Though Duckworth held onto a twinkle, Gillaspie's gaze offered nothing but white hot hatred.

"Duckworth, you are base and without respect."

"Yes, sir. I reckon that's about right."

J.B. paused to see if any more vitriol was forthcoming, but in its absence, he merely dipped his head in a polite nod.

"Now you have a Happy New Year, judge. And a comfortable retirement."

Yes, a drink across the street felt like a capital idea.

It was barely a block from the regular car stop to the house. Even closer when he was the only one on the car. On those nights, Joe Russo let him off right in front of his neighbor's walk. This night, being a bit earlier than Joe's final run, there were others aboard, and J.B. was obliged to wait until they were alone before he recounted to his brother the conversation with Judge Gillaspie. The story burned a hole in his pocket like a boy with a nickel, and he started to spin the tale of his unexpected encounter in the courthouse lobby as soon as Joe Russo clanged his goodnight.

J.B. put a gentle hand on John's arm to keep him on the porch as he completed the yarn. His brother's first response, other than laughter, was to say that "balance is restored to the heavens." John's huzzah brought a wide smile to his younger brother's face.

"Take a seat, I'll look in on the girls and get our refreshments."

Lola and Katherine were just in bed, and J.B. stuck his head in to check on each. Lola spilled out a drowsy hello and summoned her husband to the bedside.

"John came back with me. We promise to be quiet."

He punctuated his vow with a kiss.

"Katherine and I had a wonderful afternoon outing. We walked all the way to Elysian, and I got to show off the new hat you gave me for Christmas."

It had satin facing on the underside of the brim and an egret plume. It might be a small, vain thing, but it made her feel good. And was that not the point of a gift?

"I got several compliments. Give me another kiss. I love you."

After her husband pulled the bedroom door almost closed, Lola shut her eyes. Today's walk around the park was an introspective one. She could not help but see other women on the street and be glad that her husband was good to her. She knew of other women not so lucky. Not for certain, not personally, but she suspected. Lola saw poorly dressed women with bruised faces. What else could the cause be? But it was not just the physical, or the new hats, Jamie took the time to say that she was a good wife and worked hard, and someday he would give her more.

Two large nightcaps in hand, J.B. and John sat on the little porch of the house. The night was cold but dry. Each man sat under a crocheted afghan, and J.B. had another draped around his shoulders. On top of worries about noise, Lola preferred the cigar smoking to be done outside.

They talked softly, mindful of Katherine's room on the other side of the front wall. Mostly they sat mutely, listening to the industrial thrum.

"It never stops," John said. "The big machine of industry."

"I used to hate all that racket until I really sat here and listened to it. Then it became rhythmic and methodical, comforting even. Everything revolving in its circle. A calming metaphor for life."

"Jamie, I know you love to wax philosophical, but you've lost me. Our life is rarely rhythmic. It's all over the damned place. And it sure as hell ain't calm."

J.B. laughed.

"I'll give you that. Maybe it's more apropos to how we build a case. It's got me in mind of Louie Swearingen. You've worked your hind end searching for something helpful, and we are currently holding a couple of dog turds."

John started to protest, but his brother cut him off.

"Now, I'm not blaming you. I'm serious. You've looked at the victim, and Lord knows you've chased after our client and his missing alibis. That just means the answer lies with someone else involved."

John mouthed wary agreement, still feeling a bit scolded.

"I've spent more time on that case than I should have, Jamie."

"Look, I ate enough thin gravy when we were kids, John. I don't aim to do it now. And sure as shit not in court for the world to see."

Though he frequently had cause, John Duckworth did not bridle at his little brother often, but he felt the sting of criticism now.

"Damn it! What the fuck do you want from me? I've run after every lead we got. I wore out a pair of shoes looking for the girl he plugged the night of the..."

John caught himself and lowered his voice.

"...looking for the girl he was with the night of the killing."

"It was your idea, John. You were the one who wanted to go to Galveston to suss out a hoochie for Gillaspie. Well, that turned out to be right, didn't it? We didn't find one until you came up with the notion. So, you're missing the goddamn point. All I'm saying is I think we need to cast the net wider and hope we catch some luck."

John stared at his brother then took a calming inhale off his cigar waiting for his anger to subside before speaking.

"I thought we'd agreed to take the lifebuoy that'd been thrown to us."

Now it was J.B.'s turn for a thoughtful puff. When he spoke, there was resignation.

"Yes. You're right. That is the smart play, isn't it?"

The sheriff sat down to his stack of mail and lifted the opener from his desk. Almost every day's post brought a handful of pleas to release a woman's innocent son because there was no chance that her boy committed the crime for which he was accused. It was ludicrous, of course, but each letter was deeply personal and sincere. In all his years in law enforcement, Archie Anderson had never heeded any of those calls, but he read each letter through. He figured it was owed to these women, and it was always women. Their unflinching love for their boys earned them each some consideration.

As predictable as the letters were in sentiment, so were they disparate in writing craft. Some were rudimentary, the kind of work a first grade child might produce. Many were written by a third party owing to the illiteracy of the felon's mother. Every so often, Anderson received an entreaty constructed with simple, aching eloquence, but even those women with a poet's soul had their prayers rebuffed.

Archie pulled the third envelope from the pile and examined it a beat longer than usual. The address was printed in shaky block letters, not in script, and there was no return. He got the sense that it was a masculine hand. Usually men only wrote because they believed the county owed them money, and those came on printed billheads.

The Sheriff split the seam of the envelope and read. The single line of unsigned words drew him erect in his chair.

"You will find Mat Thorn in St. Landry Parish."

He examined the paper closely. Postmarked Port Barre. Clutching the envelope and sheet in his hand, Sheriff Anderson headed for the adjoining building and the district attorney's office.

Chapter 24

January 1903

Frank Prescott stretched his back to the left and then used the train car door to pull himself upright before he cleared onto the platform. He muttered what was for him an oath.

"Gol dang it."

Both he and Deputy Brooks Reed were nursing stiff backs and aching shoulders by the time they reached Opelousas, Louisiana. They had departed from Grand Central at 7:30 in the evening. Reed was hungry again by midnight, and he convinced a porter to retrieve two stale sandwiches from the closed café at Lake Charles during the stopover. They were among a knot of passengers dumped into the depot at Lafayette at 2:30 in the morning and had finally caught an Opelousas car after a few restless hours on an oak bench.

Prescott was a Texas Ranger sergeant of Company A. He did not drink and tried not to swear, nor was he any sort of pious churchgoer. He rolled his own cigarettes which was a feat in itself since his right arm was slow to respond after a knife fight at Liberty Hill some 20 years back. It was not useless, but he had been obliged to switch his gun hand to his left. His face was leathered, and he usually made his words count. Those who knew him best might say that Frank Prescott's heart carried an unpredictable fury and an ever-present melancholy.

By the time the Texans arrived, Main Street in Opelousas was bustling but not so much that grass was not sprouting at the edges of the mud street. People spoke of it as a growing town, but the wood framed buildings did not exactly smack of prosperity yet. For every beast loaded with sacks of feed and each wagon piled with bundles of lumber, there was also some shiftless sort in overalls leaning against a post.

The men found a café sandwiched between two millinery shops and ordered breakfast. The sausage was spicy and the eggs fresh, and they were rejuvenated enough to find the sheriff's office and introduce themselves and announce their purpose.

Marion Swords, the top lawman of St. Landry Parish, was a heavyset fellow sporting a full head of curly, greying hair. The bags under his eyes bore testament to the sheriff's late night, or truth be told, to a years-long string of late nights. He looked the new arrivals up and down, and leaned farther back in his chair before he spoke. His French accent was heavy on the ear.

"No shit? A real life Texas Ranger. Deshotels, you hear that?"

The deputy at the next desk gave a lazy nod. Prescott's gaze might have bored a hole in most men, but it did nothing to impress Marion Swords.

"So y'all got y'all's selves a colored fugitive?"

Swords fiddled through a small stack of papers and produced one that he waved at the Texans.

"See, y'all, we ain't as dumb over here in Louisiana as y'all might think, yeah. Now, I can tell you right now that you go wandering around on y'all's own, you going to end up stiffer than four week laundry. Gators done eat you up, you, and Mrs. Ranger will never hear tell of y'all again."

Reed knew he should look stern as the sheriff goaded them, but he could not stop himself from shifting uncomfortably. He was not a particular lover of reptiles, and he had heard old-timers talk of Louisiana giants that reached 20 feet long.

"I am happy to fix you y'all up, though," the sheriff finally said as he casually inspected a smudge on his loosened necktie. Swords then pulled out his pocket watch and checked the time as if his offer of help might soon expire.

"I got me a colored fellow. Ain't no jig in this parish so much as squat in the woods but that this boy can't tell you about it. Goddamn magic. I can't tell you how he does it. Some voodoo shit, yeah."

The room sat quiet as Frank Prescott mulled this information until Deputy Deshotels, who was leafing through a magazine, gave a loud suck of his teeth.

"All right," Prescott said. "How much is this magician going to cost us?"

"Old Spoons gets five dollars a day for tracking, which y'all going to need, and when you catch him, y'all owe him 15 dollars. You will catch your boy."

Swords punctuated the fee schedule with a chuckle.

"After that, y'all gentlemen on you own."

They found Spoons Bordelon leaned against the outside wall of an undertaking parlor taking a morning drowse. He was a small, ropy man whose appearance did not immediately inspire confidence, but he was all they had at the moment to fill in for their anonymous informant. With a down payment of two dollars shoved to the bottom of his pants pocket, Spoons offered assurances and promised he would be in touch before dawn.

He even pointed Reed and Prescott toward a cheap "White man's hotel" where they could get some rest. Since expenses came directly out of their reward money, the officers opted for a single room. They did not plan on staying there long.

The deputy leafed distractedly through a day-old newspaper from downstairs. A question for his traveling partner ruminated in his mind, but Reed did not want to disturb the man. The past two days they had spent together notwithstanding, the Ranger was still a bit intimidating, but when he returned from the outhouse, the deputy spoke up before Prescott could reimmerse himself in a book. Reed was wondering about joining the Rangers.

"Why the Sam Hill would you want to do that? State just let most of us go."

"I grew up reading the dime novels, I reckon. It seems like the life. I've been a deputy in Houston for eight years, and 90% of what we chase are drunks and dope fiends and complaints from old women."

"Most outlaws are drunks, boy. That's the way of the world."

Reed was briefly cowed, but regained his footing.

"It just feels like time for a change. I don't know."

Prescott had picked up his dog-eared book, and Reed took that as a signal that the conversation was over. When the old man then carefully laid it face down on the blanket, Brooks was briefly afraid that he had caused great offense. Instead, Prescott began talking, his face not directly at the deputy but seemingly focused on a fixed point near the door beyond him.

"Let me tell you how I ended up a Ranger. Back 17 years ago, I owned a little spread out past Lampasas. I went out to my corral one morning, and every last one of my horses was gone. Fence wasn't busted open. The gate latch had been lifted, and them mounts of mine had been stole during the night, slicker than goose dung. Judging by the boot and hoof prints, I surmised there was five of them bastards. Pardon my language. I told my wife I was going after them. We were scrabbling by on that scrub ranch. I needed those horses to work the place. On top of it, a man can't let such an affront pass, now can he?"

Prescott did not wait for an affirmation.

"I told her I'd be back soon, but I was gone better than four months. Had to rent a mount from my neighbor, on credit no less, but I found all five of them sons of perdition. Brought one in and killed the others. I recovered two of my four horses. Other pair had been sold off to heaven knows where. Not long after I got home, a Ranger name of Ira Aten come calling. He'd heard about me and my horses and wanted me to ride with him to hunt down a fellow murdered a rancher who lived next county over. I knew the old man who got himself killed, and almost didn't go on account of he was a sorry so and so, but with only two horses, well, me and the Mexican kid who helped me couldn't fully work my place. I figured the tracking pay would get me set again. Only took us three and a half weeks before we found the man swizzled to the gills behind a saloon at Pope's Crossing, New Mexico. Railroad had passed that little wide spot by, so there weren't nothing to do there but get drunk."

Prescott turned toward Reed for the first time and pointed his finger.

"The predictability of whiskey will get you every time. I got my money, but my wife had run off by the time I got back. Her I didn't bother to track. If she didn't want to stay, I wasn't going to make her. I sold off my land, took my two horses, and joined the Rangers."

Prescott stared at the print on the hotel room wallpaper so long that Reed assumed the story was over, but there was a final thought.

"You'll need lots of sand in your guts and no concerns about a home. There's some Rangers married, most of them maybe. But it ain't no life for the woman. If she's someone you like seeing now and again, you'd be best off staying put. I've only known you three days, son, but you don't strike me as Ranger material."

Prescott turned back to his book.

When the lawmen came downstairs around dawn, the hotel's owner gave Prescott a folded piece of paper and a shake of the head.

"Don't ask me. It was here when I woke up."

The note instructed them to meet Spoons Bordelon behind the city hall in the town of Melville. It also noted "6 hour ride."

"Well, shoot. We'd best get moving."

Fortified with a few hastily secured slices of bacon, a biscuit each, and a cup of coffee, the men stopped at the nearest livery where they rented three horses. Two for riding, and the other optimistically slated to carry back Mat Thorn.

Even though they attempted to hurry along, it was indeed past dinner time when they reined up at the Melville city hall. It was a modest building, to say the least. It looked remarkably like a cottage with a squat steeple plinked on top, but Bordelon was propped against the back side of, just as promised. A short roan with a splatter of corn spots across his right hindquarter was tethered beside him.

He informed them that he had located their quarry. Mat Thorn was part of a work camp repairing a levee along the Atchafalaya not far north. It was the reason for meeting in Melville. Spoons also cautioned that they would contend with swampy, jungle-like growth. Critters. Moccasins.

Brooks Reed tried to convince himself that these were more Acadian tall tales, but he steeled himself for the afternoon all the same.

Frank Prescott stepped toward a store across the way in search of food to carry with them, and the other two trailed just behind him. Spoons lingered just outside the open door.

"Y'all buy me a bag of them cracklings, it'd be much appreciated."

Brooks Reed snickered.

"We paying you five dollars a day. You can buy your own damn cracklings."

"Oh, no, sir. Most of that got to go back to the sheriff."

Frank Prescott, not more than six feet inside the building, pulled a nickel out of a small pouch and placed it on the worn counter.

"Nother bag of cracklings."

"We start at the ferry take us across to Pointe Coupee," Bordelon explained once they were outfitted with grub. "We can ride close down the Atchafalaya bank for a ways. Got to stick near the bank, though; get too boggy farther back. But we get to old Rougon's place, we cut in and follow the property line. We tie our horses back in the woods there. Last five mile or so, we walking."

Frank Prescott spit a shred of tobacco from his tongue as he eyed the Black man.

"I don't aim to leave my horse."

Bordelon chuffed a derisive breath.

"The way to that work camp's across Bayou Latenache. Twelve, sixteen foot deep."

The ranger dipped his head.

"I know how to swim a horse."

"Ain't the swimming. It's the walking. That mire like to suck your boots off as is. Horse get stuck in there sure. Y'all may ride him in, but you ain't going to ride him out. No, sir."

They crossed the river with Prescott paying the fare. Bordelon's attempts at conversation largely brought grunts from the older man, and Reed tried to follow suit. He did not wish to appear flighty in front of the Ranger. Finally, curiosity and general unease got the best of him.

"You some kind of musician? That why they call you Spoons?"

Bordelon considered the question thoughtfully.

"No, but that'd be some good talent to have."

The three men picked their way through the quaggy ground. Reed's waving at the swarms of bugs a near constant.

"Yeah, boss, mosquitoes is bad, but it's them gnats that put you in the crazy house."

Spoons laughed to himself and shook his head.

Prescott and Reed had held their coats and guns aloft as they kicked and paddled themselves across Bayou Latenache, but when they slogged onto dry land again, they each realized that they would put the jackets on again over drenched clothing. The last two or three miles was a large and uncomfortable arc gently taking them back toward the Atchafalaya.

Finally, Spoons held up his hand to halt. His voice was a whisper as he pointed to the west. Brooks Reed squinted to see the object of their attention.

"That dirt pit up yonder, everybody got to empty their wheelbarrow. Your boy be there eventually. Y'all going to stay put right there in that little mot of woods. See where I'm marking?"

Reed was confused.

"Where you going?"

Spoons looked at the deputy like he was crazy.

"Over yonder."

He pointed to the work area.

"You can't just waltz in there. It'll spook him. People round here know you."

"Some of them do. That's right. Ain't nobody say nothing. I'm just another colored man at the dirt pile."

There were too many openings in the scrub, and the lawmen were obliged to crawl the final quarter mile on hands and knees until they were secreted in their place. The signal was that the guide would remove his hat and replace it when Thorn walked to the pit.

The sun was behind the trees by the time Spoons lifted his battered Stetson and wiped sweat from his brow. He did not look like much, their prize. Clothes unchanged for many days, strength sapped from ten or twelve hours' labor, but even in the fading light, there was no missing the divot in Mat Thorn's cheek.

The lawmen burst from the brush, each with a Winchester pointed at him. On his side, the Ranger also wore a revolver. There was no fight, no words in anger. The men with guns held every card. Mat Thorn was captured.

As they untied their horses in the dusk, soaked, chafed, stung, and tired, Spoons Bordelon held out his hand to Prescott who looked at it with empty eyes. Bordelon grinned.

"I ain't asking you to shake, Mr. Ranger. I want my 15 dollars."

The Ranger almost betrayed his stoicism with a laugh, but he held fast as he counted the money out, minus the two dollar advance, and gave it to their guide who then mounted up and nosed the roan east.

"Y'all know the way from here. Don't help my reputation to ride out of the woods with no convict."

Mat Thorn had not said much of anything during the ride back to Opelousas. As he was handcuffed and securely tied to the back of a horse, he kept silent. Deputy Reed rode half a length ahead of him, and Sergeant Prescott close behind the bound man in the darkness, guns always at the ready. A half moon on a clear, cold night provided plenty of light to prevent hijinks. All three of the men shivered a bit in their still-damp clothes.

Even as Frank Prescott dug a gun barrel into his back on the depot platform and shoved him toward the baggage car, Thorn was mum. But once he had been pushed hard to the floor and was settled in with one wrist attached to a metal pole, Mat spoke up.

"What do I call you?" he asked Prescott.

"You don't need to call me nothing."

"Well, I ain't going to sit here for no 200 miles with my mouth shut."

The Ranger only stared at the rope lashing on a stack of trunks.

"Sergeant'll do," he finally said.

The exchange did not exactly open a floodgate of conversation among any of the three parties, and it was only after they had transferred in Lafayette and Thorn was again hooked up to a wall fixture that Brooks Reed turned to him. Daybreak had not yet come, and the rhythm of the tracks reminded all of them that they had missed a night of sleep. Prescott appeared to be dozing, but Thorn's eyes were open.

"You've had some run, boy," Reed said. "But we got you now. You going to hang for killing that constable. That could've been any one of us, so don't think we won't see you swing one way or another."

Thorn did not move, but Brooks was gathering a head of steam.

"Why'd you do it? What in holy hell did you think? That'd you'd get away with it? That we wouldn't find you?"

The prisoner mumbled something under his breath.

"What's that, boy? Speak up."

Mat's voice was firm but muted.

"Isgitt was a bad man. Still, I tried to walk away, but he just wouldn't let me."

The deputy was a bit incredulous.

"Wouldn't let you? He's the law. You do what the law says."

Thorn shook his head.

"A man just gets dog tired of eating some other man's shit."

"What's that mean?"

"You'd never understand it, deputy. You don't wake up every morning knowing you're some animal just going to be lifting and toting for whichever White man tells you to."

Reed sat up straighter and knitted his brow.

"That's your job, boy. It's what y'all were bred to do. That lifting and toting you talk about... y'all ain't cut out to be White folks."

Mat looked down at his outstretched legs and eyed his worn, muddy boots, then he turned back to Brooks Reed.

"I had a grandfather I knew real well. Born a slave at the Glenblythe Plantation in Washington County. Big spread of an operation. Better than 200 Negroes on that place in those days. I listened to the stories at his knee. He told me there was three kind of slaves - them that want to become White, and Lord knows I've seen a few pull that off. Then there's them who fight it every step of the way. Last bunch, the biggest bunch, is them who just get along the best they could. Things ain't changed, far as I see. I know it's the hardest road to go down, but I figure I took enough. Somewhere they made me that second kind of Negro, Deputy Reed. Y'all might see me hang, sure enough, but I'll die respecting myself."

Mat Thorn was brought back to the Harris County Jail and put into one of the maximum security cells. Brooks Reed checked him in and took him upstairs personally. Their exploits in Louisiana were front page news for the next two days. The usual journalistic embellishments were added to the capture.

The promised reward money had been eaten up by expenses. Each lawman was forced to make do with his regular stipend and a temporary boost to his reputation. Prescott shook Sheriff Anderson's hand and rode off without a word to Deputy Reed.

Over coming days, the night man took to rattling a baton against the metal of Thorn's cell during his rounds.

"Wake up boy. No sleeping on this job."

Twice in the first week Archie Anderson dispersed a knurl of drunk, angry men interested in supplying their own justice for Thorn. Truth was they were easily deterred. Breaking into the new jail was nigh on impossible without a ring of keys.

Two nights after the second incident, Thorn received a nasty cut across his forearm. A search of the cells failed to turn up any knives or shivs. The cell hammocks were chosen precisely to eliminate stray pieces of metal. For his part, the prisoner declined to name his attacker, and Anderson left it at that.

Despite rumors to the contrary that still festered in Houston's legal circles, the return of Mat Thorn alive did not affect the daily business of Duckworth & Fein. Would-be clients, most being people with grievous troubles, still warmed the wooden chairs lined along the front wall of the big room. The attorneys were busy with the current caseload and tried to avoid looking those hungry villains directly in the eye. J.B. Duckworth and Henry Fein sat insulated in their private offices, but the lawyers out front, along with jack-of-all-trades John Duckworth, were also expected to handle the job of teller and castle warden.

That was why Jed Posey kept his head down as he rose from his desk and walked to J.B.'s office in the back corner. As was the custom, he gave a compulsory knock on the doorframe and entered without waiting. Duckworth barely looked up.

"Jed."

"I may have something about the Swearingen case."

That earned a glance, but it was an annoyed one.

"That book's been read and reshelved. Money's all but in the bank. I need you pointed toward what's next."

"Yes, sir. That's how this came up in the first place."

Duckworth cocked his head to one side and motioned Posey to continue.

"We may finally have a lead on a witness, now it just comes down to us finding out who the son of a bitch is."

Posey offered what was for him a grin, but J.B. snapped at him hard.

"You don't know who it is? Well, no. Then it's not a lead, Jed. That's geology. You see that big stack of papers on every flat surface in this damned place? Those are other cases. And the firm sure as hell can't spare you running around town with a shovel looking for the right grain of sand to turn over."

Chapter 25

Trial preparation for March was often a bear. February was an off month for Harris County, but the annual March pile of criminal cases was down to more than that. Only October, which ended the long July through September recess, was busier. One long ago wag surmised that "Texas summers are so hot that scofflaws save their killing for winter."

In addition to the stacked work, there was an uncharted reef. As pleased as J.B. was to see the back side of Judge Gillaspie, his replacement was an unknown. Fermin Runnels had moved from Huntsville where he had been D.A. for Walker and Madison counties to stand for the soon to be vacated judgeship. He was seemingly content and successful in his backwater role when Gillaspie put himself forward for Congress. With a hurried glance at the tea leaves, Runnels decided to move to Houston and position himself for a prominent seat on the bench.

The man had a definite leg up. Runnels was from a connected family. His father's cousin was the rabidly secessionist governor who battled Sam Houston over the question of union. That more famous Runnels had even favored the full return of the international slave trade almost half a century after it was banned. When young Fermin Runnels came of age to enter the beleaguered Confederate army at the end of 1863, he was handed a job on the staff of Prince John Magruder. Not only well out of danger, but indoctrinated under a general who later fled to Mexico rather than accept defeat. If Duckworth longed for an open minded man on the bench, the Runnels family history was not encouraging.

Duckworth himself had gone against Fermin Runnels as district attorney three times and considered him fair. J.B. won all three of those cases and sensed no ill feelings, but he had also seen several perfectly agreeable human beings turn into Simon Legree once they donned a black robe. Scuttlebutt from those who knew him better often included words such as moody and unpredictable. The tastiest juice was a wild rumor that had Fermin killing a man in a dispute over a lover when he was young.

It was tough to picture Fermin Runnels as a Lothario these days. He was 57 years old when he took the bench in Houston, a sturdy fellow with but a fringe of sandy hair. He kept himself clean shaven. The most unsettling feature of the man was that he had one blue eye and one brown.

J.B. broached the subject of their new jurist with Harris Peterson over a drink shared in Peterson's office early one afternoon. Seeing as how Harris' clients were well-off folk who were not prone to criminal impulses, at least not the violent kind, his digs were notably better than J.B.'s walled off corner. Harris also kept something closer to banker's hours, and, consequently, if J.B. dropped in for a visit, it was usually around midday to discuss matters of their mutual investment properties. Such was the case today.

Once the personal finances were covered, Duckworth asked about the new judge.

"You know more chatter than any lawyer alive. What's the insight on Runnels?"

"You mean did he really put three pistol balls into some hapless dandy whose trousers were slung over a chair back?"

"Oh. Come on," J.B. scoffed. "That's dubious even for the old hens of the local bar."

"No. I believe it is true. The woman with the elevated knees is still around. Married to the most prominent banker in Mexia."

"Does she still accept deposits?"

Peterson threw back his head and roared loud enough for those in the outer offices to take note. That tawdry gossip was not Duckworth's concern, though.

"I was wondering if Runnels will shoot straight on this Swearingen business when it comes before him. The threats are still hanging over my head, Harris. Or I should say they're renewed since the law dragged Mat Thorn back alive."

Peterson had been much less enigmatic once Shelby Arnold made his scheme known to J.B. on Christmas night. Duckworth felt sure his friend would answer him true, and he put the fine point on it.

"I'm hoping that because Runnels is new to Houston, he may not be tainted by any pressure."

Peterson took a thoughtful sip before responding.

"On the other hand, our honorable Congressman's district takes in Walker County, so for all I know, they're thick as two ticks in a corset."

Duckworth laughed at the witticism but did not take solace in it.

The prosecution in Swearingen's case had been thrown off balance by Isgitt's killing, but they still had an unshakeable eye witness in Andy Green. The district attorney and his assistant also collected an ample stock of witnesses who were ready to testify that Louie was a lowdown drunkard with a proclivity for violence. They could back up Green's story that Johnson Montgomery had earlier run ins with Swearingen. Those were the known witnesses, but John Duckworth's sources believed that there was more. They had yet to get a handle on who. It would not be a long case that Lea presented, but it was notably stronger than the defense.

Still, there was time. Swearingen was low on the docket and would not be called for a couple more weeks, maybe three. John knew that he must redouble his efforts. It was a tight position, but it was not novel. He was a lone investigator, and though the lawyers did their own digging, John Duckworth had played the role of cavalry many times, riding to the rescue in the eleventh hour to neutralize the attack. It was just that this time, he did not know where to look.

Andy Green had not wavered, but neither was he sleeping right. It was well over a year since the night of the shooting, and he was still prone to waking at an unknown noise. Work was the same as was drinking wine with his friends. Laughter came more readily, and specific memories of his buddy Johnson started to glimmer away. The part that kept Andy awake of a night was not about his lost friend, it was only about that friend's demise.

For weeks after her visit, Andy was consumed with thoughts of Johnson Montgomery's daughter. He should do something for her, but he had no idea what that might be. She and her man looked to be doing fine. It was over two months later that he came to terms with the fact that he wanted to fill a void for the young woman, to be the father that his friend Johnson had not been. But what did Andy know about being someone's daddy? Not a thing.

He finally composed a letter filled with rather meaningless platitudes. It was painful just to put those thoughts on paper. Not knowing her address, or even if she lived in Beaumont proper, he figured to send it to the post office there as general delivery mail. Only when he went to address the small envelope did he realize he had not the slightest idea how to spell her last name. He even debated with himself as to what that name was. In the end, he carefully wrote "Helen Montgomery." Two days later, it dawned on Andy that her mama had likely taken another man's name at some point. The poor girl's surname was a tangle. There was never an answer to his Quixotic letter, and Andy guessed that it was moldering in a cubbyhole at the Beaumont post office.

Gradually, thoughts of inserting himself in Helen's life faded. They were replaced by new fears, and that skittishness, those jumps, only increased the closer the murder of Johnson Montgomery got to trial.

Judge J.K.P. Gillaspie was out of office after his run for Congress had come up short in the Democratic primary, but it did not mean that he was gone from

Houston. His presence remained a small concern to Duckworth until happy rumors began to gather strength.

J.B. was well in his cups when he noticed Gillaspie and two other men seated at a table at Lang's. He emptied the glass before him, motioned for another, and, while it was being drawn, stepped from the bar to the dining room.

"Mister Gillaspie,..."

Duckworth emphasized the civilian form of address as he hovered by the table.

"I heard you were joining a firm in Dallas. Sincere congratulations for escaping this city you must disdain ever so much."

Gillaspie sniffed at him but did not speak. The former judge turned back to his conversation. J.B. put a hand over his heart in mock pain.

"Woe is me for I have no pedestal from which to fall."

There was a momentary stiffening in Gillaspie's back. His reflex to engage passed quickly, however, and Duckworth was left to smile to himself as he walked back to his next round.

Chapter 26

March 1903

Duckworth & Fein anticipated four of their Harris County murder cases to go to trial before the month was finished. All were to be handled by J.B. Another eight alleged killers would be defended by either Henry or Sonny with the expectation that two or perhaps three would go before a jury. Scattered within the hectic March caseload were several dozen lesser crimes. The firm's reputation continued to improve, and the client list reflected it. In private thoughts that he dared not share for fear of jinx, J.B. imagined enough business to justify another clerk within a year.

With the first Monday falling on the second day of the month, March jumped out to a gallop like a race horse from the gate. The Sunday session in the big room, a planning discussion that generally ran all afternoon, began early and finished late. Henry Fein was due in court at Caldwell for the opening gavel, and he ducked out around five to catch his train. He was seeing to a deadly affray between machinists at a seed oil mill.

The remaining three attorneys reviewed cases until well after sundown. As usual, the conference produced disagreement and occasional brutal commentary on how best to handle a given client. They were, after all, lawyers. If a dispute over strategy lingered, the name partners were given the last word. That generally meant that J.B. was the final arbiter. The others accepted that fact. The Duckworth record at trial gave him the right.

When the conference finally broke up, the weary men locked the doors and said their brief goodbyes on the sidewalk. The Duckworth Brothers offered to stand the other two to a first round next door at Yadon's. Jed Posey, not a sociable type like the others, quickly demurred and strode west on Congress Avenue. The others watched him go.

"What do you imagine he does at night?" John mused.

Sonny Schlottmann did not break a smile as he answered.

"Is there a library open at this hour?"

In spite of the joke, Schlottman reminded the others that he had a long Monday ahead. He would handle several motions in town before he boarded the nighttime cars for Columbus. His first trial of the month started Tuesday in Colorado County. The Duckworths were left alone to have a few drinks before they went their separate ways.

Sonny wended his way south and east toward his rooming house on McKinney, but the thirst rose in him, too. He decided on a night cap at Tony Lazio's little saloon on Texas near LaBranch. One drink to unwind, though he had little doubt that he could fall off to sleep within the hour.

It was not a big place, Lazio's, so it was hard to miss the loud group carousing at the far end of the bar. They were having a grand time, swapping ribald jokes and challenging one another to drain their glasses. Louie Swearingen's fuzzy head rose just a tad above his companions'.

Even though he knew that a counsel of caution was in order, Sonny was too tired to confront him. It took Louie more than ten minutes to recognize his attorney despite standing less than 15 feet away. Squinting against the blur, he offered an enthusiastic wave. Sonny could only muster a weak smile.

J.B. learned of the encounter the following morning, and though he, too, had a busy day in court, he summoned Louie to the office Monday evening by telling Charlie Dixon to keep pounding on the door of Swearingen's flat until somebody answered or the law ran him off. It took nothing so drastic. Louie followed the instructions with punctuality.

Schlottmann leaned against the inner office doorframe to watch the scalding, and J.B. did not take long to spur up.

"In a couple weeks, I'll be done with you. But you, you sorry sap, you've got to live with yourself for the rest of your life. I doubt if that's very long. At least your wife'll be shed of you. In short, son, I called you here to say that as things stand now, you're fucked, and you need to start taking that seriously. If you show up in court with so much as a whiff of barley or a shadow under one eye, they'll stretch your neck."

J.B. knew full well that the epithet of "son" rankled Louie Swearingen, and he used it deliberately, but it failed to provoke a rise. Instead, Louie hung his head like a chastened child. He muttered an apology and looked to Duckworth for more.

"That's it. I got nothing else for you. Now, get. I've got more important things to do than nursemaid you."

They watched the dazed Louie Swearingen cross the office and go out the door before Sonny turned to J.B..

"Stretch his neck? That was not a bit harsh?"

"It's the result that was promised."

Duckworth spoke those words low and into the ether, then he turned to face Schlottmann. He even managed to make the ends of his moustache rise in a smile.

"I've got three more murder cases ahead of him. You know the policy. I don't intend to see any of my clients die. It's horrible for business."

Opening Mondays were spent on arraignments and motions, requests for bail. Some of the court's tasks passed in a flash, others dragged on and tried the patience. On display was a mix of stoicism, anguish, and tears. Litigants plodded in and out of the big courtroom all day on an opening Monday, but after that, things got down to critical business.

The first case on the docket in Judge Runnels court was that of Mat Thorn. No one was prepared to say how many strings were pulled to place it into that spot. Both newspapers spent two column inches to remind the public that the trial was starting on Tuesday the 3rd, but they need not have bothered. The court pews would not be empty.

There were always curious spectators for a murder proceeding. Nearly half a dozen were ghoulish old women who tatted their doilies and tutted their disapproval at every lurid detail. The same certainty held true for the handful of newspaper stringers, but when it was a trial of any magnitude, the crowd on the benches was amplified.

This particular trial merited extra interest for yet another reason – James Duckworth had decided to take the case. The lawyer tried his best to keep the thing quiet. He conferenced with Thorn at the jail well after dark, and he journeyed to Harrisburg to meet with and accept cash payment from Reverend Branch lest someone observe the man coming again to Duckworth's office. Despite those best efforts, news shot through Houston legal circles like lightning. The thunderclap that followed was occasionally just as loud.

The day after it became apparent that the game had been compromised, an unsigned note on cream rag paper arrived at the Congress Avenue office. It read simply: "Big mistake, Duckworth." The source of the implied threat was impossible to trace. All manner of strangers accosted J.B. on the street to let him know precisely what they thought about his defense of a cop-killer, and a Black one at that. Their words were never polite.

It was not the first time Duckworth had defended someone who shot an officer of the law. Many, if not most, of his clients were unpopular. Such was the plight of lawyers on his side of the courtroom, but J.B.'s belief in the notion that everyone deserved a good advocate was unshakeable. As always, his only worry was how the pressure from others would affect the verdict.

Runnels did not do him any favors. The judge shot down several avenues of questioning J.B. tried on prosecution witnesses. When District Attorney Lea, teeth figuratively clinched in seriousness over this outcome, rose to object to a Duckworth tactic, Runnels backed him more than three-quarters of the time.

In spite of it all, James Duckworth managed to portray Constable Eddie Isgitt as a man predisposed to violence against Negroes, and he did it without any Black witnesses save the defendant himself. Runnels saw to that. There were just enough White men who had watched Isgitt savagely kick and pistol whip Thorn on the night of the killing. They also testified that the lawman was the first to pull a gun.

There was no way on God's Earth that an acquittal could be had in this trial, but Duckworth saved Mat Thorn from death. He was sentenced to 15 years. There were loud hoots at the verdict. Archie Anderson was in the courtroom when it was read, and he held a rare glare on the lawyer who was generally a friend. When angry deputies tightened cuffs on Thorn and shoved him roughly toward the portal to the cells, the convict did not exactly smile, but he managed a tiny nod of thanks at his attorney. The next few days and weeks would not be easy on the man, but he had a chance to survive them.

One of J.B.'s immutable rules was "always celebrate a victory and drown a defeat." When he raised his first glass with John and friends that evening, it was definitely in celebration. This was not a usual case, and Duckworth felt that he had emerged on top. Pushed down at the bottom of his thoughts, though, was a fear for the worst when Louie Swearingen came to trial.

Chapter 27

Fourteen days after the Mat Thorn verdict, James Duckworth poured over his notes on Louie Swearingen. Some were tidily composed and other scraps in the folder were scribblings hastily jotted when a new idea presented itself. They were hard to keep track of, these random bits, but the act of writing something helped fix it in his mind.

The sun was set on this Wednesday, and, knowing that he would work for another three or four hours, J.B. was developing thoughts of ordering a sandwich from Yadon's downstairs. Twice now his rumbling gut had suggested urgency.

Swearingen was his final murder trial of the month. There were two dozen cases for other serious criminal offenses, but it was always the murders that made a defense man's reputation. After Thorn, Duckworth had won two acquittals for murder defendants, at least the way he saw it. One was a not guilty verdict. Two workers at the car wheel factory had an ongoing feud, but when one of them stove in the back of the other's skull with a crowbar, Duckworth called it self-defense. The jury agreed.

The other murder case was a plea bargain on the morning of the trial. A storekeeper had stabbed his wife to death. He was certain that he had been cuckolded. She was giving her attentions to a neighborhood dandy, he believed, a gambler, at that. On the woman's final day, Duckworth's client swore he saw the debaucher on the outside stairs that led to the residence above the store. He laid aside a sale and burst into the apartment. He found his buxom wife napping in a thin, clingy gown, or perhaps feigning sleep. Though there was no other man about, the storekeeper was insistent that he smelled lingering cigar smoke. With his wife screaming protests, he took up a kitchen knife and plunged it into her eight times. Duckworth got the charge reduced to manslaughter. The client was sentenced to four years at Huntsville or whatever P-farm they shuttled him off to, but the attorney could count it as a victory.

J.B. refocused on the contents of the folder. Still precious little sat before him, but he had certainly won cases with less. If the evidence was not on his side, he still had guile and charm. He just needed a jury susceptible to those attributes.

One thing that had not yet come across J.B.'s desk were any more repercussions or threats from the Congressman. That was certainly truer for Duckworth than for J.V. Lea.

The prosecutor walked across the street from the courthouse in the late afternoon on the eve of the trial. He had been summoned for an audience with Shelby Arnold a few days prior, and the situation was gnawing at him. Lea seated himself glumly in a visitor's chair without waiting for an invitation. Duckworth welcomed him anyway.

"Evening, J.V. Isn't this like the groom seeing the bride's dress before the wedding day? Could bring bad luck for you."

Lea did not rise to the levity.

"J.B., I've gone back and forth for four days on whether or not to tell you a word of this. I don't owe you a thing under the law. And God knows I'm happy to use anything I can to beat you. Somehow, though, this just doesn't feel right. I count you as a friend, and you ought to know what's arrayed against you."

Duckworth scratched a spot behind his ear.

"Well, it sounds ominous."

Lea sighed, repositioned himself in the chair, and rubbed at his face.

"Arnold flat told me that he had someone lined up to run against me if I failed to teach you a lesson."

J.B. laughed.

"Teach me a lesson?"

"Win the case."

Lea's tone showed exasperation.

"If I don't win this case to show you that it is better to play ball, then he and his fat cats will put their money and weight behind another lawyer for D.A. You know how that works."

"Ah."

Duckworth had fretted over what might happen to him, but it had never crossed his mind that anyone else's livelihood might be jeopardized. He was not often without an immediate rejoinder, but for the moment he sat quietly. Eventually, Lea gave a rueful chuckle.

"I'm not expecting you to roll over like a porch hound, but I wanted to let you know all the same. If Arnold and his cronies are gunning for me, they sure as shit aren't done with you. So, watch your back."

"The man got 15 years. What the hell do they want?"

This time J.V. Lea snorted in earnest.

"They wanted the boy dead. But you know as well as I do that it has nothing to do with the verdict. You showed them up. You denied them. People like that are not used to some upstart like you taking their candy, J.B."

Duckworth grinned then moved toward the sideboard and his bottle of Old Taylor.

Jury selection for the Swearingen trial happened on a bright Thursday morning. It was the sort of March day Texans crowed about to their northern relatives, if they had any. Sixty-eight degrees and sunlight streaming through the fourteen-foot tall windows despite the double banks of polished shutters. Mockingbirds and cardinals sang from the ash tree on the courthouse lawn almost loud enough to be a distraction.

Duckworth had been eyeballing the panel of 70 men for faces that were familiar from downtown bars. His client was a likeable sort, and the lawyer knew that the best men he could choose were those who had bellied up to Louie Swearingen's bar. To a drinking man, an attentive bartender held the keys to relaxation and the magic wand that might wave away his problems, at least for a few hours. They could be as much an angel of mercy as a nursemaid with her cool, soothing cloth.

Sadly for J.B., the district attorney frequented the same downtown bars, and the same faces that seemed recognizable to Duckworth were the first nine strikes made by Lea.

In his observations from the first three passes for jury selection in Fermin Runnels' court, J.B. had concluded that the judge was not one to brook bellyachers seeking to be dismissed from jury duty. That also did not please the defense man. A juror who desperately wanted to be done with the process was, more often than not, someone who held the opinion that the sheriff would not have arrested a person if they were not guilty of the crime. Those jurors saw their lives as too busy and important for either civic service or nuanced reasoning.

When Runnels declined to excuse a farmer who pled that his wife was at home deathly ill with a cancer in what he described as her "lady parts," Duckworth cringed. The ruddy-faced man returned to his seat so filled with fury that his eyes welled with tears.

The prosecution wanted a jury of God-fearing men, those from the farther flung reaches of the county. He asked every last one of them to share their views on temperance. J.B. was forced to use all of his paltry strikes to weed out the men who spoke most frequently of Satan or the demon rum, though several slipped through. Duckworth's suggestions that such men were predisposed against someone who served liquor were shot down by Judge Runnels one after another.

"The court assumes that a man who knows his Bible can act with fairness," the judge said the first time J.B. made an attempt to strike with cause. After that, Runnels merely said "Denied."

Seven of the men on the final panel were farmers or ranchers in communities that ran from Gum Island to Sheldon. That included the poor fellow with the dying wife. They were most decidedly not people Duckworth would have chosen in this circumstance. There were two railroad workers, and it did not escape

J.B.'s notice that those men shared a profession with the victim. Two store clerks, one perpetually sour-faced, and a burly blacksmith from Almeda completed the panel.

When the twelve selections were sworn, Judge Runnels admonished them to be on good behavior and make up their own minds based on the evidence presented, not on the opinions of their friends. His final statement before adjournment for the afternoon was exactly what Duckworth feared.

"The trial will begin promptly at 9 A.M. tomorrow morning. Be in your seats by quarter till."

Opening arguments came on a Friday. Many judges, especially those who could find some leeway in their dockets, were loath to start a long trial on Friday. Even if there was a Saturday court session, Duckworth despised the practice. It robbed him of all momentum. Moreover, it left the jurors loose to roam among the town's blather, giving a chance for any manner of crank to gain his ear. Duckworth wanted each juror held close to the breast once a trial started, so near that he alone could whisper what to think.

Fermin Runnels, though, was new to the bench. He had not learned the rhythms of the big city courts, and was no doubt alarmed to see the calendar of days turn to the twenties with a stack of business still to be transacted. He would learn in time, perhaps, but he was not there yet. When one trial ended in Judge Runnels' courtroom that March, the next one was expected to begin forthwith, whether J.B. liked it or not.

The gallery was filled. Nora Swearingen sat directly behind her husband, and it pained her that she could not be closer to hold his hand. Her mother and sister Mary flanked her. No other relatives of the defendant were in court for the first day of trial.

Though a few of Johnson Montgomery's friends would have liked to attend the trial, they were welcome in the courtroom only as a witness or defendant. They could also not leave work.

The way James B. Duckworth saw it, a defense lawyer's job in an opening statement was to lay out the case before the jury point by point but without giving away the magic, as if showing a spinning top to a child. That meant alibis, alternate theories, other motives, and a fair-sized dollop of condemnation aimed toward all the people involved with the prosecution. Oft times for Duckworth, he treated it as if the child was in on the joke. He saw jurors being entertained by the defendant's lawyer as a key to winning.

The first of those options was a blind alley where Louie Swearingen's case was concerned. It had been a bane to the entire office, but in the 18 months since the crime was committed, no one connected with Duckworth & Fein had succeeded in establishing an alibi for their client. That was saying quite a bit for a defense firm long suspected of stretching the blanket when it came to the finer details.

As for alternate theories, they were a favorite of J.B., but the most ready-made one of his career had already been rejected. If any second thoughts crossed his mind, though, he never spoke them out loud. Still, he dropped a mention of the underhanded business, even it did fly over the heads of the jury.

"There were people who wanted me to blame this killing on somebody else, if I'm being honest. And I'm always honest."

Duckworth paused for a moment to scan the courtroom pews.

"I decided not to pursue that approach for a very simple reason. Louie Swearingen didn't kill anybody. He is the son of a long time lawman, a product of a good and honest Texas farming community."

He looked at the jury box for emphasis, particularly picking out the farmers as he delivered that last sentence. Then he dug in.

When his own case was weak, he could ill afford to let the prosecution's line of attack get a toe hold in the minds of jurors. There were things that he might reserve for his closing in a different situation, and he would no doubt reiterate them when the time came. By closing arguments, he would know precisely what he needed to combat, and the last thing a lawyer wanted was to give the other side a good idea. Yet, Duckworth was sure he needed to be fast out of the gate, so he set to dismantling the points he expected to be hearing.

"Now, Mr. Lea over yonder is hellbent on winning this case."

Duckworth raised his hands in fair admission.

"It's his job, and he's good at it. I've known Mr. Lea for a long time, and he is a fine man but competitive. I'm not saying he'd cheat, but if he was behind in a footrace, well, let's just say I've seen some other lawyers trip on accident."

Lea did not smile at the gibe. Fermin Runnels fingered at his gavel. Opening arguments generally came with a cooper's barrel full of latitude, but the judge was weighing Duckworth's words all the same.

"He's going to bring out a witness…," J.B. told the jury. "…Who will swear on his very soul that he saw my client shoot his friend."

As much as a good defense attorney liked to humanize his client by repeating his name, J.B. thought it bad form to utter the name too close to words like shoot or murder.

"This witness of theirs may be firmly convinced in his mind of what he saw, but he will also tell you that it was pitch dark. We'll want to find out how long he saw whoever it was that fired the shot. I'm as anxious to know that as y'all are, but I can tell you it wasn't long. So, we'll all pay rapt attention when we get to that answer. I know this – remembering details about someone you see from a distance on a dark night is not easy."

Duckworth held up both index fingers.

"I'm going to ask each one of you to shut his eyes for a second."

They were slow to respond, and after ten of fifteen second, fewer than half of the twelve jurors took him up on the offer, but the lawyer could only wait so long. He went ahead.

"Now think about that woman with the big hat on the center aisle in this courtroom. What color is that hat? What color is her dress? How about her hair? Go ahead, open your eyes."

Often when J.B. tried this trick in his opening or closing, he observed jurors shaking their heads or muttering to themselves. This group of men were hardened against such frivolities, so he reminded them that eyewitnesses were notoriously unsure and often wrong, then Duckworth forged on.

"Here's another thing – once they make it past that witness, Mr. Lea's case will drop like a barrel over Niagara Falls. He will be out of things to say, though he will no doubt keep talking. The fancy legal term for that phenomenon is 'not having doodly.'"

The dry goods clerk loosed a silent chuckle, but seeing he was alone, he quickly retreated to his sober expression.

"As far as I know, the prosecution doesn't have a gun that they can wave around and tell you 'This is the murder weapon.' Now, that's important in a murder case. Before you convict a man of murder, you ought to know exactly how he committed the crime. If the prosecutor can't answer that question, then I'd say it's likely they've got the wrong man."

J.B. took a deep, audible breath to signal a new point.

"Why do I say that? Why is that so momentous? Because you can't convict a person of a crime if there is a reasonable doubt. That means if any reasonable man like you twelve on the jury here can foresee a circumstance where someone else committed the crime, then you have to let the defendant go. And if the prosecution can't tie a weapon to the man they're trying to hang, I'd say that creates a reasonable doubt."

Duckworth paced two steps away then turned back toward the jury to drive home a last thought on the matter.

"Louie Swearingen doesn't even own a gun. And I promise you the police checked."

J.B. noted that two of the jurors looked at the defense table when he mentioned his client's name. It was not much, but he welcomed any sign that they saw Louie as a real person.

"All right, let's think about the why here."

He drew out the word "why" as if it had four syllables.

"They're going to tell you that Louie Swearingen, an amiable young man who is fast with a grin and a cool glass of beer, went halfway across the county because he suddenly recollected some fellow he had a run in with half a dozen years ago. Does that make sense to any of you fellows?"

None of the twelve men moved a muscle or twitched an eye.

"From what I hear of the man who got shot, fifteen minutes with him would make Job give him a blinker. He never shut his gob. Bone box rattling a mile a minute and unshakably right on every point. Well, that's just down-right annoying. It wears awful thin."

J.B. pointed a finger at the jury box.

"You all know someone like that, and after a pint or two, for those of you so disposed, you all want to give him the rib tickler. No, sir, there is no motive for my client that two or three hundred other men didn't have but more so. Other men who had more recent affrays. That is just pure common sense."

Duckworth had one final point to make. To do so he stepped even closer to the jurors, near enough that he could shake hands with a few, if he so desired.

"Gentlemen,..."

The left end of his moustache rose impishly.

"...And I use that term without knowing y'all very well. Aside from the fact that Louie Swearingen did not shoot anybody, there is one prime point that you need to remember throughout this trial, and especially don't forget it when you get into that jury room. The law never looked at anybody else. They made up their mind on the night of the killing. Took one look at the body, talked to one person, and pinned it ever after on my client. That's not the way things ought to work. To ensure justice, you need the prosecution to act like your wife in a jewelry store, take a good gander at every piece in the cases."

A raucous laugh enveloped the courtroom, and even Judge Runnels smiled down at his desk top. Duckworth accepted his adulation, but was happiest to see one or two jurors finally shaking their heads just before he delivered his zinger. He needed that foundation to build on.

Back at the office that evening, a Western Union boy leaned his bicycle against the high sidewalk and mounted the stairs from the street. All of the lawyers were hard at work at their desks. The busy March docket was winding down. The small town courts had largely concluded their business for the session, but there was still another week of full court days left in Harris County. When the Western Union waif came through from the corridor, only Sonny Schlottmann looked up. Hearing J.B.'s name, he pointed the boy toward the back corner office without comment.

After he fished out a nickel for the waiting lad, J.B. tore open the envelope. He pursed his lips and nodded once to himself. John Duckworth may just have tracked down a true ace in the hole witness up at Dayton. J.B. read the two-word wire a second time. "Unxpctd luck."

Chapter 28

Louie looked fresh in court on Monday morning. His gray checkered suit was crisply laundered, and his shirt collar was new. Nora had splurged for a shiny new watch fob to make her husband look prosperous. Taking in the overall appearance of his client, Duckworth, arriving from his office across the street, greeted him with a terse smile.

"Morning. I must say you look ready to go."

"I've gone without drink for three days."

J.B. raised an eyebrow.

"That'll make a good impression with these pious jurors."

"Truth be told Mr. Duckworth, I'm looking forward to letting one go."

The lawyer gave Louie a patronizing pat on the forearm.

"We need to win the case first, son. There's not a lot of whiskey in jail."

Louie did not get a chance to look crestfallen, but his expression turned tense nonetheless as he watched his father come through the heavy courthouse doors. Without comment, the young man tucked his chin and sought his place at the defense table. Nora offered only a wan smile before following.

Big Lou Swearingen was in for his son's trial albeit a few days late. The morning train carried him in from Sealy. The marshal glad handed his way across the teeming lobby. He greeted a passing bailiff like an old friend and seemed to know a few other bystanders, or at least gave the politician's impression that he did.

His hearty slap on the back immediately annoyed J.B. The elder Swearingen maintained a smile in his eyes as he squeezed Duckworth's hand, though as a lawman, he had formed an indelibly negative opinion of all defense attorneys many years earlier.

"So, you're my boy's lawyer."

"So, you're Louie Senior."

The left corner of Swearingen's mouth lifted in defiance of the words that came out.

"No, I'm Louis. But you can call me Big Lou."

"Mmm-hmm."

The big lawman opened with general small talk then pivoted to platitudes about concern for his son's well-being. On most days, Duckworth would ignore such things. He dealt with untruth and exaggeration constantly and had long ago learned to choose his battles. Thousands of bald-faced remarks lay unanswered at Duckworth's feet, but something in the breezy manner rubbed him wrong.

With the height differential, J.B. was obliged to look up to meet the taller man's gaze, but he was far from intimidated. Without betraying any specifics, he made it clear that the strained nature of the relationship was known to him, but Big Lou plowed ahead with conversation that suggested everything was rosy between him and his boy. Finally, the lawyer summed up his thoughts.

"So, it's nothing personal. You were just embarrassed by him?"

Duckworth did not wait for an answer. He merely headed toward the courtroom.

The prosecution case was methodical and afforded few variations from what the lawyers at Duckworth & Fein discussed at the previous afternoon's conference. J.V. Lea started by painting Louie Swearingen as a bad drunk, a man known to be mean. Though he had carefully placed temperance men in the box, this was a drinker's case, and the prosecutor hoped that the jurors would hone in on the evils of John Barleycorn.

To achieve this point, Lea called three witnesses. He opened with a pinch-faced older man who had lived at the boarding house on Hardy Street. It was a shrewd move to start with someone who could not be painted as a wet. After establishing the man's connection, Lea got quickly to the meat of the testimony.

"Mr. Perkins, what were your observations of Louie Swearingen's behavior when he lived at your address?"

"He was a drunk!"

The old man was hard of hearing after years of factory work, and as a result, his words were unnaturally loud.

"Can you give us more specifics?" Lea asked.

"He come home late, loud as all get out. Singing to himself, bounding off the walls, and if you hollered for him to pipe down, he was apt to snarl like some hound and bite your damn hand off."

Judge Runnels looked askance at the profanity but said nothing.

Lea elicited a few more stories from the old man, the worst of which was the tale of Louie urinating on the front steps of the neighboring building. When the district attorney was through with his questions, Perkins pushed himself up from the chair with a heavy grunt, but Duckworth stopped him.

"I had a couple of questions, too, Mr. Perkins, if that fits your schedule."

The old man sat back down with a loud harrumph.

"Can you tell us about the other residents there on Hardy Street?"

"What about them?"

"How was their behavior? Did you get along with them?"

The old man waved his hand to swat away the very thought.

"Bah! Bunch of drunks and ne'er-do-wells, the lot of them."

If there was any code within the fraternity of bartenders, the next two men belied it. First was a former barman from the Cabinet. He related four separate instances that he recalled of Swearingen in fistfights at that establishment. At least some were instigated by Louie, and each resulted in expulsion from the premises.

"Why didn't you ban him altogether?"

The witness looked at Lea as if he'd dropped a few marbles.

"Well, he was fine when he came back the next time, and he had good money."

With different jurors, Duckworth might have stressed how many times Louie drank at the Cabinet without incident, but that was not the play here. The best J.B. could get out of the witness in rebuttal was that dozens of other patrons were involved in occasional scraps. Even with that, two or three men in the box were already showing a visible distaste.

The next witness up was Sam Carr, the friend-turned-extortionist from the Turf. At the defense table, Louie braced himself for mention of the dubious alibi, but it was not forthcoming. Instead, Lea led Carr through a painstaking description of the nightly transformation he observed in Louie Swearingen. He was "a model bartender at the Turf" and "well-liked by everyone," Carr told the court with a dramatic injection of pity, but when the two were out on the town after work hours, things regularly took a darker turn.

Dripping faux concern, Carr offered a half hour of specifics. In the most damning of the stories, Louie broke a man's nose as he beat him into a bloody mess on a dirty barroom floor.

"I've no doubt he would have killed him, if his friends hadn't pulled him off," Carr said.

"What prompted that fight?" Lea asked him.

"Nothing of significance. It never is, I'm afraid. Always something trivial."

In the front row of spectators, Nora Swearingen kneaded her fingers and stared at her lap. Two rows behind, her father-in-law's gaze bored a hole in the back of his son's head.

On cross-examination, Duckworth asked Carr if he and the defendant were still friends. The answer came with ironic brightness.

"Chummy as can be, me and Louie."

"Well, we shall hear what he has to say about that."

From his seat, Louie Swearingen smoldered with rage.

The D.A. next moved on to a trio of Black men testifying about some specific cases of trouble when Louie worked in Harrisburg at the small Anchor bar. They were railroad men who drank with Johnson Montgomery and saw him most every day. Each was called in turn, and a bailiff pointed them through the courtroom gallery where they were not welcome to sit. Lea, hedging his bets with the jury, started his questioning by making clear that the men knew their place.

"Now, at this bar, y'all never stirred up trouble by trying to drink inside, did you?"

"Oh, no, sir. Colored folks drank in the little wagon lot out back. Got our beer out the rear door there."

"And you remember Mr. Swearingen when he worked there?"

"Oh, yes, sir."

"What was memorable about him?"

"He stands out with that ...well, his hair. Some of the White folks used to tease him, and Mr. Louie, he didn't cotton to that."

"So, he had trouble with White folks and colored, then?"

Duckworth rose to his feet.

"Objection. Mr. Lea might as well have a halter the way he's leading the witness."

A murmur of glee rippled through the gallery, and Judge Runnels grudgingly mumbled his sustainment.

J.V. Lea restated his question and elicited exactly what he wanted – affirmation that Louie Swearingen had been mercurial and sometimes difficult during his time at the Anchor. On some occasions, there had been violence.

The second of Montgomery's co-workers, a ropy, light-skinned man named Rufus Golden, singled out his friend as a favorite target.

"Johnson struck him wrong, I reckon."

"Did the trouble between them happen often?"

"More than most, I suspect, especially among the coloreds. Mr. Louie, he'd get fed up with Johnson's whooping and mouthing and holler for him to 'shut up.'

It turned physical a time or two. Laid hands on him twice I recollect and chased him half down the block another time."

"Do you think it was personal?"

Golden, who had avoided any looks at the defense table, finally stole a glance in that direction.

"Tough to say. Tough to say."

J.B.'s cross followed much the same pattern with each of the first two witnesses. He cajoled and befriended as he sought to dispute their statements, taking great pains and using multiple questions to underscore the passage of several years and the frailty of a man's memory. He not too subtly asked about the education of each man in an attempt to play upon the prejudices ingrained in the jury panel. None of it fazed either of the witnesses, nervous as they might have been. The third man up proved different.

When Dory Cooper took the stand, Duckworth changed his tack in hopes of finding more favorable wind. His job was to disrupt the testimony that the prosecution elicited, and so far all the traction belonged to Lea.

"You worked with Johnson Montgomery for a long time, didn't you?"

"Yes, sir. Better than ten years and likely more."

"Maybe even 12, 15 years then?"

Cooper let go a friendly laugh.

"Maybe. Like the man says, 'time flies.'"

"Knowing him that well for that many years, wouldn't you say that Montgomery was a grating and annoying person and even more argumentative and obtuse when drunk?"

Dory Cooper was either the most comfortable and adaptable of men or an innate actor. He responded without a hint of embarrassment.

"I'm afraid I don't know what that word means, Mr. Duckworth."

J.B. returned Cooper's easy smile.

"Which word was that?"

"Well, since it was new to me, I can't rightly repeat it either."

The witness gave a music hall mug toward the tittering spectators.

"Obtuse?"

"Yes, sir. That's the one."

Fermin Runnels shot a stern look into the giggling gallery.

"It means stubbornly insensitive and deliberately acting like he doesn't understand."

Cooper let go a loud chuckle.

"Oh, yeah. Then Johnson could be obtuse, all right. Obtuse. That's a good one. I'll have to remember that."

At the prosecution table, Lea cringed.

"That sounds like just the kind of man who would infuriate everybody around him, make even his friends spitting mad."

Dory nodded deeply.

"Ain't that the truth. Johnson could be all of that."

A tinge of sadness had crept into Cooper's words, and Duckworth sensed it. He would not pull back on the reins.

"Johnson make you mad enough to want to fight him on occasion?"

"Oh, I reckon so. Sure."

J.B. raised his fists for effect.

"Same with his other friends we heard from? They ever want to plant one right in his phiz?"

"Sure did."

"Y'all ever get so mad at Johnson's lies and bluster that you just wanted to kill him?"

Dory Cooper's face turned philosophical as he paused for the first time to frame his answer.

"You know, Mr. Duckworth, I suspect we all felt that way. But we never made no move to do it. Johnson was our friend, and in my way of thinking, you take your friends as they come."

Like most good criminal lawyers, Duckworth & Fein had their insiders scattered across half of Texas. If the district attorney filed a subpoena, the lawyers on Congress Avenue usually heard about it in due course. It was different with officers of the law. The D.A. simply sent a runner telling the given badgeman to be at court at an appointed time. So, when Lea called for Deputy Constable Ben Simmons, J.B.'s first thought was to wonder what it was all about. A moment later, he knew just what was coming.

Simmons was there to introduce an assertion from the late Eddie Isgitt about Louie Swearingen threatening to kill Johnson Montgomery. It took Lea only three establishing questions to lead the deputy there, and a twinkling after that J.B. was on his feet.

"Objection. Hearsay, your honor."

J.V. Lea's response was immediately at the ready.

"A casebook exception to the hearsay rules, your honor. The declarant is clearly unavailable."

Duckworth spoke angrily knowing it was ill-advised.

"That's the declarant's own fault."

Lea turned directly to his colleague even though he was speaking to the court.

"I believe it was one of Mr. Duckworth's clients who killed him, your honor. A client who was convicted of murder right here in this court."

J.B. took a half step toward his friend, his hackles raised.

"If that client had been a White man, it would've been called self-defense."

Fermin Runnels banged his gavel hard.

"That's enough. Let's adjudicate one case at a time, gentlemen. Your objection is overruled, counselor."

J.B.'s glare switched from Lea to Runnels.

"Approach, your honor?"

Alone before the bench, Duckworth kept his voice low but made little attempt to conceal his ire.

"This isn't law school, judge."

"How would you know. You never went."

Duckworth's face betrayed only an instant of surprise before a storm of pique rose in his dark eyes. The momentary flicker was enough to make Judge Runnels beam with satisfaction.

"That's right, counselor, I heard all about your dubitable background."

J.B. nodded once.

"All that you heard may well be true, but I'm still smart enough to know the difference between theoretical horse manure and some poor kid who's being railroaded by a dead man."

Runnels' grin had turned sour.

"Step back, Mr. Duckworth. I made my ruling."

Bade to continue, the district attorney turned again to Ben Simmons.

"Now, deputy. Please share what the late Constable Isgitt told you."

Simmons leaned back in his chair, smugly milking his moment in the limelight.

"Well, he told me that boy over there,..."

He used the condescending word as he pointed even though he and Louie were roughly the same age.

"...he said he was going to put a bullet into the colored fellow."

"Meaning the victim Johnson Montgomery?"

"Yep. Johnson Montgomery."

Lea paused to look the jurors in the eyes before continuing.

"Did Constable Isgitt say what the cause of their trouble was?"

Simmons languidly scratched the back of his neck.

"He reckoned it was just because that jig was so mouthy."

"So, you'd describe it as a personal grudge, then?"

"Yep. That's a good way of putting it. That colored boy was a troublemaker. I run across him myself a couple of times, and he was just an uppity..."

Lea cut the editorializing short.

"Thank you, Deputy Constable. That will be all."

J.B. was slow getting to his turn at the witness. He stopped to riffle through a few papers on the desk, pretending to read something.

"Mr. Simmons, you used the phrase 'put a bullet into the colored fellow.' Were those the exact words that Mr. Isgitt used when he told you the story?"

Simmons dropped his chin at an angle like a schoolmarm ready to scold a recalcitrant child.

"He might have said that your man over there wanted to kill him, but the result was the same. It would end up with one dead coon."

"And what were the exact words that Mr. Isgitt used to describe the difficulty between my client and Johnson Montgomery? And please be careful to use the exact words."

The deputy shifted forward in his chair.

"Well, now, I can't recollect the exact words, at least not to swear to. But I sure as hell, sorry, sure as heck, know the gist of what Eddie was telling me."

Duckworth gave an understanding nod.

"Were you drinking when this story was shared?"

"No."

"You positive about that?"

"I don't recall."

"Did you and the constable often have a pop or two of an afternoon?"

"I wouldn't say often."

Simmons had started looking past J.B. toward the courtroom door.

"But sometimes?"

"Maybe, sometimes. I don't know. That was more than a year ago."

J.B. let that remark linger.

"Yes. That was more than a year ago."

After the luncheon adjournment, the prosecution introduced testimony that placed Louie on his way to Harrisburg, potentially galled about being spurned by a girl. Carl Dumler was every bit the happy gossip on the stand as he had been with John Duckworth months earlier. There was no denying that the German was universally likeable, and the rosy glow of the man's face suggested he had enjoyed a pint or two at lunch. Even the tea-totaling farmers found a certain charm.

For reinforcement, the D.A. called Deputy Sheriff Bernhard, but this time Duckworth had slightly better success with the hearsay rules. Still, at least half of what the dour deputy had to say was admitted into the record.

Lea was almost ready for his star witness, but there was one more piece he wanted to present to the jury first. Rudy Kubicek, one of Louie's childhood running buddies from Austin County, was there to testify about Louie Swearingen as a teenaged marksman.

Kubicek was very apologetic about his presence. On his way to the stand, he even stopped at the defense table to extend his hand and tell Louie he was sorry, but the judge gaveled him down hard with a threat of contempt if he tried to speak directly to the defendant again. Fermin Runnels was definitely running a tight courtroom.

Rudy's hangdog resignation about testifying against his friend and the rhythmic monotony of his Moravian-accented English did not make him the most compelling witness of the day, but when he said Louie had the steadiest aim among the boys of Kenney and could "shoot the eye out of a sparrow at 60 yards," it was damning. At the defense table, Swearingen could only sigh and slump.

Duckworth did not try to ingratiate himself with this witness but rather he cut directly to the bone.

"Did he ever enter those contests dead drunk?"

Kubicek looked dumfounded.

"We were just 12 or 13."

"I take that as a no."

J.B. was unsure how the next bit would play, but he could not ignore his hunch.

"How did you get here today, Mr. Kubicek?"

"I rode in on the train this morning with Marshal Swearingen."

Louie snapped his head around to the gallery. The space where his father had been sitting was occupied by a non-descript clerk holding his bowler on his lap. Duckworth, meanwhile, was forging ahead.

"So, Louie's own father is tampering with witnesses for the prosecution?"

The district attorney was standing and pleading "your honor" even as Rudy Kubicek stammered on about being subpoenaed. Duckworth's moustache twitched upward ever so slightly as he sat.

"Nothing more for this witness."

The climax of the carefully crafted case against Louie Swearingen was Andy Green. It was strong stuff, the ironclad eyewitness, about the worst thing a defense lawyer could run up against. The prosecutor felt so too, and he had his questions meticulously plotted in order as if the story of conviction was already written in ink.

As the tale of that night was unfolded, even J.B. could not deceive himself into denying that Green was a sympathetic storyteller. Several on the jury were rapt. One of the simpler-looking farmers leaned so far forward in his seat that Duckworth wondered if the man might fall off.

"Johnson had been going on like that for some time. I'd learned to let his conversation drift in and out, mind you. Like a man learns to do with his wife, I reckon. But then he started on about oil wells, and that got my attention. It was a relaxing give and take until Poochie, our little mongrel, till he started growling at something just beyond the bar ditch. I looked up and that's when I saw Mr. Louie, ...Mr. Swearingen, that is, I saw him plain as day. One instant later – BOOM!"

The last word came so loud that most of the spectators in the courtroom gallery jumped. Several of the jurors did the same including one of the store clerks who was listening with his eyes closed. Standing just in front of the prosecution table, J.V. Lea could not help but smile.

J.B.'s goal today was to change Green's story, but barring that, he desperately needed to at least interrupt the flow. He tried to introduce any doubts he could, pulling out every trick, but he could not shake Andy Green's assertion that he saw Louie Swearingen shoot his friend.

The darkness of the night of the killing was a cynosure of his questioning.

"There was only a quarter moon that night at best," Duckworth stated. "Maybe just a sliver, and there were trees along your street. That's barely any light at all. How can you possibly swear to who you saw when it was gloomy like that?"

"He weren't but 15 yards away."

"In the shade, in the dark, Mr. Green!"

"Not like he was a stranger, sir. I knew the man."

"Pshaw, Mr. Green. You hadn't seen my client in almost a decade."

"Fellow notes people, Mr. Duckworth. City ain't that big you don't see folks around. Mostly, though, us poor people can't afford to forget them that's done us wrong. No, sir. We can't afford it."

So it went with every frustrating topic until Duckworth was bound to give in. He sat down with his head high and a forced twinkle in his eyes as if he had the prosecution case right where he wanted it, but in truth, he could not even summon a signature quip on which to end his cross-examination.

Louie Swearingen spent a restless night. He wanted a drink so badly that he got a case of the itch. At first he stared at the wall, thoroughly unable to fall asleep. Try as he might to blame it on the attempt to retire early, he quickly devolved into a bundle of worries. Despite the cool night air blowing through the open window, he twisted and adjusted the bed linens until he was hopelessly tangled in the sheet.

Nora could not sleep for all of his tossing. Several times she tried to soothe her husband with a soft word or touch, but by one o'clock, she was as frustratedly exhausted as he was. Louie huffed from the bed not long after, pulled on his pants and shirt, and not-so-quietly shut the door on his way out.

Chapter 29

The second day of the trial began with a very different looking defense contingent than Monday had seen. There were dark circles under Louie Swearingen's eyes when he arrived. His suit was the same as the day before, but the pants had seen a rough few hours. Someone had half-heartedly tried to rub out a food stain on the right thigh. The jacket and vest looked much better, but the brightness of the watch fob was gone, it perhaps having been mislaid.

Nora Swearingen could best be described as sullen that morning. The sleepless night showed in her face. The Reaves deputation was down to Nora's sister Mary. Louie's father was nowhere to be seen.

James Duckworth still had to put on a case for the defense, of course. Since they had never produced an alibi for Louie Swearingen, the path forward was unreassuringly simple - disruption. The only way forward for the defense was to sow doubt. Big handfuls of doubt.

The court clerk announced the case, and Fermin Runnels spoke without fanfare.

"We're in session, and it's your turn, Mr. Duckworth."

"Defense calls John R. McNally."

District Attorney Lea also had access to the subpoena list, more reliable access than Duckworth & Fein. Knowing this and wishing to obfuscate his defense blueprint as much as possible, Duckworth preferred to circumvent the system and make his own arrangements for summoning witnesses to court. When his trust of those witnesses was thin as carbon paper, however, he was not left with much choice. Several of today's planned witnesses fell decidedly into that category, and, as a result of the grudging transparency, Lea did not waste a minute before he tried to stop the defense case before it ever left the womb.

"Permission to approach, your honor?"

Without being invited, J.B. walked to the bench with the prosecutor.

"Your honor,..." Lea began. "It's my belief that opposing counsel here is about to try to blame this murder on the late Constable Isgitt, and I don't think that's a reasonable defense. I think it's unnecessarily cruel..."

Runnels held his palm up toward Lea.

"Is that true, Mr. Duckworth? Is that where you're fixing to go?"

"It is, judge. I believe it's perfectly..."

Again, the jurist stopped the statement in midsentence. He looked out at the spectators. To a person, they stared back at the little conclave. Runnels tapped his gavel on the podium top.

"Ladies and gentlemen, I'm going to need to have a little talk with the attorneys in my chambers. Y'all hold tight for a second. Members of the jury, no talking among yourselves or to anyone else."

It was the first time Duckworth had cause to enter the criminal court judge's chambers since Runnels took over. Little was changed from Gillaspie's office. The large oak desk stood in the same place. J.B. did notice that the place of honor behind it was occupied by an ornately framed proclamation from the Office of the Governor. He could not read the details, but he had no doubt that whatever honor was bestowed on Fermin Runnels came courtesy of his blood relationship and had nothing to do with merit.

Lea began speaking as soon as the door was closed behind them.

"Judge, there is no cause to drag Constable Isgitt's name through the mud again. He has a widow and orphaned children."

Both lawyers were standing, but Runnels had found his chair. Duckworth offered Lea his most cynical look before turning toward the judge.

"It's my right," J.B. said. "To show an alternative story of the crime, your honor."

Runnels pointed at him.

"This is my court, and I get to decide what rights you'll exercise within."

"Come on. It's the law. I'm entitled to put on a defense."

"I don't care what other judges let you do, Mr. Duckworth."

Runnels looked back at Lea.

"J.V., in spite of any inclinations I may have to protect the reputation of a slain officer of the law, you're going to have to give me something better than hurt feelings."

"We just went through this two weeks ago, judge. Mr. Duckworth tried to pin everything but the rape of the Cubans on Constable Isgitt…"

Lea could not resist a look directly at his friend.

"…and he lost. I call that asked and answered. You can't let him keep using the constable as a whipping boy forever."

Up to this point, J.B. had not fully believed that his friend the district attorney was genuine about his argument, but he now saw the competitive fire in Lea's face. This was repayment for the D.A.'s failure to hang Mat Thorn, and it was serious. Moreover, it was Lea doing everything in his power to preserve his job. The bile rose in Duckworth's gullet.

"What you can't do is stop me from presenting my case, and I say someone else committed this murder. Someone, I might add, that Mr. Lea already introduced into this trial. You cannot deny me. The appeals court would laugh that kind of ruling out of the room and halfway to Bastrop, and you know it."

The judge bristled.

"Don't you dare threaten me, mister."

J.V. Lea sought to tamp down the feelings even as he soberly summed up his argument.

"It's the exact ground we went over at the other trial, your honor. Denigrating a murdered lawman places an undue burden on his family. It prolongs their heartbreak over the loss of a husband and father. They deserve some kind of respect and standing."

"That's sentimental claptrap. It's horse shit. There is no basis in the law! None. The day begins anew on every trial. I'm entitled to this defense."

"There you go with entitlement again. And you will watch your language in my chambers."

Runnels rubbed his face hard before asking J.B. a question.

"Do you have real evidence to present or will this be smoke signals to the jury?"

Duckworth's nature begged him to vehemently argue. It cried out for more passionate snideness, to put this thick-witted judge in his place, but he swallowed it all down.

"Real evidence, your honor."

Runnels sucked in air through his teeth.

"You're on a short lead, Mr. Duckworth. A damnably short lead."

John McNally was an Irishman who ran a small grocery at Harrisburg, had done for several years, and he was well known and liked in the community. Purely out of thirst last fall, John Duckworth had stopped there in search of a bottle of Coca-Cola. He had lately become a devotee of the stuff. While cooling down with his soft drink, the investigator casually stated his business, and got a bucketload more than he expected.

The testimony that J.B. wanted on the record was that the potential murder rifle was borrowed from the grocer by Isgitt. For months, it had been the only contravening evidence that Duckworth had. It still was not much, but it might well stand up if Lea failed to ask to right questions.

When J.B. handed over the witness, Lea asked the obvious: Why had this just now come up? McNally shrugged.

"Nobody come out and asked me till that other fellow's brother did. Poor old Eddie is dead now, ain't he? Bless his soul. I didn't reckon it'd matter spreading his business."

Unable to glean anything else for his side, Lea breathed in loudly as he turned to the prosecution table but stopped just short of taking his seat. He turned back toward the witness who was rising.

"One last question. Had Mr. Isgitt ever borrowed your rifle before?"

"Well, I reckon a time or two. Aye. The man loved to hunt."

Duff Voss was a natural contrarian. J.B. knew him from his time as a constable in Fort Bend County before both men moved to Houston. Voss was now with the Houston Police and one of the few officers on good terms with Duckworth. A close observer of such things might notice that Voss had testified for a Duckworth & Fein defense before when the firm wished to lend a respectable law enforcement voice to their case. In spite of their earlier connections, it had been Jed Posey who stumbled across the bridge to the Swearingen case.

On the stand, Voss swore that he heard his fellow lawman Isgitt say he had been having trouble with Johnson Montgomery. When District Attorney Lea objected on grounds of hearsay, J.B.'s moustache twitched up on both sides as replied.

"The declarant is unavailable, your honor."

Fermin Runnels wore a lemon-sucking expression when he overruled.

"Isgitt had beaten Montgomery with a pistol butt once for sassing him," Voss testified. "Don't blame him. I know the kind of man Montgomery was."

"And what kind of man was that, Officer Duff?"

"That old buck loved to run his mouth and that didn't sit with E.P. He was a mean son of a bitch, Isgitt was. He didn't brook sass."

Duff unleashed a mischievous grin.

"Pardon, your honor."

Since losing his objection over hearsay evidence and Eddie Isgitt, James Duckworth had become a convert to the notion. He sent John back to Harrisburg on Monday evening with instruction to find anyone willing to say a bad word about the dead lawman. Gene Soujourn had been a regular drinking companion, and Soujourn also liked to talk. J.B. was more than willing to let him.

"Did you know Eddie Isgitt well, Mr. Soujourn?"

The red-nosed witness looked much less at home in the courtroom than he did in a barroom. A glance at the rural jurors confirmed that they sensed the same. Despite appearances, Soujourn seemed fully sober this morning.

"Oh, yes. I knew Eddie since he come to Harrisburg. Passed many a night with him in one establishment or another."

Oblivious to some of the jurors' sensibilities, Soujourn shot the box a wink.

"During the many friendly discussions you had with Mr. Isgitt, did he ever speak about the charges against Louie Swearingen?"

"He did. More than once."

Soujourn paused for thought a second or two before adding more.

"Eddie flat told me one night that Swearingen didn't do it."

Just like before, Lea rose to his feet and reiterated his hearsay objection. J.B. looked straight at the district attorney.

"For Chrissake, if the guilty man was alive, I'd ask him, but this is the best I can do."

Runnels gaveled him down.

"We went over this not long ago in my chambers, Mr. Duckworth. You'll watch your mouth in my court. And save your assertions for your closing. I won't warn you again. The next time, you will owe this court both money and hard time."

By far the most solid piece of the defense was Floyd Moore, whom John found in the small town of Dayton while investigating for another case. Once again, John's disarming inquisitiveness paid off. In this case, as had happened dozens of times before, Floyd Moore had been following the Louie Swearingen case in the newspapers. Luckily for the defense, Moore had a conscious, and something was gnawing at it. When he realized who John was, Moore spilled unprompted.

The night of Johnson Montgomery's killing, Moore was drinking with Isgitt in a saloon at Harrisburg during a stop on his way toward Pasadena to stay with his relatives. Moore's sister and her husband owned a little farm not two miles beyond the Pasadena townsite. They primarily grew strawberries and figs. "Seven acres," Moore proudly elaborated.

"I come through Harrisburg regular. There's a comfortable saloon there, and it's a good stopping point," Moore told the court as J.B. set the scene. "Man'll be needing refreshment about then. It's a long way from Liberty County."

"That's where you met Mr. Isgitt?"

"I'd drank with Isgitt before. Yes, sir, I liked the man."

"And that night, what happened?"

"I stayed until midnight, I reckon, then I said my goodbyes and started in my buggy down the road toward Pasadena. Got maybe a mile, no more, before deciding it was too late, that the family was likely asleep. I turned back to Harrisburg and got accommodation at a rooming house. I'd stayed there before. Like I told you, it's a long drive from Liberty County."

"Did anything happen as you were headed back to the rooming house?"

"Yep. I heard two shots from a distance, and right after that, I saw a man riding away at great speed. And I knew him to be E.P."

"E.P being Mr. Isgitt."

"That's right."

Moore went on to explain that Eddie Isgitt came to him in Dayton the following week. On pain of their acquaintance, Isgitt begged Moore to keep quiet.

"Why would you agree to break the law like that?"

Moore quailed a bit at the mention of illegality. He cleared his throat before continuing.

"I didn't think of it like that. It didn't seem very important, I guess. E.P. talked about the shooting when I saw him again. He didn't outright admit to anything, mind you, but he did tell me that the chump who would get blamed was just some dipso who had it coming. But he told me the fellow'd never be convicted."

Duckworth sounded his agreement and built a dramatic pause.

"Why did Eddie Isgitt shoot Johnson Montgomery?"

"I suspect he didn't like him. Enough so that he just wanted to kill him."

The D.A. raised his hand as he stood.

"Objection, your honor. That's speculation. The witness clearly has no idea about motive for a crime that almost surely never happened."

"Yes, yes. Sustained. Stick to the facts, Mr. Moore. No commentary. The jury will ignore that last exchange."

J.B. reframed his question.

"What did Isgitt tell you when he came to see you?"

"He hemmed and hawed for a good while, but finally he come right out and asked me to never say a word to anyone about anything I might have seen that night. I'm a man of my word, Mr. Duckworth. I've kept quiet all these months."

"Very honorable, Mr. Moore. Tell us exactly what changed your mind then."

"Well, your brother, John, came to see me about another matter."

Once again Moore furtively cleared his throat.

"I'd been keeping up with the story, the Louie Swearingen story, in the Houston papers. Things were starting to look like he might really go off to prison. That didn't seem right. I wrestled with it all, but finally concluded that it was more consequential than old E.P.'s reputation."

Yes," Duckworth said pointedly. "A man's freedom is very important."

Facing the first real questions against his case, J.V. Lea went after the weak points he heard in Moore's testimony.

"Now, you said that Constable Isgitt 'hemmed and hawed' when he spoke to you. I want to be clear as day on this, so help me out. Did he ever actually admit to shooting Johnson Montgomery?"

Floyd Moore took so long to answer that Lea gave him a verbal nudge.

"Mr. Moore?"

"I heard you. I suspect I should say that he never came out and used those very words, but there was no mistaking what he meant."

"But he never admitted murder?"

"He asked me to keep mum, and that's what he was talking about."

"So, he never admitted it. Thank you. Let's move on to something else."

Next, ever mindful of the jurors he had maneuvered so artfully to empanel, Lea hammered the fact that all of Moore's interaction with Isgitt had come in a bar.

"How about you tell us the real reason that you decided not to drive on to Pasadena. It wasn't the hour, now was it, Mr. Moore?"

"What do you mean? It was late. My sister wasn't liable to be awake by the time I got there. She has three little children."

"But you were drunk, were you not?"

Moore was defensive.

"Well, we'd been drinking. All of us had."

Lea repeated his statement.

"You were drunk."

J.B.'s objection was perhaps louder than it needed to be.

"He's testifying for the witness, judge. At this rate, we'll only need Mr. Lea."

"Sustained. Make it a question, Mr. Lea."

The district attorney nodded at the bench before turning back to Moore.

"So, you'd been drinking, then, as you say. Wouldn't that effect your eyesight in the dark while you drove on country roads?"

With all his might, Duckworth inwardly willed Floyd Moore to understand where the prosecution was headed, but it did not work. Moore jumped into the small snare with enthusiasm.

"Yeah, it was pitch dark. Like I said, I didn't think it was a good idea to drive on to Pasadena."

Lea looked toward the jury box as he asked his question.

"Then how, Mr. Moore, if it was that pitch dark, and with you having been drinking all night, were you able to positively identify Constable Isgitt as the man you saw riding away?"

Moore stared back silently at the prosecutor as he fished for a response.

"Well, he come to see me in Dayton, didn't he?"

"We only have your word about that, Mr. Moore."

The D.A. turned back toward his table.

"Nothing else, your honor."

"I'm hungry and I'm wagering the jury is, too. Planning for this afternoon, do you intend to call your client as a witness, Mr. Duckworth?"

"I'm undecided on that, judge. First I'd like to recall Andy Green for some more questions, and since he's not in court, I'll need an adjournment until tomorrow to get him here."

Again, the prosecutor had something to say about it.

"Your honor, Mr. Duckworth made no headway with that witness yesterday. I sincerely doubt there's anything new. This smells like just a delaying move. I don't know what it's about, but I can promise you it's a ruse, your honor. As Gladstone said, 'Justice delayed is little more than justice denied.'"

This time Runnels's frustration showed against the prosecution.

"Oh, it's half a day, Mr. Lea. Give it a rest. Court is adjourned until nine o'clock tomorrow morning."

Chapter 30

Whatever flurry of mild hope yesterday produced, Duckworth was in a foul mood Tuesday night as he sipped a drink alone in his private office. Once again, every note and scribbled thought about Louie Swearingen's case sat open in front of him. Any way he arranged things, it boiled down to one backbreaking and irrefutable fact - the prosecution still had a dead set eyewitness. Lea was correct in his final objection of the day. The notion of recalling Andy Green was primarily done for delay. J.B. absolutely did not want to reinforce Green's adamance in front of the jurors, but he needed more time to think.

The biggest question tormenting him was whether to call Louie to the stand. On the one hand, he was a likeable young man. Shortcoming aside, Swearingen's father was a respected lawman. Louie was newly married to a very pretty young wife at whom all the jurors had likely leered.

On the negative side of the ledger, the one carrying the most weight in J.B.'s mind at the moment, he was hesitant to call Swearingen because Lea would pick him apart with tales of drunken debauchery. Given a fire and brimstone jury panel like the one he faced, Duckworth was hemmed in tight.

At almost nine that night, little more than twelve hours before the start of a court day that would seal Louie Swearingen's fate for at least the next several years, J.B. settled on a compromise. He would recall Andy Green, something that carried its own share of risk, and if that did not bring any satisfaction, he would stick his hand into the fire and call Swearingen to the stand. The way Duckworth reckoned, if he could not shake Andy Green, Louie was bound for prison anyway.

He locked the door to the Congress Avenue offices and caught an uncrowded car that would take him within three and a half blocks of the jail. He needed a subpoena to ensure Green's appearance the next morning, but he did not trust Ben Simmons to serve it. Archie Anderson wanted Louie to have fair shake. His man would cost extra since he would need to be on the road well before dawn, but J.B. knew it was his best chance to have his witness shown into the courtroom when he called the name.

In his office at the jail, Anderson made the phone call right then and assured Duckworth that it was a reliable man.

"He'll see to it," the sheriff assured the lawyer.

No drink was offered and no invitation into the quarters was forthcoming, but Anderson lingered for just a moment debating whether to say what was on his mind.

"Lou Swearingen came to see me Monday afternoon. He knows you don't think much of him."

J.B. liked Sheriff Anderson, and he did not want to insult the man. He was unsure how to respond.

"Did he say much?"

"Not much."

There was another hesitation.

"The man does care about his boy and wants to see him cleared."

Again, it was Duckworth's turn to consider his words before he spoke. Anderson was right. Big Lou did not impress him, and he did not think much of the man. If he were to be blunt, J.B. might say that Big Lou Swearingen's thoughts or desires did not hold an iota of interest for him. Instead, the attorney nodded solemnly and thanked Archie Anderson for his help. It was getting late, and he would need to catch the next streetcar headed north toward home.

Andy Green's work crew was generally at their appointed site by half past six in the morning. The crew had only just arrived when a sheriff's deputy appeared out of the fog along the track siding. They had not noticed the small rig pull up on the road some 50 yards west, so Brooks Reed's arrival was a mild shock. The deputy vaguely waved the piece of paper.

"Andy Green. You've been recalled to testify. I need you to come with me now, son."

Dory Cooper just shook his head as he turned toward Andy.

"I thought you were done with that?"

Green ignored his friend and looked incredulously at the deputy. His inclination was to be deferentially compliant with any lawman, but his words did not follow that pattern.

"I can't just go back to the courthouse. I have a job."

"Stop your bitching. I talked to your bossman. How the hell do you think I knew where to find you?"

Most often, J.B. Duckworth preferred to sit alone with his client at the defense table, but he had asked Jed Posey to accompany him today. Posey was not needed for any reason, but having two lawyers flanking Louie Swearingen gave an appearance of added gravitas. It might make a difference with the jury, but he doubted it. Mostly, Posey was there to add slightly more weight onto the back of Andy Green. Besides, J.B. thought to himself, the young man might learn a new trick or two.

Duckworth opened his attempt to bust the state's key witness by trying to shake Green into a contradiction from his previous details, but, three questions in, the D.A. was on his feet.

"Asked and answered, your honor. The defense counsel went over all of this two days ago. So did I, for that matter. This is wasting the court's time."

"I agree with you, Mr. Lea. Mr. Duckworth, if you don't have anything new to ask the witness, you need to climb down off the horse."

There was no surprise in the objection or the ruling, and J.B. took it in stride. It had been worth a try.

"Happy to move on, judge."

He turned back toward the witness chair.

"Now, Andy. You weren't here yesterday, but there were several witnesses who made a good case for the idea that Mr. Isgitt shot your friend on the porch that night. What do you think about that?"

It was the first time Duckworth had mentioned any circumstance of the murder in the courtroom. It was poor form for the defense to remind the jury of the details, but J.B. was already far out on his limb. It was too late to worry about it breaking.

"Can't say. I know what I saw."

"Mr. McNally, who owns a grocery store out by where you live, he said he loaned a rifle to Mr. Isgitt right before the shooting. Are you saying Mr. McNally is a liar."

The questioning was making Green uncomfortable, but not as much as it was bothering J.V. Lea. The district attorney suspected where J.B. was headed, and he almost knocked over his chair when he stood to raise another objection.

"Your honor. What Mr. Green thinks about Mr. McNally has no relevance here."

Runnels scratched the underside of his chin. He scowled at the defense lawyer but left the door open.

"Would you care to rephrase that, Mr. Duckworth?"

"Certainly, your honor."

J.B. turned back to the witness.

"Do you know anything about Mr. Isgitt using a rifle on the night of the shooting?"

"No, sir. I just know what I saw."

Andy looked down at his lap.

"Duff Voss is a policeman. On the force here in Houston. He said that Mr. Isgitt told him about the trouble he had with your friend Johnson and that Isgitt flat hated the man. So does that mean that Officer Voss is a lair?"

"I'm not calling nobody a liar, sir. I wouldn't do that, but I know what I saw."

Lea's desperate objection was almost shouted as he tried to drown out Green's answer.

"Judge, we just went over this."

Duckworth did not wait for a ruling. With a nod and a disdainful wave of his hand, he took a step toward Andy Green and posed his next question.

"There was a fellow we found from up in Dayton. Up there just on the Trinity River, and it turns out he was drinking with Mr. Isgitt that night. Right after the two of them split to go their separate ways, that Dayton fellow heard two gunshots. Bang! Bang! And then he saw Isgitt riding away in a right damn... in a darned hurry."

Green stared at his shoe tops, and he rubbed an itch on his right pinky finger, but he did not reply.

"There's more to that story. A few days after that, Eddie Isgitt come to that fellow, the one from up in Dayton, and begged him not to tell anyone that he had shot Johnson Montgomery through the eye."

Andy's voice was a choked whisper, but he raised his eyes to meet Duckworth's if only for a moment.

"I saw what I saw."

J.B. rubbed his hands together and stepped even nearer to the witness box. On the one hand, he wanted the jury to see Green's face, but raising the pressure was paramount.

"Do you know what perjury means, Andy?"

Looking downward again, Green managed a slight nod. Almost simultaneously, J.V. Lea began to rise with another objection, but Fermin Runnels, his gaze firmly on the witness, sternly motioned the D.A. back down. James Duckworth could continue.

"When you come here, into this courtroom, you put your hand on the Bible and swear to tell the truth. The truth is very important in our system of laws. Everybody knows that, but what they don't mention is that if you lie to this court, you can go to prison for a long time. They can put shackles on you and haul you off to some..."

Duckworth might have gone on longer with his tale of horror, but water had begun to fill Andy Green's eyes, and he struggled to keep it from brimming over. He did not look up as the truth started to quietly flow.

"He caught up with me that night. Roughed me up some at first, then he reached in his pocket and give me money to keep my mouth shut. Twenty dollars. Lot of money, twenty dollars."

"Who did?"

Green could not quite say the name, so Duckworth did it for him.

"Eddie Isgitt? Isgitt gave you money?"

"Mm-hmm. Then I got afraid that he would take it back. I was scared to even spend it, and it was like the man could read my mind. One night he stepped out of the shadows and stuck a pistol under my chin. I could smell that he'd been drinking. He was unsteady, and that gun was wobbling, and it worried me even more. Man said if I ever breathed a word he would kill me but not till he had killed off people who mattered to me most."

Andy lifted his face.

"I believed him. I believed he would do just that."

J.B. took a moment to smooth his moustache.

"You had run-ins with Isgitt before?"

"Mr. Isgitt had his fun rousting colored drinkers. I seen him beat grown men with sticks. He hit me back of the head with a pistol butt once. I wasn't doing nothing. Just being."

"But he was dead, Mr. Green. Why would you be afraid of him still? Why would you lie to everyone once Isgitt was dead?"

"He's the police, sir. When one of them goes away, there's another one right behind him to pick up the kicking just where the first one left off. He weren't the first, and Lord knows he won't be the last."

Green stared earnestly at the lawyer for a second.

"Man like you, Mr. Duckworth, you don't know what it's like to deal with the police."

A few titters rose from the gallery.

"Oh, more than you know, Mr. Green. More than you know."

Though many failed to get the joke, those who were laughing, those who had read of the lawyer's not infrequent difficulties with the badgemen of Texas, could not stifle the noise. J.V. Lea could not help but join in the initial laughter, but quickly regained control of himself. When decorum was regained, Runnels directed Duckworth to go on.

"I thought Johnson Montgomery was your best friend."

Andy let go a sad sigh.

"Yes, sir, he was."

"Yet you were satisfied to see his killer walk free?"

"Friend memories don't mean much if you're dead."

Duckworth gave Green a single, firm nod then took his seat. District Attorney Lea passed on his opportunity for cross with only a wave of the hand. J.B. was satisfied. Louie would not take the stand.

Given a few minutes to rethink his position, and despite the crush of disappointment, Lea was not about to let the matter go, not with his career riding on it. When J.B. rested his case and Fermin Runnels pointedly asked the D.A. if he wished to continue, Lea answered with an emphatic yes as if the question was an absurdity. Final arguments would commence after lunch.

Duckworth's closing ran crisply in order of the witnesses he had presented a day earlier. He began with a recapitulation of the violent tendencies of E.P. Isgitt. There was even a one sentence tribute to the imprisoned Mat Thorn. On the bench, Fermin Runnels blanched a bit, but he did not stop Duckworth's summation.

Next J.B. laid out the scenario where Isgitt borrowed the murder weapon from the grocer McNally. Whether that was with cold-blooded murder already in mind, or an unfortunate coincidence aligned with a hunting trip, Duckworth could not say, but he made clear to the jury that it did not matter. He mentioned Duff Voss briefly to reinforce that there had been specific trouble with Johnson Montgomery.

Floyd Moore's testimony was recounted in detail but not at great length. Lest anyone fail to understand that the constable had tried to cover up his crime. Then it was time to sum up the change in Andy Green's story. Duckworth felt that the momentum of the case was on his side. This was not the time for a drawn out closing argument. He looked carefully at the jurors.

"Andy Green was scared, gentlemen. Scared half out of his britches that a man of authority, a lawman no less, was going to come back and kill him one night. 'Stepped out of the shadows.' That's the phrase he used. For a year and a half, he was dead afraid to tell the truth of what happened, that a lawman had murdered his friend right before his eyes. That is a scary thing. It would scare you or me. You know it would."

"You saw a minute ago that it took some good bit of coercing to get the truth out of him today. But it finally came out. The truth came out. You can see the man was genuine. You are smart men who know the difference between truth and a lie. Andy Green finally found the courage to tell the truth this morning. Eddie Isgitt killed Johnson Montgomery. Shot him in cold blood. Y'all need to let Louie Swearingen walk out of here today a free man. He did not commit murder."

J.V. Lea's final argument was not as perfunctory as Jed Posey expected. The young lawyer even shot a small look of surprise at the senior partner, a look that was ignored. His boss anticipated nothing less than a best effort.

Lea looked at his temperance jurors when he rehashed Louie's many drunken transgressions. At the defense table, both Duckworth and Posey noticed with unease that some of the men were still bobbing their heads in agreement. J.B.

wondered if they were prepared to dismiss out of hand anything said by a Black man, no matter which side of the case it fell on.

As to that change in Andy Green's story, the D.A. spent a great deal of time pointing up the fact that Green had steadfastly maintained one and only one version of events for 18 months. Rather than run from the change, Lea tried to turn the suddenness into an asset.

"Gentlemen, I ask you, would not the most plausible story be the one that a person has presented for the longest time. I cannot begin to suss out Andy Green's motives for changing his tale, but simple logic dictates that there is a reason other than what was outlined only a few minutes ago. It could be a reason hidden to us still. Maybe the man fears someone who coerced him to change his story. My office may well want to look into that matter, but I do implore you, as you do your duty as jurors, not to dismiss out of hand the unwavering story that Andy Green told for a year and a half. That he unmistakably saw Louis Swearingen, Jr. fire two shots into Johnson Montgomery's head."

Lea resumed his seat having stopped short of saying words to the effect that a case should not hinge on the whims of a Negro witness, but Duckworth feared that the undertone was clear.

Fermin Runnels' instructions were brief. A few of the jurors took a last look at Louie Swearingen as they filed out of the courtroom. Though the lawyers filtered out to other tasks, the courtroom gallery remained largely filled. People were loath to lose their place as the denouement of the story stood so near. Jed Posey returned to the office, but, as was his custom, J.B. adjourned to a nearby bar for a drink and a bit of grub while the jury deliberated.

Duckworth's hope was that Andy Green's change of heart would be compelling. If that was the case, the jury would return quickly. Accordingly, he ordered only a roast beef sandwich and a beer.

The final arguments for both sides had gone quickly. When J.B. walked into the Opera House Saloon, there were still remnants of the lunch crowd, but now they were gone. A few hearty drinkers lingered, standing at the bar. Duckworth had joined them, but he had been forced to slow his beer consumption lest he be tippy when they did get called back.

The light had dimmed inside the saloon with its tall east-facing windows by the time Justice of the Peace Walter Malsch arrived for his usual afternoon pints. He took up a spot next to J.B. and the two chatted affably until the runner from across Fannin Street finally arrived to summon Duckworth back to court.

To J.B., a man who dearly loved the trappings and ceremony of the courtroom, the announcement of a verdict always lacked a certain fanfare, and thus was the case when the foreman of the jury, a gray little farmer from somewhere on the east side of the county, said the words "not guilty."

Louie Swearingen let out a loud breath and sank back into his chair. Behind him, his wife Nora squealed and clapped three times.

On top of his other concerns, on the most visceral level, having an almost assured victory snatched from his grasp rankled J.V. Lea's pride greatly. He knew full well that he would be past it tomorrow or the day after, but for now, he had no words. He stepped to the defense table with pursed lips and a curt nod. The handshake between the two lead attorneys was brief and without any congratulatory commentary. Duckworth understood fully. Murder cases were competitive. The two men would be hoisting a glass soon enough.

Big Lou reached over the railing and shook Duckworth's hand. He then gave a firm handshake to his boy, but neither of them spoke. Whatever emotions may have existed, they did not come out. The senior Swearingen exited through the rear of the courtroom without a backwards glance. No doubt Louie's mother would be relieved.

When Louie Swearingen regained his breath, he hurried around the railing and wrapped his wife in a tight embrace then they shared a most welcome kiss. Decorum be damned. He then got a hug from his sister-in-law and her mother. Mary Reaves was seeing a new beau, and she had brought him to the courtroom in anticipation of her sister needing manly support after a bitter verdict. Even that stranger got a hearty grip from Louie, even though he had never met the man. Erv Reaves failed to show up for the last day of the trial.

With the family celebration done, Louie reached across and grabbed Duckworth on each shoulder.

"Thank you, Mr. Duckworth. Thank you. I know I wasn't a big help, but thank you."

Swearingen, with the eternal optimism of youth, felt that everything was now assured of being okay. Nora was pregnant, and Louie had a feeling it was a boy. Any future tribulations were the farthest thing from his mind.

The small group walked out of the courtroom together and stood in the upper lobby. Louie's face suddenly grew serious, and he asked a final question of his lawyer.

"Who took the shot at our apartment?"

"Isgitt, I imagine."

"And do you really think he killed that colored man?"

Duckworth looked Louie in the eyes.

"Who else?"

Swearingen could not hold his gaze at first, but then brought his eyes level and nodded.

"Why?"

J.B. thought about the question for no more than a twinkling

"I once had a smart policeman, one of the rare few of that profession, tell me that people commit murder for only three reasons - love, money, or revenge, but I think that's a pile of bullshit. That leaves out self-esteem and doubt. The unquenchable lust for power. My observation is that there's a hundred reasons some fool thinks he needs to kill somebody. Most of them are tough for other folks to figure."

If Duckworth thought that his philosophical words would stir any reverent appreciation, he was wrong. Louie's wide grin had returned, and his wife's arm was hooked through his own.

"We're going to the Turf. Mr. Lusk told me to bring everyone. He didn't say he was buying, but I'll stake you to a couple myself."

"I doubt Charlie's buying," Duckworth noted with a cocked head. "He's got to recoup your legal fees."

Louie felt his face go warm.

J.B. then turned to Nora, and a smile raised the great moustache.

"Keep him off the whiskey, will you?"

"Yes, sir."

She tightened her grip on Louie's arm and shot the lawyer her best Cheshire grin. He gave her the expression he considered his client smile. He held it until the couple reached the top of the marble staircase and began their giggling descent. Duckworth watched them go and spoke aloud to himself.

"Christ almighty, but I need a drink."

Duckworth did not join the Swearingen crew at the Turf, nor did he retire to the office for more work or opt for a quiet evening at home. He stayed true to his belief that one should always celebrate a victory or drown a defeat. Consequently, he and his brother, Sonny Schlottmann, Harris Peterson, and Henry Fein were soon laughing around a table.

Things were going swimmingly five rounds into their small fete at the Acme Saloon on Franklin at Travis. The owner, Mike Callaghan, was keeping them well-oiled, and various other lawyers, court clerks, and one ever-gregarious fire captain had come in and out of the party.

Business for Duckworth & Fein was steady. Next month, the long-deferred Mitchell case was finally expected to go to trial, and J.B. would be part of it. He was third chair, but there was little doubt he would find a way to assert himself.

As the table of carousers grew larger and louder, breaking up into smaller knots of conversation, J.B.'s thoughts turned for a moment to unanswered questions. He had never truly figured out the extent of the cabal arrayed against him or whether there was some vague string that connected that group to Gillaspie and the threats over his Waco trouble.

Harris Peterson was sitting next to Duckworth, and he asked about the trouble suddenly written on his friend's face. When J.B. was done quietly spilling his thoughts, Peterson stuck out his lips and rubbed the back of his knuckles in thought.

"Does it matter? There'll always be someone trying to pull you down. It's the nature of climbing the ladder."

Duckworth could not stifle a little smile as he picked up his whiskey glass and clinked it against his friend's.

Author Notes

I t's in the disclaimer, but it always helps to remind some folks that this is a work of fiction. The characters are my creation alone, even when I used real names. The real people who share names with my characters were dead a century or more before now, and I did not know them personally. I have, however, used the historical record to create their personalities and actions in a manner that I find reasonable based on what is knowable. There is plentiful research behind my choices. In a few cases where characters were patterned after a combination of real people, I altered the name slightly to clearly differentiate from the historical figure.

Which things were nudged along by true historical murders and crimes? A man like Erv Reaves did manage to get himself shot in a grocery some months after he had killed his daughter's boyfriend. And there was a constable who was the basis for E.P. Isgitt, and he experienced similar fracases and killings. There was also a killer of that constable who eluded the law until he was nabbed near the Atchafalaya River. The details of his pursuit are largely made up. The historical record on all of these long-dead men is pretty clear, but as I said, mine are fictional characters. Newspaper accounts and court records can tell you lots about what happened, but they rarely ascribe motives and feelings. By the way, the real life killer of that constable was sentenced to 20 years in prison, and he was paroled after nine years of good conduct at the Harlem and Imperial prison farms. So, Duckworth does mimic history when he saves the killer from hanging.

The places in the book, on the other hand, were very real. I spend a great deal of time and research effort so that the characters in these pages can grab a quick lunch in real restaurants like Jim Wing's, hole up in actual seedy hotels like the New Florence, and drink in real bars which are numerous in this world. Duckworth buys some Christmas wine at a real liquor store that was indeed on the same block as his office. I even went down a little rabbit hole to see what might have been the plentiful vintages, though there are no 1890s bottles in my cellar... if I had a cellar.

Houston, as the soon-to-be third largest city in the U.S., has changed a touch since the start of the 1900s, but a few of the buildings I mention still exist. To make things easier for those who have not spent decades digging in its archives, I have crafted a map to help place some locations.

I hope the world I have created for James Buchanan Duckworth and his associates feels real and gritty. I started my career in history in the realm of non-fiction through both books and documentaries, and I believe those years and that previous work gives me a little bit of a leg up. Accordingly, I work hard to make the first decade in 20th century Texas as historically accurate as possible. That includes issues of race. There is no way to talk about American history without talking about race. No matter how much some people may wish to bury their heads in the proverbial sand, our nation has a heartbreaking history. I think we are stronger as a people when we understand what things were like, so I try to create a fictional world that is true to the time period. It is only with knowledge of how things are that we might gain a measure of empathy and understanding for what someone else might endure. Contrary to what some may say, empathy makes us much better humans.

The other thing I want to talk about is language. Ours evolves more than many of us realize, at least until you get older and have next to no idea what young relatives and TV characters are talking about.

In the past hundred twenty-five years or so, we've added tens of thousands of new words and phrases to American English and thousands of other words have fallen out of favor. As I write, I spend a good deal of time digging in various sources in the attempt to stick to words that were in use during the first decade of the 20th century. That goes for narrative as well as dialogue. Finding those colorful idioms for the characters to use is great fun, and I want even my descriptions to keep the reader in the world of Texas circa 1900.

Often times the right word today was not around even that relatively short time ago. I couldn't let Duckworth come up with a lawsuit strategy, game plan, or battle plan because, according to what I found, those terms were not around, or at least not in wide use. Likewise, English speaking folks did not have empathy until after WWII. No one in the U.S. had a mantra. People were not even having nightmares, though their dreams could certainly be disturbing. So, I looked for alternative and era-appropriate ways to convey those ideas.

The 1920s and 1940s provided a ton of the slang I grew up hearing from "old people," but that doesn't mean a person in 1901 would understand the phrases. One that surprised me a little was that folks did not have a snack at the start of the last century. They may have had a bite or a morsel of something, but that just sounds a tad effete. Instead, I just had J.B. grab some grub while the jury was out. Grub is a fine word that dates back to the middle ages in the sense of digging and was applied to eating, first as a verb, by the 18th century.

I don't want to spend too much time on all this since not everyone is even a slight grammar nerd, but some of the etymology makes for great trivia. People in the 18th century were four times as likely to use the word noxious as we do today. They blamed noxious vapors and miasma for many diseases. Nowadays, the word is not very popular, though I suggest it applies nicely to much current political discourse.

Once or twice, I've had friends call me out on using modern words in these novels, and they turned out to be wrong. There are always surprises, and some words we feel are our own actually come from centuries past. William Congreve was making rockets for the British starting in 1808. That's how they show up in the lyrics to our Star Spangled Banner. And data, well that fine word did not come along with computers. It dates to at least the early 1600s.

I could go on, but for your sake, I won't.

Book Club Discussion Questions

U se these questions to facilitate group discussion.

1. Who was your favorite character and why?

2. Which character did you dislike the most and why?

3. What was the most memorable or shocking scene in the story and why?

4. How did the author explore themes such as justice, truth, deception, or morality?

5. Did the book challenge or change your perspective on race at the start of the 20th century? If so, in what ways?

6. How relevant or relatable are the themes in *A Convenient Scapegoat* to society today?

7. If you could travel back in time to Texas in 1900, what would you do or see?

Mike Vance is available for a 30-minute visit with your book club via your remote meeting platform. An honorarium will be needed. Contact Mike through the website at www.mikevancewriter.com to talk about scheduling and honorarium. Thanks.

Acknowledgements

S ome of the research on this novel dates back to historical non-fiction work I did many years ago, and there is a long list of wonderful folks at places like the Houston History Research Center, Houston Public Library, and the Harris County Archives who helped with that. Many other libraries and archives around Texas also helped in those days. Of course, during my misspent youth I researched and compiled copious notes about Texas locales and people during this period, and I still write non-fiction Texas history, so those helpers each contribute pieces of these fictional puzzles.

During work on this specific book, I was helped greatly by Laney Chavez who was then the Harris County Archivist, and Annie Golden and Barbara Estrada who also work at the archives there. They helped hunt down pieces to help me recreate Harrisburg circa 1900.

Several new folks provided details or answered questions during the time I was writing this novel. Those include: Schyler Rhea for expertise and detail on the grasses and ecology of native Texas prairies at the start of the 20th century. The Hon. Ken Wise and the Hon. Mark Davidson for allowing me to toss out a few legal history questions. Some of my fellow members on the Austin County Historical Commission, particularly Bill Hardt, served as a sounding board about the early community of Kenney.

Though I didn't bug them in person, thanks must also go to the folks at Portal to Texas History and all of their member libraries who supplied many thousands of old newspapers to peruse. The same goes for those who make old Sanborn maps digitally available at the University of Texas Libraries. It especially is true of the digital city directories available from my forever friends at the Houston

History Research Center, Houston Public Library. The world cannot survive in any sort of hospitable, intelligent, forward-moving form without libraries. Please support them in all ways.

Lastly, endless thanks go to my beta readers and editors for providing feedback. They confirm my relative sanity in creating the stories. Those people include Elizabeth Price, Marsha Franty, Tony Cavender, and Eliot Tucker. Unlike me, those last two gentlemen have decades of experience as attorneys, and their thoughts on the legal profession are absolutely invaluable. My wife, Anne, read the book and provided copy editing at a reasonable price. Finally, as before, Chris White, my pal since high school and a longtime professional author, has generously given his time so we could talk shop and swap ideas in hopes of making these labors of love profitable. The jury is still out on that one.

Sign up for the newsletter
at the bottom of any page
at www.mikevancewriter.com

If you want to know more about any of Mike's books, including finding loads of extras, the website is the place to go. You'll find plenty of biographical details, some pertinent maps for the Duckworth Historical Crime Novel Series, and dozens of interesting photos and videos.

Please follow MikeVanceWriter on Patreon, Facebook, YouTube, and Instagram.

Don't forget that one of the biggest favors you can do for any author is, if you enjoyed their books, leave a positive review of their books.
Thanks so much for your support.

www.ingramcontent.com/pod-product-compliance
Lightning Source LLC
Chambersburg PA
CBHW021038310726
48969CB00006B/1708